Praise for Tom ..

"Abrahams has a writing st
down to the very last detail...a
torture you with suspense."

"Tom Abrahams' writing is
trumpet's call, never more so than on the pages of his novel Allegiance, where the stakes are as big as Texas."

—Graham Brown, New York Times bestselling
author of The Eden Prophecy.

"With echoes of heavyweights like John Grisham, Abrahams rolls out the plot with precision and attention to detail giving us believable characters unlike so many of the other post 9/11 cookie cutter thrillers that clog the genre."

—E-Thriller.com

"If you like Robert Ludlum, Vince Flynn, Brian Haig or any of the great political thriller authors, Tom Abrahams is an author you need to discover today."

—Rabid Readers Reviews

"In a rising sea of political conspiracy novels, Abrahams' SEDITION stands out as one of best I've read in several years."

—Steven Konkoly, Bestselling author of
The Perseid Collapse & Black Flagged

"Packed with detail and plot, Abrahams' Sedition reminded me of some of John Le Carre's work. Maybe RUSSIA HOUSE or TINKER, TAILOR, SOLDIER, SPY."

—International Bestselling Author Marc Cameron

OTHER WORKS BY TOM ABRAHAMS:

Sedition

Allegiance

www.tomabrahamsbooks.com

ALLEGIANCE BURNED

A JACKSON QUICK ADVENTURE

TOM ABRAHAMS

A POST HILL PRESS BOOK
ISBN (trade paperback): 978-1-61868-888-0
ISBN (eBook): 978-1-61868-889-7

ALLEGIANCE BURNED
A Jackson Quick Adventure Book 2
© 2015 by Tom Abrahams
All Rights Reserved

Cover Design by Ryan Truso

Post Hill Press
275 Madison Avenue, 14th Floor
New York, NY 10016
http://posthillpress.com

For my *nuclear* family; Courtney, Samantha, and Luke

PROLOGUE

"The best weapon against an enemy is another enemy."
—Freidrich Nietzsche

Dr. Paul Wolf never felt the bullet, but he saw it coming.

The matte black steel barrel of a semi-automatic Fort-12 was pushed so close to his right eye his retina registered the explosion inside the chamber, and the optic nerve sent a final message to his brain.

Wolf's body slumped to the floor of his laboratory nearly five thousand feet below the Cherozem soil of South Dakota. A dark red puddle spread from his brutalized head, staining his lab coat a violent shade of pink.

Wolf's assassin fired a second bullet into his body, thumbed the safety on the left side of the Ukrainian-made weapon, and surveyed the subterranean lab. It was a small space with white floors and walls. The bright Hydragarum medium-arc iodide overhead lighting was intended to mimic the blue undertone of daylight and help the room's visitors forget they were merely four hundred feet shy of being a mile underground.

He was surprised at how easy it was to access the lightly guarded complex, given the importance of the work there. The Sanford Underground Research Facility was, from the surface, a modest red brick building adjacent to a five-story white silo. At the top of the silo in green lettering was the facility's original name, Homestake.

A seven dollar surface tour earlier in the week, courtesy of the Homestake Visitor Center, provided the killer virtually everything needed to carry out the mission. The tour guide had taken the group into the main building and shown them the Yates Shaft hoist room. The guide mentioned all sorts of interesting experiments studied deep underground. He did not mention Dr. Wolf or his lab, but the assassin knew where to find both.

Two days of surveillance from a gray Ford F-150, the most common car in the state, revealed what the cheap tour did not; the security rotation and the fastest routes from the complex onto highway 85. It also led to the Iron Horse Inn in nearby Deadwood, a favorite hangout for some of the technicians at Homestake. For the cost of six whiskey sours, ten plays on a dollar slot, and a room for the night, he nabbed an entry passcode, a couple hours of companionship with a horny technician, and a wicked hangover.

On the night of the mission, he parked the F-150 in a space farthest from the building. With one bullet from the Fort-12 and the passcode, access to the A-framed building housing the Yates Shaft was almost effortless.

Inside the building he moved silently to the cage-like elevator that would descend forty-eight hundred feet straight down. The fourteen thousand pound cage was nine feet tall and could carry ten thousand pounds. The assassin engaged the motor to lower the cage, and the wire ropes groaned into action.

As the cage hummed its way deeper into the Earth, the air cooled and dampened. The dim light inside the cage did little to ease the assassin's usually unshakable nerves. When the ride ended and the cage rattled against the floor, he inhaled deeply, sucking in the humidity, and stepped into the narrow hallway.

To the left was a corridor that split into a Y, leading to a lab module conducting research on dark matter. Beyond that was what they called the FAARM and a temporary clean room.

He turned right.

The hallway forked almost immediately, but he knew it was a large loop and either path would work. Walking to the left, he checked the Fort-12, made sure the chamber was loaded, and approached the Majorana Demonstrator. An exhaustive intelligence file told him the M.D. was where researchers were working with pure copper for their experiments. A few steps beyond it was a large, suspended water tank. The researchers called this the "can", part of a highly sophisticated instrument unlike any other in the world. Beyond the cylindrical tank, against a white wall framing the support poles, was a narrow ladder. The assassin moved with purpose to the ladder and felt around the back of the fifth rung, finding an almost imperceptible lever.

The lever pulled to the left, and part of the wall behind the ladder hissed open. The doorway was only eighteen inches wide and five feet in height. He slipped through the opening and into Dr. Wolf's hidden lab.

"Hello."

The scientist, sitting at a table at the far end of the lab, spun to see his executioner aiming a gun at his head. "Wait!" Wolf protested, waving his hands and raising them over his head. "Who are you?"

Without turning from the prey, he pressed the pneumatic lever next to the doorway and waited for it to close before moving closer to Wolf. The scientist was alone.

"Who are you?" Wolf asked again, his eyes darting around the lab looking for an answer or for help. He found neither as the intruder put the gun to his right temple.

"Shhhh," the assassin put a finger to Wolf's lips. "No talking."

Wolf tried to grasp his reality. In front of him, a sleek figure in black held a deadly weapon to his head. Face obscured by what looked like a ninja mask, the scientist could see only a tubal device above the man's right ear and black eyes which told Wolf he would not leave his lab alive. He would die a mile beneath the Earth, buried without ceremony.

"Tell me," the man whispered, "where is it?"

Wolf, obeying the earlier command, said nothing.

"You may speak," he pushed the barrel against the side of Wolf's head.

"Where is what?" The scientist shook his head. Tears welled in his eyes.

"You know why I'm here," the assassin said. "You knew I'd be coming."

"It's not here," Wolf admitted. "I don't have it."

The quick admission surprised the intruder. Maybe this would be easy. "Where did you hide it then?"

Wolf said nothing.

"Where?" A jab with the barrel. "You've got five seconds." Maybe not so easy.

"I don't, I don't..." Wolf stammered.

"Five."

"Please!"

"Four."

"I really can't—"

"Three."

"Okay, okay—"

"Two."

"It's not in one place!" The scientist closed his eyes and pressed tears down his cheeks.

"What does that mean?" The assassin dragged the Ukrainian barrel across the scientist's face and planted it against his eye.

"It's in several places," said the scientist, his hands shaking from fear. "I separated it."

"Where?"

"I...I can't—"

"One."

"Please! Don't!!" Dr. Wolf opened his eyes in a last desperate, futile plea for mercy.

The gunman pulled the trigger and, with a pop that echoed against the solid walls of the lab, it was over.

Maybe, with more time, Wolf would have coughed up the needed information, but there wasn't time. The mission guidelines were clear: find Wolf, get him to talk quickly, and kill him within thirty seconds if he hesitated. It would send a message to the others. They didn't need Wolf. A confession from the good researcher was a bonus, but unnecessary. They already had leads. They knew where Wolf had traveled and who he'd visited.

After the second shot, the assassin found the hard drive that was the real target of the mission. It was in a drawer to the left of the scientist's body. It was white, like everything in this ridiculous tomb. He checked the serial number on the back of the drive and matched it to the number committed to memory before removing a head mounted 1080p digital camera and inserting it into the USB slot of the dead scientist's desktop computer. The five hundred gigabyte memory within the camera recorded the entire mission from the killer's perspective. Whoever found the body would find the video, and that video would find its way to the people who most needed to see it. Unless, of course, the video upload led to the discovery of the murder.

How much fun would that be? he thought, checking the lab one more time before slipping out of the exit and sliding it closed with the pull of the hidden lever.

Sixteen minutes later, he was just another late night traveler on highway 85, headed west toward Wyoming.

PART I

NUCLEUS

"The fear of death follows from the fear of life.
A man who lives fully is prepared to die at any time."

—Mark Twain

CHAPTER 1

The silent alarm flashes and vibrates against the hardwood floors next to my mattress. There's somebody in my apartment. It's 4:36 AM.

The adrenaline shocks me instantly awake and focuses my attention. From under my worn feather pillow, I wrap my hand around the synthetic grip of a Smith & Wesson Governor revolver. It's loaded with shot shell and is excellent from close range.

As I've practiced countless times before, I quietly roll off the mattress onto the floor and then slide away from the locked bedroom door. Underneath the door, in the narrow gap above the floor, is the erratic beam of a flashlight. There's no sound. I push myself to a squatting position.

Resting on the balls of my feet, I press my back against the wall. To my right is the bathroom, a shelving unit is on my left. With my left hand, I reach onto the second of three shelves and grab a familiar four-inch canister and place it on my lap. Still holding the pistol at the bedroom door, I reach back to the shelf and pull down a TM-X thermal camera.

My bedroom is dark, barely any light from the single window peeks through the cheap metal blinds pulled down for privacy. For a moment, I close my eyes and hold my breath, listening for the intruder or intruders who are here to kill me.

Nothing.

Crouched like a baseball catcher, I inch my way to the bathroom door and position myself two feet past the opening into a shadow. I lean forward onto my knees and lay the gun on the cold tile next to a pedestal porcelain sink.

Grabbing the canister, I pull the large ring from its top and roll it toward the bedroom door. Smoke pours from the top of the paintball tactical smoke grenade, filling the bedroom as the door blasts inward, followed by the repetitive thump of at least two silenced semi-automatic weapons.

From my position in the bathroom, the attackers can't see me. They're maybe ten or twelve feet from me when I pull the thermal camera to my left eye and secure it with a homemade head strap.

The room fills with shades of green and in front of me, next to the mattress on the floor, stand two neon green images. At their armpits, heads, and rifles, the green transitions into a yellow and pink heat signature. Both look like large men. I level the pistol at the pink image to the right and pull the trigger. A spray of pink shot shell hits the target and he stumbles back. I fire again and shift my weight to my left. The second man is confused, peppering the room with bullets, unable to see the direction of my fire. Another two quick pulls of my trigger and he's on the floor with his partner.

The smoke starts to dissipate and I have two shot shell bullets left. Deliberately, and with the help of the camera, I quickly eliminate the distance between me and the two men. Standing over them, I pull the trigger twice more, emptying the Smith & Wesson and ending their assault.

The acrid smell of the grenades fills my nostrils, I taste fireworks before the haze begins to lift.

It's 4:38 AM.

The sound of gunfire likely has police on their way. I walk to the bedroom closet opposite the shredded mattress on the floor and flip on the light. Sticking to the plan, I get dressed in a dark, long-sleeved cotton

T-shirt and some black Nike sweatpants. From the top shelf, I pull down some slip-on Merrells.

It's 4:40 AM.

In the corner of the closet, behind some hanging dress shirts, there's a black rucksack already packed. I unclip the top and pull open the drawstring closure to check the contents.

There's another smoke grenade can, a Gerber Bear Grylls survival kit, a bottle of water purification tablets, an Intratec 9MM Luger, two box magazines holding 50 rounds each, a box of shot shell for the Smith & Wesson, an extra pair of Merrells, a Garmin eTrex handheld GPS, a blue metal box with a combination lock, three rolls of duct tape, and a pair of photochromic Ray-Ban sunglasses.

In a side pouch there's a large plastic bag containing forty-thousand dollars, two fake driver's licenses, matching passports, and the key to a safe deposit box. Another pouch contains a Spyderco four-inch military jackknife, car keys, an extra shirt, black military surplus cargo pants, some socks, and a couple of pairs of underwear. The TM-X thermal camera, with its head strap, fits into a third pouch next to four smart phones.

It was only a matter of time before my planning paid off.

Still, it's surprising how fast they found me. I'd paid six months' worth of rent in cash to sublet this crappy one-bedroom. Nobody knew I was here. Or so I thought.

There they were, though, on my floor; paid killers sent to end my life because of what I knew, what I'd done. Both men looked like the others who'd chased me: short cropped hair, thick necks, and rounded shoulders. They were anonymous contract workers assigned to terminate someone they didn't know. I was a target.

I am a target.

It's 4:42 AM.

There are sirens wailing in the distance. I slug the rucksack on my back, pull a polyester Under Armor beanie onto my head, tuck the Governor into my waistband, and walk out into the night. Six minutes ago I was asleep and dreaming.

***

I leave my apartment building through a rear entrance, expecting more resistance on the way out. There's none and I shrug the rucksack into a more comfortable position on my back as I make my way through the quiet, if low rent, neighborhood in Alamo Heights. The streetlights flicker from neglect as I pass Deerwood Drive. It's a couple of hours from sunrise, so most of San Antonio is asleep. Still, it's surprising there's nobody following me.

A woman with earbuds and a leashed black Labrador named Henry jogs past without noticing me as I turn right on Eisenhauer. She's two minutes behind her normal schedule.

The number fourteen bus that services Alamo Heights should be at the Eisenhauer/Austin Highway stop at 4:43AM. It's the third stop on the route and if it's on time, which it usually is, I'll be long clear of the dead bodies in my bedroom before anyone finds them.

For four months, I've gotten to know this part of the city as well as possible— the streets, the bus schedule, the traffic patterns— anything that'll help me escape easily and without detection. I've carefully blended into the fabric of the community, familiarizing myself with people and places without ever revealing anything real about myself. It hasn't been easy.

My face was plastered all over the news for weeks after I was involved in a televised shootout. Then the whole thing with my boss made it hard to slip out of the spotlight. However, time has helped. With every passing day and week it seems like my anonymity is slowing returning. That is, except for the douchebags who keep hunting me and trying to kill me.

A green Honda Accord turns left off of Eisenhauer into the parking lot shared by an Express Lube, an Asian Buffet restaurant, and a Goodwill store. Curt Eugene is on time for work, parking the Honda ten minutes before he raises the garage bay at the lube shop.

Millie Fong's battered Jeep Cherokee is already parked at the side entrance to her restaurant. She's up to her wrinkled elbows in crab Rangoon.

The bus is on time, squealing its way to a stop. I climb on, notice a woman sitting in the seat nearest the door, and take a seat on the third row behind the driver. It's a new driver, a guy I don't recognize. He nods and pulls shut the door lever before easing into the sparse pre-dawn traffic. I've got twenty-four minutes until I'll transfer to the forty-four bus at Flores and Houston.

The attackers worked for F. Pickle Security Consultants. I'm pretty sure of that. They had that look about them, ex-intelligence dudes. They were sent by my former boss, the Governor of Texas, and his friends.

When I ratted out their conspiracy of bribery, fraud, and murder to the media, they ended up in prison and I had a target on my back. In the last eighteen months, they'd tried four times to kill me: the Florida Keys, Santa Fe, Toronto, and now San Antonio.

Every time, I'm waiting for them. Every time, I get better at protecting myself and escaping to the next hiding place. I never get back my rental deposit.

They usually attack in two teams of two, however. This time there was only one team. They had no backup. That doesn't fit with their typical method of operation.

It doesn't fit.

The woman sitting near the door has her back against the window. Her angular profile gives her an athletic appearance. Her black hair is pulled back into a short ponytail underneath a Spurs baseball cap. She's cradling a large backpack on her lap that covers her chest. She's looking toward the driver, who glances at her before his eyes flit to the rearview mirror and me. The woman, whose body is turned toward the aisle of the bus, hasn't glanced at me once. Her focus is on the driver.

Something's not right.

"Good morning." I nod to the woman, trying to get her attention. "It's early to be up isn't it?"

She looks at the driver before shifting to me. "I'm sorry?" Her eyes narrow and her right hand slips behind the backpack.

"It's early," I repeat with a toothy grin. I don't have time to get the Tec 9 from my bag. The revolver will have to suffice. I've got six shots. I carefully slip the weapon from my waist and hold it against the seat with my left hand. It's ready to fire.

"I suppose," she says, her eyes still betraying some confusion.

"What do you do?" I ask. The driver takes a longer look at me in the mirror.

"What do you mean?" The woman shifts again. Her jaw tenses.

"For a living," I say. "You know, what's your vocation?" With my right hand I grab one of my bag's shoulder straps and grip it tightly, shifting it onto my right leg.

"I'm a consultant," she says, nods almost imperceptibly at the driver, and reaches for the chrome pole that separates her seat from the entrance steps. "Now!"

The bus decelerates quickly, sucking me from my seat into the seat back in front of me on onto the floor. I'm stuck, but I still have control of the Governor. The bag falls on top of me.

Thump! Thump!

Two large holes spit through the innards of the seat back inches from my head.

Thump! Another shot rips the seat and grazes my right arm.

I let go of my rucksack and kick it out into the aisle, scrambling onto my back so I can see underneath the seat. There are a pair of black boots angled toward me near the entrance steps. She hasn't left her seat yet!

I extend my left arm under the seat and aim for the boots. I pull the trigger.

The sound of the shot shell expanding into the cabin is quickly followed by a loud scream.

"I'm hit!" she yells, firing again. "My ankle!"

Thump! Thump! Thump! She returns fire but the pain is affecting her aim. The shots whistle past the top of the seats and crack into a window a few rows behind me.

The bus lurches forward into gear, so I roll onto my side and switch my aim toward the driver. Two pulls of the trigger elicit expletives and a groan. The bus accelerates and then slows again quickly, causing the woman to fall from her braced position in the front.

Her hat falls off and she hits the ground face first. I can't see her face, but she's dropped her semi-automatic, which tumbles down the aisle out of her reach. She looks up and meets my eyes right as I pull the trigger. She doesn't scream this time.

The bus is starting and stopping like the driver is experimenting with a manual transmission and can't work the clutch. He must be hurt. He's moaning and talking incoherently. I roll onto my back and manage to pull myself up, peeking around the side of the seat into the aisle.

The woman is dead or dying, her blood creeping toward the 9mm. Her left hand is twitching. She's not a threat.

I pull myself into the aisle and, crouched low, inch forward toward the driver and pick up the gun with my right hand. It's warm from the six shots she fired, and from her blood, which is sticky on the barrel. I slip the Governor back into my waistband. The bus rolls to a slow stop.

"Who sent you?" I call to the driver, moving to the seat behind him, the 9mm aimed at the back left of his head.

He moans and shakes his head, his chin dropping to his chest. He's in bad shape. The lower back of his seat is riddled. The shot shell pellets probably punctured his lungs. I can hear a wheeze rattle from his open mouth. Somehow he managed to slam the bus into park.

"Who sent you?" I press.

"I..." the driver starts. But he can't finish. "I...." He sighs and spits his final breath.

I inch around to his side and see the problem. He's got a large entry hole underneath the shirt pocket on his left side. It's about the size of a 9mm.

His partner killed him.

We're stopped at an angle against a curb, blocking the left lane of traffic. It's 4:48 AM and still dark. There's no crowd gathered outside yet. I tuck the 9mm next to the revolver and use the seat backs to hop over the dead woman in the aisle. The blood pooling around her hasn't reached my backpack thankfully. I grab the pack and sling it on. It feels heavier.

Hopping back over the woman, I almost slip and fall back onto her, but regain my balance and pull the lever to open the bus door. I carefully step off of the bus onto the grass lining the curb. I'm not sure where I am. Nothing looks familiar. I turn left and start walking quickly away from the bus, like one of those scenes from an action movie. I don't turn around, half expecting the bus to explode behind me for effect.

I've marched maybe a block when a black sedan pulls up alongside me and slows to my pace. Instinctively, the revolver finds its way into my hand. I raise it as I turn to face the window lowering from the rear passenger door.

"Get in the car, good man," says the familiar voice in the back seat. "You're liable to catch your death out there."

CHAPTER 2

"How did you find me?"

It's 4:54 AM, and my body sinks into the wide leather seat with the exhaustion of a full day.

"I've told you before, Jackson Quick, I can find you whenever it suits me," the man laughs and sips from a white china cup. The cup is dwarfed in his thick, swollen hands. "And this morning," he continues. "It suited me."

"Yeah." I rest my arm on the rucksack next to me. I'm facing backward in the limousine, my back against the partition separating us from the driver. "I find the timing a little coincidental for my liking."

"Trifles light as air are to the jealous confirmations strong as proofs of holy writ," he smirks.

"Shakespeare?" I say more than ask. "A little trite, even for you, isn't it?"

"Perhaps." He leans forward to rest the cup on a saucer. "But you know, Jackson, I am not much for coincidence. I much prefer the idea of divine intervention."

"God complex much?" I reach for the bottled water in the cup holder to my left. The cap twists easily and I pull a swig into my mouth.

"Your wit is only outdone by your arrogance," he says. His hands are resting on his knees. He's in a well-tailored dark blue suit with a yellow ascot. "I'm truly shocked you've lasted this long."

He's right. It's a miracle I've survived as long as I have. I should be dead.

I screw the cap back onto the bottle. "So what do you want?"

"Cut to the chase," he laughs. "That's what I love about you."

His eyes meet mine. I don't blink. He senses I'm not saying anything else until he tells me why I am in his car.

"I have a job for you."

So there it is. Sir Spencer Thomas has a job for me.

The last time he saw me, we were in a bar in Austin. He offered me a beer after trying to persuade me into joining him in his never-ending battle to fight for either the righteous or the highest bidder. It was one or the other. I can't remember.

I do remember his self-proclaimed Robin Hood once held me captive, tortured me, let me go, and then saved my life. He lied to me and then offered to protect me. He worked for the man who used to be my boss and who now wants me dead.

We have a complicated relationship.

"I told you months ago, Jackson," he reminds me, "you cannot protect yourself from the reach of your enemies. I have the ability and inclination to keep you safe. That is, if you listen to my proposition and take me up on the offer."

"I'm doing fine on my own," I lie.

"So it seems." His eyes glance at the bloodstain on my right arm.

"Why me?" I ask, self-consciously rubbing the nick on my arm. "I'm no Special Forces guy. I don't have any covert training. I'm a regular guy trying to survive."

"Men like you," he nods, "the ones trying to survive? They're the most effective, I've found at getting the job done." His lips curl into a smile. "It's not business for you, Jackson. It's, as you said, survival, and survival is perhaps the strongest of all motivators."

I swallow past the dryness in my throat and gulp down some water. He's right. Eventually, my former boss will win. His goons will kill me.

Until then, I'm not really living anyhow. From one cheap hiding hole to another, I keep looking for peace. I can't find it.

Sir Spencer *does* have resources. He has money and powerful friends. He's connected to the good and the bad. If there's a man who lives in shades of gray, it's Sir Spencer. I do believe him when he tells me he can keep me alive. Plus, there aren't a lot of options. It's not as though there were limos lining the curb to pick me up.

"If I do this," I say, "and I mean *if* I do this..."

"Yes?" His eyes widen. He knows I'm ensnared.

"Can you help me disappear permanently?" I need to get off the hamster wheel. I want normalcy.

"Of course." He leans forward and extends his meathook of a hand. "Jackson, my good man, I can make you disappear."

***

"Still flying the Embraer Legacy?" I ask Sir Spencer, stepping onto the asphalt runway, inhaling the sting of jet fuel, and climbing the fold-down steps onto his ice white jet.

"Oh yes," he laughs from behind me. "It's too convenient a toy with which to part."

"Hello again, sir," curls the drawl of a thin blonde in a tight blue skirt at the top of the steps. Her hair, as it was the last time I flew with Sir Spencer, is pulled against her head in a loose bun. Her lipstick is more subtle than I remember. Her blouse is not.

"Sally Anne, is it?" I smile and slide past her close enough to replace the jet fuel tang with her perfume and step into the familiar cabin.

To the left is a wet bar with a refrigerator, a wine cooler, and a microwave. Farther left is the lavatory and the cockpit, its dual controls lit with green and red. To the right is a cabin awash in ivory leather and walnut trim.

Along the right side of the aircraft, stretching most of its length, is a long sofa. To the left are four pairs of captain's chairs. Two face forward and two face the rear of the aircraft. There are walnut tables between them. At the rear of the jet is a pair of recliners.

My mind flashes to my last flight on this plane. A brief trip from west Texas to Austin, during which the Governor of Texas admitted to me he'd used me in a complex scheme.

He'd struck a deal with a handful of energy companies to prevent his political rival from using new technology to enhance the efficiency of fossil fuels. Money changed hands; people died.

"We are warriors, Jackson," he'd spun his warped rationale. "It's a battle between what's right for Texans and what's not. We're on the side of good here. Our economy feeds off the energy industry. We survived the recession in '09 because of oil and gas production. President Obama said it, 'We're the Saudi Arabia of natural gas!' We can't let anything affect that."

"He meant the United States as a whole," I told him. "I don't think he was talking specifically about Texas."

"Get your head out of the sand, boy," the Governor sneered. "Texas *is* the United States if you're talking energy of any kind. Hell, we're ahead of the Socialist Republic of California when it comes to wind energy production. *Wind* for goodness sake. Our economy, the nation's economy, would be impotent without what the energy folks do for us. Those so-called 'environmentalists' are traitors as far as I'm concerned. You can't have it both ways."

Now he's in jail and I'm living life in a prison.

"Music, Jackson?" Sir Spencer gripped his thick hand on my shoulder and shuffled past me to his recliner. "Anything you prefer?"

"Linkin Park?" I request, knowing he's unlikely to have it in his iPod playlist.

"Ha!" he snorts as his heft sinks into the leather chair. He pats the seat next to him. "Have a seat, good man. Have a seat."

He pulls a remote from the table next to his seat and thumbs through his options. I drop my pack on the floor and sit in the recliner next to him.

"Hmmm," Sir Spencer squints and presses his selection. "What about this?"

The strains of a violin fill the cabin.

"This isn't Linkin Park."

"Clearly," he says, his eyes closed. "This is Marin Marias."

"Violin?"

"Violin and harpsichord." He gently waves his right hand in the air, his fingers dancing. "Beautiful isn't it?"

"Eh."

"Please, good man," he opens his eyes and narrows his brow. "This is genius. Before Marin people didn't see the harpsichord as an instrument worthy of anything other than solo performance. He looked beyond the obvious."

"And?" I don't share his love for classical music or harpsichords.

"And this is so ahead of its time. It's called music for the Sun King."

"I'd still prefer *A Thousand Suns.*"

"Linkin Park?" he asks, his hand still keeping rhythm.

I nod as the music stops, interrupted by the pilot.

"Welcome aboard," his voice crackles through the speakers. "We'll be leaving Stinson Municipal Airport here in a minute. We'll taxi onto runway twenty-seven and make our way under partly cloudy skies to Ellington Field in Houston. The temperature there is a muggy eighty-five degrees with a slight chance of rain. The trip is a quick one hundred and seventy-three nautical miles. It should take us a little less than forty-five minutes in the air."

"Houston?" I don't want to step into the lion's den. "Why Houston?"

"We have a meeting there." Sir Spencer hands are resting on his knees. The music begins again and he smiles, exhaling lightly. "At Nanergetix Corporation."

***

Nanergetix's world headquarters is a tall, blue, reflective glass building in part of what used to be Enron's campus on the southwestern edge of downtown Houston. The company was founded and run by Don Carlos Buell. He wanted to be governor. He wanted to change energy. He wanted a lot of things before an assassin, hired by my then boss, put a bullet in his head in front of a live television audience.

"Why are we here?" I follow Sir Spencer through the revolving door and into the building's lobby. "You told me on the plane I'd find out when we got here."

"All in good time, good man," he says without turning around. "All in good time."

I can't stand this self-righteous knight. His condescension and double-talk make me want to puke. Or shoot him. Or shoot him after I puke. He's my ticket to normalcy, though. He can make me disappear. So I'll tolerate it.

"Excuse me." He bellies up to the reception desk. "Excuse me there, sir."

A uniformed security guard looks up from a bank of flat screen monitors and raises his eyebrows. He doesn't say anything.

Sir Spencer shrugs. "Well, that's not the kind of southern hospitality I would have expected."

"Can I help you?" The security guard frowns. He's unimpressed by the well-dressed Brit with the receding hairline and expensive veneer smile.

"Much better," says Sir Spencer. "And yes, good man, you *may* help us. We're here to see Bella Francesca."

"Are you now?" The guard sounds dubious. "And you would be?"

"Sir Spencer Thomas and guest."

"Is she expecting you?" The guard pulls a thin red three-ring binder from a drawer and opens it. He runs his finger down what appears to be a list of expected visitors.

"Yes," Sir Spencer winks. "She is."

The guard's finger stops and runs along a line of text. He looks up again at Sir Spencer and glances at me.

"You the guest?" he asks with a chin nod.

"Yes," Sir Spencer intercedes. "That's Chester Bennington. His name should be there too." I try not to chuckle.

The guard looks down at the list and then picks up a phone in front of him while scribbling something in the binder.

"This is Fitzgerald in security," he grunts into the phone. "I have a Mr. Thomas and a Mr. Bennington in the lobby. Can I send them up?" He pauses. "Okay then." He hangs up.

"You can go ahead," he says, suspicion leaking from his stare. "The elevators are to your left. Take one to the sixtieth floor. There will be someone to greet you when you get there."

"Thank you so much, Mr. Fitzgerald." Sir Spencer pats the desk and then herds me toward the elevators. When we're out of the security guard's earshot, I grab Sir Spencer's arm.

"Chester Bennington?" I tug him to a stop. "Really?"

He smirks. "Well we couldn't use your real name. You're a wanted man and one can never be too careful."

"Yeah," I acknowledge. "But Chester Bennington is the lead singer of Linkin Park."

"As though the good Mr. Fitzgerald would have known," Sir Spencer winks, pulls himself from my grip, and strides toward an open elevator.

As I follow him onto the elevator, I count the seventh and eighth security camera we've passed since getting out of the car in front of the building. A fake name won't be enough to keep me hidden from those who want to find me, but it keeps my name off the paperwork.

***

The elevator doors whoosh open to reveal a large woman in a lime green pantsuit and a headset awaiting us on the sixtieth floor. She smiles, revealing what I imagine is a piece of her breakfast stuck between her gums and upper front teeth.

"Good morning, gentlemen," she says without dislodging the embedded food. "Welcome to Nanergetix. I hope your flight was uneventful."

"It was quite good." Sir Spencer motions to his teeth with his fingers and smiles.

The woman blinks and runs her tongue along her teeth. She smiles again, silently asking for approval.

"You got it, dear," Sir Spencer nods.

"Thank you," she blushes and then turns to lead us down the hallway, her high heels clicking on the cream-colored travertine floors. Her hips swing back and forth quickly, matching the rhythm of her feet on the polished stone.

The walls are lined with photographs of Don Carlos Buell, each of them framed and featuring a plaque detailing the story behind the picture. His smile is nearly identical in each one of them. It's hard for me to reconcile the man grinning in the photographs with the image of his stunned, bloodied face burned into my memory.

The end of the hall opens to a large office with floor to ceiling windows looking west toward Eleanor Tinsley Park and the edge of the tree-lined mansion estates of River Oaks. The panorama holds my attention until Sir Spencer grabs my shoulder and turns me toward a woman whose ice-blue eyes are more intoxicating than the view.

"Bella, I'd like you to meet the man we discussed." Sir Spencer draws me toward her. "Jackson Quick, this is Bella Francesca Buell."

Buell?

"Hello." I extend my hand and she reciprocates, eyes searching mine. She's looking for something.

"Hello," she said, her lips spreading into a demure smile. "It's a pleasure to finally meet you." She lets go of my hand and motions toward a seat across from a large glass desk.

"Will that be all, Miss Buell?" Lime Green Pantsuit asks, adjusting her headset.

"Yes, Brenda, thank you." Bella Francesca slinks around the desk and sits on the edge of a large white leather office chair. She grabs the edge of the desk and pulls herself toward it. Brenda leaves the office and closes the door behind her.

"Buell?" I ask the obvious question without really asking it.

"I'm his daughter, Mr. Quick," she says. The kindness in her eyes has given way to a steely glare. "His death left me in charge of his company." She crosses her legs and brushes the wrinkles from her lavender skirt. Then she fiddles with the oversized Cartier watch on her left wrist, as if the red soles on the bottoms of her shoes didn't already give away her taste in expensive accessories.

"I see the resemblance," I acknowledge through a smile. Her dark hair and strong, attractive features resemble her father's. Her olive skin is flawless, and she's maybe thirty years old. "I'm sorry for your loss."

"You were there, Sir Spencer tells me," she glances at him and then back at me, "and I remember seeing you in some of the news footage."

Is that what this is about?

Sir Spencer is looking down, his eyes pinched between his fingers as if he's fighting off a headache.

"Yes," I admit. "I was there."

"I understand," she shifts forward on her elbows, leaning into me, "you, in turn, killed the man who killed my father."

"Yes."

"Tell me about that," her eyes narrow. "I've read the news accounts, of course, but I want your perspective."

"I'm not sure what to say."

"I can take it," she leans back again. "I'm a big girl."

I suddenly feel as though the temperature in the room was cranked up fifty degrees. "Well, my girlfriend, at the time turned out to be an assassin, a sharpshooter. She was working for your dad. She had a partner named Crockett. The two of them betrayed your dad. They decided to flip and work for my boss, the governor. I don't know if it was a money thing or what, but they flipped. My girlfriend was killed."

"I'm sorry to hear that."

"Why are you sorry?" I ask. "She flipped on your dad."

Bella rubs her lips lightly with the tip of her middle finger as she considers the question. She exhales. "I'm sorry for your loss. I'm not sorry she's dead." She's a straight shooter like my ex, apparently.

"Fair enough."

"So continue." She waves her fingers at me as if to shoo me away.

"After she died, Crockett worked on his own. I figured out he was gunning for your dad. I tried to stop him. It didn't work. I was a couple of seconds too late. But before he killed my boss, I shot him."

"So you risked your life." She points at me. "You put *your* life in danger to save *my* father, when he might not have extended you the same courtesy?"

"Ha!" Sir Spencer interrupts. "Please, Bella! 'Might not have'? We know he wouldn't have helped out poor Jackson here. Who was Jackson in the scheme of things? He was considered collateral damage by his mentor and employer. His girlfriend betrayed his trust. Your father, who did not know Jackson, would not have risked his life for anything of the sort. He—"

"Point taken," Bella cuts in. "A poor turn of phrase."

"Speaking of points," I interject, irritated with being spoken of as if I'm not here. "What is all of this about? Why am I here?"

"I was getting to that," says Sir Spencer.

"Was this job to play storyteller for the poor little rich girl?" I stand up from my seat, motioning at Bella.

Her jaw tightens at my description of her. She folds her arms across her chest and leans back in the chair, almost pouting.

"Unfair," Sir Spencer says softly. "That's rude and uncalled for, Jackson."

I palm the sweat from my forehead. "I don't see it that way."

"Miss Buell was merely using this opportunity to gain some perspective on the man she wants to hire for a critical role," he explains. "And frankly, given the death of her beloved father only months ago, I don't blame her."

"I don't like being called collateral damage," I huff.

"She didn't call you that," Sir Spencer stands to face me. "*I* did. And it was in reference to the way in which your beloved governor saw you."

"The same governor who hired *you*," I said, pressing my finger into his shoulder. "*You* were working for him when her father was killed. You were on that team. So how is it you're now in this woman's good graces? How is it you're playing headhunter for Nanergetix?"

"As I've told you before," Sir Spencer says softly, returning to his seat, "I am an equal opportunity consultant. I work for whomever—"

"Has the most money?"

"Touché," Sir Spencer nods. "In many cases, yes. It is also of great import, however, I share a certain amount of fundamental ideology with my partners."

Bella abruptly stands from her seat and walks around the desk toward Sir Spencer. "I'm not sure he's the right man. He's fiery, yes. He's smart, agreed. But I don't think he's the one."

"We have limited options," Sir Spencer says. "It's not as though we have people banging on your door to help you. A typical operative wouldn't be motivated by the amount of money you're offering."

"Maybe I should offer more?" Bella shrugs her shoulders and sits on the edge of the desk between Sir Spencer and me. "This is too big a job for an overly sensitive amateur."

"Hold on," I interject. "I'm right here! Stop talking about me in the third person! And you can't fire me from a job I haven't even accepted yet."

Sir Spencer nods silently and rubs his chin. He sits back against the chair, releasing a whoosh of air from the soft cushion. "We've gotten off topic here. And I made a mistake by allowing you to question Jackson about what he saw in your father's final moments. We need to keep this to the mission at hand."

"Which is?" I still have no idea what is going on. I'm here in a high-rise with the daughter of a dead energy titan turned politician and a snake of a kingmaker who holds my life in his hands.

"It's complicated," says Sir Spencer.

"And why wouldn't it be?" I ask, the sarcasm oozing.

***

"So you're telling me I'm going to skip around the globe looking for little pieces of some formula?"

"It's not exactly a formula," clarifies Bella. "It's more like a process."

"Oh," I laugh snidely. "That's better."

"I understand from your perspective, there's no difference," says Sir Spencer, who's helped himself to a drink from Bella's office wet bar. "However, given what's at stake, the subtle differences are important."

"Sure. Whatever. Explain to me what's so critical about this process?"

Sir Spencer leisurely stirs his drink with his left pinkie and then sucks it dry. "Suffice it to say that the process involves what are called 'solar neutrinos'. It is world-changing. The scientist who cracked it is dead. He was killed."

"Before he died, he took precautions," adds Bella. "He separated the steps of the process and hid the elements in different places. That way, no one person would have the entirety of the research."

"There are a lot of people who want this research," says Sir Spencer. "People who have and will kill for it."

"What does it do? This neutrino process..."

"It's energy related," Bella answers. "And it dips into the communications arena too. There are a lot of layers. I can explain the details later."

"Who owns this *process*?"

"I do," says Bella. "Well, Nanergetix does. The scientist who was killed, Dr. Paul Wolf, was working for us in an undisclosed underground location."

"Somebody disclosed it," I say. "Or he wouldn't be dead."

"Therein lies the rub," says Sir Spencer. "You're not the only one looking for these disparate parts. It's a bit of a scavenger hunt."

"So I need to find all of the missing pieces and give them to you before someone else finds them?" I ask. "And then my job is complete? Then I can go about my life and start over?"

"Yes," say Sir Spencer. "That's the deal. You find the entirety of the process, deliver it to me, and I become your best friend."

"How many parts are there?" I ask, standing from my seat.

"We think there are four," says Bella. "But you're not doing this alone."

"What do you mean?"

"I'm coming with you," she replies. "You won't recognize what you're looking for without me. And I need you to keep me alive."

"Uh huh. That brings me back to the question I asked you in the car, Sir Spencer. Why me? Why am I the one who'll keep her alive? I don't have those kinds of skills."

"I knew that question was *again* forthcoming," Sir Spencer wags his finger at me as he backs his way to the wet bar. "The answer is again, quite simple."

Sir Spencer pours another three fingers of scotch and takes a healthy sip before answering the question. Bella gives him a look that tells me she's growing impatient of the theatrics.

"It is foremost you are motivated by fear, Jackson," he says, without acknowledging Bella's glare. "That's why you've survived no fewer than a half dozen attempts on your life in the last four months."

"How do *you* know?"

"That's beside the point." He swirls the highball glass and sniffs the scotch. "Suffice it to say that I do." He takes a sip. "Then there is your history of travel."

"What do you mean?"

"There was that vision quest across Europe during your less-than-focused early twenties," he says.

"The lost years between your failed stint as a radio deejay and the fortuitous foray into Texas politics."

"What does that have to do with this? And how do you know about that?"

"Good man," Sir Spencer peacocks his way from the bar toward me and takes his seat, "when are you going to learn? My methods are...my methods. How this is relevant is simple. You spent significant amounts of time in two of the cities we believe hold at least two of the pieces to the puzzle. You know the streets, the haunts, ways to extract information. Am I correct?"

"I dunno," I shrug my shoulders. "What two cities?"

"Odessa, Ukraine," says Sir Spencer, "and Heidelberg, Germany."

"Seriously?"

"Quite seriously," says Bella, no hint of humor in those hypnotic eyes of hers. "I received a partial message from Dr. Wolf before his death. He gave clues to at least a couple of the hiding places."

"This is all a bit too convenient," I say, smelling a rat. "This scientist doesn't want anyone to know how this process works, so he spreads parts of the formula all over the world, then he sends you some secret message that hints at where they are?" I shake my head. "It sounds to me like he didn't trust you either, Bella. Either that, or you're not telling me the whole story. This whole thing, it doesn't add up."

Sir Spencer exchanges a furtive glance with Bella. Neither of them say anything.

"I'm out." I make my way towards the door. "I'm gonna need my bag from your car," I tell to Sir Spencer without turning around.

The smiling portraits of the dead Buell blend together as I stride past them to the elevator. I step onto the elevator and wait to turn around until the doors slide closed behind me then glance up at the television monitor above the bank of floor buttons. There's no volume, but I recognize the scene on the screen. It's a bullet hole riddled bus, only now the bus is surrounded by yellow crime scene tape and is swarming with police. Large crowds are standing around, watching the investigators try to piece together what happened. The words scrolling across the bottom third of the video read: *Early morning shootout, bus crash in San Antonio leaves two dead. Police searching for suspect, consider him to be armed and dangerous.*

The screen fills with a new image and I hit the red emergency stop button. The elevator screams to halt and a loud bell rings an alarm. On the screen, with the words *DOUBLE HOMICIDE SUSPECT* beneath it is a color surveillance photo of my face.

CHAPTER 3

I should have known better. I should have known to rip the bus camera from the windshield and take it with me. But I didn't. I left the best piece of evidence against me sitting in that bus. It doesn't matter that the woman on the bus fired first. As far as the cops are concerned, I killed two people and ran. I'm royally screwed. I end up behind bars anywhere in Texas and I am dead. The governor will see to that.

Against the annoying ring of the alarm bell, I weigh my options. I can continue down to the first floor, exit, grab my go-bag from Sir Spencer's car, and try to disappear. Or I can head back up to the sixtieth floor and take my chances with a couple of dangerous liars who want to use me in some sick spy game to who-knows-what end.

Not much of a choice.

"Hello," a voice blares through the speaker in the elevator. The alarm stops. "Hello, this is security. Is everyone okay?"

Think, Jackson. Think!

"Is everyone okay?" the voice repeats.

"Yes," I answer. "I'm the only one in here. I hit the button by mistake. I'm okay."

The voice tells me to remain calm and explains which buttons to push to restart the elevator. I take a moment and then grab the phone from my front pocket and dial a familiar number. It rings once.

"News 4 Houston," answers the man on the other end of the call. "George Townsend."

George is a television investigative reporter. He helped me send the governor to jail. He's risked his life right alongside me. If he knows there is a potential story in it for him, he'll do anything I ask him to do.

"George," I whisper. "This is Jackson. I need your help."

"When don't you need my help?" The reporter laughs, clearly not sensing the urgency in my voice.

"Really," I stress. "I need you to do some digging for me."

"Okay. What is it?"

"Sir," the security voice echoes in the elevator. "Do you need me to explain the restart procedure again?"

"Uh, no. I've got it. Thanks."

"Where are you?" asks George.

"In an elevator," I explain. "Long story."

"It always is," George says. "Is this about the governor? You know he's appealing the conviction."

"No, it's unrelated," I explain. "Sort of."

"Sort of?"

"Shut up and listen for a second!"

"Sir?" The security guard again. "I can override the system from down here if you'd like. It'll take a couple of minutes."

"Okay," I agree with the guard. "That's fine. Maybe that would be easier."

"You're stuck in an elevator?" George asks.

"Yes."

"Okay sir," the guard says through the speaker. "It'll be a moment and then you'll resume your trip down to the first floor. Hold on to one of the rails against the wall please, the elevator will jerk into motion suddenly."

"Okay, thanks," I call toward the speaker. "I appreciate it."

"How'd you get stuck?" George asks.

"Not important. You got a pen?"

"Yep."

"Okay then," I exhale. "I need to you look up Bella Francesca Buell. Find me everything about her I can't find with a Google search."

"The C.E.O. of Nanergetix?"

"Yes. Also, I need you to do some surface digging into a scientist named Paul Wolf. And if you can, cross reference something called solar neutrinos, whatever they are."

"N-e-u-t-r-i-n-o-s?"

"Yes," I repeat. "I guess so. Get it to me in a pdf file I can read on my phone. I don't want unsecured links I have to click."

"No please or thank you?" George laughs again.

"I'm a little stressed at the moment. I may have gotten myself into something here and I need to know more about what it is."

The elevator groans to life and it starts moving downward again. I almost lose my balance and quickly grab onto the stainless steel rail against the back wall.

"Gotten yourself into something?" George asks, his computer keyboard clicking away in the background. "Did you ever get yourself out of anything?"

He knows I've been running for my life for the last year and a half. He helps me when he can, but I try not to over involve him. He's in danger enough with his almost weekly reports on the governor's illicit schemes and the fallout, and it's only his high profile that keeps him alive.

"Not really," I admit. "But maybe this something will help me with the other something."

"I'll get this stuff to you as soon as I can, okay?"

"Thanks, George. I appreciate it."

"I know you do. By the way, were you on a bus in San Antonio this morning?"

"Can I trust you?"

"Hmmm," he pauses and then laughs again. "Probably not."

"Then no," the elevators door slide apart at the first floor, "I wasn't."

***

As soon as the elevator doors open, I press the button for the sixtieth floor and the doors close again. There's not much of a choice here, but I'm going with door number two. On my own, I'm as vulnerable as I've been in months. With the resources of both Sir Spencer and Bella I've got a better shot, regardless of whatever it is they're *really* trying to get me to do. I don't trust them. However, Sir Spencer was right when he told me I needed him. As much as I hate admitting it to myself, I do. He's got connections and access that I don't. He can help me, he says, once I'm done with this job.

Truth be told, I've got no way of knowing if I'll survive this "scavenger hunt". I've no guarantee he'll follow through with his promise to help me start a new life, free of bullets and blood and betrayal. I've been burned before and I survived.

The elevator doors open on the sixtieth floor and I'm greeted immediately by Bella Francesca Buell. We both jump back a step, surprised to see each other.

"I was coming to get you," she states. "I—we—really need your help."

"Sir Spencer convince you of that?" I ask, stepping into the hallway.

"I convinced myself," she says, walking back toward her office. "Sir Spencer is persuasive, but the decision is mine alone."

"I still don't trust what either one of you are telling me, but I don't really have a choice."

"He tells me you're not *quick* to trust anyone, pardon the pun." She laughs nervously, her edge softened.

"Ah hah," bellows Sir Spencer's voice from the end of the hall. "There he is! See, Bella? I told you the prodigal son would return."

I roll my eyes. "I was gone all of five minutes. I was just telling your conspirator I don't trust you, but I don't have a choice."

"See yourself on the news did you?" He laughs. "Such a silly mistake, good man. You know better than to have left the security camera intact aboard that bus."

"How did you...?"

"Bella has a row of television monitors on the back wall of her office," he says, stopping a step too close to me, always skilled at making me uncomfortable, keeping me off-balance. "No sooner had you walked out when your handsome visage pops up on three of them almost simultaneously. Such a pity."

It takes everything in me not to punch him square in his smug Anglican jaw. I clench mine instead and walk past him into Bella's office. I spot the row of LED televisions to the right. I didn't notice them before.

I'm really off today. I'm missing the little things.

"So then," I sit down in one of the chairs opposite the desk, "what's the plan?"

"You and Bella will take my plane to South Dakota," Sir Spencer says. "There, you'll rendezvous with a friend of hers who should make your lives a touch easier."

"How so?"

"He's former military," Bella tells me. "He's a contract employee of Nanergetix, a consultant who wears a lot of hats."

"Any of those include killing people?"

"They include advance intelligence," she answers. "He'll provide us with scouting reports of what we can expect ahead of our arrival...well, anywhere."

"Why South Dakota?"

"That's where Dr. Wolf was killed," she says. "And there may be some additional information we need to find."

"Okay then," I stand from the seat. "Let's go."

***

"Here you go, Mr. Quick," Sally Anne, Sir Spencer's flight attendant, hands me a Diet Dr. Pepper in a leaded glass. "Is there anything else you need?"

"No thanks," I take a quick sip of the drink before setting it on the table beside me. "I'm good."

Sally Anne turns her attention to Bella, who is sitting in the large captain's chair next to mine at the rear of the plane. "Ms. Buell, would you like a refill of your espresso?"

"In a few minutes, please," she says. "Thank you, Sally Anne."

The flight attendant nods and walks to the front of the aircraft. Sir Spencer is reading the newspaper in a mid-cabin seat. He's been in his own world since takeoff.

Bella turns her attention to her iPhone. I notice a small white square on the back of what looks like a Vera Bradley case. Charlie liked Vera Bradley.

"You have the Tile app?"

"Uh," she flips over her phone to look at the square plastic stuck to the case, "yeah. I'm always misplacing this thing, so I ordered a couple of these things. I've got one on my keychain too. It works pretty well." She flips the phone over and goes back to thumbing through whatever it was she was reading.

Tile is like a beacon. Stick one to anything, and with the help of a cell phone app, I can locate it. The trick is, if it gets too far away, I have to hope other people using the app are nearby. Then their phone locates my tile and relays that information to my app. It's pretty crazy technology but it seems to work. I bought a few of them when they came out and like them.

"So, Bella," I shift to my left and face her, "tell me more about solar neutrinos and why this process is so important."

"It's complicated," she sighs and clicks off her iPhone. "I'll keep it as simple as I can."

"Thank you Obi Wan. If you made it too *complicated* for me, my head might explode."

"That's not what I meant," she blushes. "I meant it's not easy for me to explain. I'm not a scientist. I'm a businesswoman."

"I'm kidding with you."

"Oh," she says. "All right then." She brushes hair from her cheek and then pulls it back behind her ear.

Apparently her sense of humor isn't nearly as appealing as her appearance. It's difficult not to stare at her. She's *that* striking. The more time I spend with her, it's all the more noticeable. I find myself intentionally avoiding eye contact with her. I don't want her to think I'm a creeper.

"Go ahead," I offer. "I'm listening."

"So," she begins. "The sun is powered by nuclear fusion, right?"

"Right."

"And there are byproducts of that process," she explains. "One of those byproducts is an invisible particle called a solar neutrino." She holds up her hand and pinches her fingers together, as though that helps me understand how tiny these *invisible* particles are. "Fusion, in case you didn't know, is when two atomic nuclei merge, or fuse, into one nucleus."

"Okay."

"Well, without getting too deep into this," Bella says, "during the fusion process, there is what's called beta decay. That's essentially the conversion of a neutron into a proton accompanied by the release of an electron. When that electron leaves the atom, its energy should match the energy missing from the atom it left behind."

"Clarify that. My mind is exploding."

"Okay," she says. "So, you have an atom with three parts. One of the parts becomes charged and another one of the parts leaves. It's like subtraction, kinda. Three minus one should equal two, right?"

"Right."

"Well, it doesn't in this case. There's something missing. Instead of three minus one equaling two, it equals one and a half. Or it equals one. Whatever. It doesn't calculate. So scientists discovered the missing part is what's called a neutrino. It's the missing energy that escapes the fusion process. And it flies through space onto the Earth and gets absorbed."

"Absorbed into what?"

"The Earth."

"So why are these neutrinos important?"

"As far as I understand it," she says, "neutrinos are one of the fundamental particles of the universe. They're similar to electrons, except they don't carry a charge. They're not negative, not positive. So they can travel a long way without being affected by other charged particles. They really can travel through anything."

"Like radiation?"

"Good question!" She leans forward, eyes widening. Bella seems excited I may be getting this. "Yes! Like radiation but with one big difference. Radiation doesn't necessarily travel well through water."

"And neutrinos do?"

"Yes. Neutrinos, as I said, move through anything. So, they have the potential to carry 'things' with them as the move. Even through water."

"Okay," I shake my head, "now you lost me."

"Neutrinos have the potential to carry information with them. If you can encode a message in the neutrinos, they could take that message from one place to the other. If you take a bunch of these neutrinos, concentrate them, and then blast them in a beam in a particular direction, they can deliver those messages much faster than other forms of communication." Her eyebrows arch, looking for any indication of my understanding of the physics lesson. "The real application here is underwater, in the ocean. As I mentioned, radiation doesn't travel as well as neutrinos do. Neither do radio waves. Right now, submarines use a low frequency wave to communicate, but to do that they have to surface or use trailing radio antennas."

"So...?"

"So," she shakes her head condescendingly, "that makes them vulnerable to detection. The point of a sub is to remain *undetected.*"

"Understood."

"If you could use neutrinos, which pass through everything, you could send messages to these submarines from very long distances without compromising their positions. It's tactically a game changer. And since two-thirds of the Earth is covered in water…"

"If the neutrinos pass through everything, wouldn't they pass through the subs too?"

"Yes and no. Scientists figured out a way to actually make the hull of the submarine a neutrino collector of sorts. Without giving you too much information to digest—"

"Too late."

"Right," she laughs. "Well, scientists embed the neutrinos with these other particles that are charged. By measuring those charged particles they can, essentially, 'catch' the neutrinos in the subs. But there's a catch."

"Always is."

"This whole neutrino communication thing is cutting edge, and so the messages can only flow one way."

"What do you mean?"

"The subs can only receive messages. They can't send them," she says. "Or at least they *couldn't* send them."

"Your scientist figured out a way to send them from subs?"

"Yes," she nods excitedly, "he did. He was really the first one to perfect the reception of those particle transmissions, building off some work done by guys at Virginia Tech and N.C. State."

"My dad went to N.C. State."

"Oh," she says, completely disinterested. "So, building off that work, he perfected the transmission of the neutrinos to the subs. At the same time, he was able to design a portable, lightweight neutrino transmitter that would allow submarines to transmit encoded messages faster and farther than ever before. It's revolutionary."

"Instead of the looking for these puzzle pieces all over the world why don't we go find the portable transmitter? Wouldn't that be easier?"

"It would," she says. "Except it hasn't been built yet. The puzzle pieces are the blueprint and instructions for the transmitter. Without those pieces, we can't build it or use it."

"I see." I get it. This isn't some formula. It's not just a process. It's much bigger than that. "If the wrong people get a hold of it, that could be a problem."

"A huge problem. If the wrong people find these pieces, they'll sell them off to the highest bidder. They could end up in the hands of the Russians or the Chinese."

"Or worse," I add.

"Or worse." She leans back against the leather of the captain's chair. She takes a last sip from her coffee cup and then holds it up. "Sally Anne," she calls, "could I please have a refill on the espresso? I need the caffeine."

"Of course, Ms. Buell." Sally Anne hurries toward us, smiling the entirety of the short trip to the rear of the cabin. She takes the empty cup. "Anything more for you Mr. Quick?"

"No thank you."

"I'll be right back, Ms. Buell," she says. "Black with no cream or sugar, correct?"

"Yes, Sally Anne, thank you."

Sally walks to the front of the cabin, her hips swinging in the skirt that leaves little to the imagination. My eyes follow her until she turns into the kitchen adjacent to the cockpit.

"Nice," Bella scowls at me. "So typical."

"What?"

"You know exactly what."

CHAPTER 4

Rapid City, South Dakota is not what I remembered. It's beautiful; the dense forests, jagged hills, deep blue, cloudless skies. But aside from the grumble of the occasional passing Harley, it feels almost uninhabited.

"We should be there in about thirty minutes," Bella says. "It's a quick trip to the monument."

We're in the back of a rented Chevy Suburban. The driver is an older man with a snow white mustache. His face resembles the weathered outcrops of granite poking out from behind the trees and brush that line US-16. He's listening to an AM country station on the radio. Merle Haggard.

My phone buzzes in my pocket. It's a message from George Townsend, the reporter. I touch the screen to reveal the text.

lots of good info. call me when u can talk. i sent some prelim stuff 2 ur email. pdf like u asked. talk soon -gt

I thumb a quick response.

just got off a plane. can't talk now. will look at pdf and call l8r. thx.

"Who's that?" Bella nods at my phone.

"Nobody."

Her eyes narrow, but she doesn't say anything.

"So," I say, changing the subject before it gets uncomfortable, "what's the deal with Sir Spencer?"

"What do you mean?"

"He left us here and flew off to wherever. How do we get around once we're finished here?"

"I have a plane on standby," Bella says. "It'll be ready when we are."

"What is it? A G6? I've always wanted to fly in a G6."

"What are you, a hip hop mogul?" she laughs. "No. It's not a G6. Those planes are sixty million dollars new and they hold eighteen passengers. I don't ever need anything that large."

"But you shopped one, obviously. Don't act like I'm the only one who thinks they're cool. And I've been shot at more times than 50 Cent, so that gives me street cred."

"It's a Bombardier Global 5000, good enough to get us to Europe nonstop," she replies without expression. "And you're a child."

I smirk and turn to look out the window. The trees have given way to the granite. The hills framing the horizon poke at the sky with their jagged, irregular peaks. They're mesmerizing as we whir past one after the other. It's almost like standing on the beach, watching the ocean meet the sky in the distance. My mind drifts, hypnotized by what's out there, what awaits me.

***

My dad, when he was alive, loved the outdoors. He was an expert marksman who relished the kick of a rifle, but never put a bullet in an animal. And the summer before he died, he and my mom had brought me here to South Dakota.

Our true destination was Wyoming and Devils Tower. I wanted so badly to see it up close after my dad and I watched Close Encounters Of The Third Kind on cable. I'd begged for months to take a trip there. Sloppy molds of the laccolith, made with my mother's homemade mashed potatoes, were a poor substitute for the real thing.

I remember seeing it for the first time. We were in a rental car, heading west on US Highway 14 from South Dakota. There was little but prairie and rolling hills for most of the two hour drive, but over a rise, miles from the monument itself, we saw it. Like a singular casino in the Vegas desert, the Tower grew unnaturally from its surroundings.

As we drove closer, and the Tower grew taller, the excitement built. Even my mom and dad were giddy at the prospect of hiking around the monument and learning more about it.

My mom turned around in her seat to face me. "You know, Devils Tower was the country's first national monument. And when they made it official, on paper, someone left off the apostrophe in Devil's. They never bothered to change it."

"The devil's always in the details," my dad laughed. He glanced at me through the rearview mirror, a big grin plastered on his face.

"You're too funny," my mom said, playfully shoving my dad's shoulder. "Always one with a joke."

We laughed and kept teasing one another until we pulled up to the monument's entrance. On either side, outside of the gate, there were alien-hocking souvenir shops. Apparently I wasn't the only one whose trip was inspired by closing scenes of Close Encounters.

My dad paid the park entrance fee and got a glossy brochure he handed to my mom. The road to the Tower wound to the left, past an open field pocked with prairie dog holes. I pressed my face against the window and caught a glimpse of a couple of them poking their heads out from the dirt.

"Those prairie dogs aren't well-liked around here," my dad remarked. "Ranchers hate them and will use them for target practice."

"Why?" I asked. "They look harmless."

"They ruin the crops, the soil, make it tough on their herds," he said. "They're nuisances."

The road spun back to the left and uphill into dense forest. I rolled down my window and could feel the air getting cooler. A motorcycle grumbled past us, the driver with both hands on the handlebars of his.

"Are we gonna hike around the Tower?" I asked excitedly. "There a couple of paths we can take."

"I don't see why not," my mom looked at Dad. "We came all this way. It'd be silly not to take in the full spectacle of an alien landing site."

"Mom," I protested, "there were no aliens here. It was a movie."

"I know it was a movie, Jackson, but you can't definitively say aliens have never landed here. Can you?"

"Well," I looked at my dad in the rearview mirror, who was smirking, "I can't definitively say they haven't. But there's no proof they did, either."

"So you'd need to see something to believe in it?" my dad interjected. "You're a show me kinda guy?"

They did this a lot, my parents. They'd challenge my reasoning, my beliefs. I'd make a declarative statement and they'd refute it, or call it into question.

I remember my dad telling me I should never quantify anything as being the best, unless I knew it was better than all of the other alternatives. Otherwise, he said, I could only contend it was as good as any other alternative.

"I guess that means you're as good as any husband in the world," my mom had reasoned. "Since, I've only been married to you, I can't say you're the best. I haven't been married to all of the alternatives."

My dad told her she was right. She kissed him and told him that, without having married anyone else, she knew him to be the best. She didn't need empirical data.

But she played along with him every time he challenged me. She took his side, pushing my critical reasoning skills.

So there, in the rental car, climbing the road to the base of Devils Tower, I had to admit I could not disprove the existence of aliens. It was possible they'd been to Wyoming. And actually, that thought, that possibility, made the hike around the Tower all the more enjoyable.

***

Envision a prototypical United States Marine. Picture his barrel chest, Popeye-like forearms, and ramrod straight posture. Now age him thirty years. Pencil in crows-feet and scowl lines. That's Mack Mahoney, with some slight differences than what you're probably imagining.

He shakes my hand with a vise of a grip. "Hello, Quick. I've heard a lot about you." We're standing in the back of the outdoor amphitheater at Mt. Rushmore. Four presidents are eavesdropping, but other than that, there's nobody around. The evening presentation doesn't start for a few hours.

"Thank you."

"I didn't say what I'd heard was *good*. I said I'd heard about you."

"Oh." *Awkward.*

"That's not fair, Mack," says Bella. "I didn't say anything negative about you, Jackson. Mack, how is your wife?"

"She's in remission, six months. So it's day by day, really. Thanks for asking, Bella," he turns to me again. "I make you uncomfortable, don't I?" he asks, still holding my hand.

"Well," I consider the question. "Yes."

"What is it?" he asks, letting go of my hand. "Is it that I'm black, that I have vitiligo, or that I'm missing a leg?" The intensity of his stare outdoes anything else that might put me off balance. I glance down at the hi-tech prosthetic extending beneath his pressed khaki shorts.

"It's the vitiligo, and you're missing a leg." I keep my eyes locked on his.

"Not me being black," he says, no hint of expression. "That doesn't make you uncomfortable?"

"No more than me being white with two legs and no viral skin condition makes you uncomfortable."

Mack Mahoney takes a step back and folds him arms. He looks me up and down as though he's taking inventory. Then he nods and a smile slowly spreads from one cheek to the other. "You'll do, Quick," he says. "You're a straight shooter."

He has no idea.

He slaps me on the shoulder and I exhale. So does Bella.

"Let's sit," Mack says. "I only got one good leg to stand on and it's tired." He motions to the nearest bleacher and we sit, Bella and I on one row and Mack on the one in front of us. "I like coming here when I'm in the area. Every night they honor veterans. They invite us up on stage and let us say our names, our branch of service. We always get big applause. It makes me feel good."

"It's kinda in the open isn't it?"

"So?" Mack grunts.

"So, Mack," Bella adjusts the conversation and her lavender skirt, tucking her right foot behind her left ankle. "What can you tell me I don't already know? And why are we meeting here?"

"They're still here," he says. "The trigger man is gone, but the team is hanging around. They're waiting on you. Here at the monument, we have privacy. They may or may not know you're here already. But they can't watch you here."

"What do you mean?

"Whoever killed Wolf is gone," he says. "But there are clearly others working with him who are sticking around."

"How do you know this?" I ask.

"Surveillance," he says. "I've got a handful of wireless cameras staking out popular parts of Lead, Custer, and Deadwood. There are security cameras I've accessed, and I've got facial recognition software on my computer. I can distinguish the locals from the tourists and the tourists from the hired guns. I spent a career doing this."

"How do you know none of those hired guns aren't the killer?" I press. Bella looks at me and nods at Mack. He looks unsure about answering me.

"Body types," he finally answers. "I've got the surveillance video from the security cameras at the Homestake mine, where the lab was. Whoever that dude was, doesn't match these other guys. Satisfied, Quick?" His question is a directive to stop asking any of my own.

This whole conversation seems choreographed, like it's for my benefit.

"Yes." *No.*

"Okay then," he turns his body more toward Bella. "There are three or four of these guys hanging around. They're looking for you, Bella, even though they don't know it. They're here to clean up."

"Clean up?" Bella asks. "I don't understand, Mack. They killed Dr. Wolf in a lab nobody was supposed to know about. They've got at least part of the process and a head start on finding the rest of it."

"You saw the video," Mack says. "You saw what they did to Wolf from the killer's perspective. You heard the questions the killer asked. You know what it is he wanted."

"Yes," says Bella. "We saw it because the killer uploaded it into Wolf's computer. He left the video camera attached to it."

"Why do you think he did that?" Mack asks.

"So we'd see it," says Bella. "So that we know what they know."

"So you'd know what they want you to know," says Mack. "Whoever is behind this wants you here."

"The video was bait?" I ask.

"In a way," Mack replies. "You don't upload a video directly to the company server and then tag the executives unless you want attention from them."

"Then I shouldn't be here," says Bella. She stands and brushes her skirt. "I'm not clear as to why I'm here, Mack. You could have easily told me this over the phone."

"I could have," says Mack, pushing on the bench to stand.

"Then why didn't you?"

"Because there's a reason they want you," he says, shifting his weight to his good leg. "And I want to know what that reason is."

"Now *I'm* bait?" she asks. "You'd have me come here to be a sitting duck, a target? I've known you since I was a little girl, Mack. I don't get this."

"You wouldn't have come here if I told you the operational hazards," he says. "And I wouldn't have had you come here if I couldn't keep you safe."

Bella considers what he's selling and folds her arms in front her. She looks at me for guidance. I shrug. I'm along for the ride, despite being wary about where it's taking me.

However, I think something is… off.

"You said it," Mack points at Bella. "I've known you since you were no higher than my knee, since I had two good knees. Do you really think I would risk your life?"

"I guess not," she shrugs.

"Good," he says. "Then let's get to work and find out why it is they want you."

***

Sitting alone in the front of the Chevy Suburban while Mack and Bella ride in the back discussing the details of his plan, I've finally got time to check the browser on my phone and find out what George Townsend emailed to me.

I log into my email on a secure server. There's a new message from George:

Jackson— I found a fair amount of info on Bella Buell. She doesn't try to hide. I also found some basic info on solar neutrinos. What's the connection between Buell and neutrinos? Whatever it is, it's not obvious. There's nothing I could find that put the two together. Call me when you can. -GT

At the bottom of the email are two pdf attachments. I tap the file attachment to open the first one:

BELLA FRANCESCA BUELL**

DOB: 09/25/85

BIRTHPLACE: HOUSTON, TEXAS

EDUCATION: UNIVERSITY OF TEXAS, B.S. BUSINESS
RICE UNIVERSITY, M.B.A.

PARENTS: DON CARLOS BUELL (DECEASED), MARY JOHNSON BUELL

EMPLOYMENT: NANERGETIX CORPORATION, HOUSTON TEXAS

CRIMINAL BACKGROUND: N/A

MARITAL STATUS: SINGLE, NEVER MARRIED

PASSPORT:VALID, UNITED STATES OF AMERICA

DRIVER LICENSE:VALID, TEXAS

CHL:VALID, TEXAS

PERSONAL NET WORTH:$165,000,000 USD (ESTIMATED)

NARRATIVE/PERSONAL: BUELL WAS A CHILD OF PRIVILEGE. A/B STUDENT AT PRIVATE CATHOLIC SCHOOLS IN HOUSTON, TEXAS. SHE COMPETED IN EQUESTRIAN EVENTS AS A TEEN. SHE IS AN ADEQUATE SNOW SKIER. AT 17 SHE WAS CERTIFIED TO SCUBA DIVE. SHE IS ALSO A LICENSED PILOT, THOUGH SHE IS NOT INSTRUMENT-RATED.

NARRATIVE/PROFESSIONAL:BUELL WAS HIRED BY NANERGETIX, HER FATHER'S COMPANY, IMMEDIATELY AFTER OBTAINING HER M.B.A. SHE WAS AN EXECUTIVE LEVEL SPECIAL ASSISTANT, REPORTING DIRECTLY TO THE C.E.O., UNTIL HER FATHER'S DEATH. SHE ASCENDED TO C.E.O. OF NANERGETIX DESPITE INTERNAL FEUD WITH C.F.O. AND C.T.O. BOTH RESIGNED AFTER BOARD OF DIRECTORS SELECTED BUELL. SHE HAS MAINTAINED COMPANY FOCUS ON EMERGING ENERGY TECHNOLOGY AND NANOSCALE/MICROSCALE RESEARCH.

**ALL INFORMATION CULLED FROM READILY AVAILABLE PUBLIC RECORDS/ DOCUMENTS/NEWS ACCOUNTS

Bella puts her hand on my shoulder. "It must be interesting."

"It is," I click the home button and turn off the phone. "It's all about you. Really fascinating stuff."

"Oh really?" She leans forward, trying to look. "What's it say about me?"

"You're nosy," I slip my phone into my pocket, "and you should put on your seatbelt."

"Huh," Bella slides back into her seat, tugging on her belt, and fastening it. "That's not a lot of information."

"It's enough for now."

She doesn't believe what I'm telling her. She doesn't trust me, which I find frustrating and ironic. As far as she's concerned, *my* life's an open book. She's the one collaborating with Sir Spencer, a man who months ago was working against her father. She's the CEO of a company with secret underground labs and scientists being killed for their intellectual property. She's working with a leatherneck turned counter-intelligence operative who knows how to hack security cameras and entrap contract killers. Nothing about her adds up, and the information George Townsend gathered doesn't clarify anything.

But I'm the untrustworthy one.

"So where is it we're headed?" I ask.

"The bar in Deadwood," Mack answers. "That's where we'll meet up with the two guys looking for Bella."

"Got it," I nod and take a deep breath. This is going be a long day. It already has been.

I woke up to the sounds of two nasty dudes trying to kill me, took a near fatal bus trip, flew to Houston, then South Dakota, and I'll end the day trying not to get killed by two more nasty dudes in a bar.

Mack hands me his iPad. "Take a look at this. You need to memorize these faces.

Mack's plan seems simple on the surface, but it's not. With his facial recognition software, he's identified two men who've repeatedly entered the same seven or eight bars and restaurants in Custer, Deadwood, and Lead. In the surveillance video he's gathered he's learned those men are carrying photographs of Bella. They're showing them to hostesses and barkeeps and they generally get blown off.

At one bar in Deadwood, however, the bartender seems interested in helping the guys. They exchange money and phone numbers. He gives them drinks. Of course there's no audio, but the video is compelling enough, to make that bar our point of attack.

On the iPad are digitally enhanced still frames of the two men. They look like most of the contractors who've been chasing me for the better part of two years. Both of them have their hair cropped high and tight, they wear starch-creased Dockers with tucked golf shirts that accentuate their thick necks and expansive biceps. Around their necks hang aviator sunglasses, even at night, and their watches are military issue. It's their casual look.

"The plan is the plan?" I glance at the driver. I don't want to say anything I'm not supposed to say.

"Yes," says Mack. "And you're fine to talk about it. Duke here is a friend of mine."

Duke smiles at me from underneath his prickly mustache, nods his head, but says nothing. He turns his attention back to the road ahead.

"Okay," I say. "Nice to meet you, Duke."

Duke nods again.

"We go into the bar and find our seats. After we order, you signal Bella to come in and sit alone at the bar and order herself something. We assume the bartender will alert the two bad guys. They arrive. We do our thing and flip the script on them."

"Yes," Mack says. "Though it may require a little improvisation, depending on what the subjects' intentions are."

"What does that mean?" asks Bella. "I thought you *knew* their intentions?"

"Common sense dictates they want to talk to you," says Mack. "Otherwise they could have sent people to Houston to take care of you."

"That raises a good question," I point out. "Why would they wait for Bella, or anyone for that matter, to come here? Why wouldn't they do whatever it is they plan on doing in Houston, where Nanergetix is located?"

"Couple of reasons," Mack says. "Less of a police presence here. Less security. More remote. And they know someone, like the head of the company, is going to come check out the lab. It's clear the killer was in and out. He had limited time in the facility. So if he missed anything, somebody from Nanergetix will find it. And the fact that he uploaded the video onto a computer and then sent it to a distinct distribution list, tells you what they want."

"That's a lot of guessing," says Bella.

"You're only now figuring that out?" I ask. Duke snickers.

"Look," Mack huffs, "I like how you're a straight shooter. I said that. But I don't need your sarcasm. You're a grunt here. I'm in command." He unfastens his belt and uses my seatback to pull himself close to my ear. "I'm paid a lot of money to gather intelligence and act on it," he barks. "Right now, we've got a dead scientist, we've got a call for an executive to come visit, two contractors are searching bars and restaurants for the C.E.O."

"Thanks for the refresher," I mumble. Despite Mack's experience, expertise, and apparent devotion to Bella, something tells me this isn't so clear cut. It's a gut feeling.

"Regardless of what's right or wrong in my theory, we need to find those two contractors," Mack snaps. "We need to learn what it is they *know* and what it is they *don't.*"

"We're here," Duke interjects with a voice deeper than Sam Elliott's.

The wood framed building looks like it's straight out of the Old West. I half expect Wild Bill Hickok to stumble out from between the batwing doors at the open air entrance to the bar.

"Are you in or are you out, Quick?" Mack grunts. "I need to know now if I can count on you to follow my lead. You buy in or you fold."

I unbuckle my belt and turn past Mack to look at Bella. Even though I don't think I trust *her*, I need to know if *she* really trusts Mack. Her eyes plead with me to back off and let Mack do his thing. She bites her lip and nods.

"Okay," I concede. "I'm in. I'll do what you say. But if I sense the need to improvise, as you suggest, I'm doing it."

"Deal," says Mack. "Let's do this."

CHAPTER 5

Mack and I are sitting in a booth near the entrance to the bar. The green vinyl seat is split, the foam cushion poking through. There's Scott Joplin, or some other kind of ragtime music, playing through the overhead speakers. The place is a dive and the air conditioning is either non-existent or non-functional.

My revolver, freshly loaded with shot shell, is tucked into the small of my back. Mack is carrying a Beretta M9. Between the two of us we've got twenty-one shots, even though Mack doesn't know I'm armed.

The club sodas on the table between us are sweating, the ice cubes long melted. I've only taken a couple of sips of mine when Bella strides in through the doors.

She surveys the place, ignoring us to her right, and then walks left to the bar. She pulls herself onto a stool and sits. The bartender, the one in the surveillance video, descends on her quickly and takes her order. She pretends not to see him make a phone call from the opposite end of the long wood laminate bar at an old mechanical cash register.

"He's calling them," Mack says. "They'll be here in a few minutes."

My eyes are on the barkeep. "How do you know?"

"Most of the action is here. There's not much to Lead. Custer's pretty quiet at night. So I'm guessing here, but I bet they're close by."

The bartender pulls a tap and fills a glass mug with an amber colored beer. He wipes the head with a coaster and then walks the drink back to

Bella. She puts some cash on the counter and he takes it, thanks her, and then walks back to put the money in the register.

There are seven other people in the bar. Two women and five men. The women are with two of the men at a table near the bar. They've been drinking a lot. Two other men are at a table between us and the front door. They're in an intense conversation, shoveling their way through nachos and downing bottled beer. The fifth man is at a booth in the far corner of the bar, watching cable news on the television hanging high on the back wall. His back is to me.

I doubt any of them are threats.

Underneath the television are twin doors. One is the men's room, the other the ladies'. It doesn't appear as though there are any exits other than the front door.

One way in and out.

Behind the bar, hanging on the mirrored wall between the house and call brands is an autographed baseball bat. I can't tell who signed it, but that bat could be an issue. My guess is that the bartender has something underneath the bar as well. A shotgun maybe. He's a big dude too; six feet tall, maybe two hundred fifty pounds.

He could be a problem.

"They're here," Mack says under his breath. "My three, your nine o'clock."

Both men are wearing the same Dockers pants from the video stills, but this time they're wearing jackets. Even though they're light windbreakers, it's still too hot to be wearing anything more than a short-sleeved shirt.

"Time to go." Mack gets up from his seat. He walks toward the bar and then exits through the batwing doors, swinging them as he leaves the bar. He'll be waiting outside, making sure nobody leaves the bar with Bella.

I shift the revolver into the front of my waistband, get up, and walk to the bar to find a stool between Bella and the door. Both men have chosen a table right behind her. One of them, with salt and pepper hair, raises his arm to get the bartender's attention. He's the senior of the two operatives.

I glance over at Bella. She takes a sip of the beer she's been nursing and wipes the condensation off of the bar with a napkin. She's fidgeting.

I glance into the mirror behind the bar and see the bartender at the table talking to the men. One of them motions toward Bella and the barkeep nods. Neither of them order anything that I can tell. They're biding their time.

The two couples sitting at the table next to them get up to leave. One of the men hands the bartender some cash and the group noisily walks out of the bar. That leaves the nacho guys at the table near the door and the television watcher in the rear booth.

The bartender takes the cash to the register, which he pops open and shut, and makes his way toward Bella.

"Do you need another beer?" he asks with a sheepish grin. He glances past Bella to the men at the table behind her and then back at her.

"No thanks," she says. "I'm fine."

"How about you bud?" he points at me. "You need something?"

"I'll have another club soda please. More ice this time."

"You betcha'." He pulls a glass from under the bar. "It's hot as blue blazes here. Can't get the A/C cranking hard enough." He shovels some ice into the glass and then sprays it full of soda water. "I swear it feels like Africa in here," he laughs and slides the drink to me. As he gets closer I can see the beads of sweat at his temples and on his lip. It's not the heat that has him sweating.

"It is pretty warm," I say. I raise the glass, thanking him, and take a gulp. Then I get up from the bar and walk back to my table. I have a better vantage point from the booth and am less visible to the two men casing Bella.

When I reach my seat and slide in, the nacho dudes get up and leave. The batwing doors are still swinging when one of the jacketed thugs approaches Bella at the bar, the one with the salt and pepper hair, and sidles up to the stool on her left. I can't hear what he saying to her, but the bartender has slipped to the far side of the bar, pretending to be occupied with receipts.

Something's about to go down. My right hand slides onto the handle of my revolver and pulls it from my waistband.

Bella says something to Salt and Pepper, her attention on him. He glances past her shoulder as she's talking and looks at his blond-haired partner, who stands, pulls something from inside his jacket and steps quickly to Bella, then turns to face me. They don't want to talk.

Time to improvise.

In one motion, I'm up from my seat and pulling the trigger twice at Blondie before he has his hand out of his jacket. The loud cracks of the revolver are followed instantly by the man's scream as he falls over a chair and on the floor. His knees are blown and he's out of play.

I swing the gun to the man at the bar and then back to the man on the ground, trying to cover both of them. The one at the bar is too fast, he grabs Bella by the hair and pulls her onto his lap, swiveling to face me. He has a gun jammed into the right side of her neck.

"Hey!" the bartender yells. "You didn't say anything about guns. You didn't say there'd be guns!"

"Shut up!" yells Salt and Pepper. "You!" He nods at me, not letting go of Bella's hair. "Drop the gun. You aren't gonna win this."

The pistol is leveled at his head. I don't know if I can get the shot off without risking Bella, and with shell shot in the chamber, chances are she'd be hit. I should have brought the Tec-9. It's in my pack in the trunk of the Suburban.

"I can't do that," I tell him. "You know if I drop this gun, you kill me and then you kill her."

"I don't want to kill her," he tightens his grip on Bella's head. "She's got information I need."

"Why the gun to her head?"

There's a flash of indecision in his eyes. A millisecond of self-doubt. We're in a Mexican standoff and he knows it. I'm not lowering my gun; he's not letting go of Bella; his partner is rolling around on the floor. I take a step toward him.

"This is how it's going to go," I tell him. "You're going to let go of her hair, you're going to lower that gun. And we're going to talk about this."

"Not happening," he says and, while still gripping Bella with his left hand, swings the barrel of his semiautomatic toward me.

Before he can pull the trigger, the bartender tries to grab the baseball bat from the wall. He's too slow.

Salt and Pepper spins and fires at the barkeep, hitting him in the shoulder and shattering the mirrored wall behind the bar. I dive to the floor and slide next to Blondie, who's passed out from the pain, and try to grab his weapon from inside his jacket. I'm too slow.

By the time I grab the weapon and turn on my back to aim it Salt and Pepper, he's gone. With Bella. Just like that. I scramble to my feet and, armed with Blondie's 9mm, stumble through the swinging doors in time to see a Chevy Suburban squealing past me and into the darkness. Bella's gone.

Mack set us up.

***

The bartender is lying on the floor amidst the broken glass behind the bar. The customer watching television in the back booth is on the phone near the register, presumably calling the police.

I grab a rag from the bottom liquor shelf, kneel down, and press it against the bartender's bleeding left shoulder. He's breathing heavily, as though he's trying to whistle. His eyes are squeezed shut.

"Keep this here and press hard," I instruct. "This will slow the bleeding until the ambulance gets here." He nods and keeps breathing in and out through pursed lips.

"What the hell happened?" The television watcher is off the phone and stepping towards us. "Who were those guys?"

"I don't know." I stand up and peek over the bar at Blondie, still unconscious on the floor under a table. "But I'm gonna find out." I hop up on the bar and swing my legs over, then jump down. "You called the cops?" I turn back to look at the customer, whose eyes are like saucers. He's pale and shaking a little bit. He nods, slack jawed.

I kneel down next to Blondie. He's lying on his side, blood soaking through his Dockers at his knees and shins. I was at close enough range that the shot shell struck a pretty narrow pattern. He might not walk for a while.

I start digging through his jacket pockets, first the left and then the right. I need transportation.

Bingo!

I pull out a cell phone and a set of keys looped to a remote and a rectangular Lucite tag, the kind of keychain rental car companies use. I flip the tag over to read the faded writing on the paper slip inside the tag; Make/Model: Ford Fusion Energi SE. Color: Silver

I put the keys and the phone next to me on the floor and shift closer to Blondie's head. His hair is matted with sweat, his lips are blue. He's in shock. I should elevate his legs, but I don't want to mess with the mangled knees. There's nothing I can do really. But I need information from him before I bolt. So I slap him.

"Dude!" I slap him again and his eyes flutter open. "Who hired you?"

He mumbles something and then winces in pain. I grab both side of his face and lean down to look him in the eyes.

"Focus!" I speak slowly. "You were shot in the knees. You'll be fine. An ambulance is on the way."

He groans and his eyes close again. He must be losing more blood than I thought. Maybe a fragment hit an artery. He's turning gray.

"Who hired you?" I apply light pressure to the sides of his face.

Tears leak from his eyes but he doesn't say anything. There's the faint sound of a siren. I've gotta go.

"Hey," I call over to the customer. "Bring this guy some water or something. Keep him awake."

"Why should I help him?" the guy yells back at me. "He tried to kill us."

"He tried to kill me," I shoot back. "Not you. Now get over here. I need to go."

"Fine," he raises his hands in surrender. "I'll help him."

"What about me?" cries the barkeep from behind the bar. "What about me? I'm bleeding to death."

"Keep pressure on the shoulder," I call back. "You'll be fine."

I grab the keys and the phone and push my way through the batwing doors. The sirens are getting louder. The ambulance, and the police, will be here any second.

To the left, across the street, is a parking lot. There are a half dozen cars in it. Walking towards the lot, I hold out the car remote and press the unlock key. The lights flash on a silver sedan. I adjust the revolver in my waistband and jog across the street toward the car.

I've got to find Bella.

The car is parked facing the street. Sitting in the driver's seat, I can see the first police car pull up to curb outside the bar. It's a black and white Dodge Durango, and the officer jumps out of the SUV with his gun drawn. Less than a minute later two more cops pull up, followed by an ambulance. Though it's hard not to watch the action across the street, I've work to do.

I unlock my phone and slide my finger to the Tile application. The app opens and I enter my name and password. The screen changes to a list: LAPTOP, BLUE BOX, GO BAG.

I press GO BAG and the screen slides to show me a photograph of my rucksack. I press the screen again to reveal a map. It takes a couple of seconds, but then a pin pops up on the map with the location of my rucksack. The back of the rented Chevy Suburban. Bella is in the Suburban with her iPhone. She's got the *Tile* app. Her phone should help me locate my bag. As long as they stay within one hundred and fifty feet of each other, I'll be able to find her.

The locator pin is static. So I'll have to keep refreshing the map as the Suburban moves. I do at least know they're headed south on US-85. The pin is right next to the Whistler Gulch campground.

I hit the ignition button and the car hums to life. It's a hybrid, I guess, so it's super quiet rolling past the wailing emergency vehicles outside of the bar. Driving past, I can see paramedics on the barroom floor tending to Blondie. He'll be fine. He'll have a limp, but he'll survive.

In less than a mile, I'm on Cliff Street, which turns into US-85, and I hit refresh on the Tile app. The pin is further south, about two miles ahead of me on the highway. I pick up speed, passing the campground. It's dark outside now, the clock in the Fusion telling me it's 8:36PM. I've been up exactly sixteen hours and I'm running on adrenaline. My eyes burn, my stomach's upset, and I need a shower I'm unlikely to get.

The Tile app tells me the Suburban, or at least my bag, is getting closer. It's only a mile away. There's no landmark indicator on the map, but a couple of quick taps on the refresh button tell me they've stopped moving. They're parked somewhere.

Less than a minute later, I find exactly where they are, why they wanted Bella, and where they're taking her.

Homestake Mine.

***

After figuring out how to turn off the headlights and the running lights, which is no easy task on the Fusion, I slow roll into the parking lot outside of what looks like a complex of buildings with a grain silo at one end. I'm thankful for Blondie's eco-consciousness. The Fusion is almost silent against the freshly paved asphalt. I roll down the driver's side window and smell the tar.

Ahead of me are three or four vehicles, clustered together, at the end of the parking lot closest to the silo. The lot is dark, except for a couple of spotlights shining off of the sides of one of the buildings. I press the brake, put the car in park, and turn it off. I'm protected by the dark and there's no need to call attention to myself.

I check the Tile app again. The pin is gone. They must have moved her from the Suburban. But I'm close enough now that, once I spot the

SUV and get within a couple of hundred feet, I'll find the bag and the Tec-9 stashed inside of it.

Climbing out of the car, I crouch low to the asphalt, looking for the Suburban. It's not with the other vehicles parked in the yellow glow of the flood lights. Burning from sleep deprivation, my eyes have trouble adjusting to the dark as they scan the less visible parts of the lot.

With my phone in one hand and the Governor in the other, I move along the lot looking for the SUV. I'm closing in on the cluster of cars and trucks near the silo when the pin appears on the Tile app map. It's to my left, and as I slowly, quietly move that direction, a ping.

My bag!

The SUV is parked by itself in what might be the darkest part of the lot. I would have missed it, if not for the app telling me where to look. I turn off the phone, slip it back into my pocket, and quickly move to the Suburban's tailgate to pop it open.

It's unlocked, the hydraulic hiss of the lift gate the only sound as the interior light illuminates the rear interior of the SUV. There it is. My bag.

I quietly unsnap the top and loosen the draw string. Inside the bag, I find the Tec-9, a fifty round box magazine, and a shot shell box. Placing the Tec-9 and the magazine next to the bag, I pop open the revolver in my hand and drop the four remaining shot shell from the Governor into the box. The box and revolver go back into the bag and I sling the pack from the SUV and onto my shoulders.

The Tec-9 feels familiar in my hands and, despite its notoriously cheap construction and propensity to jam, I love it. It's a nice, lightweight machine pistol that is accurate at close range. The sites suck, but I'm not a sniper so I don't care. And I keep it clean, so it doesn't lock up on me as much as it does for others who don't take care of their weapons. True, it's not the Governor, my true weapon of choice, but the Tec-9 has saved my life too many times to count now.

The long, thin ammo cartridge pops into the magazine catch and it clicks. I pull out the Tec's operating handle from the safe position and then pull the handle all the way to the rear, engaging the striker. It's ready to fire. I pull the shoulder strap over my head and reach up to pull the lift gate closed when there's a noise coming from *inside* the SUV.

Releasing the lift gate, I step back quickly and swing the Tec-9 into my hands. "Who's there?" A lump spontaneously materializes in my throat, my breath shallows.

The response sounds like a grunt and it's followed by a hand reaching over the rear seatback, gripping the leather.

"Who is it?" I repeat. "I've got a gun pointed at you."

No response.

"Bella?" I'm trying to keep my voice low enough so nobody aside from the person in the SUV hears me. "Is that you? Are you okay?"

Another moan. Stepping closer to the back of the SUV, I get my answer. It's not Bella. The hand is too masculine and too dark, except along the knuckles where the skin is varying shades of pink skin.

The hand lets go of the seat back and waves weakly at me before disappearing.

Leaving the lift gate open, and the Tec-9 trained on the back interior of the SUV, I walk around the left side to the rear passenger door. In one motion, I pull open the door and take two quick steps back. Mack Mahoney's head falls back, his left eye swollen shut and bruised, his right eye half closed. He moans again and mumbles something unintelligible.

I sling the Tec-9 over my shoulder, and grab his shoulders. "Mack, it's me, Jackson. What happened?"

He's heavy, almost dead weight, and he barely helps me sit him up. It's evident he was jumped. There's a lump on the back left side of his head, his nose is bloodied, his bottom lip is swollen. He mumbles again. He's not going to be much help.

"Okay, Mack, I'm gonna ask you 'yes/no' questions. Nod your head or shake it. You don't have to talk."

His neck is limp, his chin against his chest, but he manages a nod.

"Were you jumped when you left the bar?"

A nod.

"Was it someone you knew?"

Another nod.

"That mustache, Sam Elliott guy, named Duke?"

He nods with a shrug. Maybe he's not sure.

"Anyone else jump you?"

Mack shrugs.

"Was Bella with you?"

He nods.

"Was she conscious? Was she okay? Did they hurt her?"

A grunt. To many questions at once. I take a deep breath and exhale slowly.

"Was she okay?"

A shrug.

"Was she hurt?"

Mack shrugs again.

"Did they take her inside the mine?"

He nods.

"To the lab?"

Another nod.

"Okay. I'm gonna help you here, but I need to get to Bella first."

"Uh huh," he nods again before laying his head on the seat back.

"Do you think you can get up? I want to get you over to my car and out of this one."

He shakes his head and grunts again, rolling his neck back and forth on the seat back.

"Okay then. I'll leave you here. I'm going after Bella now. Be back as soon as I can. Hang in there." I slip off my pack, and pull out the Governor. I flip open the cylinder and fill it with six shot shell. Mack may or may not be trustworthy, but I can't chance making the wrong decision. He could be useful down the road, and given the condition of his face, he's probably still on Bella's side. That means he's on my side for now. He gets the gun.

"Use this if you need to," I wrap his left hand around the revolver. "It's loaded with shot shell. They'll spray like shotgun shells. You don't have to be accurate."

He looks down at the gun and manages a weak chuckle.

"Not everybody's weapon of choice," I acknowledge. "But it'll get you out of a jam."

He tries to say something, but he gulps past what I imagine is a knot in his throat and the pain in his mouth, and he gives up.

"Don't worry about it," I reassure him. "You're welcome. Don't lose it. That gun's my favorite."

I make sure his legs are clear of the door and I close it. He's pretty badly beaten up, but he'll be okay. Maybe.

***

Among the complex of buildings, the only one showing any signs of life is the silo and the A-framed building attached to it. Its lights are on and from a distance it appears there's a security guard sitting in a chair next to the entrance.

Still hidden by the darkness of the lot, and maybe fifty yards from the door, I kneel down and shove the Tec-9 into my pack. No need to call more attention to myself than necessary. Especially in the dark. After hours. At a secret research facility. In the wake of a murder.

My mind cranks through the possible explanations I can feed the guard. None of them sound viable.

As I approach the door and the guard, it's obvious I won't need anything to get past the guard. His blue and gray ball cap is pulled low over his eyes, his arms hanging at his side. To the left of his brass nameplate, which reads S. TILLEY, there's a dark burgundy stain on his gray uniform shirt. His eyes are fixed, staring past me into the dark lot.

I kneel again and whip out the Tec-9. I open the front door to the building with my foot. It's unlocked and pushes inward against a rush of cool air from the large open space inside.

At the far end of what looks like a combination of an office and a machine shop, is a large cage. The cage is an open enclosure that houses an elevator shaft.

There's no elevator though, which means Bella, Salt and Pepper, Mustache Duke, and whoever else, are at the bottom of the shaft.

There are no up and down elevator buttons. There's no obvious lever or switch. But on the left side, there's an electrical box. Inside the unlocked box are a series of breakers. Next to each of the breakers are Dymo labels, one of which reads EMERGENCY RETURN.

I flip the breaker and there's an immediately rumble on the inside of the cage. The large wire ropes on either side of the cage are spinning, whining almost, as they pull the elevator up from the floors below.

What seems like three or four minutes pass before the elevator, not much more than a cage itself, clangs to the opening above ground. I flip the emergency return breaker to its original position before sliding open the gate, closing it, and engaging the motor from the inside.

I have no idea where this thing is taking me or what I'll find when I get there. The elevator churns below ground, and I pull the Tec-9 and aim its Swiss cheese, ventilated barrel at the gate. My finger sits on the trigger, ready to pull.

CHAPTER 6

Devils Tower is the core of a volcano that never erupted. Or maybe it's not. That was my favorite of the many explanations as to what formed the rocky tower thousands of years before my parents took me there.

After I sat through a ranger's talk and walked through the museum display at the base of the tower, my dad agreed to hike around the tower through the piney trail that surrounded the monument.

"We've got a couple of options," my dad said, struggling with a park map. "There's the Red Beds Trail, which is pretty long. And there's the Tower Trail, which is shorter, but takes us closest to the tower. It even looks like you might be able to climb some of those big rocks at its southern base, Jackson."

"I'm up for whatever," my mom said. "I've got on good walking shoes. You boys lead the way."

"Tower Trail is good, Dad," I told him. "I want to climb those rocks. Plus, it's better to be closer to the tower."

He clumsily folded the map to shove it the breast pocket of his hiking shirt. "Everybody got their water bottles?"

My mom and I exchanged nodded and the trek began.

I remember the temperature changing almost immediately as we approached the base of the tower, the tall Ponderosa pines creating the bed of the hiking path with their dead needles, and providing shade that kept the sun at bay. They were beautiful and imposing, acting as sentinels for the tower.

"Look for a walking stick," my dad suggested. *"I bet you'll find a good one here."*

"Why do I need one?" I was two or three steps ahead of my parents. They were holding hands.

"For walking," my dad chuckled.

I stopped and turned around to look at him. My mom was rubbing his bicep with her free hand, her wedding band glinting against a thin beam of sunlight sneaking through the needled canopy. "I can walk. My knee is healed. Why would I need one?"

"Your knee is fine, yes." He glanced at the leg I'd spent months rehabbing in the wake of a torn ligament. "But a walking stick is about a lot more than helping you walk."

"What do you mean?"

"Well," he rubbed my head with his right hand, "sticks are walking aids. But throughout history they've also been used as signs of power. They're good weapons too"

"Weapons?" Now he had my interest. He and I already shared a love of guns and crossbows. But sticks? This could be beyond cool. Old school ninja cool.

"Yep. In Egypt, the type of stick you carried said a lot about you. Were you a farmer or a king? Among other things, the stick would symbolize that position. The same was true for tribal chiefs. He pointed up to the southern side of the tower. "The Native Americans who worshipped here, they had sticks. The bigger the dude, the bigger the stick."

"What about the weapons?" I pressed. "How were they weapons?" We were getting close to an outcropping of large rust colored rocks on the southern base of the tower. It looked as though a giant had chiseled grooves into the side of it, and these rocks were the chipped pieces.

"Think about it, Jackson," he challenged me. "How could a stick be a weapon?"

"I guess you could use it defensively." I held my hands out in front of me, pretending to grip a large stick. "You know, to block a knife or a sword."

"Good one," my mom said.

"Or," I switched hand positions, one clenched on top of the other, "I could hold it like a sword if it had a pointed end."

"You sure could." My dad stopped walking and looked down at me. "You could also hide a weapon in the stick. If it has some sort of special handle on the top or if it's hollowed out in the center."

"Oooh!" My eyes widened at the possibilities. "I hadn't thought of that." Hands on hips, I scanned the area in front of us, the forest to either side. "Do you see a good stick?"

"You choose," he suggested. "I bet you'll find one that'll do the trick."

Off to my right, before we reached the rocks, there was a stick that looked right. It was two, maybe two and a half, feet high, and it bent into a natural handle at one end. The other end was torn, revealing a sliver of the yellow pine underneath. I grabbed it from its place among leaves and needles and brushed it off. It was sturdy and maybe a couple of inches thick. It was dry but not brittle. The knots along its side gave it character, almost making the stick look wise. A stick worthy of kings and warriors, that's what it was.

"What do you think?" I held it out to my dad without testing it out first.

He took it from me with a smile. "This is a fine stick," he said. "Nice balance, great handle, a really fine choice, Jackson." He handed it back to me and I gripped the handle, putting my weight onto it.

I used the stick to climb the first couple of large igneous boulders. My parents walked around the rocks, staying on the path which wound east toward a sheer cliff. I hopped from boulder to boulder, using the stick to help me avoid falling into an imaginary river of flowing magma. I was too old for imaginary friends, who'd long since left my mind, but not too old to play make believe. I was the hero, battling the elements to save the world from evil. One wrong step and I'd slip into molten lava; evil would triumph.

"Hop down!" my dad called from the edge of the trail. "Your mom wants a picture."

Putting the quest on hold, I climbed down and, carrying the stick like a rifle, charged to the photo spot. My dad's pager beeped.

"Really?" Mom asked in exasperation. "Now?"

"Hang on." Dad pulled the pager from his hip and checked the alphanumeric message. His eyes narrowed and he sighed.

"What?" Mom asked, trying to read his expression.

"I've got to take this," he said. "Give me two minutes."

"Two minutes," she held up two fingers and shot him a look that suggested even one extra second on the phone would be too long.

He walked away from us, back towards the rocks, and opened up his flip phone. He checked the pager with one hand while he dialed his cell with the other, then turned his back and lifted the phone to his ear.

"Who's that?" I knew the answer.

"Work," she said. "It's always work, right?"

"Yeah." I pulled the stick up and held the handle next to my cheek. I aimed the opposite end of the stick off into the distance, beyond the edge of the cliff and out toward the valley and mesas below. The green and yellow fields were spotted with young pines, the edges of those plateaus framed with what looked like red clay. It was like something from a postcard.

"Boom!" The stick rifle kicked against my face. "Bulls-eye!!"

"Good shot!" my mom said. "What are you aiming for?"

"The target," I replied without looking away from the vista expanding below us. "Always the target."

From the corner of my eye I could see Mom looking back toward my dad. She examined her fingernails and then placed them to her lips and began chewing. Nervous habit. It happened a lot when my dad got a page from work. It usually meant he was about to leave us for "emergency business". He had a lot of "emergency business" for being a technology consultant. But not this time.

"Hey," Dad said, rejoining us. "I'm back."

"That was four minutes." My mom gently shoved his shoulder. "What did they want?"

"Nothing much, just checking up on me."

"They're never checking up on you," she said. "They always want something from you. When do you leave?"

"Not until the day after tomorrow," he said, trying to avoid eye contact with me. "You know as well as anyone, darling, that when work calls I have to answer."

"That means we have to cut the trip short." My mom, master of the obvious.

Dad, his eyes betraying guilt and disappointment, looked at me, and then put his hands on my shoulders. I was holding the stick like a divining rod and had turned my attention to the dirt under my shoes. My dad was a good father. He did the best he could, and whenever he had the time, he spent it with me. Trips to the gun range, out into the country and our own private waterside retreat, and to the movies to see the latest PG-13 rated action flicks.

He traveled a lot though. They weren't the kind of trips for which my mom and I could plan. They came with a couple of days or a couple of hours' notice. When he was gone, it might be for a week. It could be a month.

Looking back, my mother was incredibly supportive. She never complained beyond the initial protest. "I signed up for better or worse," she'd say. "And the better outweighs the worse." She was always there, which made it more tolerable. When Dad was gone, Mom was around. She indulged my track meets, my obsessive interest in music, my love of guns. She carted me to and from whatever. I always told her how much I appreciated all she did for me. I never left the house or hung up the phone without telling her how much I loved her.

But she wasn't dad. She knew it. He knew it.

"I'm really sorry, Jackson." He knelt down, hands still on my shoulders, his eyes searching to meet mine. "I didn't plan this. It can't be helped."

"It's okay." My eyes focusing on his face, I could see how genuinely hurt he was at having to abbreviate our vacation. "I get it."

"We still have this tower to conquer," he said with a forced smile. "Mt. Rushmore is tomorrow. Then we can check out the buffalo at the state park before we head back."

I nodded. I knew he felt bad.

I also had a gut feeling he wasn't telling me something.

***

The elevator rumbles to a stop at the bottom of the shaft. The wire cables dance for a couple of seconds after the ride ends. They sound like sound effects from a laser fight in *Star Wars*. The hallway outside of the elevator is brightly lit and empty. There's an odd mixture of humidity and air conditioning that smells almost like grass after a rainstorm.

I shrug my pack onto my shoulders and adjust the Tec-9 shoulder strap. The machine pistol, with its fifty round magazine, is comfortable in my hands.

The corridor is narrow and, to the left, it forks. To the right, there's a single hallway. I turn right, expecting an easier path, and almost immediately find another fork.

Great.

Eenie-meenie-miny-moe....

I take the left path and walk slowly, heel to toe, panning right to left with the Tec-9. Every couple of steps, I stop to listen. Only the sound of what must be enormous air circulators are hissing and humming overhead.

I'm about to turn around and take one of the other hallways when I notice what looks like a large water tank about fifty feet in front of me. The corridor ends at the cylindrical tank, which is suspended from the ceiling and framed by a couple of metal floor to ceiling ladders against the rear wall.

This part of the hallway feels like a "clean room". The walls are white and bathed in a bright, off-putting artificial light. I stop at the tank and reach out to touch it. It feels cool against my sweaty hand. There's a rapid, though faint, vibration coming from inside the tank.

I'm lost for a moment, considering the uses of the upside-down, vibrating cylinder, when there's a noise from the other side of the tank. I close my eyes and listen.

There it is again!

Both hands are on the gun again as I pad my way to the wall behind the tank. Deliberately, I press my ear to the wall.

From the other side of the wall, I can hear people talking. It sounds like one man and...no...two men. Two men are talking.

A third voice...higher pitched...maybe a woman. Two men and a woman. Their voices are muffled, so I can't understand what they're saying. The men sound agitated, one maybe more than the other. One of the voices is much deeper and resonant.

It's gotta be Bella, Salt and Pepper, and Mustache Duke.

There's no obvious connection between the hallway and the other side of the wall. It could be that they took another corridor and I'll need to backtrack. Before I waste that much time, however, I need to exhaust my options. Bella and Mack talked about the lab being undisclosed, a secret underground location.

Backing up a step, my fingers search the wall for a door seam or an entrance. At first I don't find anything, so I start to climb the ladder against the wall thinking there could be an access panel along the ceiling.

On the fifth rung, my hand feels something protruding off the back of the ladder. I hop off the ladder and look closer, seeing a lever.

My left hand is hovering over the lever, my fingers dancing, playing an imaginary piano, ready to unleash whatever this hidden lever operates. My right hand is wrapped around the lower receiver frame of the Tec-9, trigger finger engaged. I take a deep breath in and out through my nose and I flip the lever to the left.

The wall behind me opens with a loud hydraulic hiss. The doorway is narrow and short, maybe five feet tall. Instinctively I slide to the side of the door, pressing my backpack against the wall.

If I try bursting into the room, I'm at a tactical disadvantage. If I wait, whoever comes through the awkward door loses the upper hand.

Sliding down the wall, resting my butt on my heels, I listen for any sound coming from inside what I now know is Dr. Wolf's lab.

"Did you do that?" says Salt and Pepper. "Did you open the door?"

"Why would you think I did it?" That's Mustache Duke, his voice sounds closer to the opening. "I'm standing here with you. Both of my hands are on the girl here."

"Go check it out," says Salt and Pepper, clearly the leader. "I can watch moneybags here while she gets us what we need."

I inch my body farther away from the door. I'm next to the ladder, hoping that I'm far enough away from his peripheral vision that he'll be completely in the hallway before he sees me.

"For the last time," Bella snaps, "I don't have what you want. I'm looking for the same thing, okay?"

"I don't buy it," Salt and Pepper again. "Duke, go check out the hallway."

"Fine," he grunts through his moustache. His heavy boot steps approach.

Sliding my back up the wall, I swing the Tec-9 to my left hand, turning it backwards and gripping its barrel like a knife. I hold it, extended, in position above the opening. It's five pounds feeling more like fifty, given my awkward stance.

"I'll be back," says Duke. "It's probably nothing."

With my right hand I grab the fifth rung of the ladder to feel for the hidden lever. I find it as a shock of white hair ducks through the opening.

"Pssst," I whisper right as Duke clears the door.

He snaps his head toward me and her looks up in time to get the back end of my machine pistol slammed down into the middle of his forehead. Before he crumples to the floor, I twist the lever to the right. The door hisses shut at the same instant the back of Duke's head cracks against the floor. He's out cold.

I sling the Tec-9 back to the right side of my body and move to Duke's head. There's already a dark purple, rectangular bruise between his whisker-like eyebrows. He's slack-jawed, his tongue hanging from his open mouth. From behind his head, I grab his armpits and drag him away from the secret wall-opening.

Now what?

I figure I've got a couple of minutes before the door slides open again and Salt and Pepper peeks through it looking for his partner, so I crouch down beside Duke, put my pack on the floor next to me, and dig through his pockets.

He's wearing a tan hunting vest over a black T-shirt and some jeans. There are six pockets in the vest, and one of them holds a cell phone and a Bluetooth headset. Another contains a Leatherman in a belt loop pouch. His wallet has a couple of hundred dollars in tens and twenties. I pocket the cash and the keys to the Suburban before stuffing everything else into my pack.

I'm only three or four feet to the side of the secret opening, shouldering my pack, when the door hisses open. I don't have time to react with the Tec-9 before Salt and Pepper squeezes through the opening facing me, his semiautomatic 9mm leveled at my chest.

***

Salt and Pepper's face contorts with confusion, his eyes narrowed and darting between me and Duke's limp body on the floor next to me. That moment it takes for his brain to process what's happened is enough time for me to close the distance between us and tackle him. My momentum carries him backward into the bottom of the suspended tank, which hits him with a hollow thud between his shoulder blades.

He grunts, all the air escaping his lungs, and we tumble to the floor beneath the tank. I land on top of him, and grab his face with my right hand, gripping it like a basketball. I drive my left shoulder into his right arm, forcing his gun free.

Struggling to keep my position, my neck gets yanked sharply to the right. He's grabbed the Tec-9 strap and is blindly tugging, trying to gain control of the pistol with his left hand.

He gets his hand around the barrel, and I hit the magazine catch release under the trigger. The 50 round cartridge drops out of the magazine catch and into my hand. Fighting against the strap's pressure cutting into my neck, I grip the magazine as tightly as I can and jam it into the right side of his head.

It stuns him and he loosens his hold of the pistol strap. I grab the strap at my neck and yank it over my head, freeing myself from it. Rolling back to straddle him, I grab his ears and slam the back of his head against the floor. His eyes flutter, he gasps, spit bubbling along the side of his mouth, and he passes out.

I don't think the blow to head killed him. He's still breathing, and I collapse on top of him, rising up and down with his labored breaths.

That didn't go as planned. Then again, I didn't really have a plan.

The left side of my neck feels burned. My right hand aches almost as much as my left shoulder. My lower back feels bruised, probably from the pack banging against it during the scuffle. It's like I can feel the pain-numbing adrenaline leaking from my body, replaced with a rising wave of nausea and exhaustion.

Hand to hand combat is not my thing.

"Jackson?" a meek voice calls out. "Are you okay?"

"Uh huh." I gather my strength and use Salt and Pepper's body to push myself up. "You?"

Bella nods, her eyes revealing a fear I hadn't seen from her in the long day we'd spent together. She's bent over, her hands pressed against the secret opening.

"This formula, or whatever it is, it must be valuable, right? You've got all kinds of crazy going on here."

"Did you find Mack? Is he alive?"

"Yes, he's okay. He's still in the Suburban. I left him a gun." A ping of dizziness dances through my head, blurring my vision for a second, before I regain my balance.

"How did you find us?" Bella steps through the opening, stepping carefully around Salt and Pepper. "I mean, how did you know they'd bring me here?"

"I didn't know," I admit. "I used the Tile app on my phone. There's a tile in my bag here, and I remembered your cell had the app too. It told me where you were."

"Really?" she asks in surprise. "I can't get that thing to work if I'm more than fifty yards from it."

"You gotta have someone else's phone near it," I explain. "It relies on a lot of people having the app to work right. Not perfect yet. Just got lucky."

Bella notices Mustache Duke laid out on the floor to her left. "How'd you do that?"

"Tile app."

"Funny." She shoots me a disapproving look. "What now?"

"Now you tell me a little bit more about what it is were up against here." I bend over to grab the magazine and the Tec-9 from the floor. "You know a lot more than you've told me. I deserve some additional information." I point the pistol at one body and then the other.

"Fair enough," she sighs. "You've earned it."

***

Salt and Pepper moans before jerking his eyes open and sucking in a gulp of air. He looks unhappy.

I wouldn't be happy either if I were duct taped to a lab table.

"You're not going to get away with this," he threatens, his voice hoarse.

"That's kinda overdone isn't it?" I'm sitting in a rolling desk chair a couple of feet from him. Mustache Duke is on the next table over, same treatment, still unconscious.

"I mean really," I push against the floor with my heels and roll toward our irritated prisoner. "*You're not going to get away with this!!*" I mock. "That's so overdone."

"You're in way over your head," he croaks, trying to clear his throat.

"I'm not the one taped to a table. So…there's that."

He winces and presses his eyes closed.

"Head hurt?" Bella appears on the other side of the table. Salt and Pepper doesn't say anything.

"The tables are turned," she says.

"Nice turn of phrase," I wink at Bella. She smiles.

"As I was saying," she turns her attention to Salt and Pepper, "I'm the one asking questions now. And you're going to answer them."

He clenches his jaw and struggles against the tape I used to bind him, but he says nothing.

"Who are you working for?" Bella folds her arms. "Who sent you after me?"

No response.

I stroll up to the table, find the swollen bruise on the right side of his head, and press into it with my thumb. Salt and Pepper squeezes his eyes shut and bites his lower lip against the pain, trying to move his head away from the pressure.

Bella softens her voice and moves next to his ear. "Here's the deal. Nobody is going to come looking for you. This lab, despite being breached, is still relatively hidden. If we leave you here, strapped to this table, another sticky piece of duct tape over your mouth to keep you quiet…" She holds her hands as if to say, *Oh well…*

I pick up my remaining roll of tape and rip off a piece long enough to cover Salt and Pepper's mouth. The sound of the tape tearing from the roll is still echoing in the lab when he breaks.

"Okay!" he blurts out. "Hang on a minute. I need a second to collect my thoughts."

"Is it a second," Bella asks, "or a minute? When I get to one, that's it. We leave you here with your buddy over there. When he dies, and I don't think it'll take very long without a doctor, it'll get ripe in here pretty quick."

"But—"

"Occasionally dead bodies make noises," I chime in. "They grunt or groan, maybe even squeak. That'll be fun with the lights off, right?"

Bella shoots me a look that suggests I stay out of her interrogation. She's in CSI mode or something.

She holds up her fingers. "Five."

"Okay, wait!"

"Four." She folds her thumb against her palm.

"Seriously!"

"Three." Bella tucks her pinkie.

"Blogis!"

"Blogis?" Bella folds her arms. "Is that who sent you?"

"Yes," he says. "Liho Blogis."

"What kind of name is that?" I ask. "Is that a man or a woman?"

Another laser beam from Bella. "And who are you?" she asks Salt and Pepper.

"Sal," he says. "Salvador Pimiento."

"What exactly is it, *Salvador*, that Blogis wanted you to get from me? Why did he hire you and send you here?"

"He told me that you had information about a valuable process," Sal swallows hard, his voice still cracking from the dryness in his throat. "He said it was worth a lot of money."

"And?"

"And that the process was in pieces." He swallows again. "Can I get some water?"

"We don't have any," she snaps. "Keep talking."

He blinks hard a couple of times, a tear rolling across the bruise on his temple, "He said you had part of it, he had part of it, and that you probably knew where more parts were hidden."

"Why did he think that?"

"I dunno." Pimiento turns to me. "He figured that the lab had stuff in it. And he knew that if it did, somebody would come to find it."

"You didn't know it would be her?" I ask, avoiding eye contact with Bella. "I didn't know for sure," he says. "But I had good intelligence it would be her."

"Intelligence?" Bella barks. "What intelligence?"

"It makes sense," Pimiento says. "You're the head of the company, the lab is super top secret. Why wouldn't the head of the company come to check on her huge secret science experiment?"

"You didn't say that it made sense," I push. "You said you had intelligence."

"Blogis," he closes his eyes and coughs. "Blogis gave me everything."

"Where is Blogis?" I asked. "Why isn't he here?"

"Ha!" Pimiento laughs through another cough. "*Here*? Blogis? Nah. He wouldn't do this level of work. He hires it out."

"Where is he?"

"I dunno. Ukraine somewhere, maybe. He's Ukrainian. Or Russian. Not sure."

"Ukraine?" I remark. "What a coincidence!"

CHAPTER 7

Mack is in the same spot I left him; sitting in the back of the Suburban, six shooter in his hand. The passenger side rear door is open. He doesn't look great, but he peps up a little when he sees Bella trailing behind me.

"Hey," he manages, "you made it back."

"We did," Bella sighs. "How are you?" She leans on the door and peeks her head inside the SUV. "Are you going to be okay, Mack?"

"Yeah. I've been through worse."

I step to the back of the SUV and toss in my backpack, which now holds my Tec-9 and Sal Pimiento's loaded 9mm Sig Sauer.

"We're taking you to the hospital, Mack." She puts her hand on his shoulder before gently pulling a seatbelt across his body. "You need to see a doctor."

"I'll be fine," he protests, tugging on the shoulder strap.

I slam shut the SUV tailgate.

"Could you be louder?" Bella snaps. "We don't need attention from anyone right now!"

"Thanks for the tip," I mumble, walking to the driver's side and hopping into the driver's seat. The blood from Max's nose is almost tracing the pigment changes above his upper lip. His lower lip doesn't look any better. "Mack, how's the bump on the back of your head?"

"Uh," he reaches back to find it and winces when he does. "Oooh. It hurts. Like I said, though, I'm good to go. Let's hit the road."

"Bella's right," I say, "you need medical attention. We're dropping you off at the hospital between here and Deadwood. It's, like, two minutes away."

Bella shuts his door and gets into the front seat next to me. "Really, Mack," she says, "you're of more use to us once we know you can think straight."

He doesn't say anything as I crank the engine, making sure the headlights and running lights are off until we're out of the parking lot.

"Think I can call now?" Bella asks me.

"Wait till we're out of the lot," I suggest. "We need a little bit of distance between us and those idiots."

"What happened down there?" Mack asks.

I glance in the rear view mirror at Mack. He's backlit from the building lights behind us. "First, you tell us what happened to you."

"I got jumped."

"By whom?" I ask. "Your buddy Duke?"

"I got jumped from behind, so I don't know. I guess it had to be Duke if the other guy was in the bar with you."

"Had to be Duke," Bella concurs. "When Pimiento shoved me into the car, Duke was in the driver's seat and you were slumped over, unconscious."

"All I know," Mack says, trying to speak clearly through his swollen lower lip, "is that I walked out of that bar and *BOOM!* Next thing I remember is Quick giving me his gun and telling me he'd be back."

"Oh yeah, I'm gonna need that back when we get to the hospital."

"Here you go," he leans forward and places the pistol on the center armrest between Bella and me. "What happened down there, Quick? Where are Duke and the other guy?"

I take my right hand off of the wheel and put the gun inside the center armrest compartment. "Bella, you want to tell him?" I flip the headlights on and pull out of the lot onto the highway.

"When we got here," she explains, "both men took me by the arms and essentially carried me into the building."

"They killed a guard," I add.

"Yes," she says. "They shot him when he asked for identification. Then we got onto the elevator and down to thc lab level. They knew the lab was down there, but didn't know exactly where."

"You told them?" Mack asks.

"Of course I told them," Bella says, irritated by Mack's question. "What was I going to do? They'd have killed me if I didn't."

"You took them to the lab..." I prompted.

"Yes," she nods, "I took them to the lab. Once we were inside they started asking me questions. They wanted information."

"What kind of questions?" Mack asks. "What information? Did they say who else had seen the video of Wolf's assassination?"

"That's a weird question," I interject.

"Pimiento seemed to think I had additional pieces to the process," Bella says.

"Additional pieces?" I ask. "How did they know you had *any* pieces?"

Bella purses her lips, processing my question before dismissing it. "They just did. They knew I had a part of the process and that there are three, maybe four, other components out there."

"What did you tell them?" I press. "Did you tell them you have more than one piece?"

"No," she answers, "because I don't. I only have the one section. But they thought that I had more information than that, and they knew I was going to Ukraine."

"They *knew* you were going to Ukraine?"

"Well, they mentioned Odessa, so maybe they didn't know. But it seemed coincidental. I remember thinking to myself that they knew and wondering *how* they knew."

"So they didn't necessarily *know* anything," Mack interjects. "They may have the same information you have. If they're affiliated with Dr.

Wolf's killer, then they know everything he knows. He took the hard drive."

"What hard drive?" I ask.

"There was a hard drive that Dr. Wolf kept in his lab," Bella tells me. "There was a list of contacts, people he trusted. It also contained GPS coordinates to a half dozen locations where he might have left the missing parts of the process."

"Now this Liho Blogis guy has a list of people and places which will lead him directly to the entirety of the process. If that's the case, how are we even in the game?"

"That's where it gets complicated."

"Oh," I say mockingly, "'cause it's not already complicated." I pass a Best Western hotel and turn the SUV to the right, pulling into the emergency parking lot of the Lead-Deadwood Regional Hospital. There are a lot of empty spaces, so I pull up next to the entrance and park.

"There are two hard drives," says Bella. "One of them is full of false leads. One has the real information."

"You've got a scientist who was so paranoid about the secret work he was doing in an underground lab he took the time to separate this process you keep talking about. Then he sent the pieces all over the world."

"Yes, but—"

I hold up my hand to interrupt her. "Wait. That's not all. His paranoia extended so far as to then create two lists of hiding places and the people who would validate them. One of the lists, though, loaded onto a hard drive, is fake."

"Are you finished?" Bella pinches the bridge of her nose with her forefinger and thumb.

"Not yet. It gets better. Our job, as I *now* understand it, is to find one of those hard drives and hope it's the right one. Because our lethal enemy, a Ukrainian named Liho Blogis, already has one of the drives and at least one part of the process."

"Now are you finished?" Bella narrows her eyes. "May I please speak?"

"Go ahead."

"You are right that I've not been entirely forthcoming with information," she admits. "That said, look at it from my position. I met you this morning. You were recommended to me by a man I trust barely as far as I could throw him. Am I supposed to divulge everything to you?"

"Well—"

"Ah, Ah!" she stops me. "My turn. You gave me the talking stick. There is more still that I haven't told you. It's not mission critical, as Mack would put it. But if that information becomes critical, I'll share it."

"Whatever."

"As I said," she sighs, "there are two hard drives. Yes, Blogis has one. The killer stole it from the lab right after he killed Dr. Wolf. But *we* have the other drive."

"Who has it?"

"I do," Mack says.

I turn to look at him.

"It was in Wolf's home," he said. "For some reason Blogis' team never searched Wolf's home. Maybe it was a lapse in intelligence or follow through. But there was a second drive in his house in Custer. I found it under a closet floorboard in a fireproof safe, within hours of his death."

"Blogis' people never went there?"

"They may have *gone* there," he says, "but they didn't search it thoroughly enough. If they had, we'd be out of luck."

"Where is it now?"

"I'll tell you in a second," he says. "You never told me what you did with Duke and the other guy."

"We left them strapped to the tables in the lab," Bella says.

"You left them there to die?" Mack's eyes widen at the thought.

"No," Bella laughs. "We're not killers." She looks over at me. "At least, I'm not. I called the head of security and told him they were there. He's handling it."

"Like he *handled* Wolf's body?" Mack asks.

"Exactly," she says. "And by the way, Jackson, when you were up on your soapbox there a minute ago, you kept hammering home that Dr. Wolf was paranoid, as if he didn't have reason to be."

"You're pretty stupid for being so smart, Quick," Mack snorts. "There ain't a day that goes by where a man shouldn't be worried, especially if what he's doing can make people either rich or powerful or both."

***

"Can you hear me?"

My phone is connected to the Suburban's speakerphone. It's after two o'clock in the morning, and Bella and I are parked on the tarmac next to her plane, which is getting refueled. We're briefing Sir Spencer

"I hear you, Jackson," Sir Spencer answers. He sounds like he's in a tunnel. "Is Bella there with you?"

"I'm here," Bella leans toward the speaker. "I can hear you."

"Very good," he says. "I understand you were at sixes and sevens much of yesterday. Am I correct?"

"What does that mean?" I ask. "I don't speak *knight.*"

"Sorry, good man," he chuckles. "I should say you were a bit mixed up, as it were. Am I right?"

"If by mixed up," Bella answers, "you mean betrayed, kidnapped, and dragged underground..."

"You should know something about that," I add after Bella doesn't finish her thought.

"Pardon?" Sir Spencer says, feigning ignorance.

"Nothing," I wave off Bella's look of confusion. "Doesn't matter. What does matter is what you know about our issues in Deadwood."

"I don't know much more than you," he says against the distinct, ambient sound of ice clinking in the background. "I am aware that Bella's associate Mr. Mahoney is hospitalized and you have the second hard drive."

"How do you know this?" Bella asks.

"Suffice it to say that I do," Sir Spencer replies. "Though I suggest you really should pay your head of security a salary more commensurate with the work he performs."

Bella asks through clenched teeth, "You bought him off?"

"I enabled his willingness to be forthcoming," Sir Spencer says. "He also told me that Jackson did quite a job rescuing you from those nasty men who...what was it...'dragged you underground'?"

"I did what I'm being paid to do," I interject. "What else?"

"It may be fortuitous that you'll be stopping in London on the way to Odessa. There might be some good information for you there."

"What do you mean?"

"Do you remember a man you met there a couple of years ago? You delivered an iPod to him at the Texas Embassy restaurant?"

"I remember." The man was one of the energy industry contacts the Governor of Texas sent me to meet. I handed him an iPod containing what I later learned was bank transfer information. He was part of an illicit conglomerate bribing the Governor to be friendly to their interests. He stuck me with the tab for a margarita. "His name was Davis."

"Yes!" Sir Spencer's a little too excited. "Good memory, Jackson, very good memory!"

"What about him?"

"He can be of some assistance," he answers. "Call me when you land, and I'll arrange for a quick meet."

"But he worked for the governor. Why would he be helping us? The governor and his friends want me dead. This sounds like a set-up or something."

"It's no *set-up*, Jackson," he sighs. "He was never implicated in the scandal, nor were his compatriots. The governor's scheme was merely a means to an end for Mr. Davis. And what was on that iPod has as much to do with your mission today as it did to your mission then."

Bella's eyes are squeezed shut. She's clearly lost. "I don't understand. Someone who was involved in a plot *against* my father's work, against

Nanergetix, is now willing to help us? Who is this person? And how do solar neutrinos fit into some scheme two years ago?"

"All in good time," Sir Spencer says. "You asked several questions, Bella. All I can tell you at the moment is that Davis is willing to help you. As for who he is, he is a man who, like me, plays the odds. His friends are those who will benefit him most. He is no longer in the oil business, as it were."

"How do the solar neutrinos fit in with the iPods?" I ask. "I thought I was delivering bank information to him and to the others."

"Yes and no," Sir Spencer says. "To some, as in our good friend in Alaska, it was merely bank transfer instructions. But to Davis, there was more encoded into that little music player than a series of numbers."

"What else?" I ask.

"Not now," Sir Spencer says. "I've got to run. Busy, busy. We'll speak when you touch down in my homeland." The line goes silent.

"What exactly have you told him, Bella? How much does he know about this whole thing? None of this smells right to me."

"Well," Bella shifts uncomfortably in her seat, "to be honest, now I'm not sure how much he knows. His reach is a lot longer than I assumed it was."

"Ha!" The chuckle escapes before I can stop it.

"Why is that funny?""Sorry, I don't mean to laugh. I'm surprised that you're only now figuring out how connected and untrustworthy Sir Spencer really is."

"I thought, I mean, I *think*, I can still handle him." She sounds as though she's trying to convince herself.

"Maybe."

"Maybe what?" She leans back against the door, away from me.

"Maybe you're handling him," I say. "Maybe he's playing both of us."

She considers what I'm suggesting then says, "We have a flight to catch."

"Aren't we going to look at the hard drive?" I ask. We do need to know what information it contains and determine whether or not we have the real one or the red herring.

She nods and opens the passenger door then steps out onto the tarmac. "I need some sleep first, though. I'm running on fumes. We've got plenty of time once we're in the air."

"*You're* running on fumes?" I roll my eyes. It's 2:35 AM, almost twenty-four hours since my odyssey began. I haven't slept. I haven't eaten anything of substance. Still, there's no way I can sleep. As Sir Spencer would put it, I'm at six and sevens.

***

Bella's plane, the Bombardier Global 5000, is maybe the most amazing plane ever. It makes Sir Spencer's jet look like an Antonov turboprop.

The maple trimmed interior has eight mocha colored, fully reclining leather chairs. Next to my seat, which faces the rear of the cavernous cabin, is a pullout maple work station. There's in-flight wireless and satellite television. The yellow and black Nanergetix logo, an upper case N surrounded by the interlocking triple oval atomic symbol, is on the carpeted floor and on the lavatory door.

It'll make the flight to Odessa, Ukraine with a brief stop in London. We've got nine hours until we land and, fifteen minutes into the trip, Bella is asleep. Next to her is a laptop bag, in which she's got a computer and the hard drive.

On the desk in front of me is a porcelain dish with a variety of fruits and cheeses and a tall glass of iced Diet Dr. Pepper. I pop a couple of cheese cubes into my mouth and pull out my cell phone.

I remind myself to toss this phone when we land and pull out one of the burner phones from my pack. I'll also need to use one of my remaining identities to get through customs. Flying a private jet has its privileges, but I'm told avoiding passport control is not one of them.

With Bella asleep, it's the first chance I've had to look at the second pdf file that George Townsend sent me. I've also got a pair of text messages from him that I missed in the midst of our adventures in South Dakota:

jackson—please call. need 2 talk. learning more about buell and neutrinos. Gt

jackson—have u looked at files yet? need to talk asap. have more info. gt

The wireless signal on the plane is strong, and I message him:

george—sorry. can't talk. looking at files now. send more info when u can. pdf again. with buell! text is best way to exchange info. jq

A couple of finger touches on the screen and the second file George sent me, the one detailing neutrinos, opens in a pdf.

SOLAR NEUTRINOS BACKGROUND INFORMATION

Nicknamed "ghost particles", solar neutrinos are particles emitted in both nuclear reactions and decay. Neutrinos are believed to be the only particle that escapes from the sun's core without interaction. They are a product of nuclear fusion and account for missing energy produced during decay. The sun produces >200 trillion, trillion, trillion neutrinos per second.

Neutrinos are low energy with a mass of nearly zero. 60 billion neutrinos pass through a square centimeter of the Earth each second.

Neutrino experiments are ongoing at research facilities in Homestake Mine in Lead, South Dakota, Creighton Mine in Ontario, Canada, Ino Peak Cave in Theni, Tamil Nadu, India, CERN Physics Lab in Switzerland, FERMI laboratory in Chicago, Illinois.

FERMI scientists in 2007 and a CERN conglomerate in 2011 claimed to have measured neutrino speeds in excess of 186,292 miles/second. The greater scientific community doubts this is possible.

Neutrino experiments also indicate a theoretical probability of sub-surface/aquatic communication. First proposed in 2009, then attempted successfully in 2012, neutrino-aided communication would allow for submariners to communicate with one another or with those on the surface.

Neutrino experiments also suggest further applications are theoretically probable in areas of nuclear fission detection. But experts suggest this is folly and not possible for at least three decades.

—MORE INFORMATION AS/IF IT IS ATTAINABLE

George's notes aren't much more than what Bella already told me, but at least they confirm her information. I wouldn't have known whether or not what she was feeding me was legitimate or not. Now, at the very least, I've confirmed what she told me about neutrinos. My phone buzzes. It's a new text from George.

jackson—got ur msg. sorry u can't talk. will send new info when i can. busy day. might be a little while. if u can talk would be better. gt

no problem, I text him, *will call if can. jq*

I take a sip of the Diet Dr. Pepper and then pop a red grape in my mouth. They don't really taste good together.

Bella is still asleep, a white blanket pulled up to her neck, her chair in full recline. She's a pretty woman, beautiful actually. Even asleep, with her mouth catching flies, it's hard not to watch her.

What am I doing with her? Why am I on this odyssey, as Sir Spencer called it?

I can't figure out, for the life of me what it is about this deal that doesn't seem right. I don't know which parts are missing or where they'd fit.

Let's start with what I *do* know. With my eyes closed, I start piecing it together.

Bella's father was a mega-rich oil magnate, who supposedly turned on the industry, founded Nanergetix, and went green. He wanted to produce chemically altered oil that would outperform traditional crude. Then he announced he was running for Governor of Texas. It seemed counterintuitive. Who would want to a run a state whose primary industry you were trying to dramatically alter in a way that would hurt profitability? He did, apparently.

When it looked like he was going to lose, he hired people, including my-ex girlfriend, to shoot him and make it look like an assassination attempt. In the meantime, he was keenly aware that my boss, his political rival, was working hard to undercut his new altered oil product.

He knew that my boss was running some sort of scheme to pump the energy companies, for money, with my unwitting help, while at the same time promising them he could "undo" the increased efficacy of the new, better oil product. A lot of people died; a research scientist, my girlfriend, a bunch of ex-spook contractors, my friend Bobby.

Then Buell was killed. I exposed my boss with the help of George Townsend, who got the big story and Peabody Award he wanted. My boss went to prison, along with an energy executive I'd met in Alaska. She didn't trust me and wanted me dead. That hasn't changed.

I went into hiding, unsuccessfully attempting to return some sense of safety and normalcy to my life, until Sir Spencer found me and connected me with Buell's daughter. She'd teamed up with him for some unknown reason, despite his association with my boss prior to her father's death.

He convinced her that I, for some reason, would be an asset in her search for some secret, world-changing process involving neutrinos. Now here we are, in a private jet, speeding toward Europe.

Once we land, we need to piece together the pieces of the process before some rival killer, Liho Blogis, finds them and gains control of the world-changing process...a process that lets submarines communicate better?

None of this fits together. There's more to it. Everyone is holding back from me; Sir Spencer, Bella, even Mack Mahoney.

They all know something that I don't.

***

Mysteries are nothing new to me. Since my parents' deaths, I've lived a series of chapters without endings; one two-dimensional character after another floating into and out of my narrative without any depth or purpose. With time and distance, my parents devolved into two of those characters, their existence becoming a slideshow of memories I warp for the better each time they play through my mind.

The only constant, the only reality, is a handful of photos and mementos I keep in a blue lockbox. It was my only real possession through the years of foster care I endured, my link to a fairytale long forgotten.

The contents of that blue box are clues to what my life could have been, what my life was supposed to be. I often find myself playing out the scenarios I imagine, almost as though I'm writing a *Choose Your Own Adventure* book; if jumping to page seventy-three doesn't work out for me, I can always go back and skip to page eighty-six for a different ending.

More than that, though, the trinkets help me think. They can act as clarifiers, muses cutting through the fog in my mind.

Bella is still asleep. I pop open the box on the desk in front of me and pull out a chess piece, a pawn, my father kept on his desk at home. He told me it was a reminder to him that a good foot soldier is always important. It's carved from black marble, and feels cold in my hand. I rub the smooth rounded top of the pawn with my thumb and reach into the box for another memento.

My mom's wedding ring is simple. It's a thick gold band. On the inside of the band, are the inscribed words "WITH ADORING LOVE". She never wore a diamond, telling me that dad had wanted to give her one for their engagement, but she'd resisted. She told him a simple band on the day they got married was enough, and that he'd reluctantly agreed. But for their first anniversary, he'd bought her a pair of huge diamond earrings. I keep them in the box too, sealed inside an envelope, which finds its place on the desk next to the ring and pawn.

I fish out a lone shotgun shell, and sit it upright on the desk. It was my dad's, and I snuck it from the house when the movers came after they died. It was under his gun safe in his study closet, a lone red shell left behind.

At the bottom of the box is a small, unlabeled brown leather album, large enough to hold the two dozen 3 ½ x 5 inch photos in its plastic sleeves. I slide it out of the box and flip it open.

The first photo, my favorite, always punches the air from my lungs. It's of my mother, my father, and me in Key West, Florida, a large red, black, and yellow marker framed between us and the crystalline water of the Atlantic. The ocean looks as though the varying shades of teal were painted in stripes with a brush, each line lighter than the one above it until they meet the pale horizon.

Emblazoned with a triangular logo for The Conch Republic at the top, the marker proudly announces that the spot is ninety miles to Cuba and is the southernmost point in the Continental U.S.

My mom is dressed in a yellow tank top and white shorts, her left arm around my lower back. Her eyes are hidden by her large tortoise shell sunglasses, and her smile is genuine. My father has his right arm draped over my shoulders. He's wearing reflective aviators, his hair cropped short, a deep tan accentuating the white of his teeth. His other hand is in the pocket of his cargo shorts. His Guy Harvey t-shirt features a marlin on the breast pocket.

I'm in the middle of them, beaming and clearly content. My arms are around my parents' backs, my hands wrapped around their hips. My nose and cheeks are pink from too much sun on board a waverunner earlier in the day. I'm standing on my tiptoes, heels off of the backs of my cheap flip-flops. My sun-kissed hair is lighter than usual and unkempt the way Norman Rockwell might paint a young boy after a day at the beach.

The trip was a quick one, a couple of days together after my dad had finished some business in Miami. We'd crammed a lot into that mini-vacation. I could still taste the coconut oil used to cook the conch fritters we ate at sunset, overlooking the water from our outdoor table.

I flip past the photo to a handful of my father and mother before they married, while they dated, and then a couple of my mom pregnant with me. Then I get to the reason I opened the box in the first place.

There's a photo of my dad's college rifle team at N.C. State. He's on the far left of the photograph, his arms behind his back, chest puffed out. The rock solid team member with a mop of curly hair next to him had his elbow leaning on my dad's shoulder. The photograph looked similar to the iconic U.S. Army platoon photographs from Vietnam or the first Gulf War. I always smile at that picture. On the back of the photograph "Wolfpack Rifle Team" was written in pencil. The year was nineteen eighty something. The last number was faded, as were the names of the team members.

The next few photos are of my dad on business trips. He didn't often pose for photographs when he was out of town. He didn't bring his camera with him, as far as I knew. But every now and then, he'd bring home a snapshot or two that someone else had taken.

The first is my dad standing with his arms folded in front of his chest, his knuckles behind his biceps to make his muscles appear more impressive. His lips are pursed, his eyes slits against the sunlight hitting his face. Behind him is a large metal statue of a woman with her arms raised, a sword extended from one hand, a shield held by the other. The woman's expression in the photograph is serious, contemplative, not unlike my father's. The statue is enormous, at least two hundred feet tall, and it sits atop what looks like a cone shaped visitor's center with glass windows encircling the bottom.

She's wearing a long pleated dress, belted at the waist, and a cloak that drapes down her back. She's masculine, almost asexual aside from the hints of breasts at her chest. On the shield there is a hammer and sickle, the emblem of the defunct Soviet Union, encircled by ears of wheat and topped with a lone star.

I flip the photo and look at the back. The ink has faded to gray and pink where my father scribbled "Mother Motherland, Kiev, Ukraine".

The next photo is also in Ukraine, but this one is south, along the northern edge of the Black Sea. My father is sitting on a set of steps, flanked by tourists and street vendors, who've parked themselves along the wide stone edges of the steps. Behind my father is a woman selling wooden nesting dolls, her head wrapped in a bright yellow floral scarf. She's photobombing him with her road map of a face, worn by what I imagine were years of street hustling and farming. The folds in her face are as thick as the roll in her midsection. She looks pained, but manages a wide-eyed gap-toothed smile directly into the lens.

My father has his elbows on his knees and he's looking past the camera to the sea. He's sitting on the Potemkin Stairs, a boulevard sized stairway from the Port of Odessa into the city. For more than one hundred and fifty years, they've served as the official entrance into Odessa. The photograph is taken from below my father, up the staircase, giving the illusion of endless steps upward.

I've had dreams about those steps, trying to climb them, never reaching the top. In the dream it's like I'm running up the down escalator. Not a pleasant dream.

On the back of the photograph my father has scribbled "Potemkin, Odessa, Ukraine". There's no date. A third photograph has him raising a glass of what I imagine is vodka in the booth of a restaurant. On a wall behind him is an advertisement for a brand of beer in large green and gold Cyrillic lettering.

I never knew why he was there other than "business", why he posed for the photographs, or who took them. It was those photos that made me want to spend time in Ukraine, find some connection with my dad. Now I'm on my way back under much different circumstances, my pack filled with weapons and survival gear instead of socks and underwear.

Bella rustles in her seat, stretching her arms above her head, and I hurry to stuff my belongings back in the box. She doesn't notice, yawning and rubbing the sleep from her eyes.

"Good morning," I say. "Or good evening. Whatever it is."

"Hmmph," she grunts, "I passed out there for a while. Sorry about that."

"Not a problem. Look, we need to check out that hard drive and find out what, if anything, on it is reliable."

"Good idea," she stands up, stretches again, and goes to grab the bag next to her seat toward the rear of the jet. It's hard not to notice when she bends over in that skirt, but I avert my eyes and shove the lockbox back into my pack.

She pulls out her laptop and the white hard drive and sets them on the table between us. It takes her a second to power up and connect the drive. She smiles at me over the top of the computer, but the expression on her face quickly changes, her mascara smudged eyes narrow with confusion.

"That doesn't make sense," she says. "I don't get it."

"What?"

She spins the computer around and shows me the contents of the hard drive.

It's empty.

PART 2

REACTION

"To educate a man in mind and not in morals is to educate a menace to society."
—Theodore Roosevelt, 26th U.S. President

CHAPTER 8

"They're pretty amazing aren't they?" my dad asked from the back of an open air Jeep Wagoneer. We were on a guided tour of Custer State Park, the last outing of our vacation cut short by his work. "You don't get a sense of how big and powerful they are without seeing them this close."

"They're majestic," my mom added, a bit too enthusiastically, sensing my misery. "I didn't expect to think that."

"Majestic is a really good word for 'em," said the tour guide through his headset. "They are truly underappreciated for their beauty. I like that word, majestic."

The guide, who was driving, wore a dirt and sweat stained straw cowboy hat and a plaid wool shirt. He probably hadn't shaved in a couple of days, the rough beard most noticeable on his chin.

"Their poop is majestic," I said, my chin resting on the edge of the Wagoneer's interior where the window should be. "And by majestic, I mean huge."

"They are buffalo, Jackson," my dad said, not acknowledging my moping. "If their poop was anything but majestic, wouldn't you be highly disappointed? Seriously, son, buffalo poop is impressive."

He elicited a reluctant giggle from me and took advantage.

"Did you see that one, Jackson?" He pointed to a large bison flipping its tail against its scarred haunch. "It took a leak that I swear might cause flash flooding in some places."

"Okay, Dad, I get it. I should stop feeling sorry for myself and enjoy the time we have together. It's not like you want to go to work."

"Smart boy." Mom squeezed my shoulder. "Your dad does the best he can, Jackson. But he does have to work. It's not like we're rich."

"I get that," I said. "It's just…"

"What?" my dad asked, turning around from his seat in the front of the Jeep.

"I'm gonna turn off this road here," the tour guide said. "It's gonna get a little bumpy for a moment. You'll probably see some varmints out there. Like those pesky prairie dogs."

"Sometimes it feels like you pick work over me and Mom," I said, slumping against the worn vinyl seat back. "You know, when you travel all of the time."

"Your dad—" My mom stopped when Dad gave her a look.

"It's okay, hon," he said to her. "I got this." He turned his body toward the driver/tour guide so he could look me squarely in the face, hold my attention. "Jackson."

"Yeah?" I sighed, bouncing against a divot in the dirt road. My head almost touched the sagging lining on the Wagoneer's ceiling.

"Sorry about that folks," the guide apologized. "Got a couple more coming up. Nothing too rough. We may catch some antelope up on the right, catching a nap under that tree."

"You know very well that you and your mom are the most important things in the world to me," my dad said, bracing himself against another bump. "I have a job that pays pretty well, it allows us to do a lot of nice things as a family. But one of the trade-offs is spontaneous travel."

"Couldn't you find another job?"

"I could," he glanced at Mom and then back at me. "I guess so. But what I do is very…"

"Specialized?" my mom suggested, a weak smile on her face.

"Yes," Dad agreed. "My work is specialized."

"What do you do for a living, the tour guide asked, "if you don't mind?" He looked at my dad, both of his thick, calloused hands on the wheel, and smiled.

My dad shifted uncomfortably in his seat, adjusting his seatbelt as we bounced across another divot in the road. He looked back at my mom for her approval, which she tacitly gave.

"I'm a technology consultant."

"What's that?" the guide asked. "Is it like a computer expert?" He laughed nervously, as though he didn't want to seem uninformed.

"Exactly!" my dad grinned. "I make sure the computers and other electronic devices companies utilize work properly and can interface or synchronize without glitches."

"Who's the company?" the guide pressed, jerking the wheel left to avoid a hole in the road. "IBM? GE?"

"No," my dad chuckled. "It would be nice to work for one of those companies. Again, I'm a consultant. So I don't work for the same company for very long. I go where the work is. The group I'm working for right now is a privately-held firm that has some government contracts."

"Government stuff," the tour guide nodded his head up and down, processing it, "you don't say? Must be good work if you can get it." He smiles again.

"It is, even though it sometimes means being away from my family without much notice."

"Hey," the tour guide says, "there's the antelope I was talking about. That's the momma. There's a little baby there too. They're tucked behind those shrubs underneath the tree." He stops the Jeep about fifty yards from the lone tree in a vast, rolling prairie. We're off the road in wheel high grass.

"Look, Jackson!" My mom scooted over against her window. "Come here, look out this side."

"The antelope is a cousin to the deer," the tour guide explained. "Unlike the deer, which grows new horns every year, however, the antelope keeps them permanently. It's their primary form of defense against predators. The momma there, she usually has one baby at a time. Sometimes they'll have twins, but it's rare."

"They looked scared," I said.

"That's cause they probably are," said the guide. "Even though they're used to seeing us around here, the momma is her most vulnerable when she has a baby with her. Remember, they're a big mammal, so they make a good meal for a predator."

My mom was mesmerized. "They look like statues."

"They get like that," the guide said. "That baby calf is gonna stay still. It thinks it's hiding. Though if we get too close, it'll run. They do that. They hide until they're on the verge of being discovered. Then they bolt and hope they can run fast enough to get away."

"Do they always get away?" I asked.

"Nope," said the guide. "They might get away fifteen times or twenty. But eventually the hunter is gonna get most of them. Luck always runs out, sorry to say."

***

Bella arms are folded, one hand at her mouth. She's biting her thumb, pacing back and forth along the aisle of the jet.

"Ms. Buell," the flight attendant asks, "is there something I may get you? You seem anxious."

"No thank you," Bella says, walking past her without stopping.

The slight woman appears to my left. She's maybe thirty-five or forty. Her years in the air have dried out her skin, and fine lines accentuate the space between her cheeks and lips. Her forehead bears the stress of too many turbulent flights, and her makeup barely conceals deep circles under eyes. She's past the line of being too thin, her blouse and dark blue skirt swallowing her narrow frame. As she reaches for my glass, I notice faint yellow stains on her index and middle fingers.

"I'll be happy to refresh this for you, sir," she smiles, highlighting what I guess must be the wrinkles of a longtime smoker, the hint of gravel in her voice further confirming the assumption. "Diet Dr. Pepper, right?"

"Yes please, that would be great." Diet Dr. Pepper is the crack of all soft drinks.

She takes the glass, along with the nearly empty snack plate. Bella passes me three more times before the flight attendant returns with a refill. I take a long swig.

"I don't get it." Bella stands in front of me, next to the desk. She's rubbing her bottom lips with her fingers. "Why would Mack give me a blank drive?"

"Let's go over this again," I say. "Who told you about the hard drives?"

"I knew that Wolf was storing information on external drives," she says. "Our information technology group knows that he plugged in multiple external drives and downloaded files that no longer exist on his computer in the lab."

"Can they retrieve the files from the computer?"

"They've tried," she says. "But he went into the master file table and used some sort of third party eraser program. He also used a command prompt and then the *S-DELETE* function to ensure that everything was gone. All that exists is a series of random number sets. The IT guys are stumped."

"And the IT guys know how many different drives Wolf used?"

"Yes," she says. "Two drives."

"If the data is gone from the computer," I ask, "then how do you know what is really on those drives? Is it possible that what he put on the drives is not the information you think it is?"

"The files he dumped were named *Neutrino Bid List One* and *Neutrino Bid List Two*. That kinda gives it away."

"We've established that two external hard drives have information on them, that your scientist was not at all creative with file names, and that each drive likely contains different information, right?"

"Uh huh," she mumbles, the tip of her thumb still in her mouth, not reacting to my sarcasm at all.

"You believe the disks contain lists of names and locations of possible buyers for this underwater walkie talkie stuff, right?"

"It's not exactly a walkie talkie," she corrects. "It's more like—"

"I get it," I interrupt. "My point is, the disks are different."

"Yes."

"Who told you this?"

"IT," she says. "They told me one of the files was loaded onto one of the drives, and the other file was loaded onto the other drive."

"Then, clearly, Bella," I rationalize, "one of three things happened here."

"What?" She says it like she doesn't really want to hear the answer.

"The IT guys lied to you. The hard drive got erased. Or..."

"Or what?"

"Or Mack gave you the wrong drive." I lean back in my seat and finish what's left of my third Diet Dr. Pepper.

"Why would he do that?" Bella sidesteps to the chair facing mine and sits down, crossing her legs and tugging on her skirt to pull it down. "Mack wouldn't do that."

"Are you sure about that? Your head of security wasn't entirely loyal. Sir Spencer gave him some cash and he rolled."

"That's different," she said, clearly not liking the implication.

"How so?"

"Mack is..." her eyes are searching for the right words, "I don't know. He wouldn't betray me like that."

"You'd like to think he wouldn't," I suggest, "but you're not sure about it are you?"

"I'm not sure about anything, Jackson. I don't know which end is up here. We're going to land in London with nothing. We have no leads. This hard drive, for whatever reason, is blank. It's useless."

"Remind me then, if we have *no* leads, why are we going to Ukraine? Who suggested we go there?"

"Well," she looks at me, the confusion still floating in her eyes, "remember that intercepted message I told you about? The one from Dr. Wolf?"

"Yeah," I respond, "except I thought you said it was a partial message you *received* from Wolf. You never said it was intercepted."

"I did receive it," she says. "I never said it was intended for me."

"You did," I point my finger at her. "You said he sent it to you."

"Semantics," she shakes her head. "Bottom line: it was sent to a scientist there who *was* working with Wolf at one point. They worked together in Germany. Now this guy is in Ukraine. He has a place in Odessa. I've met him once, briefly. So we're starting there."

"Where'd you meet him?"

"At a party with a bunch of researchers, " she says. "Does it matter?"

"What does he look like?"

"I don't remember," says Bella. "It was for a moment at a party. What's your deal?"

"Can you trust what this guy will tell you, *if* we can find him?"

"I don't know, Jackson. I don't know," she closes her eyes as she speaks. "It seems to me, we can't trust anyone."

I completely agree.

CHAPTER 9

London's Biggin Hill Airport is about twelve miles southeast of the city's center. It's apparently dedicated to serving large business jets, which is evident as we taxi past a seemingly endless row of white aircraft, most adorned with a corporate logo on the tail.

The V-shaped runways frame a massive, impossibly green field. The edges of the airport are decorated with large trees that mask the surroundings, except for the occasional red roofs of neighboring homes. A large hangar sits aside each of the two runways puddled with water. The skies are thick with gray clouds that look ready to dump more rain on us.

"How far to the meeting place?" It's the first thing I've said to Bella in a couple of hours, both of us too tired and too anxious to talk. My watch reads 5:45 PM local time.

"Forty-five minutes by car. Sir Spencer suggested we meet this Davis guy in a public place."

"Where exactly?" I ask. "And how are we getting there?"

"I hired a car," she peeks her eyes above the top of the magazine she is reading. "It should be here already. We're going to meet at the Marble Arch on Park Lane and then get on a tour bus."

"A tour bus?"

"Yes," she hides her eyes but not her sarcasm. "Got a better idea, Jackson? You know, you could have made the call to Sir Spencer."

"I don't have a better idea," I admit, "but a moving tour bus makes it difficult for us to leave the meeting if it turns sour."

She exhales dramatically and slaps the magazine down onto her crossed legs. "Jackson, I don't understand you. You didn't give me any suggestions before I called Sir Spencer. I'm doing the best I can here, okay?"

"You're right," I say. It's consistently the best thing to say to any woman, I've learned, when I'm interested in diffusing an argument. "I'm thinking out loud. We'll be fine."

She glares at me, not buying my surrender, and unbuckles her seatbelt. "It's time to go," she says. "Where are your weapons?"

"Inside my bag here," I motion toward my rucksack. "Why?"

"They're illegal here," she tells me. "As is the ammunition I imagine you're packing."

"What do I do?"

"You'll need to leave them on the plane," she says.

"I don't think that's a great idea. Sir Spencer, a man neither of us implicitly trust, set up this meeting."

"We don't have a choice," she says. "I can't risk us getting arrested and stuck in a British police station because we're carrying guns."

"What do you suggest?"

"Do you have any other weapons?" She glances at my pack. "A knife or something?"

I nod and open up a side pouch on the pack, rifling through socks and underwear to pull out a black Spyderco folding knife. "Like this?" I flip open the four-inch blade.

"Just one?" she asks.

"Just one," I stuff the socks back into the pouch and close it.

"I guess it'll do," she says. "It'll have to. Leave your pack here. Let's go."

I grab one of my fake passports and a burner phone, slipping both of them into an empty pocket. My old phone and ID get tossed into the trash bin on my way out.

Bella leads me off the plane and into a waiting car, a white Range Rover. There's a driver and an additional security guard sitting in the left front seat. Both men look like Jason Statham; balding, muscular and thick-necked, with chauffeur jackets that fit a half-size too tight across the chest. Neither of them say anything as we pull away from the jet and onto a road called A233.

"Tell me about Davis," Bella says. "Who exactly is he?"

"Good question," I answer. "I'm not one hundred percent sure."

"Tell me what you know."

"I met him a couple of years ago. I was working for the governor and he had me delivering iPods all over the place. The iPods had information on them that the governor wanted to secretly get to these people."

"Banking information?" She leans in toward me, lowering her voice.

"Probably. The one I delivered to Alaska had banking information. I saw it. But the ones I took to Venezuela, Brazil, Florida, Nebraska, Oklahoma, Louisiana...here to London...I'm not sure."

"That's a lot of iPods," her eyebrows arch. "And you never thought to ask what was on them?"

"I thought to ask," I chuckle, "but I also thought better of it. I was so happy to be traveling, to be trusted with some 'important mission', that I didn't really want to know what I was doing. Of course, I never thought it would rise to the level that it did. I never thought it would cost me my life." Out the window, we zip by what look like Tudor style apartment homes, a young couple sitting at a bus stop.

"You're still alive," she points out.

"Yeah. But this isn't *my* life. I lost that the minute I handed that first iPod over to Davis."

She looks at me, the slightest hint of pity in her eyes. "We'll get your life back."

"I'm not naive enough anymore to believe that. It is what it is. I just want to stop running. That's the only reason I'm here."

"Got it." The pity disappears from her eyes. "Tell me more about Davis please."

"I met him at a Tex-Mex restaurant," I tug on my lap belt, loosening it a little bit. A sign that reads *Bromley* flies by to my left. "He showed up, told me his name was Davis, which I am pretty sure was an alias. We talked for a maybe a minute. I asked him what he did for living. He told me his job was 'whatever needed doing'. "

Bella frowns. "Sounds like something Sir Spencer would say."

"It does," I say. "Sir Spencer said he's a man who plays the odds. So maybe they have a history I don't know about. I do know, as Sir Spencer mentioned, that Davis was an energy executive. He was involved in the big conspiracy to hurt your dad's business."

"What energy company?"

"I don't know," I say. "I never found out. Why the twenty questions? What're you thinking?"

"I'm not thinking anything," she snaps, a defensive, sharp tone in her voice. She catches herself and lowers the volume again. "I'm wondering a couple of things."

"What things?"

"First of all, what information could he possibly have that would help us? And second, is he dangerous?"

Those are good questions.

"I don't know the answer to either of those questions," I admit.

"Are you any good with that knife?" Bella glances at my pocket.

"Let's hope we don't have to find out."

CHAPTER 10

The Marble Arch is across the street from a McDonald's, a Pret A Manger, and a Thomas Cook travel agency office. It's probably not what architect John Nash imagined when he designed the arch to be an entrance to Buckingham Palace. Instead of some grand adornment for the royal home, it now sits on the edge of Hyde Park, across from the home of the Big Mac.

Bella points through the arch and across a plaza. "The buses are over there. That's Cumberland Gate." We jog through the gate, splashing through puddles to a row of red double decker buses. Amidst the evening rush of cars and taxis, one of the buses is stopped, its doors open next to a man who I assume is the ticket taker.

"Excuse me," a voice says from behind us. "Excuse me, Mr. Quick?"

Bella and I turn around to see a man holding three tickets in his hand. He's dressed in a long-sleeved dress shirt, underneath a windbreaker, and slim tailored pants. On his head is a dark blue pork pie hat. He looks a little like Walter White, from the television show *Breaking Bad*, only without the eyeglasses. He smiles, revealing his crowded, yellowed teeth. "Mr. Quick, good to see you again." He offers his empty hand.

"Mr. Davis." I shake his hand, studying his eyes, which give away nothing. "Hello again."

"Miss Buell?" He offers her his hand, which she takes with a smile. "I have our tickets. Shall we?"

He gestures toward the bus and follows us on board, handing our tickets to the man at the door. The bus is mostly empty, save a handful of people crammed into the narrow seats. A few of them are wearing the cheap earbuds offered with the accompanying audio tour.

"How about upstairs?" Davis suggests. "We might have a bit more privacy up there." He says the word 'privacy' with a short 'i'.

I climb the narrow stairwell up to the open air of the double decker. The wet seats are empty, not a single rider up here. The intermittent drizzle is enough of a deterrent to keep anyone from the top deck.

When Davis' head peeks through the stairwell, Bella and I are standing at the back of the bus, facing the front. She doesn't look thrilled about sitting in water, so I take the sleeve of my shirt and rub one of the seats as dry as I can.

"And who suggests that chivalry is dead?" laughs Davis. "Quite a gentleman, Mr. Quick."

Bella slides into a seat next to the outer guardrail and I sit next to her. Davis sits across the aisle, turned toward us. The bus pulls away from the curb and into traffic.

"Ladies and gentlemen," the tour guide's voice booms through the large speaker at the front of the bus, "we'll be taking the red tour, that's the city sightseeing tour. It's a two hour, fifteen minute drive, though you are most welcome to depart at any of the stops and rejoin the tour on another of our buses at any point today or tomorrow. Your tickets are valid for the next twenty-four hours."

Davis leans his right elbow on the seatback in front of him and turns his body toward us. "Mr. Quick, I recall that the last time we met, you indicated it was your first trip to The Old Smoke."

"I recall," I said, "that you stiffed me on your margarita."

"Very good!" He smiles broadly and laughs. "I did, didn't I? Quite rude, I suppose. Forgive me my trespasses, then, will you?"

"I suppose."

"Good then." He checks his watch. "So," he looks up and the smile disappears from his face, "I understand from our mutual friend that you have something for me."

"Really?" Bella leans forward so she can clearly see Davis. "We understand you have something for *us*."

"Hmmm," Davis knits his brow, his narrowed eyes dancing between Bella and me. "That's interesting. What would I have for you?"

I slip my left hand into the pocket of my sweatpants, gripping the jackknife. "Our mutual friend tells me that there wasn't only banking information on that iPod I gave you. He says there was something relevant to Nanergetix's latest project."

Davis stares at me, expressionless. He taps his fingers on the seat back, but doesn't say anything.

"What do you know about neutrinos?" Bella blurts out. "What can you tell me about Dr. Wolf's work?"

Davis blinks, wincing almost. It's the kind of facial tic that tells me he has no idea what we're talking about. His jaw sets, the tension in his face growing obvious.

Sir Spencer set us up. He lied to Davis. He lied to us.

"You don't know what we're talking about do you?" I ask.

"Perhaps," he says coyly. "Perhaps not."

"What information did you think we had for you?"

A smile snakes across his face again, this one much less amiable than the one before. He's not giving up anything. He's trying to figure out why he's here, like I'm processing what Sir Spencer was trying to accomplish by getting the two of us together.

"Up ahead," the tour guide's voice blares from the speaker, causing all three of us to jump, "you'll see Downing Street to the left. It's through those wrought iron gates. That's the home of our Prime Minister. Please don't confuse it with Baker Street, the fabled residence of literary detective Sherlock Holmes." The bus slows in the traffic and then brakes suddenly.

"We'll be letting on some guests here," he adds, "and if you'd like to hop off at this point, you're most welcome."

"Should we get off the bus?" Bella whispers into my ear. "I don't like this."

"I don't either," I try not to move my lips or take my eyes off of Davis and still slip the knife from my pocket and onto the seat between Bella and me. I have a bad feeling I'm going to need it.

***

"Why are you here?" asks Davis as the bus lurches forward. "Why is it you think you're here?"

"We want information that can help us," Bella says. "Our friend tells us you can do that. He says you can help us."

Davis chuckles, still rapping his fingers on the seat. "You know, Mr. Quick," he sneers, "I knew you were in over your head when I met you in that restaurant. It was apparent to me then that you had no idea about the grand scale of things. You trusted the wrong people then, and you're trusting the wrong ones now." From his right jacket pocket he pulls a handgun, a semiautomatic, and levels it at my chest, concealing it beneath the seatback.

"Are you kidding me?" I mumble to Bella. "No guns," I mock her. "We might get arrested?"

"What are you saying?" Davis demands. "Don't make any moves that might force me to pull the trigger."

"Just commenting on gun laws," I say.

How am I going to get out of this? I brought a knife to a gunfight...

"You owe me, Mr. Quick," he says, "and it's quite a bit more than the cost of a margarita."

"For what?"

"Your little stunt, your betrayal of your boss, cost me immeasurably," Davis answers, the gun's barrel bouncing in rhythm with his speech.

"You weren't implicated," I say. "You've had no trouble. Why do I owe you?"

"What do you owe?" he laughs "What trouble have I had?"

"I lost the millions of pounds that I fronted your boss," he spits. "Money that my bosses were not happy to lose. So they sacked me. And the technology your boss was trying to thwart, *her father's* technology," he points the barrel at Bella and I shift my body to block her. "it's going to market. Better, more efficient fuel, is the scourge of the petrol industry. It was my job to help stop that. I failed. I'm a pariah. I can't find work."

The bus slows and stops.

"We've arrived at the Tate Modern, a wonderful museum," the guide advises. "If you'd like to take a look, now's your chance. Hop off here and hop on another bus at your leisure."

"We're still years away from perfecting the nano-enhanced—" Bella tries reason.

"Pipe down!" Davis snaps, his eyes widening and nostrils flaring. "It's going to happen. Everyone knows it. Don't try to sell me a false bill of goods Bella Buell." He says her name with the disdain of an ex-lover. "It's only a few months from market. And whatever this *neutrino* business is, I am certain that it too would only serve to pain me further."

"Why are you here then?" I ask, though I already know the answer. The bus pulls into traffic.

"I'm here because our mutual friend offered me an opportunity to exact a measure of closure," he says. "It's something about which I've thought these last months. The addition of Miss Buell wasn't even part of the fantasy, but it's a gift I'll treasure."

Sir Spencer wants us dead? Why would he want us dead?

"You know there are video cameras everywhere in this city. One is bound to capture you killing us."

"You won't get away with it," Bella adds.

"How trite," Davis says, "and really it doesn't concern you, does it? Does it matter if I am caught after you're dead and buried?"

At the moment he raises the gun, I push the release button on the Spyderco sheath, popping open the blade, and sidearm it toward Davis. It's too late. My ears ring from the crack of a single gunshot and I grab my chest to find where I've been hit but find nothing.

My knife is stuck into the seat behind Davis.

I missed!

Davis, however, is slumped over, bleeding from his head or neck. His pork pie hat is upside down in the aisle. From my peripheral vision, I sense something to my left as Bella screams. There, moving deliberately from the stairs to Davis, gun smoking, is our driver, Jason Statham number one. He steps within a foot of Davis and fires another quick shot at the disgraced energy executive, then whips his neck to look at Bella and me.

"Time to go," he tucks the gun into the shoulder holster beneath his suit jacket and turns back toward the staircase.

I grab Bella's hand and pull her out into the aisle. She shuffles toward the stairwell, holding onto the seats for stability. I jimmy my knife from the seatback, step over Davis' hat, and follow Bella to the first deck.

The bus is stopping when I reach the bottom of the stairs and our driver is hustling Bella onto the street. I quickly follow.

"What was that?" I call to the driver, who's now five yards in front of me. "What happened?"

He ignores me, but Bella turns around and reaches back to me as she keeps walking. I catch up and grasp her fingers. They're cold but they feel familiar, comfortable.

The driver continues walking at a hurried pace, weaving between umbrellas and newspapers held above people's heads. It's raining again and hard to keep track of him as he maneuvers his way through the crowds walking the wide sidewalks.

Behind us, maybe a block or so back at the bus, there's a woman's scream followed by men yelling. The temptation to turn around is instinctive, but Bella squeezes my hand. Both of us resist, weaving through commuters who've stopped and turned to look.

We've walked maybe a quarter mile when a white Range Rover squeals up to the curb ahead of us and to our right. Statham number one doubles back and hops in the front passenger seat while Bella tugs me to the SUV.

"Get in," the driver, now a passenger, says to us when Bella opens the rear passenger door. She climbs in and slides over so that I can get in and shut the door. My hand is on the handle, pulling it closed when the Range Rover jerks into traffic and merges with the cabs and buses navigating the nasty, wet streets of central London.

"What was that?" I'm out of breath and pushing the rain from my forehead and into my hair.

Neither Jason Statham says anything. The killer Jason pulls out a cell, punches a series of numbers, and then hands the phone to me. It's ringing when I put it to my ear.

"Jackson?" The voice makes me want to crawl through the phone and strangle it. "Is that you, good man?"

I don't say anything. A gray BMW, a London police cruiser, speeds by us on the right, siren blaring and blue lights flashing. A green and yellow checkerboard ambulance is close behind.

"I'll take your silence as a 'yes', then," Sir Spencer chuckles.

Take it as a 'Screw you!', you manipulative ass.

"How was the sightseeing tour?" he asks. "I understand one learns something new every time."

***

"Mr. Davis was a fly in the ointment, Jackson," says Sir Spencer. "He needed to be dealt with."

"You used us as bait?"

"That's such an unfortunate turn of phrase," Sir Spencer answers. "I prefer to suggest you were an incentive for Mr. Davis to show himself."

"What do you mean?"

"He was not a happy fellow," Sir Spencer explains. "He'd informed me that there might be other arrangements, other deals, he might be willing to divulge to the authorities should I not satisfy his needs."

"Needs?"

"Oh, for heaven's sake, Jackson," he huffs, "must I spell it out for you?"

"Yes."

"Fine, then. This is a secure line, I imagine?"

"Is this line secure?" I ask Jason Statham number one. He nods. "Yes," I tell the knight, "it's secure."

"He wanted you dead, Jackson. He blamed you for the failure of the governor's plot. You were, after all, the only living person, aside from the governor, involved in the scheme."

"*You* were involved," I correct him.

"True," he says. "But I don't count. I'm involved in everything."

"He never had any information about the neutrino process?"

"You're not so quick sometimes, Jackson," the knight belly laughs. "Of course not. I only told you that so that you'd lead me to him. I told him that I'd give you to him for his disposal if he'd forego his incessant threats."

"We *were* bait," I conclude. "And he almost killed us both."

"Characterize it however you want, Jackson," he chides, "but he didn't kill you. You're alive and well."

"This little side trip of yours wasted a lot of our time. We need to be looking for pieces of the process, not unwittingly doing your bidding."

"Who contends those are mutually exclusive propositions, Jackson?" There's a click and the line goes silent.

"Hello?" I pull the phone from my ear to look at the display. "Hello?" Jason Statham number one reaches for the phone, which I hand to him.

"He set us up?" Bella asks. "He used us to kill that man?"

I nod silently. The rabbit hole is getting deeper and the Mad Hatter seems to be the only one who knows how far it drops.

***

"We'll be landing in Odessa, Ukraine in approximately thirty minutes," Bella's pilot announces, waking me from a dead sleep. "The local time there is 3 AM."

I've spent most of the three and a half hour flight trying to get some rest. My guess is, though, that I've gotten an hour's sleep at best. Through the fog, my eyes focus the digital display on my watch, which has already adjusted to the two hour time change: 3:02 AM.

What is that...like...6PM yesterday back home? Wherever home *is...*

My knee aches, my lower back hurts, my neck is sore.

Bella is asleep in her recliner. She's changed clothes, ditching the business top and lavender skirt for a pair of jeans and a long sleeved silk blouse. She's also kicked the pumps for a pair of Nike running shoes. Her hair is pulled back into a ponytail, her makeup less obvious. Not that she needs makeup.

My burner phone indicates I have a signal. I move away from Bella and dial. It rings twice.

"News 4 Houston," the familiar voice answers. "George Townsend."

"George," I say in hushed voice, "it's Jackson."

"Jackson?" He sounds surprised. "I don't recognize the number. How many phones do you have?"

"Not enough. So what's the additional information you have about neutrinos and Bella Buell? I read what you sent."

"We're on the air, you know," he says. "It's right at six o'clock. I've got a live hit in about fifteen minutes."

"Can you spare five?" I ask. "And skip the makeup?"

"Very funny," he deadpanned. "I've got a minute."

"What's the deal?"

"Why are you whispering?" he asks.

"I'm fine right now, though I'm not in a place where I can speak freely. I'd prefer to listen."

"Okay," he says. "So here's the deal. As you know, this neutrino stuff is being studied for subsea communication, right? Well, I mentioned the fission detection stuff too in that brief I sent you. That could be the real key here. The submarine walkie-talkie crap is probably a red herring."

"I don't understand." I look toward Bella to make sure she's asleep. So far, so good. "Red herring?"

"Maybe that's a stretch," he concedes. "They probably are interested in that as a real money maker. The United States Navy alone would pay big bucks for that. You sell it to other countries too, even our allies, and you're talking billions."

"Then what?"

"I don't think that's the real end game of this neutrino stuff."

"Why not?"

"This is a stretch here," he admits.

"Enough with the teases. You're burying the lead here."

"There was some research in 2010 that some French researchers published about this. They contended that using what they called a neutrino beam, they could detect hidden nuclear reactors. You know, in countries that don't like us. They have these nuclear programs that officially don't exist, but everyone knows they've got stuff going on."

"How does this help?" I ask quickly. Bella is getting restless.

"Think about it, Jackson," he says. "If we, or anyone, could detect where a country was hiding its nuclear reactors, that would put us at a great strategic advantage."

"What you're saying is if we knew where these hidden reactors were, we'd have a stronger case to stand up and say, 'Tsk, tsk, tsk. We know you have a nuclear reactor. Our special neutrino beam told us you do!!'. C'mon, George. That can't be it. Convincing the world a special beam of invisible, nearly massless particles from the sun can tell us where secret nuclear reactors are hidden is about as likely as convincing the O.J. Simpson jury that DNA evidence is real."

"That was a throwback reference," he laughs. "It sounds like a stretch, but here's the interesting part. One of the participants in that 2010 study was the CEA, a French technological research organization. They get most of their funding from the French government, but they have a lot of partners all over the world. One of those being Nanergetix."

"What do you mean by 'partner'?" I ask. Bella's eyes are still closed, she's pulled the blanket up to her chin.

"They gave them millions of dollars, Jackson. Now I gotta go. If I find out anything else or have an update, I'll let you know. In the meantime, when you get a chance, Google what's called a SNIF detector."

"Thanks, George," I whisper. "I appreciate it."

"Yeah," he says, "I still don't know what all of this is about, or how you've managed to get yourself involved. I expect the exclusive interview, though, when it's all over."

"Right, like that's gonna happen."

I hang up, grab a Diet Dr. Pepper from the wet bar next to kitchen at the front of the plane, thank the sky waitress, and head back to my seat for landing.

Nuclear detection. Is that what this is really about?

CHAPTER 11

The streets in Odessa are empty except for the thick fog rolling past our car. There's no sign of the ongoing conflict between Ukrainian loyalists and pro-Russian Separatists who've taken over the eastern part of the country.

Having wasted an hour at customs negotiating the appropriate "tariff" for our belongings, it's after four o'clock in the morning. With the help of a local translator she hired, Bella negotiated the shakedown and paid two thousand hryvnia, the equivalent of about two hundred and fifty dollars.

"You know," she says as we pass an afterhours nightclub with a few people milling about the entrance, the glow of their cigarettes cutting through the fog, "that jerk at customs could have asked me for any amount of money and I would have paid it. He asked for next to nothing."

"It was probably a lot to him," I say. "What's the average income here?"

"It is not very good," the translator interjects from the front passenger seat of the car. "I am working security for my job. My payment is one thousand two hundred hryvnia. That is maybe, one hundred fifty U.S. dollars."

"Is that a day or a week?" Bella asks.

"That is what I am getting paid in a month." He smiles, yellow streetlights flashing a glow across his round, clean-shaven face. He is bald with thick, black eyebrows. "This is why I am doing the extra work, yes?"

"I understand," she says. "I'll pay you better than that. Don't worry about it."

"I am knowing that you are paying big cash." He rubs his fingers together to indicate the riches he expects to make from this job.

"Big cash," Bella smirks and plops back against her seat.

I lean close to Bella and whisper into ear, "Maybe you shouldn't have said that you'd 'pay anything' in front of this guy. Where did you find him?"

"My father hired him a couple of times. His name was in the rolodex."

"You still use a rolodex?"

"Figuratively." She rolls her eyes, her face lit by headlights from an SUV behind us. "It was in the contacts on his computer. You know what I meant."

"I'm trying to lighten the mood, Bella. It's four o'clock in the morning and we're in eastern Europe on a wild goose chase. Thought you might like a laugh."

The car slows to a stop at an intersection, waiting for another car to pass.

She looks out the window at the rows of three-story high apartment buildings lining the street. "I would, but there's not much that's funny about any of this."

"How much farther to the hotel?" she asks the driver.

"He doesn't speak English," says the translator. "I would be telling you we are not far from hotel. Five minutes more, maybe?"

I'm focused on the car in the intersection. The thickening fog makes it difficult to make out, but it looks like the car is stopping right in front us. The lights from the SUV behind us are brighter. It's right on our tail.

I wrap my right hand around the back of Bella's neck and push her down out of the light. "Get down!!!" I draw the revolver into my left hand and the world around me downshifts into slow motion.

"Jackson, what the—?!?" Bella protests, surprised by the force of my shove, I'm sure.

The windshield shatters, glass flying into the car along with a hail of bullets. The translator's body contorts, convulsing in his seat as round after round tears through him. I duck next to Bella on the floorboard behind the front seats.

The rear window shatters and glass sprays onto our backs, into her hair. Another round of semi-automatic fire riddles the car in short bursts. My revolver is no good in this situation and we've got only seconds before they work their way around to the side of the car. We'll be trapped.

Reaching around to the front, I feel up under the driver's armpit. Fumbling around, my hand grips leather: a holster! A second later, a 9mm is in my right hand and I'm returning fire, perched low between the gap in the two front seats.

"Jackson!" Bella screams. "Jackson!"

"Are you hit?" I'm focused on the man now approaching the car from the front, emerging from the fog with what looks like a compact machine gun. He's reloading, trying to pop a magazine.

"No!" she whimpers. "What's happening?"

"Stay down!"

The man approaching the car from the front is squinting now, our headlights blinding him. I slide forward, belly first, onto the armrest between the two front seats, extending my right arm forward, aiming for the gunman's head.

Elegant.

Pop! Pop! Pop! Two shots to his face, one to his chest, and he is no longer a problem.

"Stay here!" I snap at Bella and roll into the front seat, up against the slouched body of the translator. In one quick series of motions, I lean over to the driver's side door, open it, and kick out the driver. His body tumbles to the ground in a heap, his right foot still on the floorboard. It draws immediate fire from behind the car, and I turn around, my back against the dashboard aiming for the headlights of the SUV behind us.

Pop! Pop! through the already shattered rear window.

Both lights are out and I've got maybe ten to twelve more rounds in the semi-automatic. My revolver is on the rear floorboard of the car.

"Bella! Grab my gun off the floor next to you. It's behind the driver's seat. Stay low!"

There's a figure approaching from the left, near the curb. I crawl out of the car and behind the driver's body, propping him up as a shield.

"Bella! Do you have the gun?"

"Yes!"

"Then use it! Aim for the curb!"

I roll over on the ground, facing the front of the car, just in time to see a sweatsuit clad man leveling a handgun at me.

He fires twice before I can get off a shot. The first hits the right front tire, popping it and releasing the air with a nasty, loud hiss. The second grazes my hip and settles into the driver's body right behind me.

He's approaching quickly, but I manage a burst of shots from the semi-auto in my hand. One hits his knee, dropping him. The other gets his midsection. He's alive, but crying out in pain on the street.

His cries are immediately drowned out by the sound of successive shots from my revolver....three, four, five shots, followed by the sickening sound of *click, click, click*!

I scramble to my feet and, crouched low, curl around the front of the car through the headlights, ready to fire. On the ground next to our car is a motionless body.

"Bella!" I can't focus in the dark.

"I'm okay," she cries. "I'm okay. Are they gone? Did we get all of them?"

"Yes. You can get out of the car."

Bella pops open the door, hitting it against the body on the ground, and runs into my arms, still holding the revolver. She's pressed tight against me, her fingers gripping my back as though she's about to fall. She buries her face in my chest and sobs.

"What was that?" she says, her voice muffled. "Who were they?"

"I don't know yet," I put my hands on her shoulders to release her hold on me. "We'll find out. Do me a favor, okay?"

"What?"

"Pop the trunk, grab your bag, and get into the car in the intersection. I'll grab mine after I talk to our friend over here."

Bella nods and walks around to the driver's side of the car. Moments later, she walks past me with her bag as I kneel down to start asking questions.

I put the gun on the ground above his head and grab his face by his jaw, pulling his gaze to mine. His face is compressed with pain, but he opens his eyes to look at me.

"Що ви захочете?" I ask him. *What do you want?*

"Вмріть свиня!" he spits, blood leaking from his lips. *Die pig!*

"Котрі ви працюєте?" I tighten my grip on his face. *Who do you work for?*

"Ваша мати," he coughs. "Але вона мій аматор також."

"My mother?" I ask. "She's your lover too?" Still gripping his face with my right hand, I find the wound in his abdomen and stick my left thumb into it, inducing a cry that matches the octave of the siren that's begun wailing in the distance.

"You'll see her soon, dead man," I tell him. "Ви побачите її скоро, мертва людина!"

I let go of his face and pick up the gun, pressing the hot end of the barrel into his forehead. "Котрі ви працюєте?" I repeat. *Who is your boss? Who sent you?*

He coughs again, spitting more blood onto the street, before the cough morphs into a laugh, a cackle almost, as he writhes in pain.

I walk back to the car to get my bag from the trunk and head back to meet Bella at the car.

"Зло," the dying man calls out as I pass him. Bella is already in the driver's seat of the car in the intersection. She's waving at me to hurry up. I stop and kneel down.

"What did you say?" I ask him. "Що ви сказали?"

"Liho," he laughs. "I work for Liho."

Liho, I remember, is not only the name of the man against whom we are competing, the man who apparently wants us dead. Liho is Ukrainian for the word *evil*.

***

"What did you say to him?" Bella asks. She's sitting in the driver's seat of what, close up, looks more like a small tank than a car. The back of it is emblazoned with the word *Kombat*. The engine sounds like a garbage truck.

"I asked him who he worked for." I climb into the front passenger seat. There's not much leg room with the large control console sitting mid-dash. "He reluctantly told me."

"He spoke English?" Bella's door is still open. The sirens are coming from maybe a street or two away now.

"We need to get out of here, Bella." I slam shut what must be a heavily armored door. "Close your door and drive."

She grabs the door and heaves it closed.

"Don't worry about it. Go!" The reflection of blue and red lights are bouncing off of the building to our right as she puts the Kombat in gear and accelerates into the fog.

"Where is the Bristol Hotel?" she asks. "We need to get off the streets."

"Agreed. We can't go to the Bristol though. They'll know we're coming. Turn right."

Bella spins the wheel to the right and the Kombat lumbers around the curve, its wheels squealing against the worn pavement. "How did they know we were here?"

"I'm guessing that they knew we were coming because of your plane."

"What do you mean?"

"Your pilot had to register a flight plan, right?" I explain. "Given that the goons in South Dakota knew we'd be coming here, it's not much of a stretch to figure out that they were waiting on us." My revolver is in one of the large cup holders between us. I grab it and pop open the cylinder. It's empty.

Bella's hands are shaking against the wheel, her arms twitching. The adrenaline's beginning to wear off. "I get that. They had someone at the airport tipping them off. Then they followed us."

"Probably." The violent rush leaks from my body and a wave of nausea hits me. "Turn left here."

The mini-tank rumbles past an appliance store with its interior lights on.

"That's why we can't go to the hotel. They've probably got a team there. This is not what I thought it was going to be." I gulp against the bile rising in my throat and take a deep breath before reaching between us into the back seat for my pack. It's got three, maybe four bullet holes in it. Bella's bag, sitting next to it, is riddled. From my pack, I pull ammunition for the revolver and the Tec-9, then I reach around until I find the barrel of the machine pistol and pull it into my lap.

"What did that guy say to you?" Bella questions.

"He worked for Liho Blogis." I snap closed the cylinder and spin it. "This gun will be yours for now. It's got shot shell in it. You don't have to be accurate. It'll spray like a shotgun, okay?"

"Like it did back there?"

"Yes." Up ahead I can tell the lights are from the port of Odessa. They're coming from cranes and ships lit for early morning on and offloading. "Up ahead, there's going to be a statue. It's in the middle of a roundabout. Make a right and then go a couple of blocks. Then stop in front of a blue sign that says *Londonskaya*."

"Okay." She nods. "You didn't tell me, Jackson. The guy back there, he spoke English?"

I shake my head. The lighted statue is about fifty yards ahead of us, and beyond that the Black Sea. She slows to enter the roundabout.

"He didn't speak English," I say. The back of the statue slides by her window. "Take this first right."

"So...what?" She makes the turn. "You speak Ukrainian?"

"Pull up to the curb over here," I say, pointing to an empty spot underneath a glowing blue neon sign that screams the name of the hotel. "Yes, I spoke to him in his own language."

She puts the Kombat into park. "Well aren't you full of surprises. Why the hell did I need a translator if you speak the language?"

"You didn't ask, Bella." I sling my bag from the backseat and climb out of the tank. "Let's get a room."

***

It appeared that the last time the Londonskaya Hotel lobby was updated was circa 1920. It smells the same as it did the last time I was here, a mix of cigarette smoke and potpourri. The expansive green carpet leads to a grand staircase opposite the entrance. Several large crystal ballroom chandeliers hang from the decorative tray ceiling, casting a dim glow. To either side of the lobby are large rosewood counters. There's a young girl standing behind the one to the left, smiling as we approach her. She's tall and thin, her ash blonde hair pulled back into a tight bun. Her cheekbones are dusted pink, her eyeshadow blue. She looks like a cross between a high fashion model and a Russian call girl.

"Hello," I lean on the counter with my elbows. "How are you?"

"I am fine, thank you," she says in thickly accented English. "Welcome to the Londonskaya. Do you have reservations?"

"No. Is that a problem? Do you have any rooms?"

She looks down at a ledger, running her finger along one edge. "We are very full today. And check-in is not until three o'clock in the afternoon."

The large clock on the wall behind the counter reads before five o'clock in the morning. We have three hours before our meeting with the scientist, assuming that still happens.

"What's the chance that we could get a couple of rooms for a few hours? We need two or three of hours of sleep, a shower, you know. We landed only an hour ago, flying all night to get here."

"I am not sure I am able to do that because we don't let rooms by the hour, sir."

"I understand that," I reply, a little more forcefully. "Would a generous gratuity help you find a couple of rooms until, say, eight o'clock?"

She looks up from the ledger and checks a computer screen. "I am thinking that maybe I have one room for you. The hotel is full. There is a room with two beds."

"Deal."

"I'll just need your passports and credit card please." She fakes a smile, her gray smoker's teeth distracting from an otherwise pleasant face.

"Passport, no problem." I fish into my bullet riddled pack and find my passport. "But I'll be paying for the room in cash. If that's okay with you."

"U.S. dollars?" she asks with more than a hint of suggestion.

"Звичайно," I say. "Of course."

Her fake smile melts into a real one, her otherwise whey-faced cheeks glowing pinker than the blush she's generously applied. "Я буду повернутися!"

"Я зачекаю," I call after her as she giggles into a room behind the reception desk and disappears.

"She'll be right back," I translate to Bella as she socks me in the shoulder. "Hey! What's that for?"

"Flirting?" she says. "You're incorrigible. We almost died for the second time in twenty-four hours and you're picking up desk clerks."

"Flirting?" I rub the sore spot where she frogged me. "You're kidding, right? I'm trying to get us off of the street and into a place where we can regroup. Sheesh."

"Right," she says. "What did you say to her?"

"I told her we'd be waiting for her." The truth. "Remind me the next time we start dating."

"What does that mean?"

"All I'm saying is that you seem awfully preoccupied with my social behavior given that we hardly know each other."

"My preoccupation is solely about finding the pieces of the process and staying alive. I want your attention focused on the task at hand. Nothing more. As *if...*" she huffs.

"The lady doth protest too much, methinks," I mumble, passively aggressive.

"What?"

"Nothing." I smile. "Gotcha. I'll stay focused."

"*MacBeth*, Jackson?" she shakes her head. "Lame."

"It's *Hamlet*," I correct her with a quick grin. "Act three, scene two."

Bella shoots me a look deadly enough that it would have been helpful twenty minutes ago.

"This is the room key for you, Mister," the desk looks down at the passports, "Rick Grimes and Miss Jane Smith."

"Дякую." I take the key and the passport. "Thank you. And your name?"

"Akalena," she says with another genuine smile. "Your room is on the third floor. Please remember that the checkout is at eleven in the morning."

"Дякую, Akalena." I slide five one hundred dollar bills across the counter, adjust my pack on my shoulder and start walking for the elevator. "You coming, Jane?"

"Right behind you, *Rick,*" she says. "Aren't you forgetting something important?"

"What?"

She's dangling a key from her hand like a dog treat. "The car. It's parked right in front of the hotel, and it kinda stands out a little bit, right?"

"Good point." I stop at the elevator, push the UP button, and the doors slide open. "Here's the key to the room. Go ahead and get settled. I'll ditch the car."

She hands me the key to the Kombat urban assault vehicle and slips past me into the elevator. "Hurry up." The doors slide shut.

***

Bella opens the door wearing a dark blue tank top and some gray cargo pants. Her hair is wet, her face freshly washed. "You've been gone for a while, so I assume you ditched it. I expected you back here, like, thirty minutes ago."

"Well, *hello* to you too, Bella." I step past her into the large room and toss my pack onto one of the two sagging twin beds. I rub the back of my neck and crank it to the right to crack it. "Nice room, by the way." It's decorated much like the lobby; unnecessarily ornate in some ways and completely utilitarian. The furniture is worn, the hardwood floors scuffed and scratched, but the room itself looks clean.

"It's after six o'clock, Jackson," she shuffles to a cherry, clawfoot writing desk opposite the beds. Her laptop is open. "We're running out of time before we meet our contact."

"I ditched it at a church about three blocks from here." I drop onto the edge of a bed, bouncing with the give of the mattress. "It's parked around the back, in a cobblestone alley. The keys are in a collection box at the back door."

"Then what took so long?" She's leaning against the edge of the desk, facing me with her arms folded in front of her. There's a nasty bruise on her right shoulder.

"Sorry. I did what I had to do. I needed to make sure that nobody saw me dump the tank and then follow me back here. So I took a... circuitous route."

"What does that mean?" she asked, ever the Grand Inquisitor.

"It means that I didn't walk straight back here. I went out of my way to get back here without running into any problems. I *know* what *I'm* doing."

"Why say it like that?"

"Nothing." I pinch the bridge of my nose, exhaling. "What's with you? Twenty questions? I'm not Sal Pimiento."

"What is that supposed to mean?"

"What I mean is that you're grilling me for keeping us safe, which is my job, and yet I'm really the one who should be asking the questions."

She runs her hand through her hair and then rubs it on her thigh. "I don't follow."

"One second, you're this arrogant CEO in cahoots with as shady a guy as there is. The next you seem completely out of your league. Then you're Goldfinger, interrogating Pimiento, threatening him like a professional spook. Next thing I know, you're shaking with fear after we get ambushed. Now, you're acting like a jealous girlfriend who forgot to put a tracker on my car."

Her jaw tightens.

"You seem a little bipolar, I guess."

"Why did you call me a jealous girlfriend who forgot to track you?"

"Because that's how it feels," I say. "To paraphrase Jay-Z, we've got ninety-nine problems, and making sure I don't get tailed isn't one of them."

"I mean the tracking part, specifically," she snaps. "Why would you say that?"

"It was a metaphor, Bella."

"Oh."

"Why fixate on that?" I press. "I called you Sybil and you zero in on *that*?"

"Um..." she runs her hand through her hair again, "it got me thinking. Maybe they *were* tracking us. Maybe that's how they ambushed us."

"Okay. Still, what's with you?"

"I'm not used to this action adventure stuff, Jackson," she says. "You've lived it for months now. You're accustomed to the adrenaline, the close calls, the bullets flying past you, your life flashing in front of your eyes. I'm not. One minute we're in control. The next, not so much. I worry about your focus. I don't know you well enough to know what you're thinking or what you're capable of doing. When you were gone, I worried what was going on. If that's bipolar, then that's me, I guess." She puts a hand over her mouth and closes her eyes. When they open again, tears are pooling.

"Fair enough." I push myself from the bed and walk over to her. "But let me tell you something," I'm five inches from her face, looking straight into her blinking eyes. "You never get *accustomed* to this. Ever. You just..."

"What?" She swallows past the tears. Her eyes are dancing back and forth, but never lose sight of mine.

"You just go numb." I put my hands on her shoulders, careful to avoid her bruise, and pull her into my chest, sliding my hands onto her back. She unfolds her arms and slides her hands up my back, gripping my shirt. Her heart is pounding, her breaths are short and rapid.

Her hair smells like cheap hotel shampoo, thinly fragrant. It's damp against my face. Her right hand lets go of my shirt, moves to the back my head, her fingers running through my hair.

Neither of us speak for what feels like forever, but it's not long enough. This is the first time I've felt human in months.

***

You feel better now?" Bella's sitting in the high back chair at the desk when I emerge from the bathroom. "Sometimes a hot shower can change everything."

"Or a cold one," I laugh and sit on the bed to put on my Merrells, pulling up the cuffs of my black surplus pants. I do feel better. I've cleaned, sterilized, and put a bandage on the flesh wound at my hip.

"Whatever." Bella rolls her eyes and turns back to her laptop. "I've made contact, finally, with our friend."

"Are you on hotel Wi-Fi?" I look up from double-knotting the nylon laces on the shoes.

"Yes," she says without turning around. "Why?"

"Is that safe?"

"My email program is encrypted. It's fine."

I stand up and untuck the last clean t-shirt I have with me. It's a Lyle Lovett concert shirt with a hamburger drawn on the front. It reads, *Hello? Here I am.* "What's the plan?"

"Half an hour," she says. "We meet him in the park right outside the hotel. Nice shirt."

"Thanks," I tug on it again. "Is that safe?" I step over to her and lean against the desk. "Out in the open?"

"Now who's the one with twenty questions?" she smirks.

"It's hard to control that situation," I explain. "You know, outside, a couple of blocks from where I ditched our would-be-assassins' tank car."

"You said nobody followed you."

"Right," I say.

"The truth is, we're not safe anywhere, Jackson. If Liho Blogis wants to try to kill us, it doesn't matter where we are, right?"

"I guess." I still don't like it.

"Okay then," she closes the laptop. "It's set."

"Has he been contacted by Blogis yet? What does he know?"

"He didn't say."

"We need to be careful with this guy. Does he know I'm with you or does he think you're alone?"

"I didn't tell him *you* were with me, but my messages referred to *we* and *us.* So I'm certain he doesn't think I'm meeting him alone. Why?"

"You said we couldn't trust this guy," I remind her.

"What I said," she corrects, "was that I don't think we can trust *anyone.* What's the problem?"

"He'll be worried if it's two against one, so to speak. He may be less forthcoming. He doesn't know me from Adam. If he thinks there's a potential threat, after Wolf got killed working in *your* lab, he may have eyes elsewhere."

"What are you suggesting?"

"You go alone."

"What?" Her eyes widen.

"Look, it'll be fine." I move to the window, which overlooks the park and, beyond that, the Black Sea. "Come here."

Bella joins me, peeks out at the tree lined, crushed granite path below.

"See that bench?" I point to a long bench, a man with a book sitting on one end. "That's your meeting point. I'll give you a phone. You'll be on speaker. I'll hear everything you talk about. I've got a thermal camera that acts like binoculars. I'll be your eyes from up here. Anything looks the least bit off and I can get you out of there."

"How do you warn me? I won't be able to hear you."

"I'll call you from another phone if there's a problem. It'll buzz in. You'll feel the buzz in your hand, and that's your signal to bolt."

"What if there's not enough time to signal?"

"I have a Tec-9 machine pistol. Cool?"

"Not cool," she says. "But I agree with you that this is the safest option." Bella, stands, touches my chest and moves past me toward the bathroom. "Is that thing even accurate? Your Tec-9 *machine pistol*?"

"It'll do the job. I've got some Heckler & Koch sights on it and I'm using steel cased bullets. It shouldn't jam, which is the big complaint with these things."

"That's not encouraging."

"You can do this." I grab her hand. "Remember I'll be up here watching over you."

She smiles weakly. "I know you will."

"We've got twenty-five minutes." My watch reads five minutes after seven, local time. "Then you head down there."

"I've got to finish getting ready. Give me ten minutes." She shuts the bathroom door behind her, locks it, and a hairdryer cranks to life.

Ten minutes. That's enough time.

Sitting at the desk, I flip open the laptop, which wasn't completely shut, and hit the spacebar. The monitor glows with a full screen photograph of Bella with her father. Both of them are smiling, his arm around her. They're dressed in ski jackets and framed against a snow-capped mountain range. Bella's amber goggles are on her head, covering the canary yellow wrap protecting her ears from the cold. Her nose and cheeks are adorably wind burned.

Her father's wearing a knit cap with a yarn ball at the top. His crow's feet are pressed deep at his temples from the sun reflecting off the snow. Their teeth are ridiculously white and I get the sense they're both laughing. They look happy, content maybe, like a normal family. Don Carlos and Bella, a father and his daughter on a ski trip somewhere. Black diamond runs in the morning, a fireside meal and drinks in the five star lodge at night.

Thankfully the screen lock hasn't kicked in yet and I thumb the mousepad to the internet icon and click it. Bella's face dissolves into the homepage for Nanergetix and a prompt box for secure login.

Google is bookmarked on the navigation bar. I click the link and the familiar search engine home page appears.

I type *SNIF Detector*. The screen populates with results and I pick one, an article from the MIT *Technology Review*. It's an old article, from 2010, about some French scientists who thought they could plant what they called "antineutrino" detectors off the coasts of so-called rogue nations that might have secret nuclear programs.

The author revealed that fission reactors release nearly countless numbers of "antineutrinos" every second. That gives them a definable signature which, theoretically, is easy to spot with the right technology.

The French idea was to place what they call a *Secret Neutrino Interactions Finder* – a SNIF— into a supertanker, sail the tanker to the coastline of a rogue nation, and then temporarily sink the tanker two and a half miles under the surface. The hidden tanker could, from a great distance, detect nuclear activity without the rogue nation knowing about it.

I click a link to what was probably a PowerPoint presentation and scroll past the pages of scientific gobbledygook until I find the executive summary at the end. It's in plain English and concludes the best option is hiding the detector in an oil supertanker. It also concludes that it would take a detector up to six months to confirm a large fission reactor and a lot longer to find a smaller one. What stands out to me is that it calls the SNIF detector a futuristic option, declaring it's not realistic within three decades.

Three decades?

I go back to the results page and find a few more links, and all of them are dated in 2010 or 2011. There's nothing after that.

Maybe George is on to something. There's all this hype about neutrinos, scientists around the world talking about their magical possibilities; subsurface communications, nuclear fission detectors. And then...nothing. Radio silence. Aside from a random reference about neutrino astronomy or a post-doctoral thesis posted online by some geeky genius, all mentions of practical neutrino applications stop.

Is this what it's really all about? Nuclear detection?

That would explain the violent extremes to which Blogis would go to find the pieces of the process and why Bella would work with a ne'er-do-well like Sir Spencer.

I'm beginning to think "the process" is more of an instruction manual than a process. That would make a lot of sense. After years of theory, dear Dr. Wolf was finally able to figure out how to build a neutrino beam generator that would not only be powerful enough to detect nuclear fission reactors, he also figured out how to slip it into an oil tanker. Something like that would be priceless, or at least really, really expensive. Whoever controlled that technology would have an incredible geopolitical advantage.

The blow dryer shuts off and Bella calls out to me, "Be ready in a minute!"

I close out the page, clear the history, and return her browser to the home page. "You've got a minute or two. Time for bronzer if you need it." A couple of clicks and I carefully close the laptop, repositioning it on the desk before moving to my bed.

"Very funny," she says. "I don't use bronzer."

"Natural glow, then?" I sit on the edge of the bed, trying to find a casual position.

The door clicks open and Bella emerges. "Must be." She fakes a smile. I can tell she's nervous. She's wearing her hair down, over her shoulders, which gives me an idea.

"I've got an idea that'll make communicating a little easier. It'll be better than a call to alert you."

"What?"

"Assuming he doesn't frisk you—"

"He's *not* frisking me, Jackson," she interrupts.

"Okay," I continue, "then given that he's *not* frisking you, this'll work."

"What'll work?"

I roll off the bed and reach into my pack, pulling out an earbud and a pair of burner phones. "These are my backups."

"I don't understand."

"Here's how it'll work." I push the button on the side of the earpiece and the power button on one of the cells. "You'll have your phone on speaker so that I can hear you on one of my phones. Then, since you're wearing your hair down, you can put this earpiece in one of your ears. I'll pair it with this phone," I hold up one of the burner phones, "which will be connected to this extra phone."

"We're using four phones?"

"Yes. Your phone will allow me to hear everything that's going on down there on my primary phone. If there's a problem, I can communicate with you using that earpiece and the pair of backup phones. Got it? It's a very rudimentary hidden walkie-talkie system. It'll make it easier for me to get you out of there if something goes down."

"Okay, I get it. It's a good plan."

Scrolling through the options on the smart phone, I pair it with the Bluetooth earpiece. She pulls her hair behind her right ear and inserts the earbud.

I dial the numbers for the phones and make sure everything is connected before handing her back her phone and one of the burner cells. She slips one into each of her pockets. Neither are visible with her blouse untucked.

"I'm ready," she says, moving toward the door.

I stop her with my hand on her shoulder. "Let me get this." I gently pull her hair over her right ear to disguise the earbud. "There you go. You're ready." I can feel her looking at me as I focus my attention on her hair.

"Thanks, Jackson," she says. "For everything."

"I haven't done anything except keep us alive."

"That's enough so far." Bella slips out the hotel room door and into the hall. The door swings shut behind her and I pull the security bar closed.

It's time.

CHAPTER 12

The man approaching from the east is tall and thin. He's wearing a long sleeved blue and white striped shirt and dark blue denim pants. There's no jacket and no bulge anywhere that would indicate a weapon. He steps towards Bella on the park bench almost directly across from my vantage point inside the hotel room, his arm extended.

On the windowsill in front of me are two phones. One of them is the burner phone through which I can talk to Bella. The other is on speaker, so I can hear their conversation. I've moved Bella's computer to a chair next to me and have the internet pulled up on the screen.

"It's so good to be seeing you!" Though his accent is thick, his English is intelligible.

"Good to see you, Dr. Gamow," Bella shakes his hand. "It is Dr. Gamow, right?"

"Yes," he says, planting quick kisses on each of her cheeks before sitting next to her on the bench. "Of course, of course. I was so pleased to get your messages."

He doesn't seem nervous.

"So," Bella exhales, "please tell me what you can about our mutual friend."

"You are one who goes straight to the point, Bella," he laughs. "Not a person for what you Americans call 'small talk'?"

"I guess not, Dr. Gamow," she says. "I...well, I really don't have much time."

"I am understanding you," he says. "And I am sorry for the loss of our friend. He was a brilliant man. His work was so many years past others. I miss him already."

"Yes, he was brilliant," Bella exhales again. "I miss him too, Dr. Gamow."

I whisper into the burner phone, "Bella, he's not nervous. You'll be okay. Take a breath. Calm down. I'm here watching you."

Bella takes another breath. "He was working on some very important technology for us, for my company. He was worried about its implications and so he separated his research into several parts."

"This I know," Dr. Gamow interjects. He's leaning toward Bella, his left arm draped across the back of the park bench. His legs are crossed. He's unbelievably relaxed. Too relaxed. "He told me about basics of work. He was always talking about neutrinos. Neutrinos here. Neutrinos there. Always neutrinos."

I hurriedly type *Ukraine Research Gamow* into the browser and turn my attention back to the conversation.

"I always tell him," Gamow wags a finger in the air, "you are only one who is married to neutrinos. She is not a good wife! She does not cook or clean for you! But she takes your time and your life."

Bella smiles and nods.

"But he always tells me that he's so close to something," Gamow goes on. "Always so close."

"Did he share with you the location of a piece of that research?" Bella is direct. Gamow is right, she's not one for small talk.

"Yes," he slides closer to Bella. His arm is now behind her on the back of the bench. "He tells me that he finally solved this neutrino problem of his. He says he finally figured out what nobody else could figure out. He tamed his wife!" He laughs.

I hit the *IMAGES* tab on screen before looking back through the binoculars at Bella and her contact. The Tec-9, with an aftermarket suppressor attached, is in my lap.

"He did give me a clue about where he put two pieces of the process," Gamow confides.

"Two pieces?" Bella asks in surprise. "He told you where he hid two pieces?"

"Yes," Gamow lowers his voice. "But you will never find them." A smile worms its way across his face.

On the screen in front of me are dozens of photographs of Dr. Rudolf Gamow. None of them look like the man sitting on the bench next to Bella.

I grab the burner phone with one hand and look through the scope. "Bella, that's not Gamow!"

At the instant she hears the words, her eyes bug. She looks instinctively toward the hotel and slides away from the man next to her on the bench. He grabs her hand and pulls her closer to him.

"Bella, stay there. Don't scream!!!" I warn her. "I've got this!"

"Your Dr. Gamow," the man growls without any accent, "was quite a help to me. However, I'm afraid he won't be much—"

With two pulls of the trigger, a pair of dark red spots bloom against the man's blue and white striped shirt. He slumps next to Bella and she shoves him away from her on the bench. Through the binoculars, I can see her shaking, her hands pressed to her face, covering her mouth.

"Bella, check his pockets, grab what you can, and then quickly walk away."

She sits there, hands over her face. Through the earpiece and the speakerphone I can hear her struggling to breathe.

"Bella!" I shout into the phone, snapping her to attention. "Check his pockets and get out of there."

She nods, almost unconsciously, and rummages through the man's pockets, pulling something from the front right of his pants. Twenty yards to her right, through the canopy of the park's trees, I spot two men, both dressed in light colored suits, speed walking toward her. One of them has his hand inside his jacket.

"Get out of there now!" I swing the Tec-9 to the right, leveling the suppressor on the window sill. I know I'd be better off with a rifle from this distance, but I've got what I've got. "Run!"

Thump! Thump!

The man with his hand in his jacket spins to his right from the first hit and falls, his head contorting unnaturally as the second bullet hits his temple. Lucky shot.

Thump!

The second man stumbles and falls, grabbing his left thigh. I can hear the echo of his wail as a chorus of screams fills the park from the bystanders enjoying their morning. The Tec-9 is outperforming itself.

Thump!

The second man stops grappling with his injury and doesn't wail anymore. He's dead on the crushed granite three feet from his partner.

I start disassembling the Tec-9, slap Bella's computer shut and stuff everything I can, including her duffle, into my bag. My pack is heavier than it's been and is bursting at its seams, but I sling it onto my back. One last check around the room and I bolt.

"Bella, can you hear me?" All I can hear is her breath, interrupted by intermittent whimpering. I approach the stairwell next to the elevator. "Bella, I need you to focus. Ahead of you, maybe a couple of hundred yards, is a large statue. To the right of that statue is a wide set of steps. Go to those steps, go halfway down, and wait for me. I'm on my way."

"Bella!" I call again when she doesn't respond. I turn the first flight of stairs, running as quickly as I can with the heavy pack bouncing against my lower back. "Can you hear me?"

Another flight of stairs and the pack is rubbing my shoulders raw. It's too heavy and I almost slip, but I catch myself on the handrail. Still nothing from Bella.

"Bella, I got both of them, uh, all three of them. You're okay. I'm coming to you." I grab the handrail and turn down another flight. "Go to the steps. Do you understand?" I stop on a landing to adjust the pack on my shoulders. I hear Bella's breathing, the crunch of her feet pounding against the crushed granite. Then the line goes silent. She's gone.

***

A baby carriage rolls to the edge of the marble steps in slow motion, the child's mother mouthing the words, "My baby!" underneath the strain of a violin-heavy soundtrack. The pounding of its wooden wheels alternate with the blasts of pistols and pump action shotguns, the baby inside seemingly unaware as a bullet rips through the canvas of his carriage and a pair of sailors in dress whites are shot and killed.

Kevin Costner's weapon fires a blank and Andy Garcia tosses him a six shooter and slides to catch the carriage with his legs at the bottom of the steps. The baby is saved.

"You know this scene is an homage to a famous silent film," my dad said between mouthfuls of popcorn. He presses pause on the remote. "It's based on what some might call the greatest propaganda film of all time, The Battleship Potemkin.*"*

"What's propaganda? Is it politics?"

"Yes." My dad tousled my hair. I was ten or eleven years old and had the perpetually unkempt mop of hair typical of pre-teen boys. "It's politics."

"How is The Untouchables *an homage to* The Battleship Potemkin?*" I took another sip of soda.*

"Ease up on the Dr. Pepper, Jackson," he laughed. "It's too close to bedtime and your mom will kill me." Friday night movies were a tradition, as was a can of caffeine and a bowl of popcorn. Usually my mom watched with us, but that night she was at a book club meeting so it was just Dad and me. He picked the movie, telling me it was a classic that I had to see. He let me have two cans of soda.

"It's almost gone," I smiled.

"Figures," he said. "Do you know what an homage is?"

"Is it like a copy?"

"Yes." He shoveled another handful of popcorn into his mouth. He loved popcorn and was greedy about it. "It's like a tribute."

"How is this movie a tribute to that movie?"

"Well," he shifted his weight and turned toward me on the sofa, "the 1925 movie was about the revolution in early twentieth century Russia. In real life, there was a revolt against the country's leader, the Czar. It started aboard a battleship called the Potemkin. Sailors fought against their superiors and it's said to have been the start of their civil war."

"What's that have to do with the stairs?"

"In a place called Odessa, the port where the battleship returned home, there are these huge stairs. They look like they go on forever," he said, pulling his hand from the popcorn bowl to demonstrate how far the steps extended. "They're now called the Potemkin Stairs, and in the movie, the director, a man named Eisenstein, created this really violent scene on those steps."

"How was it violent?"

"The scene is maybe three times as long as the one in The Untouchables and there are a bunch of soldiers who open fire into crowds of innocent people. They kill men, women, and children. Toward the end of the scene, which is bloodier than the one we just watched, a mother is standing at the edge of the steps with her baby in a carriage."

"Like we just saw?"

"Yes," he said, "except the mother is shot and killed, and when she falls back, her body knocks the stroller down the steps into the chaos."

"Is the baby rescued?"

"Uh, let's just say there's no Andy Garcia there to save it." My dad dug his hand back into the bowl of popcorn.

"But it never really happened, right? The baby wasn't really hurt?"

"No, it didn't happen. The director put there to represent how horrible he thought the Imperial Regime was at the turn of the century."

"Innocent people weren't killed by the soldiers, then?"

"I can't say that," he said. "There were a lot of people killed during that revolution. Then after the revolution, when the Bolsheviks took over, they killed people too."

"The people getting killed for what they believed then killed others for what they believed?"

"Yes." He picked up the remote and set in on his knee next to the bowl. "That's how it typically works, Jackson. Violence tends to keep people in power and remove them from it."

"That's not what happened in America?"

"No," he said, "that's what makes our country so special. Power is transferred from the loser to the winner without violence. That doesn't happen in a lot of places."

"I hate violence, Dad," I said. "I just don't understand it. I mean, self-defense is one thing, but hurting people because they don't agree with you is wrong. Hurting people because you both want the same thing, because you want money or power or control of things, is wrong."

"Son," he said, his hand pausing in the bowl, "violence should never be the solution. People should be able to resolve their differences, seek control, earn money, and win power without hurting others. However, violence has plagued us since Cain killed Abel. Sometimes it's just the way the world works and violence is a necessary evil. Sometimes there's no avoiding it."

I was surprised to hear my dad rationalize violence. Of course, at the time, I wasn't mature enough to understand my confusion. My dad, my saint and hero, a man who liked guns but despised hunting, was telling me that violence could be justified as a means to an end.

Sometimes...violence is a necessary evil. Sometimes there's no avoiding it.

He pressed play on the remote and the Al Capone henchmen run off, leaving Kevin Costner's Elliot Ness and Andy Garcia's Giuseppe Petri alive amidst the carnage on the steps.

***

The crowds on the Potemkin Stairs are sparse. From the top of the steps, they appear to be a series of wide landings, deceptively hiding the one hundred and ninety-two steps. Beyond the steps is the Black Sea and the Port of Odessa, framed by the large trees populating either side of the stairs.

To my left is the Duke de Richelieu Monument, a bronze statue honoring the city's first mayor. To my right, a couple of hundred yards away, are police and paramedics responding to the park. Incredibly, despite the large pack on my back and the desperation I'm sure is evident on my face, nobody pays me any attention.

I shrug the pack and start down the steps to the first landing. There's a woman selling hand-bedazzled wooden crosses. She's gripping one by its bottom, holding it out to me as though she's exorcizing a demon.

"Ви захочете купити?" she asks me if I want to buy one, telling me it's a good price. "Це - гарна ціна!"

"Ні дякую," I tell her, no, but I need her help finding someone. I surprise myself at just how much Ukrainian I remember. I haven't used it in so long. "Я потребую вашої допомоги."

"Я не дивлюся будь що." She hasn't seen see anything, she says, she's too busy with her business. But maybe, if I were to buy something, she could help. "одна рука миється інший."

I ask her how much one of the crucifixes costs and then pull out a five dollar bill, which more than covers her price. I describe Bella and ask the woman if she's seen her.

"Висока жінка. Гарна жінка," she holds her hand above her head and tells me she's seen a tall, pretty woman. She points down the steps toward the port entrance, suggesting she went that way.

"Дякую," I thank her and then hand back the bedazzled crucifix, suggesting she sell it again to someone else.

Bounding down the steps, three or four more peddlers offer me their homemade goods, calling after me as I pass by them with smiles and waves. Scanning the groupings of tourists, I don't see her. At the bottom of the steps, I turn around to look for her one more time, just in case the woman was wrong. From this vantage point, the landings disappear and the steps seem continuous up to the statue. No Bella.

Across a narrow street is the entrance to the port. It's a slim, cream-colored building with large glass panes across the length of its facade. Beyond the building is a road leading to the main passenger terminal and a tall hotel at the end of a lengthy dock. Ships line either side of the dock, a huge white cruise ship is moored to the right.

Before I walk into the cream-colored building I hit redial on a burner phone. It rings twice.

"Jackson?"

"Bella, where are you?" I turn around, looking for her. She's nowhere. "What happened? Are you okay?"

"I'm fine," she says. "I mean, I'm not fine. But I'm not hurt."

"Where are you?"

"I'm not sure," she says. "I'm in a hotel lobby."

"Hotel lobby?" I swing back to look up the steps. "You're not at our hotel are you?" If she's there, we're toast.

"I...uh...I don't know," she sounds distracted, disoriented maybe. "I just wandered here. I don't remember it. I can see the ocean."

"Okay. Just stay where you are. Find somewhere to sit down. I'll be there in a minute. Don't talk to anyone."

"Jackson?"

"Yes?"

"We're going to die, aren't we?" Her voice is even, no hint of expression or fear. She's stating a fact as much as she's asking me a question.

"Not if I can help it," I assure her. "Now stay there."

I walk purposefully through the wide opening of the cream colored building, past Uzi-wearing armed guards, and straight for the back entrance. There's an equally wide doorway on the back side of the building that leads to the main terminal building on the dock. With both hands gripping the straps of my pack I march through the opening and back into the morning sun, and merge into the throngs of cruise passengers making their way to the vendors on the Potemkin Stairs. A couple passing me on my left is speaking Spanish. There's German from an elderly man speaking to what I imagine is his adult daughter or mistress.

My head's down, and I view the spate of black socks and sandals as the Europeans shuffle by. After they pass, my attention turns to the two-story terminal building, which looks like the bridge of a large ship, to the monstrous Hotel Odessa, which towers a dozen or more stories above the end of the long dock.

It's a gleaming white building the locals hate. My bet is that's where I'll find Bella.

***

I slog through the rotating door and a blast of air conditioning greets me in the lobby of the Hotel Odessa. The cool air is almost immediately replaced with the stale stench of lingering cigarette smoke. To the left of the expansive, two-story foyer is an arrangement of chairs and tables.

In a high back, red leather chair, chewing on her thumb, is Bella. Her knees are together and she's leaning on them with her elbows. The burner phone is on her lap. She's rocking back and forth, staring at nothing in particular.

I sit in the chair next to her, dropping my pack onto the floor. "I'm here, Bella." She hasn't noticed me. "Bella?"

She snaps her head around, her eyes blinking rapidly. She stares at me before saying, "Jackson?"

"I'm here, Bella," I reach out to touch her hand but she flinches. "You're okay."

"I'm not okay, Jackson." Her eyes regain focus and bore into mine. "Don't keep saying that. That's twice inside of six hours that I've been in the middle of a gunfight. People are dying. I'm not equipped to handle this."

"First of all," I grip her hand tightly enough that she doesn't pull away again, "that wasn't a gunfight. I shot them. They didn't shoot back. You were never in danger of being shot."

"I don't buy that," she says, shaking her head. "That guy, whoever he was, he would've killed me. I'm kicking myself for not seeing this, for not recognizing immediately that he wasn't Dr. Gamow. I've *met* Dr. Gamow before."

"Yeah," I let go of her hand and slide onto the edge of my seat, "but you told me you had no recollection of what he looked like. You can't blame yourself for that. You can't blame yourself for any of this. It is what it is."

"It is what it is?" She looks puzzled. I notice her complexion is sallow. She's lost her color with the exception of the dark circles underlining her eyes. "What does that mean?"

"I mean that I knew what I was getting into here. Sir Spencer wouldn't involve me if it didn't involve death and deceit. I assumed there would be plenty of both."

She doesn't respond, her gaze aiming into the distance again.

"Wanna hand me the burner phone?" I nod at the phone in her lap. "I don't think you need it."

She blinks to attention and hands the phone to me. "It's not the burner. This belonged to the guy you killed."

"You say that like it was a bad thing."

"It wasn't a good thing, was it?" She glares at me with the same disgust reflected in her tone.

"Sometimes violence is a necessary evil. It was kill him or risk him killing you. You said he would have killed you, and you're judging me for protecting you?"

"Whatever, Jackson. I'm not judging anyone. I don't know what to do. We're gonna get killed. Or we're gonna kill more people. Or both. This whole thing is a horrible mess that I never intended."

She's not making sense. Then again, she's not accustomed to bullets flying at her face. I get it.

I flip the phone over in my hand and look at the screen. It's a Blackberry. "I didn't think people used these anymore." The screen glows to life with a push of the power button.

"You know I never intended this, right?"

"What I know," I say, my attention shifting from the phone, "is that you're freaked. You're frightened. You're probably in shock. And you've lied to me from the beginning."

There are no notes on the home page on the phone. The email's empty too.

Her eyebrows scrunch together. "How do you know I lied to you?"

"For starters," I say, "you admitted it. Second, there's no way people would be killing for some *process* that lets submarines talk to one another. It wouldn't happen." I find the call list on the phone and start scrolling. There are at least two dozen calls made within the last couple of hours, all but the last one to and from the same number.

"You're right," she says, the color in her cheeks slowly returning. "It's not only about the subaquatic communications."

"Then what's it about?"

"I was being blackmailed."

Curve ball.

"What?"

"Dr. Wolf was blackmailing Nanergetix."

Major league curve ball.

"Why?"

"He knew that what he'd discovered was a valuable military tool, and the closer he got to perfecting the process, the more he wanted to be compensated."

"What did you do?"

"At first, I tried to reason with him. Jackson, he was well paid. I made sure he knew that his compensation package was far greater than anybody else would be willing to give him."

"He didn't buy it?"

"No," she said. "He demanded even more, as in nine figures more."

"Like one hundred million dollars?"

"Like one hundred million dollars." She resumes chewing on her thumb.

"Obviously you weren't going to pay that," I say.

"Obviously," she says, "but he played hard ball. He started shopping the technology right out from under us."

"Wait. So you won't bend to his demands, and while working in your lab, using your equipment, and your money, he blatantly tries to sell your process to somebody else?"

"Yes."

"How do you know this?"

"We have corporate counterintelligence people," she says as though she's talking about the typing pool. "They informed me of Dr. Wolf's intentions."

"That's why he separated the pieces?" I ask. "For money?"

"He didn't do it to insure his safety," she says. "He did it to protect his financial interests."

"We know there are two lists on those hard drives," I recall. "One of the drives, and we don't know which one, is fake. And it doesn't matter anyhow, because we have almost nothing to go on. Mack gave you an empty drive. After we check out whatever's on this phone and then maybe the lead you have in Germany, we're lost."

"I wouldn't say that," she counters. "Based on what my people found, there are four or five pieces out there. I've got one of them. If we find one here, somewhere, and then one in Germany, that's three."

"How is it again that you have a piece?"

"It was pulled off of Wolf's computer," she says. "An IT guy found it in a deleted encrypted file. Wolf wasn't careful enough."

"And the rest of the pieces?"

"People have them," she says. "As I've said before, Wolf gave them to people he apparently trusted, people who'd hold onto them without too many questions. He had a lot of global connections."

"We're going to *steal* these pieces then? They're not yours anymore, right?"

"Technically, no," she admits. "Legally yes."

"Possession is nine tenths of the law."

"Right...." She puts her head in her hands. "It's dangerous. These are not all *good* people we're talking about."

"'Good' seems to be an incredibly relative term right now," I postulate. "Isn't it always?"

I lean back in my seat and fold my arms. "Why are you telling me this? You could have kept this from me. I wouldn't know any different."

"I'm telling you," she says, lifting her head, "because you might be the closest thing I have to someone I can trust. The more I think about Sir Spencer, the less I believe he's actually trying to help me."

"That doesn't make sense. He suggested you hire me, why would you trust *me* if you don't trust *him*?"

"You came after me when those guys took me," she said. "You didn't have to do that. There was nothing in it for you. You've killed people for me. I shouldn't be bothered by it. I should be thankful."

"That's not entirely true. If I help you get what you need, then Sir Spencer helps me disappear. He uses his resources to give me a new life. I'm in this for myself more than anything. Don't make me out to be a saint now. I'm neither that nor a devil."

"You believe him?" She's as skeptical as I am.

"Believe what?"

"That he'll help you start over, free of all of this?" She waves her hands at the room around us.

"I have no choice. I can't keep running from hiding place to hiding place. It's worth the risk on the off chance he actually follows through. In the meantime, I get to experience all of this." My arms wide, I force a smile.

Bella laughs, then plops back against the leather seat. "I don't have a choice either."

"What do you mean?"

"My father left me this empire I'm ill-equipped to run the way he did," she says, her gaze distant. "There are subplots within the subplots, schemes within schemes. Within secrets there are more secrets." She blinks and looks back to me. Her eyes are welling. "My father wasn't a good man," Bella says, wiping tears from the corners of her eyes with the knuckle of her left index finger. I offer her a napkin, which she takes. "Nobody makes billions of dollars seeking sainthood. I'm not naive, Jackson. The money in my bank account is bloodstained."

I'm surprised she's being so candid. She must feel trapped, exhausted, both...

"However, I have no choice here," she sniffles. "My father entered into agreements with people who do not care that he's dead, that he was shot point-blank on live television. I inherited the mess at Homestake, I didn't seek it out."

"You're doing the best that you can," I offer, saying something because I feel like I should. "It's not easy, right?"

"No," she laughs through her tears. "It's not easy. But what am I going to do? Wolf is blackmailing us, then he gets killed, and no sooner than that happens, Sir Spencer is at the front door offering his help."

"He came to you?"

"Yes," she nods. "He came to me. He told me that he knew about the blackmail attempts by Wolf, because he'd been approached as a possible middleman."

"He likes to be the middleman."

"So I've heard," she says. "He knew some of the players. He said he had resources to track down the missing pieces of the process. And he said all he wanted in return was a finder's fee."

"How much?"

"Twenty million," rolls off her tongue as if it's twenty cents, "give or take."

"Oh, is *that* all?"

"It seemed fair for the access he was offering. I've been running this company for eighteen months. I can handle the day to day. I'm good in the board room and with investors. Long term corporate vision? I'm awesome. But get into this corporate espionage stuff and I'm lost. I'm not my dad. Looking back, I'd have been better off paying Wolf what he wanted before all of this happened. "

"Someone made your decision for you."

"How's that?" She runs her fingers through her hair. "What decision?"

Someone killed him," I say. "Someone put you in this position before you could change your mind and pay him, right?"

"Not someone," she says. "Nobody made that decision for me."

"What do you mean?"

"*I* made the decision." Her eyes are trained on mine. She's not blinking. "*I* had him killed."

CHAPTER 13

The look on my face must say more to Bella than any words I could articulate. After telling me that she had Dr. Wolf killed, she looks down, shoulders hunched, chewing her finger. The silence between us hangs in the air like the smoke from unfiltered Russian cigarettes. I rub a burn on the arm of my chair, not sure what to say.

"You really killed him?" I blurt out.

"I said I *had* him killed."

"Who did it?"

"Mack," she says dispassionately.

"Mack? The same Mack who gave you a blank hard drive?"

"That Mack."

I rub a circle around the burn hole on the chair and sigh.

"What was that for?" Bella stops chewing and looks up at me, shoulders still hunched.

"Oh, what a tangled web we weave when first we practice to deceive."

"Shakespeare? Really? Now who's judging?"

"I'm not judging. I'm observing. And it's not Shakespeare. It's Sir Walter Scott."

She rolls her eyes.

"Why'd you kill him?"

"I'm not happy about it. I feel guilty. I...I...couldn't control him," she says. "And this process, this neutrino process, it can't get into the wrong hands. It just can't."

"Who are *the wrong hands*?"

"Wolf had two legitimate buyers. One of them, we now know, was Liho Blogis. I don't know who the other one was, but I suspect it was someone who was sponsored by the Iranian government."

"Why do you suspect that?"

"There were a couple of emails that traced back to a server in Tehran," she says. "It stands to reason—"

"Who told you about the emails?"

"Mack."

"Mack again, huh?"

"What is your problem with Mack?" she asks. "What are you getting at?"

"I'm not *getting at* anything, Bella. I just find it odd that Mack would give us a blank drive. It calls into question everything he's done."

"Maybe," she admits. "But Mack is guy who my father trusted for decades. My dad helped pay for some of his wife's initial cancer treatments. Mack killed a man because I asked him to do it. He's loyal. We can trust him. This hard drive thing was a mistake. There's bound to be some reasonable explanation."

I check that nobody is listening and lower my voice again. "What did you hope to gain by killing Wolf if you knew that he'd already split the process?"

"Again, Jackson, I was neutralizing a threat. I thought it better to have him dead than selling valuable information to the highest bidder."

"And the process?"

"I didn't know for sure," she says. "Mack suspected he may have broken it into pieces and hidden them separately. We weren't one hundred percent on that. We didn't know definitively what he'd done until the night he died."

"The night you had him killed," I correct.

"Says the man who put bullets into three people in a public park," she says, her eyes narrow.

"My point exactly."

"What?"

"You did what you thought you needed to do in the interest of self-preservation," I explain. "So did I. I've done it dozens of times since I fell into the mess. I'm sure I'll do it another dozen at least. The bottom line is, we're in this together. I'm going to do what I have to do to keep us alive, even if that means killing the man sitting right next to you. Stop wallowing in it. What's done is done. Got it?"

She nods.

Bella's still hiding something. She didn't seem fazed when I called her a liar. She never countered my assertion that the neutrino process is about more than submariner communication. The truth drips from a stubborn faucet where she's concerned. She'll tell me eventually, when she has no other choice. That moment hasn't come yet, but it will. At least I'm figuring out who she is: a beautiful, intelligent woman who operates on ruthless instinct. She'll flirt with you as she's jabbing a stiletto into your neck, and I've been a fool to think otherwise.

Bella is Charlie without the red hair or the sniper rifle.

"Now that we've established that we're both cold blooded psychopaths," I turn on the hibernating Blackberry, "I've got some phone calls to make. We need to find out where to go next."

***

"Привіт," the voice answering my call is full of phlegm. He says *hello* as if it hurts to speak. "Chernobyl алкогольний напій."

Chernobyl Liquor Store?

"Привіт," I ask. *Do you speak English.*

"Yes," he says, stretching the word into the two syllables. "I speak English. Who is this I'm speaking with?"

"My name is Eugene Curtis," the name on my lone remaining passport and ID. "Is this the Chernobyl Liquor Store?"

"Yes it is," he drawls through the phlegm. "What do you want now Eugene Curtis? You call a minute ago from this number."

"No," I say, "that wasn't me. I'm looking for something special that only your store would be able to give me."

"What is that?"

"I want whatever Rudolf Gamow would order," I say.

"You want Nemiroff Honey Pepper Vodka? Very hard to find. I have bottles for you. Good price." He clears his throat.

"Is that what Dr. Gamow would buy?"

He clears his throat again, more forcefully. "You say Gamow? Dr. Gamow who works here in the decommissioning laboratories?"

"Yes. That Dr. Gamow."

"Sorry," he says as though he's not, "I cannot help you, Eugene Curtis." He hangs up.

"We're going to Chernobyl," I tell Bella.

"Chernobyl?" she asks. "As in, the nuclear disaster Chernobyl?"

"That's where we'll find part of the process."

"Are you sure?"

"It's in a liquor store."

"They have liquor stores in Chernobyl?"

"Apparently."

"I'll call my pilot," Bella says. "What's the nearest airport?" She pulls her phone out of her pocket.

"No. We can't take your plane. I guarantee it's still being watched. We need to fly commercial to Kiev. I know the situation there is…unstable politically, but it's the best route. We can get a driver there who'll take us to Chernobyl. It's maybe a couple of hours on a lot of unmarked roads."

"Commercial?"

"Do you have another fake ID?" I pull her duffle bag from my larger pack and toss it at her feet.

"What's wrong with Jane Smith?" She reaches down to unzip the crumpled bag. "I only used it once."

I find my Eugene Curtis passport and driver's license and set them on the table next to my chair. "Yeah, but you used it to check in to the hotel. They've got your photograph on file there now. Don't think the police haven't already gone into the hotel looking for clues. There's a good chance we're both on surveillance video too. You can't use that passport at an airport."

"I don't have another one," she says. "I'm a one-fake-ID-at-a-time kinda girl."

"Great." *Not great.*

"What do we do?"

"I know someone. He'll work fast, but he's not cheap. I'm guessing you won't have Mack kill him if he asks for an unreasonable amount?"

"Not funny." She zips her duffle with the kind of force that tells me she wishes part of me were stuck in it.

I pull out my burner phone and, after I locate the number I need, dial my contact. It rings three times before he answers.

"Wolodymyr," the man answers.

"Wolodymyr, my friend. It's Jackson Quick from America. How are you?"

"Jackson Quick from America," I can hear his memory wheels spinning through the phone. "Jackson Quick..."

"It's been a while since we spoke. The last time I talked to you was maybe five years ago. You were working at a dumpy mail order bride business."

"I'm still at the dumpy mail order bride business," he says without amusement. "You insult my business?"

"I'm sorry, Wolodymyr, I—"

"Ha! I joke with you, Jackson Quick! Of course I remember you. How could I forget you? Many nights with good talks and vodka. Many nights, yes?"

"Too many."

"You ready to marry?" he asks. "I find good girl for you, Jackson Quick."

"Not today, Wolodymyr, thank you. I do need your help though."

"Of course. What can I do? What do you need?"

"I need some… paperwork."

"How many people?"

"One. But I need it immediately."

"Not a problem, Jackson Quick. You come by dumpy mail order bride business."

"Okay," I laugh, "remind me where it is."

He gives me the address and hangs up.

"We need to go," I tell Bella. "Grab your bag and follow me. We're getting you a new identity and then we're catching a flight to Kiev."

"Did you say something about mail order brides?" She pushes through the hotel exit and into the glare of the sunlight bouncing off of the Black Sea, two or three steps behind me.

"Why?" I ask without turning around. "Are you interested?"

"Not funny."

"None of this is funny." I start my march back toward the Potemkin Stairs and the city of Odessa.***

"This is it?" Bella cranes her neck to read the sign above the cracked, peeling yellow wooden door. "This is where your guy works?"

"Did you expect the Ritz?" The sign reads Американська краса.

"What does that say?" she mouths the word phonetically. "Ah-me-pu-ka…."

"American Beauty."

"Like the movie Alan Ball directed," she says.

"Alan Ball wrote the screenplay," I correct her. "Sam Mendes directed."

"Whatever." She tries the handle on the door. It's locked.

"Push the button on the right," I tell her. She presses it and there's a high-pitched tone.

"Jackson Quick?" The voice sounds like its coming from the bottom of an empty oil drum.

"Yes," I say it louder than I probably should. "It's my guest and me."

"Wait for the buzz," he says and there's a loud magnetic hum.

The surprisingly heavy door clicks open and I swing it wide past Bella. She steps inside and I follow her into a dark hallway. When my eyes adjust, I remember where I am.

We're standing in a narrow corridor, its plaster walls peeling off their pale green paint. Flecks of the paint decorate the concrete floor like confetti, especially where it meets the walls. Above us, there's a caged light dangling from a thick electrical cord that disappears into the asbestos ceiling.

On the wall to our right is a large framed black and white photograph of Yuri Gagarin, the first man in space. He's wearing a spacesuit, a white helmet emblazoned with 'CCCP' above the visor, his face expressionless.

It seems so random in this space, the only photograph on the walls of the hallway. It's without context, without reference. It's very Ukrainian, though Gagarin was Russian.

We walk past the photograph in its gilded silver frame to the end of the corridor and a single door. On the door, there is the same red, white, and blue sign we saw outside, Американська краса. Before either of us can knock, the door opens, the sign flapping against it, and Wolodymyr emerges into the hall.

"Jackson Quick!" His arms are open, ready for the traditional hug as he wraps me into a bear hug. "Good to see you, my American friend."

"Good to see you too!" I slap him on the back in the most masculine way possible. "Thanks so much for helping us out."

"Is this the friend?" His arms open for Bella. She offers her hand, and he quickly adjusts to shake it. "A pleasure to meet you, friend. Come in, come in." He ushers us into his office.

"What's with the Gagarin photo?" I ask as Wolodymyr bolts the door behind us. "I don't remember seeing it the last time I was here."

"Oh," he laughs, "it is signal for business partners. If Yuri is on wall, how you say, 'Coast is clear.'" He smiles and waves his hand like a baseball umpire signaling a baserunner is safe.

Bella's standing in the corner near the door, not comfortable enough to step farther into the large euro-modern office.

"Laika the dog."

"A dog?"

"Laika was the first animal in space," I explain. "She was a stray."

"From Moscow," Wolodymyr adds. "Without her there would be no Yuri."

"What happened to her?" Bella asks.

"She died," Wolodymyr shrugs. "Overheated." He points to a photograph in a frame identical to the one hanging in the hallway. It's hanging askew on the wall.

"That's horrible."

"Let's talk about why we're here," I say. "We need new papers pronto."

"All business today, Jackson Quick." Wolodymyr claps his hands together and rubs them like Mr. Miyagi fixing Daniel Russo's injured leg. "I like all business. Let's get you new papers pronto."

He glides across the floor to a chrome and glass desk at the far end of the room. There's a large Macintosh computer and wireless mouse alongside a thick stack of manila folders. Wolodymyr plops into a lime green, ergonomic, molded plastic chair and spins around to face the monitor. Behind the computer desk, there is a wall painted bright green.

"Come here, Jackson Quick and friend, come here." He waves us over with a cartoonish gesture and begins typing on the silver keyboard.

A variety of images are on the computer screen. There are images of photographs and documents, and at the center of the screen a round, pale face is smiling back at me. The woman has shoulder length blonde hair, large eyes, and a soft spray of freckles across her long, thin nose. She looks like she could be in her late teens.

"Who's that?" I nod at the screen and rest my hand on the back of Wolodymyr's lime green chair.

"A client. She's happily married now. Living in St. Paul, Minnesota I believe. Her new husband is doctor."

Bella stands next to me behind Wolodymyr. "Is she a mail order bride?"

"She has American husband," he says. "She wanted to live in America. He wanted pretty young wife. They both happy." Wolodymyr holds up his hands, fingers intertwined. "Everybody is winner."

"Why does she have fake documents?" Bella steps to the side of the chair and leans in to look more closely at the images on the screen.

"Not everybody is angel," he says, his fingers pecking away on the glowing silver keys. "Are you angel, Jackson Quick's friend?" He stops typing and looks over his shoulder at Bella.

Bella glances at him and then over to me. I can tell she's unsure of Wolodymyr and his black market business. "Nobody's an angel."

"And that," he smiles, "is why business is always so good for me. If everybody was angel, nobody need me."

Wolodymyr moves his hand to the wireless mouse, manipulates the images on the screen and then rolls back in his chair. "Okay, time to take photograph of Jackson Quick's friend."

"My name is —"

"I don't need name," Wolodymyr holds up his hands. "I don't want to know name. Only name is one I give you. It keeps everything clean, yes?"

"Yes," Bella nods. "That's fine."

"So then," Wolodymyr directs Bella to the Chroma key green wall behind the computer, "walk over here. Stand against wall. No smile. Look at camera here on table and I take photograph."

Bella walks around the desk, adjusting her top and bushing her hair off of her face. She looks at the wall for a second before turning toward the camera.

"On three, I take photograph." Wolodymyr, palms the mouse to control the camera. "One…two…three," he clicks the mouse and the computer screen fills with a photograph of Bella. "Is good," he says. "Come back over here. We finish quick."

Wolodymyr manipulates the photograph, altering the background, changing the color of Bella's shirt, tinting her hair a lighter shade of its natural color. He erases the faint stress line running across her forehead.

"I make you look a little younger," he says. "Fresher for photograph."

"Fresher?" Bella fidgets with her hair and folds her arms. "What does that mean?"

"No offense." He saves the changes to the photograph. "I need you to look a little different." He clicks the mouse and the photograph becomes a black and white image.

"You can't look like you took the picture today," I put her hand on her shoulder. "That's all he's saying."

She nods.

"I am thinking Swiss…" On the screen, Wolodymyr opens an image that resembles the identification page for a passport. The background is mottled pink and blue. On the top of the page and in the middle it reads *Scheiz, Suisse, Svizzera, Svizra, Switzerland.* "What languages do you speak other than English?"

"I'm pretty good with French," she says, "and I am street-fluent in Spanish. Why?"

"French is good," he says. "Italian is good too. Same with German. You are from Switzerland now. You need to speak language, yes?"

"I don't speak Swiss," she says. "And I certainly don't look Swiss. I'm not tall, pale, and blonde."

"Swiss is good because they have four official languages there," Wolodymyr slides Bella's picture into the passport page. "German, French, Italian, and Romansh."

"Romance?"

"Ro-MANSH," he corrects. "Excuse me my English. I still practice. "Romansh is old language. Comes from Latin and is mixed with German. But you okay with French. "Also," he begins to enter a false passport number in the upper right of the page, "nobody checks Swiss much. You could be from part near Italy. Not everybody looks like Abba. It's best. Yes?"

"Abba is Swedish," I interject. "They're from Sweden."

"Same thing." He waves me off and looks at Bella. "You okay with Swiss?"

"Okay." Bella leans over Wolodymyr's shoulder to watch him give her a new name.

"I give you name Analiese," he tells her. "Popular name. I put it with Muller for surname. Also popular. It rings no alarms."

"Analiese Muller?" Bella tries the name. "Sounds nice."

"How tall are you?" Wolodymyr eyes Bella from toe to head.

"Five foot ten."

"That's one hundred and seventy seven centimeters," he inputs it into the computer.

"You're tall," I comment, internally comparing my height to hers. I hadn't taken note that she was almost as tall as me.

"Gee, thanks."

Wolodymyr gets up from his chair and walks over to a cabinet on our left. He spins a combination lock left, right, and left again until the cabinet clicks open. He swings open the door to reveal stacks of documents, passports, various nations' currency in small and large denominations, and a long pump action shotgun.

"That loaded?" I ask.

"Always," he shuffles through a stack of passports. "I don't work with angels, remember? Also I sometimes work with hacking."

"Hacking?" Bella's ears perk up.

"I am, what do you call it, jack of trades?" Wolodymyr winks. "I am good with computers. People need things to happen, need to see things in computers. I open windows for them."

"Microsoft?" Bella questions.

"No windows like to let in light and air," he answers. "I help people who don't want people to know they need help. Like you."

He pulls a red passport from a stack, closes the cabinet and spins the lock. "This one is good. It's Swiss and has a couple stamps on it. Ukraine,

Russia, France, reentry to Switzerland. You are good. I add one more Ukraine with yesterday's date. It will be clean and nice."

"Thanks for doing this Wolodymyr," I say. "I really appreciate the quick work."

"No problem." He spreads the passport open and slides it into a printer. "You are friend and you pay with cash. Both are good things. Yes?"

"Yes."

"We get you out of here quick. You have plane to catch," he says. "I already make reservation. Aerosvit. Sends you straight to Kiev. Then you go wherever it is you go."

"Great! Thanks for making the arrangements."

"I also tell my friend at the airport that you pay him extra," he slips in as an afterthought.

"Why?"

"You have weapons, yes?" he asks rhetorically. "You need someone to put them in plane without questions."

I hadn't thought about it. The Tec-9 and the Smith & Wesson weren't an issue on Sir Spencer's or Bella's jets. "How much?"

"One hundred dollars U.S."

I laugh. "Okay." Thank goodness for a weak hryvnia.

"Where is it you go?" He looks over his shoulder at me as the printer hums and whirs, sucking in the passport line by line.

"Wolodymyr, if you don't want to know her name, you really don't want to know where we're going. Right?"

"Good point, Jackson Quick. Good point to make."

CHAPTER 14

Aerosvit does not fly what I would call a modern fleet of aircraft. The regional Ukrainian airline employs a lot of Soviet-era military transport planes, reconfigured for commercial flight. The empty seat in front of me folds all the way forward. And first class, as it were, is special only in that there are desks attached to the seats. The overhead compartments are open, twin lines of rope serving as the barrier for our luggage.

Even after emerging from bankruptcy, the dollars, or hryvnia, must be in short supply.

"This is commercial?" Bella asks, tightening the seatbelt across her lap.

"Not really. This is Iron Curtain commercial. It's not really typical of what you'd fly in the States."

She takes stock of the less than comfortable cabin from her window seat as we bounce against the turbulence.

"When was the last time you flew commercial?" I ask.

She purses her lips, searching her memory. "At least a decade."

"Really?"

"I guess," she says. "I really don't know. I don't take a lot of vacations. And whenever I travel for work, I take the jet."

"What about the ski trip you took with your dad? When was that?"

"What are you talking about?" She brushes her hair from her face and turns toward me, away from the window. "What trip?"

"I saw a photo of you and your father. It was on your computer screen, the home screen. It was the two of you—"

"I know the picture," she barks. "What we're you doing on my computer, Jackson? When was this?"

"This morning. In the hotel. You were blow-drying your hair."

Her eyes narrow. "You got on my computer without asking? I was in the bathroom. I trusted you. I was about to put my life in your hands." She was somehow yelling at me without raising her voice. "I was vulnerable, and you abused my trust. Unbelievable."

"I needed internet access. I don't have a computer anymore."

"You could've asked me."

"Sorry, Bella. I —"

"What did you want?"

"What?"

"On the internet. What did you want on the internet?"

"I was looking up neutrinos."

"C'mon, Jackson," she chides, looking at the passing clouds, "don't compound your deceit with a lie."

"I'm not lying. I was actually looking up neutrinos. I was trying to figure out which part of the truth *you* were keeping from *me*."

"What are you talking about?" she whips her head back to me. "What truth?"

"We're not looking to find some process that helps subs talk to one another, Bella. There's more to it than that."

Her eyes are searching for something to say but don't find one. She licks her lips.

"This is about nuclear detection, isn't it?"

She doesn't answer.

"Bella, you can't sit here and act like you don't know what I'm talking about. There's a nuclear component to this. It seems like your Dr. Wolf figured out how to use neutrino beams to find secret nuclear reactors. There was a bunch of research published about that stuff and then it stopped. It went radio silent."

"How do you know this?" she asks, her arms folded in front of her.

"I got a tip and I checked it out."

"On the internet," she says doubtfully.

"On the internet."

"Hmmph," she grunts and looks back out the window, the sun bouncing off of the clouds, creating a glare against the glass. The light on her face makes her look pale, sallow almost.

"Is that it?" I ask her. "That's all you're going to say?"

Her silence only furthers confirms that this is about more than she's willing to admit. My laptop espionage is nothing compared to whatever it is she's hiding.

"Look, Jackson," she turns from the window, her gaze a little softer than before, "you're right in believing that I haven't been entirely forthcoming regarding the full scope of this."

"You mean the blackmail part or the nuclear part?"

"I guess I was wrong about you. Neither of us is trustworthy, Jackson."

"Speak for yourself," I say. "I used your computer without asking. Now I'm untrustworthy? I don't think so. Rude, maybe. Not untrustworthy."

"Parse words however you want," she says, "but you are where you are because you betrayed your employer. He entrusted you with information that you later used against him."

"*What?*" Is she on crack? "You're telling me that I'm a traitor because I *betrayed* a lying, manipulative, power hungry killer? That makes no sense. It wasn't that long ago that you were telling me that I'm the only one you can trust in this."

"I've given it more thought." She leans into me and lowers her voice to a whisper. "Your boss, no matter how much of a monster he proved to be, trusted you. You betrayed that trust. And that makes you untrustworthy. Who's to say my moral compass and yours point in the same direction? Who's to say, at some point, I give you information that you decide to later use against me?"

It's blowing my mind, but she has a point.

"Why would I tell you everything there is to know? Let's not forget, Jackson, the man who recommended you to me is someone neither of us trusts. You're the one who keeps reminding me of that."

"You're saying if A plus B equals C then —"

"Exactly. You may save my life a million times, and it doesn't mean I can trust you."

"That's messed up." I shake my head. "How are we going to keep doing this then?"

"Doing what?"

I've heard before that adversity doesn't build character, it merely reveals it. Maybe that's what's happening here. Bella is ultimately a pampered, weak, conniving, untrustworthy snake, whose only raison d'être is power and money. She *is* Charlie. She doesn't need the rifle.

"Never mind," I say. "I understand where we are here. This is business, pure and simple. We don't have to trust each other to get the job done. As long as we understand each other." I unbuckle my belt.

"Where are you going?" she asks.

"The bathroom," I mumble. "I suddenly feel a little sick."

***

Kiev's Boryspil International Airport is southeast of the city. The domestic terminal is a small building adjacent to the much busier, and more nicely appointed, international terminal. Bella and I trudge through the crowds to the curb in front of the terminal. I'm several steps ahead of her. My pack, which feels heavier with every passing hour without good sleep, has a red tag on it marked with white letters that read Спеціальний. *Special.* My Tec-9, Gerber knife, and revolver are still inside. The ammo is there too, as is my Garmin. It was the best one hundred dollars I've spent in a while.

"You think it's safe to get a cab?" Bella asks. "I mean, after Odessa."

"We have different identities." I glance over my shoulder outside the terminal. "We flew commercial. There's no way to have tracked us here. We're fine to take a cab." My phone rings.

"Is that your phone?" Bella drops her duffel on the curb.

"Yeah." I stare at the burner phone. It's an unknown number.

"Are you going to answer it?"

I answer and immediately regret the decision.

"Jackson," the caller says, "how's the weather in Kiev?" His British accent has become like nails on a chalk board.

"Confusing," I answer.

"How's that, good man? How would the weather be confusing?" He says, though I am aware he knows exactly what I mean.

"How did you find me?" I turn to Bella, who is now mouthing "*Who is it?*" Her eyebrows are smushed together.

"Oh, Jackson," he laughs. "Do we really need to play this game again? You are always at my fingertips."

"This is a burner phone, Sir Spencer," I say his name and Bella's eyes grow wide. "There's no way —"

"There's always a way, Jackson. What have you found so far?"

"Nothing."

"Nothing?" he asks. "I find that hard to believe, what with two bloody scenes and three or four dead bodies in Odessa. You'd have thought the Czar sent his army to the steps and mowed down the Bolsheviks against a haunting strain of classical music."

"Not quite," I reply.

"So you haven't found anything yet? No parts to the puzzle as it were?"

"No."

"Then where are you off to now? You must have a good lead, right?"

"Maybe."

"Jackson," he says, "really now. What's with the tied tongue? You seem…what's the word…suspicious?"

"You've got more skin in this than either you or Bella are willing to let on. There's more at stake. Bella says Wolf was blackmailing her."

Bella shakes her head and backs up a step. "No!" she says. "Don't —"

"She says there were buyers," I look at Bella as I speak into the phone. "Wolf was auctioning his process to the highest bidder. She says Liho Blogis was one of them. Another one was Iranian, maybe."

"Iran," he says. "That's an interesting one. And Blogis you say?" His condescension zips through the wireless connection.

"Where are you?"

"At the Hay Adams in Washington," he says. "My usual room. The White House is particularly beautiful this morning. I'm watching MSNBC. Care to know what I'm having for breakfast?"

"No."

"Then let's get on with what's important," he says. "We were talking about Iran, and Blogis, and a bidding war. Much more interesting conversation than the blather on cable."

"Bella says you were a middleman. You were playing broker for an interested party when, out of the goodness of your heart, you decide to help her."

"I found it the most economically viable option," he says. "It's far less expensive, and potentially more lucrative, than the alternatives."

"Were you aware that this process isn't about talking yellow submarines? It's about nuclear detection."

"I am aware of the neutrinos' value and of Dr. Wolf's discovery. I am only surprised that…"

"That what?"

"That she told you."

"Why?"

"We'd discussed what we thought you needed to know as you assisted her in retrieving the process," he reveals. "Divulging the blackmail was a tactical decision, designed to gain your sympathy. I imagine she told you this at a moment you believed her to be vulnerable."

I press the phone closer to my ear and casually step back from Bella, who's mouthing the words, "What is he saying?" I ignore her.

I'm untrustworthy anyhow, right?

"You know, Jackson," he says, "you're getting off track here. None of what you're fretting about is pertinent to the task at hand. It's disconcerting, really, because you are quickly running out of time. And if you don't succeed, you don't get what you want."

Bella steps closer to me, her eyes asking me to let her in on the conversation.

"Wait a minute." I hold up my hand as much in response to Sir Spencer as I do to signal Bella to back off. I turn away from Bella and lower my voice. "Are you telling me that there's more she's keeping from me? That the two of you will let the information trickle out when it's tactically critical? Otherwise I'm in the dark, blindly doing your bidding?"

"Take from my suggestion what you will, Jackson," Sir Spencer answers. "You know as well as I that one functions best when one has the information necessary to complete the task at hand. Too much intelligence only creates more noise. Don't take everything so personally, good man. It's not *always* about Jackson Quick."

He has a point and I have a job to finish.

"All right," I relent, "I'll accept I'm your minion. It is what it is." I turn back around to face Bella, who's given up and is trying to hail a cab. "And you're right, I need to focus. So what did you mean about us running out of time?"

"Ahhh," he laughs, "back to what matters. Very good. Has Bella discussed with you anything about Toulon?"

"No," I catch her eye for second, before she looks away again. "What's Toulon?"

"It's a city in southern France and is home to a large military port. Quite lovely there in July during the Jazz Festival. You'd enjoy the music, and the beautiful Mediterranean scenery, Jackson."

"The point, Sir Spencer?"

"Toulon is, as I mentioned, home to a large military port. It's historically important. And it is where our friend Liho Blogis found a piece of the process."

I march over to Bella to tell her. "Blogis has a piece of the process."

"What?" she asks, turning her attention from the futility of hailing a cab. "Where?"

"Toulon."

Her eyes widen, betraying her secret.

"Jackson," says Sir Spencer, "are you listening to me?"

"Yes, go ahead."

"Toulon is also the home of the Astronomy with a Neutrino Telescope and Abyss environmental research project, also known as ANTARES," he explains. "It's an underwater telescope that measures the neutrinos traveling from space into the southern hemisphere."

"How does he know this?" Bella interjects.

"What does that have to do with the process?" I ask, ignoring her.

"ANTARES went live in 2008 after years of work. Wolf was part of the team that helped design it. They figured out a way to detect the radiation from some of the neutrinos that pass through the Earth and then into the Mediterranean, despite a lot of background radiation. Quite genius, from what I'm told. His brilliance on that project is the reason that Nanergetix selected Wolf for their work."

"He had contacts there," I conclude. "And neither you nor Bella thought to start in France, the place where he worked prior to his job at Nanergetix?"

"Are you talking about Wolf?" Bella asks. I nod. "How does Spencer know Blogis has a piece?"

"Jackson," Sir Spencer says, "these are all educated guesses. France was one option. Brookhaven in Long Island was another. Bella had the lead in Ukraine. You have a history there. We thought it the best place to start."

"You never said anything about France or Long Island. Neither was on our agenda. Germany was next, right?"

"It's one step at a time, Jackson, and you can't be everywhere at once." Bella shoves my shoulder, "How. Does. He. Know?"

"How do you know Blogis has a piece of the process?" I ask.

"There are two dead scientists. They were found floating in the Fountaine des trois Douphins."

"There are two dead scientists," I tell Bella before asking Sir Spencer, "Why would that lead you to believe that Blogis did it and that he recovered something?"

"Both scientists worked for the French institute in charge of running ANTARES, and when police went to their lab, the hard drives were ripped from the computers."

"That doesn't mean it was Blogis. There were other players, remember?"

"Yes, but Blogis has the correct list of names."

"How do you know? One drive has a false list. Maybe the French scientists were diversions."

"Not possible."

"Why is that?" I press. "How would you know?"

"Because there was no fake list," he says. "That was a ruse."

"You're confusing me, Sir Spencer." A cab pulls up to the curb and a driver gets out, walking around the rear of the car toward Bella.

"Jackson," he says, "must I spell out everything for you? There was no fake list. Wolf did have two lists on two drives. One was a duplicate of the other. When Mack killed Wolf, he found one of them and gave it to me."

"Mack gave it —"

"Let me finish," Sir Spencer cut in firmly. "Mack was working for me. I paid him to provide me whatever he recovered from Bella's contracted hit on Wolf. He found the list. I have it. The dead scientists are on that list. So was Bella's contact in Odessa, the Gamow fellow."

"Mack was working for you? So that's why the drive he gave Bella was blank."

Bella's getting into the cab. The driver looks at me expectantly, motioning to his car. I hold up a finger, asking him to wait a second.

"Bravo, Jackson."

"How does Blogis have a copy? Where did he get it?"

"I'm sure he paid someone for a copy," he says. "Or he killed someone for it. His resources are greater than mine."

"This doesn't add up. If you have the list, and you're helping Bella, why would you keep it from her? And why wouldn't we just start in Long Island? That's a lot closer than Europe."

"Oh, Jackson," he sighs. "To answer your obsessive questioning about Long Island, suffice it to say that is the least likely of places. True, there is neutrino work being done there, but the good doctor had very little connection there. Proximity is irrelevant. Now, let's go back to the beginning of the conversation, during which we discussed the strategic, restricted flow of information; a trickle here, a trickle there."

I walk toward the cab.

"I am the source from whence all information originates," he laughs. "Bella learns what I want *her* to know. She shares what she wants *you* to know. That's how this works."

I should have known.

"Now Blogis is doing some of the work himself. He has teams doing the rest of it. I believe you killed a few of those henchmen already."

"I suppose." I slip off my pack while managing to cradle the phone between my shoulder and ear.

"If he doesn't have the piece from those hard drives in Toulon," he says, "he'll have it soon."

"It's Blogis 1, Bella 1."

"Yes, in the parlance of sports, I suppose. It is up to you, then, to score a point in Ukraine. After that it's Germany."

"How many pieces are there?"

"My information is that Wolf split the process into four pieces."

"Bella has one, Blogis has one, and there are two missing."

"Yes."

"You weren't really a middleman were you? You were a bidder."

"Perhaps."

"Are you working with Blogis too?" I ask, pausing at the rear passenger door before getting in the car. "Covering all of your bases, so to speak?"

"Ha!" he laughs again. "No, good man, that relationship ended long ago. The student thought he'd become the master."

***

I could hear my parents yelling from down the hall. I was sitting on the floor in my bedroom, playing Tetris and listening to an old, rare Gary U.S. Bonds album, one on which he collaborated with Bruce Springsteen.

I couldn't tell at first why they were arguing. My parents didn't disagree much, at least not about important things. Choosing a restaurant for dinner was the most common battle.

I put down the game and ran my hands through the thick pile of the carpet, grabbing and twisting some of the strands that tickled my palms.

"It's enough," my mother said. "He's getting older now."

"What do you expect me to do?" my dad responded. "It's not as though I have a lot of options. You know that better than anyone."

They were talking about me now. My interest piqued, I slowly twisted the volume down a couple of notches.

My mother's voice had that warble in it that happens when somebody's talking and pressing to hold back tears at the same time.

"I don't understand why the decision is complicated at all," she sobbed, her voice softening enough that it was hard for me to hear. "This is your family…" there was more, but I didn't catch it.

"You're making this about one or the other?" Dad's voice was still booming. He hadn't calmed down yet. "Why is that the only choice here? Shouldn't you have considered that from the beginning, from the day I met them?"

I turned off the music and pressed on the carpet to push myself onto my feet. My right knee, recently surgically repaired, resisted at first. I pushed past the tinge of pain and quietly stepped into the hallway, a few feet closer to the argument.

At the end of the hallway, my parents' bedroom door was closed. It was late afternoon on a weekend. The sun was setting and shadows danced back and forth underneath the door from inside their room. I inched closer to their room, craning my neck to listen, to understand what it was that had them so upset.

"I'm very good at what I do," he said, "and it affords us a lot of things we might not otherwise enjoy. This house, our cars, vacations, money for Jackson's college education."

"I know —" my mother started before my father interrupted.

"Do you? Do you know we have no debt? We have cash in the bank, several banks," he argued. "How many of your Bunko friends can say that? How many PTA moms are driving around in leased cars, living in double-mortgaged homes, spending every last penny they have to pay the bills each month?"

"That's not fair. Not fair at all! There are a million jobs a man like you could hold. And because we have no debt, because we have money in several banks, now is exactly when you could afford to do something else. If there's that much money, you could take some time off. You don't have to work at all."

"Right," he said, "like that's gonna —"

"Stop!" my mother shouted. "I listened to you. It's my turn."

"Go ahead," Dad huffed.

"Your son needs you. He's growing up. He's having trouble at school."

"What are you talking about?"

"He's getting bullied."

Mom knew about that? She knew about Blair Loxley, the punk? She knew that he picked on me almost daily and that the torn ligament in my knee was no accident?

"Why would you think that?" My dad sounded surprised and less angry.

"He's had bruises on his ribs. He keeps losing his lunch money. He's losing weight. His knee for goodness sake…"

"He hasn't said anything about it," my dad countered. "He has a viable explanation for all of it."

"You don't want to see it," Mom said. "You're busy on whatever job they have you doing."

"That's not fair. How am I supposed to know if somebody's picking on him if he doesn't tell me? And why haven't you said anything until now?"

"I can't prove he's being bullied, especially if he won't admit it. Plus, you're always telling me to let him fight his own battles," she said. "You tell me that he'll never learn how to grow up if I baby him. So I back off. I give him his space."

"That's a cop out," Dad said. "You're blaming me for your inaction? You're blaming my job for my ineptitude as a father?"

I should have told them about Loxley. I should have let them help me. If I had, they wouldn't be fighting. They wouldn't be mad at each other.

"I'm not saying you're inept. I'm saying that you're absent, that even when you're home you are not really home."

"Everything is my fault," his voice grew louder again. "Is that how it is?"

"I didn't say that," Mom countered with a softer tone, making it more difficult to hear her. I stepped closer to the door. "I never said that everything is anyone's fault."

"You didn't have to say it!" Dad snapped. "It's crystal clear that I'm the problem here. My job is the problem. I'm the one who needs fixing."

"Don't be ridiculous. I knew what I was getting into when I married you, when we had Jackson. I'm not an innocent here. I'm just trying to — "

"Knew what you were getting into? What does that mean?"

"I didn't mean—"

"Of course you meant it," he said. "You were complicit! You weren't along for the ride. If anything, you were the one driving. I'm done with this conversation."

"Don't —"

"We'll talk about this later, when I'm a little less ridiculous."

The door swung open into the bedroom and my dad stomped into the hall. He almost bowled over me, not seeing me just a couple of feet from the doorway.

"Whoa!" he grabbed my shoulders to prevent both of us from tumbling to the floor. "Jackson, how long have you been standing here?"

My mom appeared in the open doorway, her face pale except for the redness around her nose. Her shoulders slumped when she saw me standing there.

"Jackson," my father repeated, "how much of our conversation did you hear?"

I shrugged, "I dunno." I stared down at the floor, unwilling to look at either of my parents. "A minute maybe," I lied.

"All right," he gently wrapped his thick hand around the back of my neck, "understand that your mother and I love each other."

"Very much," my mom added.

"But we're having a strong disagreement about some things," he continued. "It involves my work. It involves us as a family."

I focus on the curled strands of thick pile beneath my feet, some of which poke up between my toes like blades of grass. I curl my big toes, rubbing them back and forth on the carpet.

My mom stepped from the bedroom and into the hall. Her arms were folded across her chest as though she was trying to stay warm. "Jackson, we love you. And it's important that you understand that parents sometimes argue or disagree."

"We're fine, buddy." My dad extended his thumb to rub it back and forth behind my ear. "We'll be fine," he corrected. "Your mom and I are just…"

"We're passionate about things," my mom said, "and sometimes it gets the best of us."

"Do you understand?" my dad asked.

I nodded without looking up. I'd never heard them argue like that before. They'd had their moments, but this was different somehow.

"Do you have any questions?" my mom asked. "Do you want to know what we were talking about?"

"We'll tell you whatever you want to know," my dad said.

I shook my head.

Mom put her hand under my chin, lifting my eyes to hers. "Jackson, are you okay?"

This was my chance. I could admit that Loxley was bullying me, that I wasn't losing my lunch money, that I didn't fall on the track while running. He took my money. He tore my ACL.

"I'm fine, Mom," I told her. "I'm fine."

***

The Hyatt Kiev is in the center of a damaged, war-torn city. A gleaming all glass, concave structure, it stands out among old red bricks and the pale blues and yellows of the older buildings around it and the burned out shells of places not fortunate to survive the unrest here.

Kiev looks like those photographs of Yugoslavia in the early 1990s or parts of France after Germany had its way in the 1940s. There's the low, dark gray haze of smoke hovering just below the clouds. In the public squares there are piles of burnt trash, bloodstains, and splintered barricades.

Outside of the hotel's entrance there is a pair of armed security guards, likely soldiers making extra cash. They're humorless and serve as a reminder of the instability here.

Inside the hotel, the outside world doesn't exist, however. In the center of the two-story lobby is a quartet of white sofas, paired off and facing one another. They frame two low black coffee tables, set upon a large gray area rug. Sitting on one of those sofas is where I find the man Wolodymyr said would take us to Chernobyl. He's bald, sun spots dotting his head. His chin sports a reddish goatee which, with the thin mustache beneath his hawkish nose, gives him a Leninesque appearance. I have a feeling it's intentional.

"Привіт," I say, hello, and take a seat across from the man, sinking into the white leather. He's holding a cup of coffee with one hand, thumbing through his smartphone with the other. He doesn't acknowledge me.

"Привіт," I repeat. "Ми маємо взаємного товариша." I explain we have a mutual friend, which causes him to glance up from his phone.

His eyes, peeking over a pair of frameless glasses, are like so many eastern Europeans', deep set with dark circles that convey the hard, blue collar subsistence so many live. He pulls the cup to his lips and blows gently on the coffee before taking a slurp.

"Я не маю слово коду для вас." I don't have a code word for him and I tell him that I need some transportation. "Я тільки потребую їзди." I stand to leave. Bella's been waiting by the entrance to the hotel, standing with our bags. "Wolodymyr сказали ви могли допомогти. Але можливо ви не бажаєте моїх грошей."

"I do want your money," he says in good English. "And if Wolodymyr told you I could help you, then I can help you." He motions to the sofa with his coffee cup, and slides his phone into his shirt pocket.

I sit on the edge of the sofa, leaning forward. "You speak English."

"Of course," he says. "It's currency just like your American dollar. I must speak English to do business with many of Wolodymyr's friends."

"When do we leave?" I ask. "We need to be at our location as quickly as possible."

"Hold onto the horses," he chuckles. "It is late. We cannot go there at night."

"Why not?" I ask. "I thought Wolodymyr expressed to you the urgency of our trip."

Across the lobby, Bella's dragged the bags over to a chair near the entrance and is sitting. Her elbows are resting on her knees, her head in her hands.

The Lenin look-alike takes another sip from his coffee, then tongues his mustache clean. "He did." He leans back and crosses one leg over the other. "I gave him price for daytime trip. Much more dangerous at night."

"So we *could* go tonight. It'll just be more expensive."

"It is much more dangerous. The roads are not good. There is more security at night."

"I thought you had papers to get us past the security? Wolodymyr told me you had papers. That's part of the cost."

"I have papers," he says. "Those are for daytime. No papers for night."

"How much?"

"How much for what?"

"I'll find someone else." I get up again, tired of his games. I'm five or six steps toward Bella when there's hand on my shoulder. I turn around, shrugging him off.

"Five," he blinks behind his glasses. "We go now."

"Thousand?" I clarify. That's not much more than the original price.

He nods. "Five thousand, yes. Each."

"Ten thousand, then," I say, trying not to reveal any surprise at the ridiculously steep charge.

"Yes."

"Thirty-five hundred each," I counter. "That's double your original price. And we won't be needing the papers. So…"

"Four." His eyes, pupils wide, are searching mine, like an animal searching for weakness.

"Thirty-five. There are others who aren't afraid of the dark." If Wolodymyr hadn't recommended this guy, I'd be long gone.

His pupils shrink. "Okay. I take thirty-five. You ready to go?"

"Yes." I nod toward Bella. "She's going with us."

"Nice," he says. "Very nice. Maybe she goes for free."

"I don't think so. Where's your car?"

"I have new Opel," he says. "It is hatchback. You put your bags in the back when I drive to front of hotel."

"See you in a minute." I start toward Bella.

"Принесіть гроші з вами," he calls after me.

"I'll bring the money," I reply without turning around. "I have it with me."

"Good," he mumbles. "Five minutes we leave."

Bella is still sitting, head in hands as I step to her near the entrance of the hotel. She looks up at me.

"We need to talk," she says.

"Now?"

"Yes."

"I don't think this is the time or place. We've got a ride to catch."

"You'll want to hear this," she says. "And probably sooner, rather than later."

"Okay." I sit in the chair next to her. "There must be something about hotel lobbies."

"What do you mean?"

"Earlier today, in Odessa. We had a heart to heart there. Remember?"

"Yes, Jackson, I remember."

"What's the big reveal, Bella?"

"You were right in suggesting I've not been honest with you. And it's not that you're not trustworthy. That wasn't fair of me to say. I'm sorry for that."

"You're probably right to doubt me."

She doesn't know the details of my conversation with Sir Spencer. I was vague when she asked about it in the cab ride to the hotel. I only told her that two scientists were dead and that Blogis likely had a piece of the process. I kept the rest to myself. She doesn't know Mack betrayed her.

"I've been letting things drip out," she says, "a little at a time."

"I figured as much." I glance outside. A SmartCar swings into the valet lane. "Sir Spencer alluded to it."

"Did he?"

"He told me that you were only sharing with me what was needed at any given time."

"Did he also explain what's really at stake?"

"What's at stake?" I rub my eyes and lean forward in the chair.

"If we fail," she says, "if Dr. Wolf's research falls into the wrong hands..." She closes her eyes and sighs through her pursed lips.

"What happens?"

"A very one-sided World War III."

PART 3

FISSION

*"Three things cannot be long hidden: the sun,
the moon, and the truth."*

—Buddha

CHAPTER 15

"I don't think I understand what you're telling me, Bella. How could neutrinos start a nuclear war?"

"It's not the neutrinos, per se, it's what they can do. Neutrinos can move through anything."

"We already established that."

"That means that they can go through the Earth, right?" Her arms are folded now. She's in attack mode. "Scientists think they can concentrate a beam of these neutrinos and, instead of using them to communicate messages, use them to destroy nuclear weapons."

"I don't get it. I thought the real purpose, the one you were keeping from me, was to find and identify nuclear reactors. You know, Iran or Syria, places like that?"

"Well, the beam *could* do that. But that's not what Wolf was developing."

"Apparently."

"If you sent a beam that was strong enough, then it could be aimed at a stash of nuclear weapons anywhere in the world. You fire the beam and it zaps the weapons, vaporing them."

"You mean blowing them up?"

"No. The process is slow. The neutrino beam causes a chain reaction that takes time. It's more like a burnout of the bomb, degrading the nuclear fuel. It wouldn't explode, it would just...evaporate."

"Whoever controls the technology could destroy the weapons of an enemy and attack without fear of reprisals."

"Exactly." She unfolds her arms and rubs her hands on the armrests. "That's the theory."

"Except it's not a theory anymore, is it?"

"No." She shakes her head. "It'll work. The funding is there, the technology is there. It's just a matter of building it, of focusing the beam with the right amount of energy."

"Has anyone tested it?"

"No."

"Why are you telling me this now? What's your game here, Bella?"

"Game?" She jerks her neck like a clucking chicken. "This isn't a game."

"What I mean, is that you don't trust me. You said that. You've told me partial truths from the beginning. Why are you telling me this now?"

"I was unfair before," she said. "I already apologized for that. And I saw how you looked at me when we were at the airport. You turned away from me. Sir Spencer told you things you're not sharing with me."

"I'm not playing some Hannibal Lector/Clarice Starling quid pro quo with you," I tell her. "We're better off not doing that."

"I'm not asking for you to trade information with me. I don't need you to tell me what you want to keep to yourself."

"Then what *do* you need?" The Opel pulls up. Lenin gets out of the car and walks to the back to pop the hatch. "Hurry up. We need to go." I reach into the pack and pull out enough cash for the ride.

"You're working for me. You're helping me. You're risking your life for me," she says. "I mean not *for* me," she clarifies before I can correct her, "but you know what I mean."

I stand from the chair and grab my pack with one hand, her bag with the other.

She stands from her seat and follows me to the entrance to the hotel. "It's only fair that you know everything," she says, stepping quickly to catch up to me. "You should know what's at stake, how serious this is on a big scale."

"Whatever you say." I pull open the heavy door, swinging it inward and nodding for Bella to walk ahead of me. "This is really about gamesmanship, Bella. You playing all of your cards because you don't know what I'm holding. That's fine. Let's finish the job and save the world."

She walks past me to the parking lot, looking at me as though I just killed her puppy.

***

Lenin was right. The roads from Kiev, north to Chernobyl, are dangerous. They're two lane, mostly in disrepair, and often unmarked. Lenin is driving the route from memory. He speeds past a woman and her cart pulling donkey. The draft of his hatchback pulls a trail of hay into the air behind us. The woman, head covered in a bright yellow headscarf, doesn't seem to notice or care as she tugs on the donkey's lead.

Lenin takes a sharp left turn on a highway marked P-02 to head west. Already low in the sky, the sun shines through the front of the car, blinding us momentarily until our eyes adjust.

"That's bright," Bella says. She's sitting behind Lenin, who takes her cue and pulls down his visor to block some of the direct orange light. "Thank you," she tells him. "By the way, what is your name?" His car is clean, looks new, but already smells of stale cigarettes. It's a smell prevalent throughout Ukraine. Even those who don't smoke smell like those who do.

He glances at Bella in his rearview mirror. "I'm Sergei. My friends call me Lisi."

"Lisi?" Bella asks.

"It means bald," I say. "Sergei, this trip is what, two hours maybe?"

"Give or take. I get you there right after dark. I make good time and know back roads once we get to exclusion zone."

"Exclusion zone?" Bella looks me, eyebrows knotted. "That doesn't sound safe."

"The exclusion zone is area around reactor number four at Chernobyl plant," Sergei responds. "It is restricted area."

"It's safe," I assure Bella. "We're not going to be getting too close to the reactor. We might not even see it. The exclusion zone is a wide area. People work there, some still live there."

"Near the reactor that exploded?" Bella asks in shock. "People live next to the worst nuclear disaster ever? How is that possible?"

"It was people's homes," says Sergei. "They live in Chernobyl their whole lives. Where else do they go? Two hundred people live here. They are old now. Government looks other way now, calls them *Samosely*. It means *illegals*. They farm and they hunt."

"The government lets them *hunt?*"

"Government doesn't like the hunting. They crack down on hunting. Add more security for that. They also don't like people who come to steal metal scrap, but people still do it. Maybe almost every night someone comes into exclusion zone without permission."

"So, you are here a lot? You help people come."

"Maybe," he says.

"I thought the whole place was still radioactive, that it would be some sort of no man's land for a century or more. When did it happen? In the eighties?"

"Nineteen eighty six," Sergei says. "Yes. There are parts where it is worse, parts not as bad. Radiation still high, but not going to kill you from a quick visit."

"That's reassuring," Bella says. "Sergei—" A black Mercedes SUV pulls next to us, speeds ahead, then shifts back into our lane.

"Lisi, please. Call me Lisi…?"

"Oh, how rude," she says, "I'm sorry. My name is B—"

I grab her leg and squeeze.

"A-Analiese," she sputters, and pulls my hand from her leg.

"Analiese." his bottom lip curls upward as he considers it. "Is that German? You don't sound German."

"Swiss," she says quickly. "I'm Swiss."

"Your English is good. No accent like me." He laughs. His eyes dart back and forth between Bella and me. He knows.

"*Je travil dur,*" Bella says, telling Sergei that she works hard at her accent.

"*Tres bien,*" he counters. "*Vouse parlent un excellent Francais.*"

"*Merci.* You're too sweet, Lisi," she giggles.

She's playing him.

"You were about to ask me something, Analiese," he prods her and then turns his attention to the road as a large truck rumbles past us, heading east.

"How is it you're going to get us into the exclusion zone?"

"I have ways," he says. "I do it before a couple of times." He shifts his left hand to the top of the steering wheel and rubs his chin with his right. "Believe me, I am best at this. That is why Wolodymyr told you to come to me."

"You work together often? You and Wolodymyr?"

Another truck whizzes past us, shaking the Opel.

"We are both businessmen," he says. "When there is business that is good for me, he tells people to call. When there is business good for him, I make recommendation. Lots of hand washing together. There is less of it since Crimea problem in east part of country. Still, some good business."

"Capitalists," she nods.

"Maybe that," he says with a smirk. "I say we are just businessmen. Capitalism is not good to say."

"Why is that?" I interject. "Without it, you wouldn't have seven thousand dollars of my money in your pocket."

"Seven thousand?" Bella's eyes widen, her jaw drops. "For a ride?"

"Analiese, I provide very special service. It takes very special price. For me, it is good. For my country, I don't know."

"You don't know what?" I lean my right arm on the door. "If capitalism is good? How could it not be good?"

"That is not easy answer," he says. "I am clever man. This economy is good for clever people. For most people it is not good. That is why you see many of my comrades thinking that Russia is good for us. They like to give Crimea back to Russia. Maybe it's good idea." He reaches into a compartment underneath the dashboard touchscreen and pulls something from the space. "Do you mind if I smoke?"

"It's your car," I shrug.

He glances at Bella to check with her and she smiles, so he shakes loose a cigarette with his lips, tosses the pack onto the front seat, and pushes in the lighter. It pops and he pulls it to the end of the cigarette, puffing twice before replacing the lighter in the dash.

The driver's side window hums halfway open and Sergei blows smoke from the corner of his mouth toward the red two-door zooming past us. I can smell rain underneath the smoke. The air is thick with humidity and I notice the tall green trees waving back and forth, their leaves rustling against gusts of wind.

"Capitalism is not always good, yes? I remember before wall comes down. I was young. We would stand in line every week for toilet paper, milk, potatoes. Maybe some weeks we wait hour. Some weeks we are in lines all day. My mother would tell stories to us or sing songs. Other children would bring their toys. We would play chess with them on the streets, waiting to move to front of line."

"That's awful," says Bella.

"Is it?" Sergei takes another puff and blows it out the window. He reaches across his body to tap the ash into the damp air. "Every time we get to front of line we have toilet paper. We have milk. We get our potatoes. We are never disappointed. Our government always provide."

"But it was doled out," she says. "You didn't have the choice to get whatever you wanted when you wanted it."

"No," Sergei says around the cigarette dangling from his lip, "but after wall comes down we had choice and there was nothing to buy."

"How could that be with a new market economy?"

"You talk like American," he sneers, "not Swiss. Many people like the wall. We had jobs, we had place to live, we had food. When we get old, our country takes care of us." He's interrupted by a flash of lightning and loud clap of thunder.

"Wall comes down and there is no job. Place to live is expensive. Food is hard to get. We get old and there is nobody to take care of us," he shrugs. "This is why, for some, capitalism not so good. This is why you see war in my country."

"That's why you have to work hard," Bella lectures. "There are opportunities if you work hard. You cannot rely on the government for everything. Hard, honest work is rewarded."

"Hard, honest work," he laughs and sucks on the cigarette. The ash glows brighter as he inhales, then dims as he blows out. "That is funny joke."

"Why is it funny?"

"I am paid seven thousand dollars U.S. to sneak you into place you should not be. That is not honest. Thick raindrops begin to pelt the windshield. Sergei flicks what's left of the cigarette out of the window and pushes a button to roll it up. "Seven thousand dollars is maybe four times more than honest person makes in year."

"Yes but—"

"But what, *Analiese*?" He narrows his eyes. "You are Swiss and I am from Africa. You are not honest."

"Wait a —"

"You judge my country. You know nothing. You come here with your money and your secrets. You think Wolodymyr send you to me if you were honest? You come to me because you need to be dishonest. I am not fool."

"Nobody suggested you are a fool," I intercede. "She's just having a political debate with you."

The rain intensifies and the Opel's wipers whir back and forth as quickly as they can. Another flash and immediate boom rattle the car.

Sergei puts both hands on the wheel and adjusts his position in his seat. He leans into the windshield and decelerates.

He raises his voice so that we can hear him over the rhythmic pounding of the rain. "Sorry, I am passionate man. I get passionate about my country. I am sorry. I should not be rude to guests."

"It's okay," Bella says. "I meant no offense to you, Lisi." She smiles demurely.

"It's Sergei," he says. "You now call me Sergei."

He's right. He's no fool.

✳✳✳

The Opel's headlights are barely able to cut through the driving rain. We approach a red and white wooden barrier. To the right of the barrier is a large, circular white sign which reads "STOP!! Exclusion Zone" in Ukrainian. To the left is a guard house. It's dark and presumably empty. Gravel pops underneath the tires and Sergei puts the hatchback into park.

"This entrance is good one," Sergei says. "No guards here until morning." He opens his door and quickly ducks into the downpour, rain spraying into the car until he slams it shut. He disappears for a moment, then sneaks into the white glow of the headlights shining on the barrier. Next to the guard house, he finds a lever and manually lifts the barrier. It sticks in the up position and he disappears back into the darkness before slinging open his door and slamming it shut.

"We go here and we find best way to where you want to go." Sergei pulls past the open barrier and slides the Opel into park again. "I'll be back." He pushes open his door and runs past the driver's side to the rear of the car so he can lower the barrier. The door is open and rain is splashing into the back seat

"It was more endearing when Schwarzenegger said it in *Predator*," Bella jokes.

"It was *Terminator*," I correct her. She's culturally clueless.

"Are you sure about that?" she asks as Sergei, now drenched, slips back into the car and yanks the door shut.

"Sure about what?" Sergei turns to look at us over his right shoulder, his head beading with raindrops.

"That Schwarzenegger said, 'I'll be back' in *Terminator*," I say, "and not in the movie *Predator*."

"Who said it was in *Predator*?" He's clearly shocked that anyone could mistake one of the most repeated lines in movie history. "Analiese?"

"I j-just —"

"You must *not* be American after all." He thumbs the fog from his lenses. "Or Austrian."

"Whatever," she mumbles. "It's just a movie."

Sergei turns around and cranks the hatchback into drive, slowly accelerating into the darkness. There are no streetlights illuminating the road, only his headlights, which he's switched to high beam, to guide us through the deluge.

"We need the rain," Sergei comments, "but it would have been better to not happen tonight." He scoots forward in his seat, both hands on the wheel, navigating what's become a narrow two lane road with no shoulders. "It is trouble enough in dark without rain. Now, it is harder."

"Do you know where to go?" I ask.

"Yes. We are at one of southern entry gates. We need to go north."

"Will we be close to the reactors?" Bella asks.

"No. We will not be close to sarcophagus at reactor number four."

"Sarcophagus?" Bella asks.

"It is structure built around reactor four," he says. "It is old now and leaking. We stay away from that."

"Good."

"How big is the exclusion zone?" I ask.

"Twenty six hundred kilometers. That is area."

"So," I calculate in my head, "that's about one thousand square miles. Wow."

Sergei slows the car at a fork in the road, then spins the steering wheel to the left and accelerates. A flash of lightning momentarily illuminates our surroundings, revealing towering trees swaying back and forth against a milky sky.

"We are getting close to liquor store," he says in a voice loud enough for us to hear it over the pounding rain. "It is late." The clock in his car reads 9:35. "I am thinking you will find nothing there. Nobody will be working."

"We still need to go there. We can't wait for the morning."

"You say that already," Sergei mumbles.

Another flash of lightning reveals a building off to the left of the road, maybe fifty yards from us.

"Is that it?" I ask Sergei.

"Yes," he says. "That is liquor store."

"Then shut off your lights!" I snap as another flash of lightning precedes a loud clap of thunder.

"What?"

"Shut off your headlights!" I repeat more forcefully. In front of the building, just off the road, is a dark SUV. "Stop the car!"

Sergei slams on the brakes and shuts off the engine. The headlights go dark.

I lean forward, between the driver's and front passenger's seat and point to the store. "Look! In the building…" Inside the dark building are the intermittent beams of flashlights.

"They're here aren't they?" Bella asks. "Blogis' men. They beat us here."

Lightning rips through the sky and thunder crashes with a percussive *boom*.

"Sergei," I put my hand on his shoulder, "are you good with a gun?"

***

Of all the things I thought to put in my pack, a rain poncho wasn't one of them. My clothes are soaked through, mud sticking to my shoes like glue. I'm cradling the Tec-9 close to my chest, the knee-high weeds slapping against my elbows. The TM-X thermal camera is strapped to my head, the Spyderco knife is in my waistband, along with a little surprise for Blogis' friends.

Bella is still in the Opel. The situation is so unpredictable, I don't want her in the middle of it. Hopefully she's lying down in the back hatch, underneath our bags and hidden from view.

Sergei is reluctantly on the other side of the road, moving parallel to me. He's carrying my six shooter. It's loaded with shot shell, since he informed me that he's not a very good shooter. The spray of the shells will be enough to stun a target if need be, giving me time to finish the job.

He knows that when I reach the driver's side of the SUV, closest to the liquor store, he's to cross the street, crouching low, and stay just behind the front passenger's side tire.

I haven't lowered the night scope yet, afraid that a flash of lightning will blind me. So, squinting against the darkness, I inch to the rear tire of the SUV, pull out my knife, and stab it into the sidewall. The air hisses loudly when I withdraw the blade, the SUV quickly sinking off balance. At the rear tailgate, I reach underneath the SUV, finding the spare tire. I punch the knife upward, jabbing three to four times before moving to the passenger side.

Sergei is hiding behind the front tire as instructed, his back pressed against the twenty-inch aluminum rim. I imagine this will cost me extra.

I punch the other rear tire, pull the blade, and relish the whoosh of air escaping from the tire. The Tec-9 is now strapped onto my back and I use my left hand to balance myself against the side of the SUV, crouching like a baseball catcher to move next to Sergei.

"Your price went up," Sergei whispers into my ear as I stab the tire in the tread to his left.

"To what?" I ask. "I just gave you another two thousand dollars before we got out of your car."

"My shoes are ruined from mud," he looks down at his feet. "These are new shoes. Lots of money."

"Really?"

The dude is about to engage in a firefight, and he's worried about whether or not I pay him to replace footwear barely a notch above a Bass shoe.

He glares at me and licks the rain from his mustache.

"Fine," I relent. "Another five hundred," I offer, "but that's it. I need you to focus."

Sergei wipes his eyes. "Why you poke holes in tires if you kill them?"

"If we don't kill them, it'll stop them from following Annaliese. Got it?"

He nods.

"I'm going back around to the driver's side. After you hear the hiss of the last tire, I'm heading for the building. I want you to follow me, but stay maybe twenty yards back. Once I open fire, you follow me. Stay low against those windows in the front. Then hit the doorway firing. I'll make sure I'm not in your way. Whatever is moving in that building, you aim at it. You've got six shots. Okay?"

"Okay," he says before another flash of lightning jolts both of us into hunching down against the SUV. "Okay," he repeats after the thunder dissipates, "I follow you. What if they kill you? Then what do I do?"

I slap my free hand down onto his shoulder. "You're S.O.L."

"I don't understand. S.O.L.?"

"It means you better run as fast as you can."

Bella has the keys to the car. She knows that if in fifteen minutes we're not back to get her, she's to get out of Dodge.

I check my watch again. "We've got eleven minutes." I slink past him around the front of the SUV. I glance ahead to the building and see the dancing flashlights. They clearly haven't found what they're looking for, which is good.

The rain slaps the leaves and needles high above me, pecks at my skin, before the cold drops travel down my neck onto my back. Closing my eyes, I exhale and focus. I lower the goggles onto my eyes, wiping the lenses clean of fog, power them up, and backhand the knife into the front tread of the last tire. It squeals for an instant before I pull the blade and tuck it into my waistband. The air rushes from the tire and everything slows around me.

I whip the Tec-9 from my back and find the trigger. Six quick strides and I'm within ten feet of the front of the building. There are two large windows to the left, a flimsy door to the right. This close to the building I can hear the men inside. They're speaking Russian, not Ukrainian, and they're angry or frustrated.

There are three distinct voices to the left of the door and behind what I am guessing is the service counter. I'm crouched in front of the door, waiting for the next flash of lightning. I have nine minutes so I pull the surprise from my waistband, holding it tight in my right hand.

***

The smoke grenade takes three seconds to obscure the doorway. Combined with the core-shaking thunderclap that rattled the building, that gives me enough cover to kick in the door and open fire. I'm standing in the doorway, Tec-9 leveled at the counter, my goggles providing enough vision to see three figures moving quickly from left to right.

I pull the trigger, releasing three quick bursts. The figure to the right falls to the ground, wheezing. His flashlight slides across the floor to the right.

After the initial volley, I drop to a knee and slide to the left, away from the entrance. Sergei should be on his way. If I can draw fire away from the door, he'll surprise them through the smoke with shots from the entrance.

There's yelling I can't understand and I pull the trigger again, this time at a figure that seems to be partially hidden behind something. The Tec-9 kicks back against my side and vibrates, its shells popping from the chamber hitting the floor and clanging with the rhythm of the rain pelting the metal roof of the building. There's no return fire.

Through the scope, the pink glow of the man's head jerks back and to one side before disappearing behind the counter. There's only one man remaining and he's moving to the right. I scan that direction. There's some movement and then a bright flash in my eyes that brings searing pain and blindness. I fall to the ground and rip the camera scope from my head, the Tec-9 still strapped over my shoulder bangs against the floor.

He must have turned his flashlight on me!

Even with my eyes closed, a bright red light floods my vision. I'm helpless on the floor, unable to get my wits about me.

"Кто вы?!" Russian He's demanding to know who I am. At least I'm pretty sure that's what he's asking. It sounds similar to Ukrainian. "**Кто вы?!!**" he shouts at me, his flashlight must be aimed right at me. I can only imagine his weapon is too.

My left forearm is folded over my face, covering my eyes, when I feel a thick boot to my right thigh and a barrel poke into my chest. "Три, два…" He's counting down to one.

Pow! Pow! Pow!

I recognize the sound of my Smith and Wesson.

Pow! Pow!

The man standing over me screams, curses. His weapon drops to the floor and rattles. Another squeal, less violent than the scream, a breathless grunt.

Pow! Click. Click. Click.

Sergei is out of ammunition. The third man is silent.

"Sergei!" I try to open my eyes. I can't tell if they're watering or still wet from the storm.

"I'm here," he calls. "They are all dead."

"Do you see me?" Squinting through the pain, I see a shadow hovering over me. "I'm on the floor."

"Yes," he touches me on the arm and grabs for my hand like an arm wrestler. "I pull you up." He heaves me to my feet, my muddy shoes sliding on the floor. I gain my balance on his shoulder.

"Are you shot?" he asks. "Are you hurt?"

"No, I'm just temporarily blinded. I had the night vision on and that last dude hit me with a light. I'll be okay in like ten minutes."

"I see the flashlights," he says. "There are two of them. I get them."

I release my hold on his shoulder. "You need to get Analiese. There can't be but a few minutes left until she knows to leave. Take her a flashlight, then the two of you come back. We'll start looking for what these guys couldn't find."

"Okay," he pats my back. "I do that." He walks away from me and picks up a flashlight before crossing the room to my left.

"Hey, Sergei," I call to the direction of the counter, "thank you for doing what you did. Your timing was perfect."

"No problem." His voice is closer to me than I thought he would be. "But it will cost you more money."

"I know."

"You are good with gun, yes?" he asks. "You kill two of them in head. You were in the dark and killed them both. Neither of them fired a shot. You didn't break any glass. You were perfect."

"Lucky," I reply. "Just good luck."

"You are, how you say in English, *a natural?*" He's moving away from me and toward the door.

"I've heard that before." The cheap door creaks open before slamming shut. I reach out and Frankenstein-feel my way to the counter to my left. It feels like heavy wood and I lean into it, sucking in a deep breath.

Alone, in the dark and unable to see, the rain pounding on the roof has my attention again. It sounds like an endless wave crashing ashore, almost deafening. I pull the sling for the Tec-9 over my head and place the weapon on the counter. I squint again, trying to force my eyesight into focus without luck. I rub my eyes with my knuckles and then run a hand through my hair. It comes away wet and I wipe it on my pants, which are already soaked.

A flash of light seeps through my closed eyes followed by a rumble that vibrates from the counter through my arm and into my spine. Dripping wet, temporarily blind, and exhausted in the middle of a nuclear wasteland, it takes everything in me not to curl up in a ball and quit. I swallow against the lump forming in my throat and squeeze my eyes more tightly shut.

Another three people are dead at my hands. That's more than a dozen since I last got a good night's sleep: the two guys in my apartment, two on the bus, one in London, five or six in Odessa not including our driver, and now the three here.

All of this death because I chose to be an iPod mule for a politician. All of this blood because I chose to stand up for what I thought was right. All of this violence because my life, my freedom, is somehow more important to me than just accepting the death I'm rightfully owed.

It's almost as if no matter which way I turn, I'm destined for violence. From the first time Blair Loxley attacked me at my locker in grade school, this was my path. There is no clean escape. Even the high and mighty Sir Spencer can't make me disappear, unless it's in a shallow grave with a bullet in the back of my head.

A shiver runs from my neck to my lower back. It's as much from the cold setting into my body from the drenching spring rain, as it is a realization that no matter what I accomplish with Bella, my life it what it is. I'm a gun-wielding natural born killer. Pure and simple.

CHAPTER 16

"Can you see me now?" Bella has my eyes held open between her thumbs and forefingers.

"Yes." My eyes sting, fighting the dim light. "It's better."

She lets go of my eyes and I keep them open enough to see. It's been a half hour since she followed Sergei into the store. The rain has stopped, and only the occasional ping from the droplets falling off trees hits the metal roof.

"It's getting late," I say. "I'm good. We need to focus on the task here."

Sergei flips on a light switch near the door. "No need for darkness now," he says.

"Focus?" Bella smirks at me. "Nice choice of words."

"Too soon," I rub my right eye. "Too soon."

She walks around the counter for the first time. "Oh!" She jumps back upon seeing two dead bodies, the color draining from her face. "There were three of them?" She glances back at the Swiss-cheese corpse in the middle of the store.

"Yes. Three. Are you okay with this, or do you want to go back to the car?"

"I'm fine," she says. She steps over the first of the two men. "I'm getting used to this, being around you."

"See what you can find back there," I say. "We're looking for a drive, right?"

Bella nods. "Or a memory card or stick. I don't know how he delivered the pieces. The one I have was retrieved from encrypted email."

"Sergei, are you going to help?" I ask him. "Or will that cost me extra?"

He presses his thin lips into a flat smile and rubs his fingers together like Johnny Manziel. "Five hundred U.S."

I roll my eyes and turn back to the counter. It doesn't appear as though the three henchmen did much real searching. The shelf behind the counter, which extends from the floor nine feet to the ceiling is filled with unopened bottles and closed boxes of liquor.

"They were looking for something specific here," I say aloud to nobody in particular. "Otherwise they would have smashed everything."

"Maybe they didn't want to make any noise?" Bella picks up a bottle of Khortytsa Platinum.

"Sergei, check their pockets please, there may be some clues there."

"Check through dead men's pants?"

"I'm not paying you a dime more. Do it. You're out of ammo and my Tec-9 is not."

"Very funny," he says. "Okay. I check pockets. No charge."

"They were back here looking for something. They had a clue, maybe. A particular bottle."

"Is there an office or back room?" Bella asks, admiring a seven hundred and fifty milliliter bottle of Mernaya Rowanberry. "Maybe they rifled through that."

"Good thought," I agree. "See if you can find something."

Bella runs her thumb along the face of the bottle and replaces it on the shelf at eye level. She nods at me and then steps over the second body toward a dark blue curtain hanging at an opening at the far end of the counter.

"I got phone here," Sergei holds up a cell, wiggling it back and forth. "You want it?"

"Toss it here, please."

Sergei underhands the phone, looping it up into the air and into my hands. He follows it with a self-satisfied smile.

I check the phone, a Droid, and find nothing. There's no call list, no recent calls, no messages, no internet search history. "This is a burner. No help." I throw it on the floor and look back to the untouched bottles when I notice something odd.

Some of the bottles are turned backwards.

"Does this look funny to you?" I ask Sergei as he joins me behind the counter.

He's bent over, trying to find a phone on the second body. He finds one in a pocket and stands up to give it to me. "Does what look funny?"

"Hang on," I check the phone for calls and contacts. Nothing. "Another burner." I toss it on the counter. In the distance there's a roll of thunder. The storm has moved south.

"Does what look funny?" Sergei repeats, his voice a little louder.

"Sorry, these bottles." I point to a grouping of them on the right side of the counter, on the bottom two rows. "They're facing backward."

"I didn't see that before, but, yes. I guess it look funny." He rubs his goatee and nods at the shelf.

"There's nothing back there," Bella announces, coming through the blue curtain. "It's just boxes of liquor. Most of it is untouched."

"What do you mean most of it?"

"There are a couple of boxes that are open," she shrugs. "But there's no broken glass or mess back there. It's a storeroom. A place for extra stock, I guess."

"There's no office? Did you see a phone back there?"

"No," she shakes her head, "why?"

I turn to the bald, capitalist Ukrainian. "Sergei, is there a phone in here?"

"I haven't seen one."

"Why are you asking, Jackson?" Bella says.

"I called this place when we were in Odessa, remember? The guy answered. He was here in the store."

"Yeah," she says. "He could have had a cell that he takes with him."

"I don't think so." I step over a body and push my way past Sergei toward the front door. Next to the door is my pack, which Sergei brought back with him at Bella's suggestion. She thought there might be something in the bag that could help my eyes. There wasn't. But there is a Blackberry.

I fish through one of the exterior pockets, pull out the device we took off the goon in Odessa and walk back to the counter. I power on the Blackberry and hit the call button. It automatically redials the last number, the number for the liquor store. I press the phone to my ear and listen to it ring.

It rings twice before we hear it; a faint analog phone clanging with each ring. There's a phone somewhere in the store!

"Where is that coming from?" Bella's eyes widen. "Do you hear it?"

"It sounds like it's in the wall," Sergei moves toward the liquor shelves. "It *is* coming from the wall."

"Is there a pattern to the bottles that are spun around?" Bella starts picking up bottles. "Maybe the bottles have something to do with the hidden room."

I recall my conversation with the man who answered the phone at the store. He was quick to hang up, but he did mention one vodka by name.

"Honey pepper. The guy on the phone recommended honey pepper vodka."

"What brand?" Bella asks. "There are a bunch of honey pepper vodkas. There's Rada," she bends over to scan the names on the bottles, "First Guild…"

"Nemiroff!" I snap my fingers. "The guy said I should try Nemiroff Honey Pepper." I join Bella, looking for the right bottle. "He said it was hard to find."

"Nemiroff not hard to find," Sergei says. "Very popular. Big seller."

"It was a clue," I said. "I asked him what Dr. Gamow would order."

Sergei pouts his lips in doubt. "You are just—"

"I see it!" Bella points to a shelf a few inches beyond her reach. "That's it right there, isn't it?" She's aiming at an amber-colored rectangular bottle. I overstep a body to reach her and look closer at the bottle, squinting to focus on it.

Vertically along the left side of the bottle reads *Nemiroff* in gold letters. Above that, front and center on the bottle's face are the words *Honey Pepper*, the second *e* decorated with a red pepper. I reach up and grab its neck and try to pull the bottle from the shelf. Instead of lifting the bottle up and away, it pulls forward and down like a lever. Surprised, I let go and the bottle springs back into its upright position on the shelf. From behind the blue curtain to our left, we hear what sounds like the creaking of gears spinning. The sound of the ringing phone grows noticeably louder.

Bella looks at me for an instant before turning and pushing her way through the curtain. "There's a door!" she yells back to us. "It leads to another room! And…"

"And what?" I call to her, tangling with the curtain to get into the storeroom.

"There's someone inside. And he has a gun."

***

The man is sitting on the edge of a cot in the corner of the room. He's aiming his handgun at Bella and me, alternating between the two of us. His hands, gripped tightly around the weapon, are shaking.

"I spoke with you on the phone," I say, my hands above my head. "I'm not interested in hurting you. I don't want you to hurt me."

He stands from the cot without lowering his aim. Slowly, the man, who I'm guessing is in his late sixties/early seventies, crosses the warmly lit room. There is a desk against one wall, with a phone, some picture frames, and a desktop computer. Along the back of the room is a kitchenette with a dorm-sized refrigerator, stove, and a half a dozen cabinets. In the middle of the space is a square table with two chairs beneath a chandelier. The light has space for four lightbulbs but two of the sockets are empty. The man stops at the table and motions for us to join him there.

"We have another person with us," I tell him before stepping into the room.

"He stays out there," the man says. "Just you and the woman."

"Sergei," I call back into the store, "please keep watch out there. We'll be out in a minute."

"Okay," he calls back. "I do that for free."

Bella and I walk to the table, where the man has taken one of the two chairs. I motion for Bella to take the other and stand behind her.

"I'm uncomfortable with that weapon." He motions to the Tec-9 strapped to my back.

"I'm uncomfortable with yours," I respond. "I guess we'll just have to deal with it, right?"

"Deal with it? You mean, we both hold guns?"

"Whatever you say. Like I told you, I don't want any of us getting hurt."

"You want Dr. Gamow," he says. "You wanted Dr. Gamow when you called." His accent is evident, but his English is good. The man's gray hair is cropped close, almost trimmed flat across the top of his head. The trio of lines burrowed across his forehead are deep and set. His eyes are sunken, framed by dark circles and heavy lids. He's clean shaven and dressed in brown corduroy pants and a tan, long sleeved turtleneck shirt. His teeth are too big for his mouth. "Am I right about that, Curtis Eugene?"

"Yes," I nod. "My partner and I are looking for something that didn't belong to Dr. Gamow. It belonged to her." I squeeze Bella's shoulders.

His eyes dart between the two of us. "I know what you want. I know why you are here, why they were here," he waves the gun toward the wall separating his room from the store. "But I don't have what you look for."

"Why are we here then, friend?" I ask. "Why were they here?"

"I am not friend," he shakes his head. "I do not know you or this woman."

"Fair enough."

He coughs, pulling the back of his hand to cover his mouth, and then clears the phlegm from his throat. "Where is Rudolf?" he asks.

"We don't know," says Bella. "We tried to meet with him in Odess—"

"He didn't show up," I interrupt Bella. No need to reveal too much. "Then I called you. When I called, you seemed willing to help. You basically told me about the access to your — what is this place?"

"I live here," he says.

"Why?" Bella asks.

"I have no money to live somewhere else," he says. "Wall comes down, home goes away. Only place I can find work is here. Orange revolution comes and goes and still no job. Rudolf likes vodka. He helps me make home in back room. He helps me make it secret. Rudolf is a good man. He knows I live here. He is the only one."

"Why did you tip me off on the phone?" I question. "You know, with the Nemiroff reference?"

"I didn't tip you," he explains. "I try to sell Nemiroff to everyone. Big margin. Nice money."

"Who are your customers, here in a wasteland?"

"People who live and work here. Lots of people still research Chernobyl. Lots of people drink," he says. "Why do you ask?"

"Because it's odd to me that you'd have a secret home, tucked behind your store. What are you afraid of? Or what was Dr. Gamow afraid of?"

He blinks at the suggestion, his eyes almost imperceptibly narrowing for an instant,. "Nothing," he says. "I was not afraid. I just am poor."

"Men break into your business," I press. "It's late at night. They start snooping around, making noise, looking for something. You had to hear them…"

He nods.

"You don't do anything to stop them?"

"It's many men against me," he says. "I cannot do anything to stop them."

"They knew somehow you had secret room, didn't they?"

"They were looking for a way inside," Bella says. "That's why the bottles were spun."

"Somehow you were warned. You knew we were coming, at least you had to suspect that," I said. "I was straightforward about it. The guy whose phone I used to call you, he'd called too, right?"

He blinks. The gun is still shaking in his grip, despite his elbows being planted on the table.

"He got you to tell him something…"

He blinks again, more rapidly, like he's fighting back tears. "Where is Rudolf?" he asked, his voice breaking.

"They had *Dr. Gamow* call you, didn't they?" I step from behind Bella and around the table. "Then I called you and you began to worry. What did Dr. Gamow say to you on the phone?"

The creases around his mouth deepen, his eyes widen and he begins to sob. He lets go of the gun and buries his face in his arms. Bella's eyes are welling at the sight of this elderly man suddenly heaving with surprising emotion.

I walk to his side and gently place my hand on his back. He flinches at first, then relaxes against the flat of my hand. "I'm so sorry." I look across the room, noticing the framed photographs on the computer desk and it dawns on me.

Both of them are of a couple embracing. In one photo, they are toasting glasses of wine. In the second, the men look maybe a decade younger. They are in a hammock on a beach. One of the people is the man grieving in front of me. The other looks exactly like the images I found on the internet of Dr. Rudolf Gamow.

***

The man grips the bottle of Tonus-Oxygen mineral water like it's the last on the planet, gulping down the last of it and exhaling. I offer to get another bottle from the refrigerator, but he declines. His eyes are red and swollen, his nose glistening on its tip. We don't have time to coddle him, despite his loss.

"I believe you have what we've come to get." I glance at Bella. She's still sitting quietly across from the man, frowning and staring off in the distance. "Tell me what you can. Please?"

"I told him," the man sniffs. "I told Rudolf not to keep in touch with that Wolf. I told him the name fit that man. He was greedy."

"Dr. Gamow or Dr. Wolf?"

"Wolf," the man snaps. "Rudolf was too nice. He was gentle and kind. People took advantage of him. Wolf took advantage of him. I warned him that man was trouble."

"How did he take advantage?"

"They worked together at the Chernobyl decommissioning labs," he says. "There are many scientists and researchers here doing testing. They look at long term radiation impacts. They study everything."

"The labs are here?"

"Yes," he says, "they are maybe three kilometers from here. Not far. George met Wolf there several years ago."

"How did Wolf take advantage of him?"

"Wolf was always arrogant," he says, wiping his nose with the back of his hand. "He would come in here and never ask nicely for anything. 'Give me that!' he would say. 'I want that!' he would command. I never liked him." He shakes his head. "Rudolf told me Wolf was a brilliant man and misunderstood. He said that Wolf was the first man he'd ever met who was so gifted at nuclear physics and engineering. Rudolf looked up to him."

"I hear you saying that bothered you." I sound like my shrink.

"It bothered me only because I had a feeling about that man," he sighs. "He would pick Rudolf's brain and then use his ideas, you know, manipulate him. Rudolf was flattered."

"What happened after Wolf left?"

"Rudolf told me that Wolf was working in France, some underwater telescope, which makes no sense to me. But I am not a scientist. Rudolf, tried to teach me things." He exhales and his shoulders drop. He stares into space, breathing quietly, except for the slight whistle from his nose.

"Dr. Gamow kept in touch?"

"Wolf kept in touch," his stare is fixed elsewhere. "He would send cards or emails. Sometimes he would send complicated problems or formulas to Rudolf and he would work on them. Then maybe a couple months ago, Rudolf comes home, uh, comes here with a package. He says that Wolf visited him at his place in Odessa."

"Rudolf worked in Odessa and here?"

"Yes," he says. "Jobs do not pay much. Rudolf had two. One here at the decommissioning labs and one at a computer company in Odessa. CS Odessa. George is good with computers. He helped with software."

"What happened when Wolf visited him?"

"He gave Rudolf a package," he says. "He said needed it to be kept safe. He told Rudolf that he trusted him and asked him to keep it."

"What was in the package?" Bella asks, suddenly reengaged.

"I don't know," he says. "But I knew it was bad."

"Dr. Gamow didn't tell you what was in the package?" I ask.

"He didn't open it. He says Wolf asked him not to open it, to trust him. He said he would be back for it in a few months, he just needed a hiding place."

"And you believe that Dr. Gamow didn't open it," Bella asks, "didn't sneak a peek inside?"

"Yes." His eyes narrow, eyebrows drawing close together. "I believe Rudolf."

Bella leans forward in her seat.

His eyes widen. "Because I have the package here with me." He looks over to his desk. "It's in the drawer under the desk."

From behind us comes the sound of boxes sliding on the floor. Sergei appears in the doorway to the man's back room, stopping at the wooden frame. "We have a problem," he says. "Security is here."

***

The man hands the package to Bella. His fingers linger on it before he lets go. "You take this," he says. "Whatever it is, I don't want it."

"We need to go," I urge. "Is there another way out of here?"

"No," says the man. "You can go out the front. I will handle this. I know MVS."

"MVS?" Bella echoes.

"Ministerstvo vnutrishnikh sprav Ukrayiny," says Sergei. "The Ministry of Internal Affairs. They are security here."

"There are three dead bodies out there," she says. "What do we do about that?"

"I will handle." He walks gingerly to the table and picks up his gun. "We meet them outside."

We follow one another through the storage room, past the blue curtain, and into the store. Sergei has wisely turned out the lights, but the front door is open. Outside, I can see headlights and a couple of flashlights aimed at the SUV I disabled.

"Maybe they'll leave," Bella says hopefully. "They don't know we're in here."

"They know there are two automobiles out there on the road," says Sergei, "and one of them has four flat tires." He and Bella glare at me simultaneously.

"What?" I shrug. "That was a smart move."

"Let's wait here and see what they do," Bella says. "There's no need to confront them if we don't have to, right?"

I nod in agreement. "That's good. We'll wait here. But if they approach, we need to meet them outside. In the meantime, Sergei, help me move the bodies."

Even in the dark, I sense his distaste for the new assignment. Nevertheless, he trudges over to the first body and grabs the hands. I grab the legs and we grunt our way to the counter. "Let's hide him back here with the others."

We awkwardly round the edge of the counter and drop the body to the floor. The head hits the ground with a sickening crack.

"Do we move others?" Sergei asks.

"They're fine back here," I decide. "They're out of sight for now."

"There is blood on floor," he says. "We cannot hide that. No rugs."

"We'll just deal with it," I hop the counter to avoid falling over the bodies, grabbing my Tec-9 as I jump down. "That's why we'll need to meet—"

"They're coming," Bella says urgently. "What do we do?"

Sergei and I reach the front windows and look out. There are two large, burly men in dark uniforms with reflective stripes across their chests. They're walking side by side toward us, both of them guiding their paths with flashlights aimed just ahead of themselves to the ground.

"We go outside," Sergei pushes the door to open it fully. Then he says loudly to the MVS, "Добрий вечір!" *Good evening!*

The men stop and raise their lights to Sergei, who raises up his arms to block the dual-beams of light in his face. Both men have sidearms at their hips. One of them instinctively has his right hand on his holster, his stance bracing for a confrontation.

"Хто ви?" calls the holster man. He hasn't reached for his weapon.

"He wants to know who Sergei is," I whisper to Bella. We're now crouched low enough to hide beneath the window. The old man is standing at the door, holding his gun. His hand is shaking as it did before.

"Я потребуюсь довідник подорожі котра деяка горілка," Sergei takes a step toward the officers. They yell at him to stop and raise his arms.

"What did he say?" Bella asks.

"He told them he's a tour guide who wanted some Vodka," I translate. "They told him to stop and put his hands up."

"Not good," she whispers.

I quietly pull my pack onto my back. I have the six shooter in the small of my back, but I haven't reloaded it since Sergei emptied it into one of Blogis' goons. My Tec-9 is strapped over my shoulder. It's got plenty of ammo left in the oversized magazine.

Sergei puts his hands above his head, but he protests the treatment.

The officer with his hand at the ready pulls his weapon and steps carefully toward Sergei, "Ви вторгнення." *You're trespassing.* He approaches Sergei and, with his weapon pointed at Sergei's head, shines the flashlight directly in his eyes. He's holding the light with his left hand, his right gun hand leveled on his left arm. "На ваших колінах," he instructs and Sergei drops to his knees, hands still above his head.

"This is not going well," Bella whispers. "What do we —"

"Що являє собою джентльменів проблеми?" The old man bangs through the front door and out into the night asking the officers what they're doing and if there's a problem. The moon makes a brief appearance between thick, dark clouds, illuminating the tension in front of us.

The officer farthest from Sergei draws his weapon and aims his light at the old man, noticing that he's armed. He yells at the old man to drop his weapon, which he doesn't do. Instead he repeats his question, his hand visibly trembling with the gun at his side.

"What's he doing?" Bella nudges me with her elbow.

"I don't know," I reply. "Follow his lead. He's got something planned."

"Ця людина є замовник," he tells them Sergei is a customer.

The guards exchange a glance. "Упускати вашу зброю!" one of them yells. He wants the old man to drop his weapon immediately.

The old man takes a step back, off of the path that leads from the front door to the street. He mumbles something that I can't hear and then he raises the gun above his head, pointing it into the air. Both officers have their weapons trained on him, commanding him to drop the weapon.

The old man looks back toward the liquor store and calls out, in English, "Run now!!"

I grip the Tec-9 with one hand and grab Bella's arm with the other. Running low, like we're avoiding the whirring blades of a helicopter, we bolt past the old man, Sergei, and the two MVS officers before they know what's happening.

As we pass, the old man fires his weapon into the air twice, which is followed by a barrage of gunfire. It sounds like semi-automatic machine pistols. At least fifteen or twenty rounds target the old man. I'm guessing they're using Stetchkin APS handguns. They're large capacity and are in heavy use by a lot of militias in the former Soviet states. That means they've got another twenty rounds at least that they can fire at us.

"Keep going!" Sergei yells from behind us. "Start the car! You have the keys."

I'm two steps behind Bella when we reach the Opel. She fumbles with the keys. There's a burst of gunfire followed by the whizzing of bullets zipping past me. Another burst ends with the driver's side rear window exploding into a spray of glass shards.

Bella screams, covers her head, and ducks into the driver's seat. I turn around, spot Sergei running, zigzagging toward us, and return fire with a quick burst above the officers' heads. I don't need more deaths on my conscience right now. Thunder rumbles in the distance and a gust of cold wind blows through me.

Both of the MVS officers are aiming, one handed, at me. They've dropped their flashlights and it's hard to see them other than the brief flashes from the muzzles of the guns. "Get in the back seat, Sergei!" I yell to him when he reaches the car. He passes my peripheral vision and there's another round of gunfire and he gasps. I turn to see him holding his side, like he's cramping.

"I'm shot!" He struggles to find the handle to the door. His breathing is more rapid, his face contorted.

I return fire again with a short burst and, sidestepping to open the door, push Sergei inside, sliding in behind him before pulling it shut. "Start the car!"

Bella cranks the engine.

With Sergei crumpled on the seat next to me, I turn to the broken window and brace the Tec-9 on the sill. Through the scope, I target the officer who first pulled his gun.

Thump! Thump!

He falls to the ground, grabbing his left foot, and I target the second officer as Bella puts the car into gear and starts driving.

Thump! Thump!

The gun flies from his hand and he leans over grabbing his wrist. Both of them are yelling and cursing at each other.

"Did you kill them?" Bella's reflection in the mirror is flashing blue from the police car in the rearview mirror.

"No. One in the hand, the other in the foot. Both of them will live, but neither of them is coming after us."

"What about the old man?" She glances at me briefly before veering to the right at a V in the road.

"He's dead. Suicide by cop."

"I don't understand why…"

"He had nothing to live for," I tell her. "The love of his life, Rudolf Gamow, is dead. There are three dead bodies in his store. He's living illegally in the back room of a building inside the exclusion zone."

"I get it," she says. "How's Sergei?"

"I don't know. I can't see him."

Bella flips on the cabin light and I can see Sergei's injury. It's not bad. The bullet passed clean through on his left side. It almost looks like an artificial wound. "You'll be okay, Sergei."

I yank open my pack and pull out the survival kit. With my teeth I rip open a package containing an iodine soaked towelette. "This is gonna hurt, Sergei, grab onto something."

He screams when I press the towelette onto the entry wound and wipe. Bella reacts to his cry by jerking the wheel to the right and then overcorrecting. Sergei and I fall into each other and he moans.

"Please keep it on the road, Bella. He's gonna scream again. I'm cleaning the wound."

"Okay," she says, "Okay. Sorry!"

I pull out a sewing kit and some fishing line from the med kit. Incredibly, after knotting the end of the line, I slide the line through the eye of the needle on my second try and then inhale as I get ready to stitch the entry wound.

I slip the needle through his skin and across the wound. Another stitch the other way and tug. The tension closes the wound for the most part and Sergei hisses through his clenched teeth. "Almost done…" I dress the wound with a patch of gauze and medical tape against the flash of a lightning strike.

"Finished?" he whimpers.

"Halfway there." I roll him onto his back.

Sergei's eyes are pressed shut, he's breathing loudly and rapidly through his nose. "Тільки половина шлях?" he asks. There's a flash outside, followed by a loud rumble.

"Yes," I say, "only halfway."

Starting with another iodine wipe, I repeat the process on the exit wound. Then I tell him to open his mouth.

"What?" he asks.

"I'm giving you a painkiller." I pull some pills from tiny Ziploc bags. "And an antibiotic." I drop a ciprofloxacin and two acetaminophen into his mouth and push his jaw shut. "Chew and swallow. Okay, you can turn off the light," I say to Bella. "Do you know where we are?"

"No. I'm just driving."

It is raining again. Large drops pelt the car, and spray in through the broken window to my left.

I grab the passenger seat headrest to pull myself into the front seat of the car. "Sergei, spread out your legs. Rest them on my pack. It'll keep them elevated and help your heart rate."

"How did you know how to do that?" Bella asks.

"Do what?"

"Treat him," she says. "Were you in the military? Were you a medic or something?"

"Nope." We round a slight curve to the right. "I watch a lot of YouTube."

"But you had all of that stuff," she says. "How did you —"

"I've been running for my life for a while now. I'm on my own. I need survival stuff with me. I kinda need to know how to use it." The windshield wipers are waving back and forth as quickly as its motor can push and pull them, but they're no match for the increasing volume of rain falling on us.

"You've done this before? You've cleaned and sewn a gunshot wound?"

"Nope, that was the first time." As we finish rounding the corner, the dense collection of tall trees disappears and we're driving into a clearing. Then lightning flashes again, filling the sky and outlining a series of structures in the near distance, maybe five hundred yards ahead.

"I don't think we're going the right way."

"Why? How do you know this *isn't* the way out?"

"Because," another flash of light, followed by a dramatic *Boom!* and I point straight ahead at the approaching behemoth. "That's reactor number four."

CHAPTER 17

I've reached the saturation point. Really. I'm so drenched and waterlogged that the rain pounding against my head and shoulders doesn't matter. Bella is standing next me, arms folded in front of her as she likes to do, her hair matted to her head. Still, she looks beautiful. We're in a parking lot next to some administrative building facing the reactor and its decaying sarcophagus. From this distance, and without the fogged car windows in our way, we can clearly see the large rectangular shell encasing the radioactive reactor. Protruding from the frame is large single smokestack.

Beyond the reactor in the distance are two unfinished cooling towers. We see them clearly when lightning forks through the sky, reflecting off of the low cloud cover. They must have been under construction when the accident happened, the work never completed.

"What do we do?" Bella's teeth are chattering. "We need to find our way out and Sergei is no help."

"I don't know," I say. "We must be pretty far north. Sergei told us he was entering from one of the southern entrances on our way from Kiev. If I remember correctly, the reactors are toward the northern end of the zone. A little farther north is Pripyat, that abandoned town."

Another lightning strike flashes above us, followed a few seconds later by thunder. I wonder if the rain falling on us is radioactive or in any way acidic. It's too late to worry about it. I've licked my lips, sniffed in the rain under my nose, and gotten enough of it in my eyes to run a microwave if that's the case.

It feels like every pellet stings just a little as it seeps into my pores. It's like I'm becoming Spiderman after the bite, each beat of my heart sending the venom deeper into my veins. I'm no hero, though. Whatever has changed inside of me, happened long before Chernobyl zapped me. And it's not for the better, even if it has made me stronger and more impervious to pain.

"The storm is moving away from us," Bella says. "Should we just keep heading north and try to find our way out?" She wipes some raindrops from her face. "Or should we turn around, now that we know we're north of where we should be."

"If we go back, the MVS is likely going to find us. I don't think we can go back that way."

"All right," she says. "Let's try to find our way out, even though we really have no idea where we are and the GPS on my phone doesn't help. For all I know, we'll end up in Belarus."

"Wait a minute." I could kick myself. "I've got a Garmin in my pack. I just have to punch in GPS coordinates."

"Are you kidding me, Jackson? We could've used that about twenty minutes ago."

"Yeah," I shoot back, "I was kinda busy stitching up Sergei. Cut me some slack."

"Let's get out of here," Bella huffs. "Now that we have some guidance, we can find our way out of this hell hole."

I jump into the front passenger seat and reach around to the back. The pack is underneath Sergei's legs, but I'm able to reach into the top compartment and pull out the Garmin and a handful of shot shell. He's asleep or unconscious, his chest heaving up and down. I punch the MENU button on the left side, then cycle through to find our current coordinates.

51.390704 LAT 30.094278 LONG

"Great," she says. "Now we know where we are. Jackson, we need to know where we need to be."

"It needs to know where we are to help us figure out where to go. "Belarus won't work, as much I'd like to head that direction. I'm still on an American passport and don't have a visa for Belarus. Sergei may not have his passport either."

"We need to get back to Kiev, right? Why don't we just head there?"

"I've got to map us to a point that's not directly south before we head back to Kiev," I explain. "Or as I already said, we head right back to the MVS. I'm scanning the map for a town west of here. East won't work. There's a river we can't cross." Another flash of lightning sparks in the sky, but it's dimmer, farther off in the distance.

"I found it," I say. "We'll head to Ovruch. It's two hours west of here."

"That's a long way," Bella protests. "We're not going that far. About halfway there is the P02 highway. We'll catch that and then head south and east all the way into Kiev."

I punch in the route and the Garmin tells us to turn right and then right again almost immediately. "In about one point three kilometers, we're going to turn left. That's maybe two or three minutes from now."

My eyes are focused on the color screen of the Garmin, watching our coordinates change and our position on the road move incrementally when Bella accelerates rapidly, pushing me back against my seat.

"We have company," she blurts. "Somebody is following us. A couple of somebodies. And they're gaining on us."

***

Bella's not following the GPS. She's trying to outmaneuver the twin MVS patrol cars speeding behind us. As soon as she pressed on the gas, they flipped on their blue strobes atop their cars. Now they're running beside each other, the one on the left is trying to pull even with us.

"Which way do I go?" she asks. "What do I do, Jackson?"

"Keep your eyes on the road. I'll handle it." I slap open the revolver's cylinder and start thumbing in shot shell.

Bella takes a quick turn to the right without decelerating enough. The rear tires spin out from behind the Opel, screaming on the wet asphalt, and she corrects by spinning the wheel to the left. Somehow, she regains control of the car, but the inertia slams my body into the door, while Sergei falls into the space between the front and back seats, crying out in pain and cursing in Ukrainian.

"Keep us on the road!" I pick up the pistol from the floorboard at my feet, find a couple of the shot shells, and load them. I've got five shots. "I'm going to give us some distance," I jump into the back seat.

The clouds are clearing again, and the moon peeks through enough for me to see the cars pursuing us. Both of them are white Toyota Priuses. *Priuses!!* There's a pair of officers in each car. I pull myself out of the open window behind Bella, lay on my side facing backward toward the cars.

The one to the left is almost even with our rear tire. As I take aim, both men in the car lock eyes with me and panic. I fire once at the front left tire and the driver slams on the brakes.

Miss!

He overreacts and loses control of the car. It weaves back and forth, sideswiping the car behind us before spinning out into the high grass on the right side of the road.

One down. One to go.

The second car is right behind us, with a fresh dent along its driver's side. The driver's riding the edge of the road and I can't get off a good shot from this position, so I duck back inside the car and climb into the front seat.

"Please put your belt back on," Bella pleads and I oblige her, snapping the buckle. "I'm gonna speed up again and turn at the next intersection."

Bella accelerates again, trying to find some space between us and the Prius.

"Turn right. That'll give me a clear shot."

"Are you kidding me?" she asks. "This is not an action movie, Jackson."

"I've done this before and it worked."

"Why doesn't that surprise me?"

"Just focus on the road. You're doing a great job."

She nods and glances in the rearview mirror. "Good thing this is an automatic," she chuckles nervously. "I never learned how to drive a stick."

I push the button to lower my window. Standing water from the rain sprays up past the side view mirror as the front tires plow through it. "There's an intersection up ahead."

"I see it." She leans into the wheel, squinting past the beads of water on the windshield. She grips the wheel and I loosen my belt enough to twist and brace my right arm on the door.

Bella takes her foot off the accelerator, taps the brakes, and spins the wheel to the right.

The back half of the Prius slides into view from right to left, exposing the right rear tire.

Pow! Pow! Two quick blasts aimed down and to the right explode into the tire when the driver slowed to make the turn with us. The tire explodes and the car wobbles before flipping left side over right, tumbling into the intersection and following us before crashing into a culvert on the other side of the road. Bella speeds up and I pull my arm into the car, untwisting myself from the seatbelt.

Her eyes are wide, a big smile plastered on her face. "Did you see that car flip over like that? I thought it was going to slam onto the back of our car." She laughs nervously, bouncing in her seat.

"I saw it." I pop the pistol into the glovebox at my knees. "Now we need to figure out where we are." The Garmin screen glows with our coordinates. *51.091671 LAT 29.585544 LONG*

"I know where we are." She slows the hatchback to a crawl. "We're in a graveyard."

The hulking shells of Soviet-era trucks and helicopters surround us. Row after row of rusted metal, parked as if it were an abandoned military dealership. The emptiness of it puts a knot in my stomach.

"Pull the car in between those two trucks," I point over to the right. "We need to hide for a second while I figure out how to get us back on track."

Bella turns to the right and slows to a stop. She puts the car in park and shuts off the engine.

My focus returns to the Garmin and I punch in *Ovruch*. The screen repopulates with directions to the west and the highway that'll take us back to Kiev.

"Do you hear that?" Bella asks.

"Hear what?"

"Silence," she says. "Total silence."

She's right. I close my eyes and listen. Aside from Sergei's heavy mouth-breathing, there's nothing; no gunfire, no engines revving, no sirens, just silence.

It figures. The first peaceful moment I've had in the last couple of days, and it's in the middle of an irradiated graveyard at the site of the world's worst nuclear disaster.

***

It's three o'clock in the morning when Bella pulls the car into the parking lot in front of the Hyatt Kiev.

"We don't have rooms," she points out.

"Not a problem. We'll manage."

Sergei is sitting up in the back seat. His face looks almost translucent, but otherwise he appears okay. The two bottles of water we gave him after a fuel stop have helped his energy.

"This is where we say goodbye," I tell him.

"You're leaving me here?" he asks, his eyebrows knitted.

I reach into the glovebox and pull out the pistol. "Yes, him and ten thousand dollars."

"But he's hurt," Bella says, glancing back at him. "He needs to get to a hospital."

"He's not going to a hospital," I say and then turn to face Sergei. "You're not going to a hospital, right?"

"No," he says.

"Sergei flies under the radar," I tell Bella. "Going to a hospital puts him squarely in the middle of it. Plus, and no offense to you Sergei, we don't have time to deal with him. We need to get ourselves to Germany as quickly as we can. Helping Sergei beyond paying him for his trouble is out of the question."

Bella runs her tongue along her top teeth, thinking about what I've said. "Okay," she says. "I get it. Sergei, thank you for everything." She hops out of the car and goes around the back to pop the hatch and grab her bag before heading into the hotel lobby. She turns and waves to him as she spins her way through the entrance.

"Can you drive?" I ask him.

"I can drive," he says, his attention on Bella as she disappears. "I just thought…"

"Thought what?"

"That you would take me with you to Germany." He looks down at his lap, his bald head staring at me.

"Really?"

"I thought we are good team." He lifts up his head. "You, me, and Bella Francesca Buell."

"Her name is Analiese," I correct him with a wink. "She's from Switzerland and speaks native French, remember?"

"Right," he smirks before wincing from what I imagine is lingering pain. "Do you think I would help you without knowing who you are, Jackson Quick?"

"Not really," I admit. "I can't take you with us though."

"Why not?"

"You're too expensive," I laugh. "And you're hurt."

Sergei smiles and slides to the rear passenger door, pulling the handle to get out. I hop out of the front seat to assist him.

"You sure you can drive?"

"I'll be okay. It's not far from here to my doctor. He's in Troeshna."

"That's not a great part of town is it?"

"Not good place." He lowers himself into the driver's seat with a grunt. "But he is good doctor."

"Be safe."

"A little late to tell me that." He starts the engine and gingerly pulls on his seatbelt.

"Thanks again, *Lisi*."

"Ha! Good one, Jackson Quick. I guess we are friends." He rubs his bald head with spread fingers.

I open the rear door to grab my pack, stuff the pistol into the top, and break down the Tec-9 to cram it into the bag, then yank my pack from the seat. "I'm good."

As I shut the door, Sergei is already pulling away from the hotel, merging into what's left of the late night traffic and driving off to his doctor, or wherever he's really going. Chances are his "doctor" is some black market pill pusher who has little or no medical training. Sergei will pay him cash, get cleaned up, and secure a month's worth of pain killers.

Then he'll hide until he's better, until he's certain that the MVS isn't coming for him. He'll sleep with a gun under his pillow and have a go-bag stashed in his closet. I pity him for a second, telling myself I wouldn't want to be in his shoes.

I'm pushing my way into the hotel lobby when I realize, a second later than I should have, that he's actually in *my* shoes, living the same Spartan existence I've come to accept as normal.

"Jackson," Bella calls from the front desk, snapping me from my funk. "I mean, Eugene," she corrects, waving at me. "I've got some good news."

We're the only two people in the lobby other than the front desk clerk. He's a tall, thin man in his forties. He's all business, and his teeth are ridiculously yellow.

"Yes?" I smile at Bella as I lean on the front desk. "What's up Analiese?"

"They have a shuttle that can take us to the airport within the hour. And this gentleman…" she turns to the dour clerk. "I'm sorry, your name again?"

"Viktor," he burps.

"Viktor here, is willing to let us clean up in a room while we await the shuttle's arrival."

"And how much does *Viktor here* expect to receive for his kindness?" I'm talking to Bella, but looking at the Munster behind the desk.

"A room is three hundred sixty eight dollars U.S.," he says. "Plus taxes."

"Right," I nod. "But how much are you charging us?"

"A room is three hundred sixty —"

"Viktor, we both know you're pocketing whatever we pay you. We're going to be in the room for, like, an hour. So how much. In cash. U.S.?"

His eyebrows move, almost impossibly, without any other change in expression.

"Never mind," I tell him. "Let's go catch a cab," I tell Bella and grab her hand.

She stands her ground at the counter. "I really need a shower… Eugene."

"We'll get you one, now let's go." We get halfway to the front entrance.

"One hundred dollars U.S.," Viktor calls out. "One hundred only," he repeats as we turn back around.

"Deal," I smile. Everyone in this country must think a one hundred dollar bribe is the going rate. It's like Dr. Evil in the Austin Powers movies thinking that 'ONE MILLION DOLLARS!!' is a ridiculous amount of money.

I pay the money and tell Bella to go ahead.

"You're not coming?"

"I've got some phone calls to make. I'll stay down here and wait for the shuttle."

"You can make the calls in the room," she says. "I won't eavesdrop."

"First," I walk with her toward the elevator, "you *would* eavesdrop. You've demonstrated many times that you're not trustworthy, right?"

"Jackson, that's not fai—"

"And second, I'm likely to sneak a peek at your computer while you're not looking. So…"

"Jackson," she protests, "I already apologized for that. I'm not upset. Why are you being so sensitive?"

"I'm not sensitive," I lie, "I'm pragmatic."

She sighs as the elevator doors open to our right. "I'm disappointed. I thought we were past that. I thought we had an understanding that, while neither of us is the most forthright person in the world, we could work together for the common good. We're on the same team, really."

"I guess," I shrug. "Right now, I've got some phone calls to make, and I need some privacy. I'll see you down here when you're cleaned up."

"Okay, then." She steps into the elevator and pushes a button to her floor. The doors begin to close and she smiles in a way that contradicts the look in her eyes.

She's hurt.

***

I was playing in the front yard of our two-story red brick home. There were two large scrub oaks that made for a fantastic soccer goal. I wasn't much of a player, despite my speed and endurance, but I liked pretending I was a professional soccer star in make-believe World Cup matches always won on a blast in the final moments of stoppage time.

It was fall, I remember, and there were large, crispy leaves fanned out across the faded green grass separating our house from the street. They crunched under my feet as I danced with the black and white vinyl ball from one end of the yard to the other, cones from the lone pitch pine no match as defenders on my way to a certain score.

The score was tied one apiece with the clock at a full ninety minutes. I tapped the ball ahead and spun around, faking out my invisible Brazilian foe. Then, just ten feet from the goal, my left foot planted and my right foot delivered an arcing shot, bending to the left, and bouncing off the inside of the left oak. Goooooooallllllll!

I dropped to my knees, eyes closed, fists pumping in the air, imagining my teammates running to dog pile on top of me in celebration.

"Nice shot," a voice from the street said, shaking me from my daydream. My eyes popped open to see a man in a long, dark wool coat. Reflective aviators hid his eyes. He was standing behind the hood of his car, a black BMW sedan.

I pushed myself up, feeling a slight pinch in my knee, and started to walk toward the car. "Uh. thanks. Can I help you?" I stopped close enough to study the man, but far enough away that I could outrun him to my house if need be.

"I'm here to see your dad," he said in a uniquely deep voice. His hands were buried in the pockets of his coat. He stood with his shoulders back, legs apart. "I'm Frank, a friend from college."

"I'll go get him." I turned to run to the house, leaving my ball and imaginary teammates in the yard.

Before I could pull open the storm door, my dad appeared at the entry and pushed his way to the front stoop. "Go inside, Jackson," he said firmly, his gaze across the yard to the man at the curb.

"Dad, he's says he's —"

"Go inside, Jackson!" He put his hand on my shoulder and guided me forcefully past the open storm door and into the house. "We'll talk about this when he's gone."

My dad closed the storm door and marched toward the man at the BMW. The man hadn't moved. His hands were still buried in his pockets, his stance broad and confident.

I stayed at the doorway, watching the exchange between them. My father had his hands on his hips. His back was to me and he was partially blocking his visitor.

My mom joined me at the door from the kitchen. She wore a dishtowel on her shoulder and she smelled like garlic.

"I don't know. The guy, Frank, said he went to college with Dad."

"Hmmm." My mom put her hands on my shoulders. "Frank? I don't recognize him. I knew most of your dad's college buddies."

My dad started pointing at the man, who stayed perfectly still on the other side of his car. He was clearly irritating my dad, who was upset at either the man's presence or the reason for it. I couldn't tell which.

The angrier my father appeared, the more the man sank into his stoicism. He was clearly defiant. Even when he wasn't speaking, he was in control. I was a kid and could sense it. So could my mom.

"It looks like your dad isn't too fond of his college buddy," she said. "I'm going to go see what this is about. We don't need a scene in front of the neighbors."

My mom patted my shoulders and then, dish towel and all, walked across the yard to my father. The man's attention turned to her as she approached, causing my father to turn around.

My father said something to her, the man nodded a greeting to my mom, and then she turned around and walked back. She smiled at me and rolled her eyes in an attempt to ease my concern.

I opened the door for her and she stepped up to come back inside the house. "What did they say?"

"Oh," she said. "It's nothing, I suspect. The man is working with your father on some work project and he came by to discuss it. It was urgent."

"He said he was a college friend. He didn't tell me he worked with Dad."

"Well…maybe they did go to school together and also work together."

"Seems kinda weird," My gaze fixed on the man and his BMW. "That guy isn't who he says he is."

"Oh, Jackson." My mom laughed nervously. "You have such a fabulous imagination. You really do. Your dad is irritated because he doesn't want to be bothered at home."

"Really? He's always bothered with work. We could be on vacation in Wyoming and he's bothered with work."

"True, but —"

"Mom, I'm just saying that something's not right, that's all."

"You're certainly entitled to your opinion, son. But don't be disrespectful about it, okay?"

"Okay," I relented. "But let me ask again for, like, the thousandth time, what exactly does Dad do?"

"He's a technology consultant," Mom said firmly. "He works with computers. You know that. Why are you asking?"

"Do technology consultants get visits from weird guys at their homes?"

My mom purses her lips like Dana Carvey's Church Lady character and narrows her eyes. "They must," she said with a head tilt, "because your father has a weird guy visiting him right now. Now go wash up. Dinner's almost ready."

I didn't buy it. I turned back in time to see the man slide into the driver's seat of his BMW and make a U-Turn before speeding off the way he came. My dad watched the man drive off. Then he turned around, face red, and stomped back toward the front door. That was my cue. I bolted for the bathroom to wash my hands and face.

Dinner conversation was bound to be awkward.

***

"George," I say quietly into the burner phone, "it's me." I'm sitting in a corner chair in the Hyatt Kiev lobby. Bella's upstairs in a room we have for an hour.

"Jackson?" says the reporter. "I don't recognize the number. Again."

"That's how I roll," I joke.

"What do you need?" The sound of the newsroom is buzzing behind his voice. I can hear police scanners beeping. There's a loud burst of static followed by someone, presumably on the assignment desk, yelling out instructions.

"Working late?"

"As usual," he says.

"I thought investigative reporters had it easy," I tease. "One story every three months. Nice lunches every day, in at noon and home by five…"

"Right," he laughs. "I'd like that gig. But really, Jackson, what's up? Are you onto something that might mean I have to turn an extra story this quarter?"

"Maybe."

"So…?"

I'm distracted by a suited man stumbling into the lobby with a much younger woman on his arm. She's wearing a dress too tight and too revealing for a woman not expecting money on a dresser at the end of the night. He's pressing his finger to his lips, spitting *Shhhh!* as the woman giggles from obligation.

"Jackson?" he asks. "You there?"

"Yeah, sorry about that. I, uh, I need you to look up another person for me."

"What about the information I already gave you?"

"What about it?"

"What's the connection between Don Carlos Buell's daughter and neutrinos? What is Nanergetix involved in? Are they into nuclear stuff now?"

"Yes," I answer after a pause. "This is off the record for now and I'll deny it if you tell anyone about it."

"Okay."

"Are you recording me?"

Silence.

"George?"

"It's off now."

"Look, this is a complicated deal. Somehow, Nanergetix came up with a way to harness solar neutrinos and use them to detect hidden nuclear reactors." I'm not ready to tell him everything, but I want to whet his journalistic appetite enough that he'll play along.

Ultimately, George Townsend is all about the story, the exclusive get, and he'll help me if he thinks there's another Peabody, DuPont, or even Emmy in it for him.

His fingers are thumping on a keyboard. "How and where?"

"In a secret underground lab, and the scientist who perfected it is dead."

"How are you mixed up in this?" Good question.

"The process by which the neutrinos are harvested and then directed at the nuclear reactors is missing. Bell— Nanergetix hired me to find it."

"That doesn't make any sense. Why would Buell's daughter, with whom you are on a first name basis, hire *you*? You have no commensurate experience, right? Plus, her dad wanted you dead, the last I remember."

"That's complicated," I say. "She has her reasons."

"Okay. Say she does. Why are you helping *her*? That's maybe the better question."

"I have my reasons too."

"Whatever," he sighs. "Seems to me you're a masochist."

"Maybe," I tell him. "But I'm not the story. The story is this technology and that it's missing."

"It's off the record, right? It's not a story if I can't tell it."

"Well, if you help me, I can help you tell it."

"What does that even mean?" George sounds irritated.

"If it works out, and we find what we need to find, I might be able to get Bella to talk to you about it, how this could help the world."

"I'm listening…" He sounds less irritated.

"If we fail, if the process ends up in the wrong hands, there's no story. Bella won't talk about it. I won't talk about it. The biggest story of your career, bigger than putting the governor behind bars, goes *Poof!*"

"If you fail, will you be alive to talk to me?"

"I don't know."

"How can I help you, so that you can help me?"

"I need to know anything and everything you can find out about Liho Blogis."

"Who?"

"A man named Liho Blogis."

"Any other information for me?" He's typing. "Date of birth, social security number, last known address, anything?"

"Nope. He's connected to Sir Spencer Thomas though."

"The dude who kidnapped you?"

"Yes."

"You know he's almost like a ghost, right? We've been through this before. There's virtually nothing about him in public records, news archives, anything. If this Liho Blogis guy is connected to him, then he's probably a ghost too."

"Maybe. But I need whatever you can find. Your story depends on it."

"Okay," he says. "I'll get to work on it."

"Thanks, George."

"By the way, where are you?"

"Kiev."

"Really?"

"Yep. I'm headed to Germany in a couple of hours. I need the information when I get there."

"I'll see what I can do," he says, "but I can't make any promises."

"Just do it." I end the call and check my watch. The van should be here any second.

"Viktor," I call across the lobby to the glum Sleestack behind the counter. "I need your help." I slug my pack to the check-in desk.

"Yes?" His right eyebrow is arched.

"I need to ship something valuable to Germany, and I need it there immediately. Can you help me with that?"

"I can arrange for a DHL pickup. I have a shipping box in the back and they usually come for pick up around six o'clock in the morning."

"How much?"

"For the shipping?" He smirks.

"For everything."

"When do you need it there?"

"Immediately."

"Immediately is expensive."

"I'm sure it is, Viktor. Just let me know the damage."

"What are you shipping?"

"Does that matter?"

"Yes. If it's something you cannot take on a plane with you, then I am certain it will add to the expense."

"Personal protection," I say. "It's the sort of protection that airport security frowns upon."

He tilts his head, cracking his gooseneck. "It'll be five hundred dollars."

"U.S.?"

"Of course."

"What's my guarantee it gets there?"

"I put my name on the shipping voucher," he says. "I have friends who make sure it gets to you."

"Okay then. Give me the box, please. I'll pack it. You ship it. You get the money."

"Okay then," he mimics. "Where do you want this package to go?"

"I'd like to send it to Frankfurt and pick it up right after we land. Can you get the package there —"

"Immediately," he interrupts.

"Yes, thank you."

"There is DHL Packstation fifteen minutes north of the airport. I give you the address. You will find it no problem. Maybe it is there when you land. Maybe a little later."

He disappears through a door behind the desk and then emerges a minute later with a box and some packing material.

"You're prepared," I remark. I reach down into my pack to pull out the Smith & Wesson and the Tec-9.

"We have lots of business people," he says. "They have business needs."

I pull the box down onto the floor next my bag. I don't want to pull the weapons up onto the desk, and freak out Viktor. Both weapons fit neatly into the box, the ammo sitting in the gaps between the gunmetal and the cardboard. I pour a bag of Styrofoam kernels into the empty spaces, fold the box closed, and run a strip of tape down the middle.

"I will label for you." Viktor takes the box from me and slides it across the desk. "Now I need the money."

I pull his payment from the bag. My once fat roll is slimming down a little faster than I'd like.

"What's the money for?" Bella asks, coming up behind me as I am thumbing five one hundred dollar bills. Her hair is pulled back against her head, still wet from a shower. Her face is clean, without makeup except for a little lip gloss.

"I can't take certain belongings on the plane to Germany," I explain. "I'm arranging alternative transportation with Viktor here."

"Good idea," she says. "I have something I need you to add to the box. Is it too late?"

CHAPTER 18

"Bella, you actually did a great job getting us out of Chernobyl." I'm walking beside her in the Frankfurt Airport, trying to navigate the yellow, blue, and green overhead signs.

"Gee, thanks," she says. "Coming from you, that's *such* a compliment." She presses her palm flat against her chest, feigning appreciation.

"That's not exactly what I meant. I didn't intend for it to come out that way. I'm just saying you really did impress me."

"Okay, Jackson," she says, "I'll take it as the compliment you intended it to be."

We haven't really talked much since leaving Chernobyl. The drive back to Kiev was filled with silence, both of us too tired to carry on a meaningful conversation. The ride to the airport was in a shuttle with a couple of other hotel guests, so we weren't going to talk then. Both of us slept on the flight from Kiev to Frankfurt. It was the best two and a half hours of sleep I've had since waking up in my apartment three, or is it four, days ago. I can't keep track.

"We need a rental car," I say. "Once we clear customs and have our bags, I'll find a place to get one."

"How are you on cash?" She squeezes past me into the single file line at immigration.

"Getting low. I have enough for a few more days. We'll be okay."

"This won't last a few more days. It's going to be all over a lot sooner than that." She takes a step forward in the line.

"How would you know that?"

"I don't *know*." She starts to run her hand through her hair before remembering it's pulled back into a ponytail. "I'm just figuring that Blogis is already here. He's got a piece of the process. We've got two piece—"

"Speaking of which, we haven't looked at the gift we got in Chernobyl. We don't know what that is, right?"

"I looked at it." She takes another step closer to the red-vested immigration officer.

"When did you do that?"

"In the hotel room," her eyes dart to the floor, "when you were downstairs."

"Well?"

"It's a hard drive," she says, "and the only thing on it is a piece of the process."

"Really?"

"Yes."

"When were you going to tell me this?"

"I just did," she shrugs. "I wasn't keeping it from you, if that's what you're suggesting."

"Whatever." I shake my head.

"C'mon, Jackson…"

"It doesn't matter. So what's left of the process? Now that we've got two pieces and Blogis has one, as you said."

"Well," she says, "I can't tell, by looking at the information I have, which two pieces we have. So there's no way for me to know what's left."

"Sir Spencer seemed to think there was maybe one piece left."

"I guess that's possible," she acknowledges. "We'll figure that out when we get to Heidelberg. Here," she hands me her phone, "take a look at this."

"What is it?" I'm staring at a screen full of mathematical equations.

(v-c)/c = fÂt /(TOFfc − fÂt) = (2.48 } 0.28 (stat.) } 0.30 (sys.)) ~10-5.î h ∂ ϕ(r;t)=Hϕ(r;t) (1) ∂t

p^2c2 + m2c4 (2) ∂22224 î h∂tϕ(r;t)= ‾h c ⊠ +m c ϕ(r;t) (3)

2∂2 22 2 24−‾h∂t2ϕ(r;t)=−‾hc⎸⎸+mc ϕ(r;t) (4)1 ∂2 2 m2c2

c2∂t2−⎸‾+‾h2 ϕ(r;t)=0 (5) 1∂2 2

2 = c2 ∂t2 − ⎸⎸ (6) (h‾ = c = 1) 2 + m2 ϕ(xµ) = 0

(7)∂2 . ∂2 −‾h2 ϕ(x; t) = −‾h2c2 + m2c4 ϕ(x; t) (8)∂t2 ∂x2

2 ∂2 2−‾h ∂t2 ϕ(t) = E ϕ(t) (10)

"It's a screen shot of the process piece."

I hand back the device. "It's gibberish."

"Sure, but's it's part of the process. I recognize some of the equations. They're similar to the work in the other part I have."

"Why are you showing me this?"

"I don't know. I guess I don't want you thinking I'm keeping stuff from you, that's all."

"Fair enough. Hey, it's your turn." A thick, squatty woman in a red vest and short sleeved white shirt waves for Bella to step to her counter.

"See you on the other side," she smiles.

An Aryan looking man with a crewcut and thin wire-rimmed glasses calls me to his space. "Guten Morgen," he says, looking at me over the tops of the glasses.

"Good morning." I hand him my passport.

He takes the document and opens it to the identification page, "You are American…Mr. Curtis?"

"Yes, I am."

"Welcome to Germany," he says without looking at me. He references the passport while typing something into his computer. "Why is it you are visiting us here in Frankfurt?"

"Business."

"What kind of business?" He continues to type, but glances over at me, studying me.

"I'm a technology consultant. I work on computers."

He spins his chair to face me. "Where is your computer then?"

"I don't carry my own computer with me. I use whatever hardware the client provides. I'm on terminals so much during the work day, I need a break at night. So I don't usually carry my laptop with me on trips."

"What kind of laptop?"

"Excuse me?"

"What kind of laptop do you have?" His eyes narrow and he leans forward.

"Oh," I say, "A Macbook Pro. Fifteen inch."

He returns to his computer. "How many days will you be here in Germany?"

"I'm not sure," I tell him. "It all depends on the client. It could be a couple of days or a couple of weeks."

"You are aware," he informs me, "that if your stay exceeds ninety days, you will need a visa?"

"I don't expect to be here that long."

He looks at me for a moment past the point of being comfortable, tilts his head, and then punches the stamp into my passport. "Willkommen in Deutschland, Mr. Curtis."

"Danke," I thank him and move past him to find Bella and baggage claim.

***

The DHL Packstation is on a narrow residential street in what looks like an apartment building. I pull the Citroen Cactus into a curbside spot, working hard to spin the odd-shaped steering wheel back and forth.

"I'll be right back," I tell Bella. "The package should be here."

Bella is sitting in the passenger seat, her belt strapped across her chest, thumbing through her phone. "Okay," she says.

The building is an off-white stucco or plaster with a series of four-paned windows trimmed in taupe. To the left of the building there are nicely manicured hedges that wrap the corner to the intersecting street. Centered along the building's main entrance are a dozen wide concrete steps leading to a landing which runs maybe thirty feet across. There's a woman walking a pair of shepherds down the steps past me as I climb to the landing. She ignores me, more concerned with not tangling herself in the dogs' retractable leashes.

Next to the main entrance, which is a large glass and chrome door, there's a narrow glass door leading to the Packstation. Above the door there's a yellow sign which reads *DHL - 3 Furstenbergerstrasse 60322*. This is the right place.

I pull the chrome handle and swing the door open to a rush of cool air. Inside the fluorescent room is a high counter, a couple of chairs, a display rack of greeting cards, and a wall length case stuffed with shipping materials.

"Guten tag!" says the cheerful young woman behind the counter. "Wie kann ich Ihnen helfen?"

"Ich spreche nicht Deutsch. Ich spreche Englisch," I respond sheepishly, telling her that I speak English, not German.

"I speak English," she says. "It is not a problem. May I help you?" Her English is good, though peppered with the throaty crispness of her native language.

"Yes, please," I tell her and hand her my packing slip.

She looks at the slip and then at a printout on her side of the counter. She runs her finger down the page and then back up toward the top. "I don't see that it is here," she says with a sympathetic frown. "I will check in the back. We may have gotten it within the last few minutes."

"Thank you." I lean against the counter with my elbows. There's a clock directly above the door through which the clerk disappears. It's eleven o'clock in the morning. It feels like midnight. My stomach has the jitters and my eyes are burning from fatigue. I notice a coffee maker on the far side of the room, beyond the spinning display of greeting cards, so I trudge over to the half-full pot and pour some of it into a white Styrofoam cup.

The cup is warm in my hands, the steam pouring from the top as I take a quick slurp. It's strong coffee, and hot enough to singe the tip of my tongue and the roof of my mouth.

I blow on the cup, rippling the coffee, and walk back to the counter. The woman reappears from the back carrying the box I packed at the Hyatt Kiev a few hours ago.

"It just arrived." She dumps the box onto the counter with a cute grunt. "It wasn't put into our arrival system yet."

"Thank you." I reach for the box.

"I see you found our coffee." She motions with her eyes to the steaming cup. "It is typically too hot."

"Yeah," I run my tongue on the roof of my mouth, "I found that out. Thank you anyhow." I take the box and slide it under one arm while grabbing the coffee with my other. "Do I need to do anything else?"

"No," she says. "Thank you for using DHL."

I turn, with my arms full, and awkwardly find my way to the door, back into it, and push myself out onto the landing into the warm air, a muggy contrast to the overly-air conditioned office. I walk down the steps, blowing on the cup and taking another scalding sip of bitter caffeine, and step to the curb. Where I parked the car, there's a gray Audi.

Confused, I scan the cars along the curb and farther down the street to a white four-door hatchback.

I must have parked farther away than I thought.

That white car, however, is a Volkswagen, not a Citroen.

What the —? Did Bella leave me here? She's got my pack with my money, my supplies…

The burner phone in my pocket buzzes.

Still looking for my car, I put the box on the ground at my feet and fish for the phone.

"Hello?" I press the phone to my ear without looking at the screen. "Bella?"

"Jackson?" It's Bella, her voice quivering. *"Are you there?"*

"Bella, where are you? Why did you —?"

"Jackson, I need you to —" Her voice is suddenly muffled, replaced with a deeper, guttural voice.

"Jackson Quick?" A man's voice.

"Yes. Where's Bella?"

"I have her with me," he says. "She does not have with her the thing I need."

"Who are you?"

"You know who I am," he says.

"Why don't you just come and get whatever it is you need?" There's a cell phone on the edge of the sidewalk near the curb. "Why play this game?" It's Bella's phone, with the familiar floral Vera Bradley case. The screen is shattered. The Tile app won't find her this time.

"I am not careless, Jackson," he says. "You are clearly a dangerous man, and it would not be wise for me to attack you in daylight, in front of a building with security cameras. I weighed the odds and took Bella."

"That doesn't make any sense." I kneel down to rip open the top of the box, tossing the coffee to the cobblestone sidewalk. "You could've ambushed us both. Obviously you knew where we were and what we were doing."

"Jackson," the Barry White deep baritone chides, "you are dangerous but not experienced. Why would I risk taking both of you in an uncontrolled environment, when I don't know whether or not you have the process in your possession? You could die, she could die, and then I don't get what I want."

I pull out the Tec-9, reassembling it before loading the magazine. The woman with her dogs walks by, shooting me a disapproving look as she climbs the steps to the building.

"If I take the opportunity to relieve you of your partner," he continues, "then I can control the time and place you bring me the pieces of the process I desire. More control, more success."

"You're picking your spots." I pull the Tec-9's sling over my head and reach for the Smith & Wesson to reload it with shot shell.

"Exactly," he says.

"Wait a second. Your flunkies have tried to kill us at least two or three separate times. Now you want us alive? What's changed?"

"I'll be in touch."

"You didn't answer my question."

"I recommend you answer the phone. Miss Buell's life may depend on your ability to follow my instructions."

"Understood. But you're assuming I can get the parts of the process you want."

"I have faith in you." Liho Blogis ends the call.

I slip the phone back into my pocket and pull the last objects out of the DHL box; the two hard drives containing pieces of the process.

***

The DHL clerk isn't as happy to see me as she was just a few minutes ago. It could be the semi-automatic machine pistol strapped across my back. Her eyes widen and she starts waving her hands at me, but I'm already behind the counter.

"You have security cameras?"

"Yes." Her hands are over her head, her eyes twitching with fear. "Please take what you want."

"I'm not going to hurt you. My friend was just kidnapped. I need to see your security video."

"I will call the police for you," she offers. "They can come here to —"

"No!" I push my way past her into the back room. "The police will take too long. You can call them when I leave."

She maneuvers her way through the maze of yellow and red shipping boxes behind me, her trembling hands still above her head, to a closet in the far corner of the back room. "The security camera video comes to here." She points to a pair of digital video recorders with accompanying monitors.

"Which one is for the front door camera?"

She pushes a button on the DVR to the left, and the display on the monitor comes to life. On the screen is a fisheye view of the street in front of the building.

"You can put your hands down. I'm not going to hurt you. I promise."

She nods, her lips quivering, and lowers her hands. "Why do you have the guns?"

"Long story. But I can assure you I only use them in self-defense."

She nods again, but doesn't seem to be any more at ease.

"Rewind that one." I point to the exterior view. "When you see me parking my car and getting out, you can stop it."

She pushes a couple of buttons and the DVR runs backwards, the digital images on the monitor moving in reverse bursts. I see myself, armed, oddly walking away from the Packstation. Then I'm taking apart the Tec-9, closing the box, resealing the tape, wandering around backward, and walking backward into the building.

The gray Audi pulls out of an empty curbside parking spot, and a moment later the white Citroen backs into the spot. Its doors open and Bella's cell phone spills from the car, hitting the sidewalk and bouncing. Four men get out of the car, two of them from the back seats, one from the front passenger's seat, and a tall man, broad shouldered with a white turtleneck and sunglasses exits from the driver's seat. A moment later I'm walking backward and getting into the car, then pulling out of the spot and disappearing off of the screen.

"Stop!" I tell the frightened clerk. "Now play it forward. Please."

The girl hits another button and the video plays in real time.

The Citroen, with me behind the wheel, reappears at the left of the screen and slowly moves into the parking spot. I get out of the car and walk past the woman with the dogs, who turns left and waits to cross the street as a black SUV wheels into the frame.

"Pause it there! Can you zoom in at all?"

"A little bit," she says. "It gets fuzzy if I go too close up."

"Zoom in on that SUV."

She pushes some buttons on the face of the DVR. The image on the screen shifts and zooms into the SUV.

The man in the front passenger seat of the SUV is wearing a white turtleneck and sunglasses!

"Zoom in on the license plate of that vehicle please!" I tap the screen again, inching closer to the monitor to get as good a look as possible.

She enlarges the image on the screen and zooms toward the license plate. It's long and thin, like most European plates. On its left is the standard blue strip for European Union countries. The rest of the page is white with large black letters and numbers. I can read the white "D" on the blue background, indicating the car is registered in Germany. Next to the country designation is another letter.

"Is that an O?" I ask my unintentional hostage.

"Yes," she says. "That's unusual. Is this really the car you are looking for?"

"Yes." I turn to look at her. "Why?"

"The first letters of the license plate says what city the car is from," she explains. "It's one, two, or three letters depending upon the city. This one doesn't have that designation."

"What is it then?"

"The letter O means this is a diplomatic vehicle," she squints. "And that is definitely an O."

"What about the numbers after it?" I point to the screen. "What do they mean?"

"I don't know," she says. "The numbers are codes for diplomatic missions. The first numbers would tell you the country. The second number, after the dash line, would tell you the registration number."

"The number before the dash is 140," I say. "We need to find out what country that represents."

She sits there, looking dumfounded.

"I need help. My friend was kidnapped in front of your store here. I have to find her. These are dangerous people I'm talking about."

She glances at the pistol tucked into my waist and the Tec-9 hanging on my shoulder.

"I get it," I say. "I come barging in here, forcing you at gunpoint to lead me into the back room of your office. I'm not going to hurt you. I told you that. I am asking, not demanding, your help in figuring out who took her and where they might have gone."

The woman's not shaking anymore, the mascara has dried on her cheeks. She's not on the verge of hyperventilating with every exaggerated breath.

"Okay," she relents. "I'll go to the computer in the front. We can look it up maybe. But then please go."

"Deal," I follow her back into the space behind the counter in the store's main area.

She bellies up to her workspace, punches a few keys, then maneuvers the mouse to some search results. I haven't even focused on the screen when she announces what she's found.

"Russia," she says. "The car is registered to the Russian embassy."

"Is there a Russian embassy in Frankfurt?"

I'm not surprised. Blogis is working for the Russians. Putin and his brethren would be more powerful than ever if they forced the U.S. into a unilateral nuclear disarmament. We'd be vulnerable to the Russians, the Chinese, even the Iranians.

"There's a consulate," she clicks away on the keyboard. "It's only five minutes from here." She seems almost excited for me, her fear of my ridiculous weaponry momentarily forgotten. "Maybe less than two kilometers. You could walk it. It takes ten minutes if you go south on Oeder Weg. It is next big street over."

"Okay. I need two more things, and then I'm gone."

"That wasn't part of the agreement." She backs away from her computer shaking her head.

"I need a box. Or better yet, a soft mailing pouch that'll hold this." I pull the strap over my head and lay the Tec-9 on the counter. "I can't very well walk down Oder Weg carrying a machine pistol."

She hurries to the back room, returning with a large soft sided shipping pouch and a pair of scissors, which she holds up and waves. "You'll need to hold onto the gun and be ready to use it, yes?"

"Yes."

She cuts holes into the bag so that I can grip the Tec-9 while it's hidden in a nice bright yellow DHL Express pouch, the words Deutshe Post in large black lettering across the front.

"You might need this too." She tosses me a yellow and red DHL polo shirt. "If you are going to sneak into the consulate."

"Aren't you going to get in trouble for this?"

"Our cameras are off right now," she says. "I had to shut them down to look at the video for you. Now, what is the second thing you need?"

"Hold onto these." I hand her the two silver hard drives.

"I can't…" she says, despite taking them from me. "What are they?"

"They have some information on them, and I need to leave them somewhere safe for a few minutes. It'll be an hour or two, tops."

She looks at the drives and bites her lower lip. "Hang on a moment." She disappears into the back room again and then returns with a key. "This is a mailbox key. Behind you," she points with the key past my left shoulder, "there are some mailboxes that we let. You can borrow one." She hands me the key and the drives. "Number 2929."

"Thank you." I pull the shirt on over my existing one. "Really, I —"

"Please just go now." She smiles weakly. "It's good."

I stuff the drives in the mailbox, the key into my pocket, grab the package, adjust the pistol in my belt, and push my way back onto the street. I've got a strong feeling that Bella is at that consulate, but my guess is that she won't be there for long.

***

The Russian Consulate is a six-story building across from a wooded park. I'm approaching from the park, trying to surveil the situation before jumping in feet first, when my phone buzzes again.

"Sir Spencer, your timing, as always, is perfect."

"Outside the embassy?"

"Consulate."

"Regardless," he replies, "nicely done. Very quick work, Jackson."

"I won't even ask how you know where I am." I take a few steps into the park. "Clearly you know Blogis has Bella. How is that?"

"I told him where you were," his words hang in the broadband, "and then I gave him your cell number." His tone is so nonchalant I'd think he was French, not British.

"I —you…"

"At a loss, good man?" he chides. "Of course you are. I'll fill you in on a little something."

He waits for me to respond, but I'm still trying to process the fact that he handed us right to the killer who is, at the moment, the greatest threat to our mission and our lives.

"Here's how it works," Sir Spencer pontificates. "You have two pieces of the puzzle, as it were. Our dear friend Mr. Blogis has a third piece. In Heidelberg, I believe, exists a fourth piece."

"We knew this already. How does this —"

"Ah, ah, ah," he interrupts. "Wait for the full explanation."

"Go ahead."

"Thank you for the permission to continue, Jackson," he says, his voice droll against the ubiquitous clinking of ice in a glass. "Now, as I was saying, we have all of the pieces in sight."

"All of them?"

"Oh yes," he says. "Thank you for reminding me. I'll soon have the fourth piece of the process. Bella's man, Mack, he's procuring it for me. So, given that we'll all be headed to Heidelberg," he chews a piece of ice, the crunch irritatingly loud, "I needed to assure that all of us would manage a reunion there."

"Why?"

"The way this is playing out, we run the real risk of nobody having all of the pieces to the neutrino process. That would be a shame. Someone should benefit, don't you think?"

I shrink deeper into the park, hiding behind a thicket of trees.

"I told Blogis where to find you," he details. "I told him that if he took Bella, you'd give chase with two pieces in hand. All of you would end up together in one place. Then he could kill you, if he chose to do so, and possess three pieces of the process. I'd then negotiate the final piece. One of us would end up incredibly wealthy, the other unbelievably powerful."

"But that's not what'll happen," I surmise.

"Brilliant boy," he laughs, "you know me too well. It's as if we're family, cut from the same cloth."

"Hardly."

"My dilemma is that I never know where Blogis will be," he muses. "But if I can lead him to you—"

"Because you magically always know where I am."

"Exactly, I lead him to you, which leads me to him. I can grab, with as much force as needed, the piece I don't have."

"You don't have three pieces."

"Oh, Jackson," he laments. "It's just a matter of time before I have all of them. You don't care about the process really. You want your freedom. You want to *disappear*! So," he says, "you'll give me what I want to get what you want. That's what this was all about to begin with, right?"

"What about Bella?" I ask. She won't give up so easily.

"What *about* Bella? She's collateral damage in this, Jackson. Do you really believe I would lie in bed, colloquially of course, with the daughter of a man whose work I fought so hard to stop?"

Collateral damage was the same phrase he'd used to describe me in the eyes of Bella's father.

"This is business, Jackson. This is money and power and the blood that must spill to ensure the preservation, nay, the growth of both intoxicants.

Bella, that untrustworthy little demon, will die at the end of this. She was a conduit and nothing more."

"But —"

"Jackson," he scolds, "enough now. Understand that I entered into this *agreement* with her, this offer of help, only because it was so much cheaper than trying to play Dr. Wolf's ridiculously expensive game. I could not afford to be outbid. So I took the shortcut, exposed him to Bella, and offered my gentle assistance."

"And you picked me because —"

"I picked you, Jackson," all warmth in his voice evaporates, "because I know you. I know where you are and where you'll be. You're little more than a carbon-based tracking device, Jackson. Certainly, I've underestimated your gumption in the past. But let us be honest with one another. This is far above your capability. Follow Blogis' instructions, lead him to me in Heidelberg, and get your pass to lifelong freedom."

There's a click and the line goes dead.

From behind the thicket, I turn around to look at the compound. Rescuing Bella does seem like an impossible task. I could forget this and be a step closer to the anonymous freedom I've sought for months.

But can I trust that Sir Spencer will deliver?

Collateral damage.

Conduit.

Carbon-based tracking device.

Screw it. I'm getting Bella. And we're controlling the process.

✳✳✳

My dad's steak was undercooked that night. I remember the pool of dark red juice pooled on his plate, seeping into his helping of mashed potatoes. Regardless, he cut into that piece of meat with vigor, sawing back and forth on the undercooked filet for each bite.

He liked his steaks rare and bloody, but that night's offering was particularly offensive to a kid whose carnivorous repertoire consisted of chicken nuggets, hot dogs, and the occasional well-done cheeseburger.

He didn't say much until I instigated a conversation halfway through my second helping of string beans. I was chewing loudly, smacking my lips, trying to get his attention.

"Jackson," he snarled like a coyote mid-meal, "you know your mother and I have told you repeatedly not to smack your food. It's disgusting." His eyes were closed when he said it.

"Sorry," I smacked. "It's just so good."

"Thank you, Jackson," Mom said, "but your father's right. Mind your manners."

I sucked pieces of bean from between my front teeth. "Who was that guy, Dad?"

My mom looked at me and then at my dad, who was busy chewing with his mouth closed. He took his napkin and wiped a spot of juice that dribbled onto his chin. When he finished his mouthful and swallowed, which took forever, he took a deep breath before speaking.

"That was a college acquaintance of mine," he said. "We used to be on the rifle team together."

"Why was he here?"

"He and I were both hired by the same company out of college. Then we went our separate ways. I haven't seen him in a while."

"What company?"

"It was a government contractor that recruited us at N.C. State."

"A technology company?" I took note of my parents' furtive glance at one another before my dad responded.

"Yep." He took an unusually large gulp from his glass of red table wine. My dad didn't drink much, that I recall, but he always had a glass of wine with his steak. "Why was he here?"

"Finish your beans," my mom said. "You asked for a second helping. If you want dessert tonight, you need to clean your plate."

I nodded at my mom, stabbed a forkful of beans, shoveled them into my mouth, and then looked at my dad.

"He made me a job offer."

"What?" My mom's reaction told me that she knew more about this visitor than she'd previously indicated. She wasn't nearly the poker player my father claimed to be.

"It's a short-term thing," he explained. "A few weeks at most for a fairly large commission. I told him I wasn't interested."

"Good," my mom said, further giving away her hand.

"Why were you so upset with him?" I asked. "He was offering you a job, so —"

"Not the kind of job I want," my dad said firmly. "He and I had a falling out years ago. We didn't see eye to eye on the way to conduct business or for whom we should work."

"He was not the most upstanding of coworkers," Mom said.

"I thought you didn't know who he was?" I poked my fork into the final portion of beans.

"I didn't recognize him at first," my mom said. "His hair is so much shorter than it used to be."

I had an epiphany. "Wait a second. I recognize him!"

"How do you know who he is?" My dad plopped his forearms on the table, his knife in one hand, steak filled fork in the other.

"He's in that picture with you," I said. "You know, the one of the rifle team that sits on the bookshelf in your study next to the big trophy?"

Both my parents are looking at me, shocked that I've added two plus two.

"Yeah, he's the guy with his elbow on dad's shoulder. The one who dad always said was the second best shot on the team."

My dad slowly draws the fork into his mouth and sucks the piece of meat off of the tines. He chews, his lips pursed, without answering. My mom pushed herself away from the table, stood, and started gathering plates to take to the sink.

"Who's ready for some dessert?" she said. "I've got cherry cobbler and vanilla ice cream."

"I am!" My favorite dessert.

"I'll take some too." My dad's expression changed and he winked at me. "Nothing better than cherry pie, right, hon?" He looked at my mom, whose face was suddenly flushed.

"You're bad," she said. "So bad."

"Your mom makes the best dessert," Dad said. "It's worthy of a whole new conversation, right, bud?"

I got the hint.

***

Like so many buildings in this city, the Russian consulate is cream colored stone and concrete. The structure itself is austere like its homeland. At ground level there are a series of barred windows, indicating a below grade basement.

There's no easy street access to the building. There's a waist high gate at one corner of the building, which is connected to a fence that surrounds a compound of what may be four or five buildings. At the other end of that fence is a motorized track gate, intended for vehicular entry and exit. There are no guards or security visible from the street, but I do notice a pair of remotely controlled security cameras affixed to the gutter downspout which runs the length of the building.

Looking past the cameras, there's a portico with what looks like a double door entrance. Again, no visible security. And no sign of Bella. Taking a deep breath, I cross the street and step to the fencing that runs along the sidewalk.

A ligustrom hedge runs the length of the fence between the two gates. I shuffle past it, looking to my left and into what passes for a parking lot, where I get a better look at the space between two of the buildings. Squeezed between them, hidden in a narrow alleyway, is a white Citroen.

I spent the ten minute walk from the Packstation formulating a plan. Well, let's be honest, it's a close facsimile of a plan. Really, it's more like those *Choose Your Own Adventures* I apply to the what-ifs in my life.

At the vehicular gate, there's a metal call box. I push the red button and a loud beep is followed by someone answering the call.

"Russian Federation."

It's a man's voice. He asks me my business. He coughs through the question, making it that much tougher to translate what he's saying.

"I have a delivery," I say in Ukrainian. "I'm with DHL."

To the left, the lower of the two security cameras swivels toward me. I smile and wave at whoever's controlling it. He asks me who sent the delivery.

"The, uh, the Consul General in Houston, Texas." I figure that's odd enough to pique his interest and let me inside.

He directs me to the building to the left, the one with the portico, and tells me that he'll meet me at the door. There's a loud metallic buzz and the gate slides open. My right hand is carrying the DHL bag, my fingers wrapped around the grip frame. If pushed I could fire through the bag before anyone knows what's coming.

My plan is do the threatening with the Smith & Wesson, so I rest my left hand underneath the package on my waist. To whomever is tracking me with the security camera, I must look a little odd with the package on its end and my hands beneath it.

I'm actually a little surprised I've gotten this far, given the added security to Russian consulates all over the world after a nationalist mob attacked the embassy in Poland in November 2013.

I remember reading that Russia's foreign minister decided to up the ante and put armed border police at their embassies all over the world. It only sticks with me because of how surprised I was that prior to that attack, Russia protected all of its embassies with unarmed civilian security specialists.

As I approach the door, I'm greeted by a pale looking man, who couldn't be more than twenty, in a dark blue uniform and tie, a pale blue collared shirt, and a blue and green service cap with a black shiny bill. He's definitely Russian military, but he's unarmed.

I smile at him and again check the security camera, which is pegged as far to the left as it will go. I'm out of its range. Three steps more and I'm within a yard of the officer.

"Hel—" he starts to greet me, but before he finishes the word, I've pressed the barrel of the Smith & Wesson between his eyes. Both of his hands shoot straight up in the air when I strongly suggest he not move or speak.

I explain that in the package is another, much more dangerous weapon, that will kill him and everyone around him if he does anything that upsets me. He nods, his eyes as wide as moons, made to look even bigger by the dark circles that frame them. There's something about Russians and their dark circles. It's as though generations of pain and anger and vodka are stored underneath the eyes, trying to hide just underneath the surface, unaware the whole world can see them anyhow.

"Can you understand me?" I ask him. He nods.

"Where is your weapon?" My eyes don't leave his.

"I don't have it," he tells me, shaking his head vigorously. "I left it at the desk inside."

"What is it?"

"Kalashnikov AK-12."

"I'm looking for someone who came here in a white car that's parked over there," I motion my head to the right. His hands still in the air, his eyes roll, trying to see between the two buildings.

"Do you see it?" I release some pressure on the six shooter, sliding it to the side as his head turns. He nods again before turning back to face me. His service cap is set back on his head, enough that I can see the beads of sweat on his brow.

"Where is my friend?"

"I don't know," he says. "I haven't seen anyone irregular come in the building."

"You have those cameras. Did you see my friend on them?"

"I don't know."

"What do you mean, 'I don't know'?" I lean into him, the agitation in my voice designed to frighten him as much as the shot shell just six inches from his brain.

"I m-mean," he stutters in less-intelligible Russian, "I saw a group of people in that car. I saw them get out and go into that building. But I didn't see the woman. I promise you."

I pull the hammer on the revolver, its racketing click startling the young guard. He whimpers and spreads his fingers wide as he tries to hold up his tiring arms.

"You promise?" I tilt my head to one side and narrow my gaze. He nods quickly and averts his eyes like a dog in a staring contest.

"Why would you lie to a man with a gun your head?"

"I *wouldn't* lie," he says, squeezing his eyes shut. "I didn't see her."

"That's the thing," I say. "I never said my friend was a *woman*."

His eyes pop open, pupils shrinking to pinpricks, and his shoulders slump, causing his arms to drop. He's searching my face, trying to gauge whether or not I'll pull the trigger.

"Tree, dva… " I count down from three in Russian.

"Wait, wait!" he pleads. "I know where she is. They took her into that building, but they've moved her to the basement. There are passageways, tunnels, between the buildings. She is underneath us now, in this building.

"How would you know where she is once she's inside?"

"There are coded doors," he says. "We get an alert at security whenever a coded door is opened and closed. The series of doors that opened and closed within the last hour started at that building and followed the tunnels to this building."

"Take me there."

"I can't," he closes his eyes in anticipation of a gunshot reply.

"Why not?"

"Because," he's speaking more quickly, making it more difficult to understand, "there are security measures. I cannot take a delivery man to the tunnels."

"Don't worry about that. I'll handle it." Drawing the gun from his forehead, I tell him to turn around and put his hands in his pants pockets. "You tell whoever we run into that you're escorting me to the tunnels. If there's a problem, it's my problem."

He nods, and with my pistol now tucked back into my pants and the DHL-covered Tec-9 pushed into the small of his back, the security guard presses his entry card against a scanner and activates the automatic door.

The door shuts behind us and we're in a drab entryway, mint green walls and gray terrazzo flooring. There's a desk in the center with a bank of LCD monitors surrounding it like a command center.

We approach the desk, and another young guard stands at attention. He's a lower rank than the three-striped sergeant leading me into the building. An AK-12, the latest incarnation of the AK-47, is leaning up against the desk. Rookie mistake.

"I'm taking this man to the tunnels," he says. "We have a package that must be hand-delivered."

"Yes, Sergeant," says the one-stripe desk clerk. "I will alert internal security that you will be arriving in the tunnels momentarily."

"No need." He waves off his comrade. "I already have orders from our Major. He knows we are on our way."

The underling hesitates and looks at me, standing behind his superior. I can see in his eyes that he doesn't trust the situation, but he's not about to challenge.

"Yes, Sergeant," he nods. "Please have your guest sign in here at the desk."

"Sign in," my guide tells me without turning around.

I step to his left and to the desk, where the comrade slides an open binder toward me. I have the package in my right hand, overtly aiming it at the sergeant. With my left hand, I scrawl an illegible name and put DHL next to it. I jot down the time and then step back behind my escort, slipping my free hand around the AK-12, slyly carrying it so the comrade can't see it.

With that, we are on our way into the tunnels.

***

The elevator opens into a hallway that turns only left. To the right is a wall, decorated with a large Russian flag. Beneath the flag is a smaller, painted insignia of the Border Guard Service of Russia. It's a large golden conjoined eagle behind a blue shield emblazoned with a green cross. The eagles' twin heads share a single crown, one talon clutching a scepter, the other a golden orb.

I've ripped open the DHL package, tossed to it to the elevator floor, and have the Tec-9 strapped over my shoulder. I'm gripping the AK-12 with both hands as the sergeant and I step into the hall. It's a narrow passageway with low ceilings. Up ahead, there is a series of windows, the top halves of which are above grade, glowing with outdoor light through the opaque glass.

The sergeant is walking silently ahead of me, save the clicking of his boot heels on the linoleum floor. The flooring is aged, curling at the edges where it meets the peeling plaster walls. The smell is dank and rife with mold or mildew. I'm guessing from the black splotches on the ceiling tiles that it's mold.

At the end of the hall is a thick metal door with a wall-mounted security pad to the right. The sergeant waves his entry card over the panel and a red glowing light turns green. There's a series of clicks followed by a loud metal hum and he heaves the door inward. There's no security camera. Before he walks through he turns his head to the side and whispers, "There's another security check up here. It's maybe fifty meters and to the right. They will be armed. They will see you are armed. Maybe you should put down the weapons."

I'm not giving up my weapons.

What do I do? I'll be outmanned and outgunned.

"Take the AK-12 from me," I whisper back, releasing the magazine, and tucking it in my waistband next to the revolver. "It's unloaded. I removed the magazine."

"Why?" He turns toward me, still propping the door open with his hip and leg. "I don't under—"

"Just do it." I shove the rifle into his chest. "When we approach, I'll tell you what to do."

He nods and exhales. His breath smells rancid, like old sauerkraut mixed with limburger and braunschweiger. The expression on my face must give away my disgust. He jerks back and presses his lips together. He knows it's bad.

"Just breathe on the guards," I suggest. "That'll knock them out." I nod my head in the direction of the hallway, instructing him to move.

"I had dinner, I'm at the end of my shift."

I pull the Tec-9 sling over my head and carry the machine pistol vertically, against my chest, as though I'm in a color guard. It'll remain hidden from the guards until the last possible second.

About twenty yards ahead, the hallway widens and intersects with another corridor that runs right and left. Parked in the middle of the intersection is a lectern and pair of guards. Above them is a security camera.

"Act normal," I whisper to the sergeant. "Whatever the protocol would be, follow it."

He nods and waves to the guards up ahead.

"Comrades," he calls out, "I have a visitor here. He has a delivery for the female guest who arrived within the hour. Can you sign us in and direct us to the woman?"

"Sergeant," one of the guards calls back, tilting his head to his left, "The visitor is at the end of the hallway. What is the delivery? Who is this man?"

The other guard, the one who hasn't spoken yet, is built like a juiced professional wrestler. He's easily six foot five, and two hundred fifty pounds of muscle. His AK is a toy in his meat hook hands.

"He is from DHL," the sergeant says, his voice quavering. "He has a package for the woman."

The shorter guard's eyes narrow as he tries to peek around the sergeant to get a better look at me as we approach the desk. "What is the delivery, Sergeant?" He tightens his grip on his rifle and moves the barrel toward us. He swallows hard.

The sergeant starts shaking his head as we step to the lectern and the large guard's eyes catch the Tec-9 in my hands. He raises the AK and yells for us to stop. I use all of my force to shove the sergeant in the middle of his back and drop to my knees, sliding to my left and away from the larger guard.

The sergeant trips forward, stumbling into the lectern, which in turn falls back into the smaller guard. The guard's neck snaps back and his head slams onto the floor with a thud. Both men lose their weapons, which rattle onto the linoleum and slide a good ten feet from the dog pile to my right.

The large guard swings his rifle toward me. I snap off a short burst, which hits his AK, knocking it from his hands and putting a hole in his left wrist. He bellows something in Russian and lunges toward me, leaping over the sergeant, the lectern, and the other guard lying unconscious underneath both.

On both knees, I aim directly at the behemoth's chest and pull the trigger.

Click!

Another two pull.

Click! Click!

Jammed!!!

The Hulk lands squarely on top of me, pressing my shoulders to the floor. My legs fold back, wrenching my surgically repaired knee. That pain is almost instantaneously replaced with the crack of the ogre's fist plowing into my jaw. A second punch knuckles my neck just behind my ear. A third from his bloody left hand drives into my temple.

Against the ringing in my ears and his immense mass, I struggle to free myself, squirming on my back like a beetle. I somehow manage to reach my hand into my waistband and snag the Smith & Wesson.

Another blow to my head and I can't see clearly, but there's surprisingly little pain now. The adrenaline coursing through me has me on whacked out survival mode. The barbarian rears back, straddling me, clenching his fists together, as though he's about to plunge a sword into me, and drives his joined hands together into my gut, forcing the wind out of me.

The shift in his weight, and my instinctive wrench against the punch frees my left hand enough that I yank the Smith & Wesson out from under the back of his thigh. He swings down a second time and I bury the muzzle into his midsection.

Pop!

The gunshot is muffled, nearly silenced in his girth but it does little to sway him.

Pop!

The second shot does the damage. His swing into my sternum is ineffectual and he falls to the side into the fetal position, grabbing his gut and screaming unintelligibly.

I roll over in the opposite direction, feeling the drool run down my cheek and on the floor as I battle to find air. From my position on the floor I can see the sergeant scrambling to grab the loaded AK-12 farther down the hall.

Switching the revolver to my right hand, I'm able to fire off another shot.

Pow!

Shot shell sprays outward, lodging itself in the fallen lectern, the unconscious guard on the floor, and the sergeant's butt.

He cries, grabbing for his backside, loses his balance, and falls down again. From this distance, maybe seven or eight feet, the spray didn't do much damage but it'll keep him down long enough.

I suck in a shallow breath, followed by a deeper one, and push myself to my feet. I'm a little off-balance, and steady myself against the wall long enough to focus.

I've got three shots left in the Smith & Wesson and the Tec-9 is jammed. To my left, about fifteen feet from me are two AK-12s, one of them likely with a full magazine.

I stagger past the intersection toward the AK when, from the corner of my eye, I catch movement in the distance to my right. At the end of the hallway, where the guard says Bella's being held, there are two men running toward me. Both of them are armed.

Then from behind me another sound. The elevator opens and two more men, one of them the young comrade from the security desk upstairs, are marching at me with their AKs leveled in my direction.

The sound of the gunfire is deafening. Bursts of semi-automatic fire interchange with the percussion of large caliber handguns.

My dive across the hallway lands me just short of the two AK-12s. On my elbows, I inch my way to the one missing the magazine. I pull the cartridge from my waistband and slap it into the rifle, roll over onto my back, and sit up to take aim.

I've got partial coverage from the fallen lectern in front of me, which is obscuring the view of the two guards coming from the direction of the elevator and the card-coded door. They're not an immediate concern.

I press the AK into my shoulder, feeling its heavier weight than a M16, adjusting my hold for the shorter barrel. My legs spread into a wide V for balance, I tilt my head and look through down the barrel at the blur of a civilian rounding the corner to my left.

He takes the corner a little wide, slipping on the linoleum, and I trace his movement for a beat before pulling the trigger.

Pop! Pop! Pop! With surprisingly little recoil, a quick three round burst finds its target in the civilian's head, snapping his neck backward violently and he goes down.

I reset to my left and follow the second civilian as he too slips too far around the corner.

Pop! Pop! Pop! His right shoulder, where it joins his neck, disappears behind a spray of red. His momentum carries him backward into the wall.

Now back to the guards who've quickly closed their distance, the sounds of their semi-automatic fire whizzing uncomfortably close to my head. The lectern is splintering into a heap of wooden shards, one of which finds its way into my shin.

Their fire is coming in waves, not bursts. Though there must be multiple settings on the AK, I can't even think about switching modes.

I tilt my head again to aim just as a bullet grazes my shoulder, ripping a hole in the DHL shirt. Another bullet skims my bicep, drawing blood.

I ignore it, exhale, steady, and frame my target. *Pop! Pop! Pop!* The guard from the desk upstairs goes down, his right thigh shredded. He'll live as long as I didn't hit his femoral artery.

Pop! Pop! Pop! The second guard takes two in the arm, one in the hand. He's down.

Amidst a horrifying chorus of wails and cries, I find my feet again, grab the second AK-12, and march hurriedly down the corridor where I hope to find Bella.

CHAPTER 19

I've got one AK slung across my shoulder, the other at waist level and ready to fire as I approach the last door on the right.

I press my back against the wall adjacent to the door, trying to ignore the cries for help amidst the carnage thirty yards behind me.

"Bella!" I call out. "Bella, are you okay?"

Nothing.

"Bella! I'm coming for you on three. One!" I spin, kicking the door with all of my force just below the tarnished brass knob. The frame splinters and the door flies inward, hanging on only part of its hinge.

The room is empty. A chair in the middle of the space is on its side. Another chair is against the wall under the window. The pane is open. Whoever was in here is gone.

I scramble to the window and push myself against the sill and through the opening onto the ground above. I'm just inside the main pedestrian gate, where I first confronted the sergeant.

"Bella! Bella!"

"Jackson!!"

I scramble to my feet and run to the left toward the alley where I saw the Citroen.

"Jackson, help me!" I run toward the rear of the compound, toward the sound of her voice, when I see her running toward me.

Her hands are bound in front of her, her ponytail bouncing wildly behind her. "Jackson!! Jackson!!"

I lower the AK and open my arms and she runs into them. She buries her face in my chest, breathing heavily, but not crying.

"Are you okay?" I ask her, my free arm wrapped around her. There's no obvious threat.

Where's Blogis?

"I'm okay," she says. "They didn't hurt me. They just want the process, that's all."

"Where's Blogis?" My own voice is muffled, the ringing in my ears from the underground gun battle hasn't subsided.

"I don't know," she says. "He left before all the shooting happened. I was alone in a room with two other men. They ran out to get you and I got out through that window and ran for the car. Then I heard you calling and I ran back."

"Blogis is gone?"

"I don't know. I just want to get out of here."

"There were *three* men, other than Blogis, who kidnapped you. That means we're missing —"

I'm interrupted by the squealing of tires and the high pitched whine of a car engine. We turn toward the parking lot to see a black SUV bouncing over a curb, heading straight for us. In the passenger's seat is the man I suspect is Blogis.

I wrap my arms around Bella and tackle her, driving her into a hedge, and land on top of her. Despite its waxy, thorny leaves, the hedge provides cushion for us as the SUV bounds past us, its suspension clanging and creaking. The driver navigates another elevated curb and a pair of yellow concrete turtarriers marking the end of the lot's parking spaces. The AK strapped to my back bangs into the back of my head, and thankfully doesn't discharge.

I expect the SUV to turn around or back up to make another run at us, but the driver guns the vehicle toward the exit gate and plows through it onto the street. The SUV fishtails a right hand turn, tires screaming against the pavement, and rumbles off.

"Are you okay?" I ask Bella for the second time in as many minutes.

"I think so." She pushes on my chest, trying to move me off of her. "A little scratched up from this hedge. I'm okay though."

I roll off of her and then struggle to my feet so I can help pull her up, then I grab the second AK, which is a couple of feet from us, propped against the curb.

"Weird," I say, plucking leaves from my clothing.

"What?" she asks, doing the same.

"Why did Blogis take off?"

"'Cause you went Rambo on him," she says. "He lost control of the situation. I remember him telling you on the phone he likes to be in control."

"Good point. That means he'll be back. He needs the two drives and he knows we have them." I point toward the white Citroen, still parked in the alley about twenty yards from us.

"How does he know?" She follows my lead and starts walking toward the car. "I didn't tell him anything. In fact, they didn't really ask me anything, come to think of it. They just scared the living daylights out of me."

"He knows." I try the driver's side door and find it unlocked. "Sir Spencer told him." I pull the sling over my head with one hand and lock the AK-12.

"He *what?*" She pulls open the passenger's door and ducks into the seat. I lock the second AK and put both of them on the floorboard behind Bella's seat. "He's playing us, as we both suspected. It's far more diabolical than what we could have imagined." The pistol finds its place under the driver's seat. It's still got three shots in it.

Conveniently enough, the keys are still in the car, and the gas tank has plenty of fuel. We should be able to make it to Heidelberg without stopping.

"What's his play?"

"Hang on." I get back out of the car and walk around the back to get the GPS out of my pack. We're going to need it.

The highway signs in Germany don't give directional instructions. They list the names of two towns in opposite directions. If drivers don't know which town is where, they will invariably head in the wrong direction. Then they're thirty kilometers down the road before they realize they have to turn around. The GPS will prevent that from happening.

I quickly return to my seat, start the engine, and put the Citroen into drive. There's a crowd starting to gather at what used to be the front gate. We zoom past without slowing down, and bounce a wide turn onto the street.

"Okay, here's what I know…"

***

"You're kidding me." Bella looks like she's trying not to smile, but it's a combination of shock and disgust she can't conceal. "He said that? He said I was *collateral damage*?"

"He did." I follow the GPS onto the A5 toward Kreuz/Basel/Flughafen and our destination, Heidelberg. "We were right that he couldn't be trusted, but it amazes me how much I continue to underestimate him."

"He said the same thing about you," Bella says, that hint of a smile perhaps more genuine now. She tugs on the seatbelt across her chest, loosening it while she slides down in her seat. "What now? How do we avoid getting killed? Let's be honest, he's not telling you he's going to kill you because he needs you to finish the job. But once that happens…"

"I've already thought of that. I have a plan."

"You do?" She turns her body toward me with interest.

"Kinda," I say. "Don't sound so surprised, sheesh."

"I'm not," she admonishes. I glance at her and then at the speedometer. We're entering the part of the autobahn without a speed limit. I'm in the right lane going about one hundred kilometers an hour.

"Okay," she admits, "maybe I am a little. But really, what's your plan?"

For a woman who was essentially comatose in the lobby of the Hotel Odessa two days ago, Bella's holding up remarkably well. She seems to have adjusted quickly to the constant threat of violence. Since I met her four or five days ago, I can't keep count from the lack of sleep and food, she's been kidnapped twice, shot at, and chased. Now she's asking how we avoid our deaths like we're planning her *quinceañera*.

I accelerate and push the car into the left lane, past a lumbering soft-sided tractor trailer. "First of all, we're not bringing our pieces of the process with us."

"What?" Her voice slips an octave higher than usual. "Where are they?"

"In a safe place." I check the speedometer, which indicates we're cruising at one hundred fifty kilometers, or ninety miles, per hour. "They're not going anywhere."

"I don't understand," she says, her brows knitted. "What did you do with them? If we don't have them, aren't we at a disadvantage? What if Blogis just decides to kill you because he's fed up? What am I going to do if you get killed?"

I take back what I said about her handling this like a pro. I engage the cruise control at one hundred and sixty kilometers per hour. The Citroen eases into the right lane and a Porsche 911 whisks by us like we're standing still. The car shimmies from the sports car's wake. "That's a lot of questions at once. I'll take them one by one."

Bella folds her arms and glares at me. Apparently Blogis isn't the only one who doesn't appreciate losing the illusion of control.

"I left them in a post office box in Frankfurt. They'll be fine there. We're not at any disadvantage by leaving them there."

"Why not?" she snips.

I put both of my hands on the wheel as a large Mercedes hums by us on the left. "I'm trying to explain it to you, okay?"

She pouts like a tween. It's actually more endearing than annoying.

"They're a lot less likely to kill either of us if we don't have the drives with us," I explain. "The parts they have are essentially useless without the two we have. They might torture me to get the location out of me, but they won't kill me until they have it." My mind flashes to the first time I met Sir Spencer.

It was in Austin while I was still working for the governor and dating my dead ex-girlfriend Charlie. He'd drugged me and chained me up, trying to find out if I'd spill the beans on the governor's plans. He didn't get it out of me. Then again, he was actually on *my* side then.

"That torture could include killing *me*!" Her eyes widen, her pupils shrink. "You're putting me in danger by not bringing them and not telling me where they are. You know these people are ruthless. I'm collateral damage, remember?"

She has a point I hadn't considered, though I'm not letting her know I agree with her. "That's not going to happen," I say. "It won't get to that point." There's a slower moving SUV up ahead, so I check my rear and side view mirrors and dart into the passing lane. The car responds almost too quickly at this speed and I have to overcorrect to center the car in the lane.

"I missed something," she says.

"What?"

"You said *they* have pieces of the process." She shifts in her seat again, wagging a finger at me. "Who do you mean *they*?"

Oops.

"Oh," I chuckle. "Sir Spencer has a piece too. Didn't I already mention that?"

"Uh…no!" She moves her neck like a dancer in a Bollywood movie. "You said he *wanted* control of the pieces, but you neglected to mention that he has one of the pieces himself. How did he get them?"

"Mack."

"Mack?"

"Mack."

"You were right." She turns to face the front of the car and sinks further into her seat. "The blank drive was Mack's doing. He betrayed me. I don't get it."

"I should clarify something," I say, interrupting her momentary malaise. "Sir Spencer claims to have only one of the pieces. Blogis has the other. Each of them has one. I made it sound like Sir Spencer has more than —"

"Really?" she turns toward me, her chin lowered. "That doesn't make it any better." She's right again. I may have misplayed this. Sir Spencer probably does have the upper hand, no matter how this ends up. He's holding a piece.

If we somehow manage to recover Blogis' piece, that'll give us three of four. If we get the lone remaining piece in Heidelberg…

Epiphany. "Hey!"

"What?"

"What are we looking for in Heidelberg?" It's the obvious question I never thought to ask. "Where are we going exactly?"

"Wolf worked there for a while, remember?"

"Yeah," I nod, checking that the cruise control is still engaged. "So?"

"Well," she sighs, "he still has — had — a place there. He rents it out."

"Wolf has a place in Heidelberg and we wouldn't check there first?" There's more than a hint of condescending disbelief in my voice.

"Sir Spencer suggested that we start —" and it dawns on her. "Mother fu—"

"He's too good," I say. "He's probably already got that piece. He told me that Mack was procuring it for him. He wanted us in Ukraine while he went straight to Germany. We're driving into a trap."

Bella throws her head back against her seat, looking up through the skylight. "I'm not cut out for this. My father was right."

"What do you mean?" I bite. Nothing like a little impromptu autobahn therapy on the way to a massacre.

"He told me more than once, as much as he loved me, that I wasn't *really* cut out to lead Nanergetix. He said there were things I wouldn't have the *fortaleza* to do." She rolls her head on the headrest to look at me. Her eyes are welled, barely holding the tears ready to stream. "That's fortitude in Spanish," she says and rolls back to look through the sunroof. "He said there were things," she sniffs, "things I was too pure hearted to do, that it took a certain type of *malvado* to be good in business, a wickedness I could never have, no matter how hard I tried."

"That must have been difficult," I say, mirroring what my therapist must have said to me a thousand times. At least.

"Yes. I always wanted his approval more than anyone else's. To hear him say that I didn't have what it took…"

"Do you think he was saying that he didn't want to you be what he'd become?" I propose. "Is it a possibility that he thought you were too good a person?"

"I don't know." She sits up straight in her seat. "I can do this. *We* can do this, Jackson. We need to do this. We need all five pieces of the process. Nanergetix needs to control this."

"So that you can prove something to yourself?"

"No," she says. "Maybe. I don't know. Regardless, if I fail here, I'll lose my job. There are already too many people at Nanergetix who want to see me go down in flames. This would do it. The board would lose its wavering faith in me."

"I thought this was a secret? I didn't think anyone knew about this, really."

"True," she admits. "They only know we're working on something big. I promised the board a huge breakthrough that would have us drowning in government contracts."

I check our speed and look at the GPS. We've got maybe twenty minutes until we hit the exit for Heidelberg. My phone rings, vibrating against the center console between Bella and me. I glance at it and don't recognize the number.

"You gonna answer it?" Bella asks, her hands over her head adjusting her ponytail. "It's probably important."

"It's never good when I get a phone call."

She picks up the phone. "I'll answer it." She connects the call and pulls the phone to her ear. "Hello?"

I can hear a man's voice on the other end of the call, but I can't distinguish whose it is. My attention's split between Bella and the road in front of us. Both of my hands are gripping the Citroen's steering wheel. I check the rear view mirror. There's a familiar SUV growing perilously larger in the reflection.

Bella pulls the phone from her ear. "It's Blogis. He's behind us."

***

Bam!

The first time the SUV slams into the rear of the Citroen, I almost lose control of the vehicle, not believing Blogis would actually ram us. I accelerate after that first crushing hit, trying to stay ahead of Blogis and his driver. Blogis is armed.

Bella's turned sideways in her seat. She dropped the phone when the SUV hit us.

"What did he say?" I ask after I've put two car lengths between us and Blogis.

"He said he's tired of being patient." She peeks between the two front seats at our pursuers. "He says he'll get what he needs one way or the other. Then he hung up!"

I notice the SUV making another run at us. "We're about to take another hit. Hold on." I accelerate again to lessen the impact. The speedometer reads one hundred and eighty kilometers per hour. Even the slightest adjustment on the steering wheel sends the Citroen careening in that direction. Bella braces herself against the passenger door and the dashboard, locking her elbows and squeezing shut her eyes.

Bam!

Bella's body flies toward the dash before the locking seatbelt pulls her back against her seat. She cries out and reaches for her right shoulder.

Part of the Citroen is dragging behind us, scraping loudly against the autobahn's pavement and sending a spray of sparks in the car's wake.

There's no traffic ahead of us. In the rear view, Blogis is motioning for us to pull over, waving a handgun toward the shoulder.

Not gonna happen.

"You okay?" I ask Bella.

"Yeah," she winces. "That belt dug into my shoulder though. It hurts."

"This car isn't gonna take another hit from that SUV."

She nods, her face still scrunched in pain.

I check the left lane in the side view mirror. "Next time it guns for us I'm moving to the left and braking really, really fast, okay?"

Her eyes pop open in protest. I don't think that's a good idea."

"We'll be fine!"

"Just take that exit!" Bella points ahead to a sign that reads L531 Dossenheim/ Handschulsheim. "Take the exit at the last second."

"Worth a try." The front of the SUV tilts upward and the driver accelerates toward us again as I brake and slip the wheel to the right to take the exit. The SUV clips what's left of the right rear bumper, pushing the left side of the Citroen into the concrete retaining wall.

I'm going way too fast for the two hundred and forty degree looped exit, which should take us back under the A5, but the friction of the car against the concrete slows us enough that it actually prevents us from flipping over the barrier. The side view mirror is shredded and slams into my window before tumbling in pieces to the road beneath us.

I'm almost standing in my seat, my foot trying to mash the brakes through the floor while the car rumbles against the pressure of it. Bella has her palms flat against the dash, her screaming louder than the nauseating sound of the Citroen's metal grinding against the waist-high concrete wall.

I overcorrect to the right and accelerate off the wall toward the road at the end of the ramp. "It worked!" I shout, still trying to navigate the car with what might be a bent rim on the front left wheel.

Bella's face is nearly translucent with fear. Her mouth is agape, no sound coming out, and her chest is heaving. Her palms are still pushing against the dash as I decelerate at the intersection of the ramp and the street running perpendicular to and underneath the A5.

"I can go left or right here. What do you think? Left or right?" Bella just shakes her head.

I turn right, thinking we've lost Blogis and his flunky, but the black SUV reappears, speeding, in reverse, down the entrance ramp and toward us. Blogis is hanging out of the window, pushed up against the roof of the SUV. He's aiming his handgun at us. I can't tell if he's firing off any shots until one of the them hits the left rear tire.

I press the hobbled Citroen as fast as I can get it to go. I'm like Clark Griswold in the wood paneled, army green Family Truckster, wobbling on a bad rim and a flat, but there's nothing funny about this.

The SUV's tires screech angrily against the sharp right turn the driver forces, centering himself in my rear view. It's closing fast again, with four good tires and rims.

The revolver is underneath my seat, the AKs in the back seat behind Bella. None of them will do me any good until we stop. I can't risk handing over the wheel and wrecking.

I check my speed: one hundred and one kilometers per hour. 70 miles per hour.

The road curves right and the SUV drifts out of my mirror for a moment. Both sides of the road are lined with thickets of trees, their leaves green and full. I push the accelerator coming out of the curve, the trees give way to farm land, and the Citroen resists my urging for more speed. The blown tire is gone, and we're rolling on a rim. The bent front rim is causing the steering wheel to shake violently.

"We don't have much longer in this car," I say. "Can you grab the rifles from behind your seat? They're both loaded."

Bella pulls against her seatbelt, loosening the shoulder strap, and reaches around to grab the first of the rifles. She sets it in the center console, the business end facing backward, and then stacks the second one on top of it.

"I need you to hold on to one of them," I say, fighting to maintain control of the car. "I'm going to pull off the road over here." I nod ahead to a cluster of warehouses off to the right of the road. "That'll give us some cover."

She nods robotically.

"When I stop, I'm going to grab my revolver from under the seat. I've got three shots if I need them. I'll provide cover with one of those AKs while you bolt to those buildings up there. Got it?"

She nods again and grabs both rifles, setting them on her lap.

"Those rifles hold as many as thirty rounds. Both are probably less than half full. And they're set to fire in three round bursts. Flip that switch, right there." I point to the safety, which she disengages.

I see the distance between us and the SUV rapidly diminishing. "Okay, here we go." I slam on the brakes and jerk the wheel to the left.

The car spins, more aptly bounces, and stops with the driver's side facing the oncoming SUV. "Go now!!!" I yell to Bella and she darts from the Citroen, running down the middle of the road for cover until she hears me pull the trigger on the AK. I assume at that point, she'll disappear into the high grass and toward the warehouses.

I pull on the driver's handle, trying to loosen it before I grab my AK to fire, but the damage from slamming into the concrete barrier at the off ramp must have jammed it shut. I duck down, pull the revolver from beneath my seat and then push myself through the car to Bella's open door. Once I'm on the pavement, I reach back inside the car and grab the rifle.

He's not going to kill me, I tell myself. *He needs me alive.*

Clink! Clink! Clink! It's the sound of bullets cutting through the driver's side of the Citroen before the sound of glass shattering. I'm crouched like a baseball catcher with my back against the car.

Okay. Maybe I'm wrong about that.

In the distance, I can see Bella picking her way through the high grass. She's almost to the warehouses, and I haven't fired a shot yet. I close my eyes, exhale, and focus. Everything around me slows to a crawl.

Standing up and spinning one hundred and eighty degrees, I pull the rifle tight to my shoulder and set my revolver on the roof of the Citroen.

To the right of the SUV, crouched behind an open door is Blogis' stooge. He's aiming a semi-automatic pistol in the space between the door frame and the door.

Pop! Pop! Pop! He's down.

I pivot to my right, expecting to put Blogis in my crosshairs, but he's not there. I swivel back to the left and there's nothing.

Pop! A shot whizzes within an inch of my left ear.

Where the —? I drop behind the car, falling to one knee.

"I don't want to kill you, Jackson," he calls out. "You're not any good to me if you're dead."

"What do you want with me then?" I call back.

"You know this," he laughs. "You know I want the pieces of the process that you are holding. I will get them from you one way or the other. There was a tracker in the Citroen."

"I'm not giving them to you," I say. "I know what all of those seemingly meaningless mathematical calculations do when they're put together."

"Do you really now?" I still can't fix his location.

"It finds nuclear weapons and renders them useless," I say. There's no sign of Bella near the warehouses. She's hidden. If I can get to her, somehow…

"Very good," he replies. "Very good. But do you truly understand what this means geopolitically? This changes everything."

"I'm not stupid. I get it. You sell the process, you make money, and then you singlehandedly screw some nation into oblivion. My guess is that you're not looking to make a deal with Uncle Sam."

"Probably not," he says, his voice from a different location. Not closer. Not farther away, just shifting. "I'm pretty tight with Putin. Vlad and I both have a taste for German beer."

"I doubt Rouhani likes beer," I say, referring to the president of Iran. "What's your connection to him?"

"Hassan?" He laughs. "Ha! I've known him since his days as a college student in Glasgow. I get him bootlegged copies of the movies he wants to see before they're available in Iran. He screens them at Sa'dabad Palace before afternoon prayers. Great guy."

"Which one is your buyer?"

"Either one is good with me," he says. "They both know how it works. And let's be honest, Jackson, either one of them does the same thing with the gift I provide them."

He says something about American imperialism when I make the decision to bolt, crab walking at first, then dashing for the grass about twenty-five feet off the shoulder of the road.

I dive into the grass as a bullet whizzes by, landing on the AK, jamming it in my ribcage and knocking the wind out of myself.

"C'mon, Jackson!" Blogis yells again. "We were having a nice James Bond/Goldfinger conversation there. You had to go run off, ruining it!" Catching my breath, I aim the AK skyward and rattle off a pair of bursts for cover before pushing myself up to make a run for the first of the three warehouses. There's no return fire until I clear the grass and round the corner between the first two buildings.

I've got a minute, maybe, to find Bella and more cover, before Blogis catches up and ends this one way or the other.

***

Thankfully, Bella is hiding on the far side of a large tractor between the first warehouse and the steep bank of a narrow river.

"You okay?" I slide next to her behind a huge tractor tire wide enough to protect both of us from Blogis' line of sight.

"I'm good," she says, sweat beading on her forehead and chin. "Scared. But good."

"Can you fire that thing?" I look at the rifle in her hands. She makes the AK look sexier than it already is.

"Just hold it tight against my shoulder so it doesn't kick, right?"

"Yep. And that weapon doesn't have as much recoil as you'd think. You should be okay."

She nods and attempts a smile before wiping her forehead with the back of her hand and pointing to the wounds on my shoulder and bicep. "You're bleeding again. You've got a new one too." She thumbs some blood from my ear.

"I hadn't noticed. It's the adrenaline."

"What do we do now?" she whispers. "We're sitting ducks."

"We'll be fine. Trust me."

The tractor provides great cover from any direction Blogis might approach. He won't be able to see us hiding behind it. Unless he approaches from…

"There you are!" he shouts from the riverbank. Both of us are exposed. He levels his handgun at Bella and approaches slowly.

"Don't think about it, Jackson," he says, his eyes on Bella as he moves parallel to the riverbank. "I'll put a bullet in her before you release the trigger. The difference between the velocity of your bullet and mine doesn't matter at this distance. You'll kill me. I'll kill her. That's not good for anyone. Plus, I've got a soft spot for you, Jackson. I don't want this to end with your bloody, unnecessary death. The girl doesn't have to die either. But she will if you do something stupid."

Bella drops her rifle to the ground and puts her hands in the air. I don't.

I keep my AK aimed at his head, tracing his movement.

He's waving what looks like a piece of paper in his left hand as he talks. "Let's do the math. You're firing three round bursts, the rounds traveling maybe twenty-three hundred feet per second. My nine millimeter is a little slower at about one thousand feet per second. I'm less than five hundred feet from you."

"Which means you're dead in a quarter of a second."

"You're at a rifle's distance, Jackson. So test it with your handgun," he snarls. "I'll see the change in your facial muscles before your finger pulls the trigger. I'll fire at the same time you do. She'll hit the ground half a second after me."

"I don't think so." My eyes are open, the right one pulled to the scope.

"I don't care if she lives," he says. "Don't push my pati—"

Thump! Thump! Thump!

I release the trigger and through the scope see Liho Blogis jerk awkwardly back, stumbling and dropping his handgun before falling down the embankment and into the river with a splash. The piece of paper in his hand wafts in the air for a moment before spiraling to the ground.

"Holy sh—" Bella blurts.

"Walk back to the car," I say without taking my eyes off the spot where Blogis fell into the water. "I'll meet you there in a second." The AK is still pulled tight to my shoulder.

"It's useless," she says. "The tires are —"

"We're taking the SUV."

"What if there are people there?" Good point.

"Gauge it from the high grass," I say. "If it's not safe then stay there. If it is, then grab the bags out of the rental and toss them in the SUV. My guess is the keys are in the ignition."

Bella nods and starts walking quickly, retracing her steps to the road. I walk the opposite direction, to the riverbank.

The rush of the water amplifies the closer I get. The bank is steep, maybe four or five feet down at an almost vertical drop. There's a smudge of blood on the weeds and dirt where the bank meets the water. To the left, about fifty yards downriver, is what looks like Blogis' body, face down. To my right, next to his Glock nine millimeter on the ground is the piece of paper he dropped. It's a photograph.

I pick it up and, before I've even pulled the image into focus, recognize it. On the far left is a man with his arms behind his back, chest puffed out.

My dad.

Leaning on my dad's shoulder is his tall, musclebound, mop-haired teammate.

How did Liho Blogis get this photograph?

I flip it over. The writing on the back isn't faded as it is on my copy.

Wolfpack Rifle Team 1981.

Team R to L: (back) Tim Highwater, G. Graff, Daniel Petrovich, Donald Wayne, Frank Blogis, James Ellsworth (front) Sanders Long, Steve Lawrence, C.L. Eaker

Two names stand out: Frank Blogis and James Ellsworth.

James was my dad. And Blogis…could it be…?

Frank! The college buddy who visited us at the house. The guy with the BMW who upset my dad. Was Frank really Liho *Blogis?*

I flip the photograph back over, looking at the man standing next to my father. Could it be?

Did Liho Blogis know my father? Did they work together?

"I've got a soft spot for you, Jackson," he said, before I put three rounds into him.

A memory I'd long forgotten flashes into my head, along with a wave of nausea that overwhelms me and I bend over, involuntary dry heaves tearing at my stomach. The answers to my questions are dead, floating down the river.

Unless…

There was that night…before my father died. I'd forgotten about it, repressed it, until this moment. It puts together the far-flung, hidden pieces of my past and my present.

I wipe the drool from my chin, fold the photograph and tuck it in my pocket, and start marching back to the SUV and Bella.

By the time I reach the road, she's in the driver's seat, waiting on me. There's nobody around except for the dead body in the road.

She rolls down the front passenger's window. "Let's go," she says, "we've got a date with Sir Spencer."

I climb into the seat and pull the door shut. "You know where to go?"

"I've got your GPS." She nods to the display, which she's placed just beneath the dash. "We're good to go. Plus," she pops open the glove box, which reveals a silver thumb drive. "We've got Blogis' piece of the puzzle. That gives us three."

I'm listening to her, but not processing it.

Blogis knew my father? They were friends?

"Are you okay?" Bella shakes my leg. "Jackson?"

I nod.

They were classmates and coworkers? Blogis worked for Spencer.

"What happened down there?" she asks. "Is he dead?"

"Yeah."

My father…did he…?

"Then what is it?"

"Nothing." I shake loose the thoughts in my head. "Let's finish this."

***

Growing up, my bedroom was above the two car attached garage. It was the largest of the three secondary bedrooms, but was the least insulated. I always found the room too cold in the winter and too hot in the summer. And whenever the garage door rumbled open or closed, my bed rattled like a coin-operated carnival ride.

One night, not long before my parents' deaths, I was asleep when someone opened the garage door. I assumed it was my dad. He'd been away on business and my mom told me he'd be home late.

Once I shook the sleep from my head, I hopped up to go greet him. My alarm clock glowed 11:45 P.M. Too late for me to be up, but I knew he'd excuse my disobedience to give him a welcome home hug.

I was halfway down the L-shaped stairway when there was another voice, one I didn't recognize. The man was talking to my father. I stopped at the turn on the stairs and sat down to listen.

"James," he said, "I'm disappointed about this. Would you reconsider?"

"No," my dad replied. "I've made up my mind. I've got a new job. It's… out of the business, and it'll keep me at home."

"I understand the family is pulling at you," the man acknowledged. "That's why I told you long ago to divest yourself of any emotional attachments. That they would only hinder your ability to perform."

"My family has never hindered my performance," my dad shot back. From the sounds of their voices, I could tell they were in the formal living room at the front of the house. "I've never blown an assignment, missed a target, fouled up intelligence, or fallen short in any way."

"I'm not suggesting that you're not stellar at your job, James. Far from it," the man backpedals. "If you were anything other than outstanding, I wouldn't be asking you to reconsider. It's just…"

"What?"

"It's just that your wife, your beautiful wife, and your son have become liabilities," the man said. "They keep you from wanting more. They have you unable to accept some of the more… complicated undertakings we like to assign."

"I don't disagree with you," my dad sighed. "I wouldn't call them liabilities, but I've admitted to being more cautious and less of a risk taker than is necessary. My family is always in the back of my mind. That's why you knew this day was coming."

"Oh, James, good man," the visitor said, "you are right. The time has come. I understand. I'll have to make the committee understand, of course. They may not be as amenable to your retirement as I, but I'll help them understand the prudence of it."

"The committee." It was a question as much as a statement.

"Yes," the man explained, "you know, James, the committee of men and women above me. They make the ultimate decision about how to handle almost everything within the organization."

"They're the ones who chose how to handle Frank's defection?" my dad asked.

"Yes," the man replied. "But please, good man, don't refer to him as Frank anymore. Frank is as good as dead. His new family calls him Liho."

"I can't understand why he did what he did," my father said. "He was like a brother. When you recruited us, we knew we'd be a team forever."

"Is this retirement about Blogis, then?" asked the visitor. "Is it about the loss of your friend as much as it is about your family?"

"I don't know," said my dad. "Maybe. He tried to get me to flip, to work for the competition. He suggested that both sides can wear the white hat."

"We both know it's not true," said the guest, "don't we?"

There was silence between them for what seemed like several minutes.

"Jackson," my mom asked from behind me, "what are you doing awake?"

"Um," I whispered, "I heard Dad get home. I was going down to give him a hug, but he's got a guest. I didn't want to bother him. I figured I'd wait till the guest left and dad came upstairs."

My mom leaned down and put her hand on my shoulder. "That's fine. But you can't sit here on the stairs. Go back to bed, and I'll make sure your dad comes in to say goodnight."

I was more interested in the conversation downstairs than in saying goodnight at that point. "Can't I stay up?"

"No," she said. "It's a school night. Now go to bed."

I stood up and my mom kissed me on the cheek before she floated down the steps, her silk nightgown flowing behind her. She looked back at me and I pretended to turn and go to my room. When she turned the corner, I stayed there and eavesdropped.

"Honey," my mom said, "you're home! Welcome back." I could hear her kiss him on the cheek. "And who is our guest?" She was polite, but there was confusion, frustration maybe, in her voice.

"Yes," my dad said, "

it was unexpected. He met me at the airport. Carolyn, I think you'll remember the name Spencer Thomas. Spencer, my wife, Carolyn."

"A pleasure to see you after all this time," my mother said in a voice reserved for false niceties. It was the same voice she'd use when answering the phone.

"Oh, dear goodness," said Spencer, "the pleasure is exclusively mine. James, you never quite captured the timeless beauty of your wife when describing her to me."

"Really?" my mother said, as much to my father, I imagine, as to the visiting sycophant.

"Only because your beauty is indescribable," my dad said. Nice save.

"And why are you here?" my mother asked, dispensing with the pleasantries.

"He's my—" my father began before Spencer interrupted him.

"I'm his supervisor, you may well recall," he said. *"Well, I should say his former supervisor. Your good man here has just informed me of his impenetrable choice to resign his position."*

"With my full blessing," my mother said. *"That means it's official, Jim?"*

"Yes," my father said. *"Just some paperwork."*

"It's but a formality," said Spencer. *"We will certainly miss him. We'll miss you too, Ms. Carolyn."*

"And why would that be, Mr. Thomas?" she asked. *"You just met me."*

He belly laughed. *"Oh, but it feels as though I've known all of you for a lifetime. James here, of course you, dear Carolyn, and that lovely little boy of yours, Jackson."*

Seventeen days later, my parents were dead.

CHAPTER 20

Old Town Heidelberg is a medieval maze of coral topped Gothic and Renaissance buildings. The streets are narrow, uneven, and filled with tourists. The Haupstrasse, which runs the lengths of the old town, is for pedestrians only. East of the town is the Heidelberg Castle. It reigns over the city atop its perch, guarding against would-be attackers from the Neckar River that flows east to west into the Rhine. It's humid in the late afternoon, the sun shining on the side of the castle facing the town.

"How much of a climb is it up there?" Bella asks. She's holding a note that was stuck to the door of Wolf's German pied-a-terre. "The note tells us to be there at sundown."

"That's probably a couple of hours from now. The climb won't be bad. Just a lot of steps. Let me see the note again?" I stop in front of a shop selling glassware, knives, and various sized flasks of Absinthe.

"It hasn't changed since you looked at it last," she says, handing over the note.

Nicely done, Jackson. You've arrived a bit late. But you're here nonetheless, and with that, I assume you've avoided or assuaged our mutual friend. Now to the business at hand. I've already recovered the package here, so you may forego the effort. Meet me for a sunset toast at the castle. We'll tip glasses and sip to a future as bright as the sun.

-SST

"What an ass," I mumble loud enough to draw a reaction from Bella. "You just figuring that out now?" she smirks. "What's your plan?"

"I'm figuring it out." I lean on the thick brown wooden window frame of the shop. "You have any ideas?"

"Not really. You've been the brains of the operation from the beginning."

I wipe the sweat from my forehead with the back of my forearm. "Yeah, that's why we're where we are."

"Hey," she lightly thumps my arm "we're alive. We've got sixty percent of the process. Blogis is dead."

"We're alive, Blogis is dead," I mimic. "You sound like Obama during the 2012 election, *"Detroit's alive, Osama Bin Laden is dead!!"*

"I never believed either of those things," she smiles. "But that's just me."

"You know," I say, half-seriously, "when this is all over, we should hang out."

"Take a vacation." She licks the beads of sweat off of her upper lip. "The tropics somewhere? A beach. A flavored rum drink. That kinda thing?"

"Perfect," I wink.

"I'll hold you to it," she smiles. I can't tell if the sudden blush in her cheeks is from the humidity or the simmering heat between us.

I've heard that extreme situations often draw people together, intensifying their emotions for one another. I thought it was crap, made up to make action movie romance seem plausible. Maybe not.

"This is the first time you've smiled since...well...since Blogis went into the river," she notes. "What's up? You hardly spoke on the way here."

"There's a lot going on here. A lot I don't fully understand. It's no accident that Spencer picked me for this. None of this is an accident."

"What do you mean?"

"I don't really know what I mean. We can talk about this later...on a beach."

"Okay."

"I do know Spencer's not going to give up the piece he's got".

"Back to business then?" She takes a swig from a bottle of water she bought at a fruit stand a block back. She offers me a sip.

"Yep." I swallow a gulp then hand back the half-empty bottle. "We've got to figure out what we do."

"Well, for starters, we don't have the pieces with us. That puts a kink in his plans to get all of the pieces together."

"That's assuming we ever intended to give him the other pieces, which we didn't."

"Good point." She takes another sip of water, finishing it. "I really need us to end up with all four pieces of the process. I'm counting on you, Jackson."

My phone buzzes. It's George Townsend. "Give me a second," I tell Bella and walk a few steps past her and into the crowd along the Haupstrasse.

"George," I say, "you're late."

"What?" he exclaims. "Jackson? This you?"

"Yep. You've got info on Blogis? If so, it's a little late."

"How so?"

"He's dead." An elderly woman, arms full of groceries, smiles at me as she passes.

"What?" he asks. "When?" He's banging away on that keyboard of his.

"Recently." A young couple, both of them in green camouflage army fatigues, walk by me hand in hand. Her head, hair pulled into a tight bun, is on his shoulder.

"I do have some information for you. I was getting ready to send it to you, but I needed to know where to send it. The only number I had for you was this one. And frankly, I'm shocked you answered it."

"What information do you have?" A man with bifocals is sitting at a cafe table about twenty feet from me. His wiry hair is shoulder length and gray. He's blindly peeling an orange while reading a newspaper.

"Uh," he pauses, "you want it over the phone?"

"You can send it in writing too. But I want what you've got right now." A teenager is at the edge of the street, playing Hacky Sack by himself.

"Okay," he says. "Liho Blogis is an alias. A guy with the feds hooked me up with some basics."

I'm staring up at the castle, my back to Bella, people shuffling by me on either side. Some of them are speaking German, others French, still more English.

"He's known as Liho Blogis, Frank Blogis, Frank Blessing, and a couple of other names. Whatever he's called, he's on the terrorist watch list. He's in his fifties or sixties. They don't know exactly how old he is. They do know he's pretty high up in the cartels that run the Eastern European black market. He's essentially got his own syndicate that provides protection, weapons, drugs, money laundering. He used to operate on U.S. soil for some private consortium that had tacit government approval, but after the wall fell, he shifted a lot of his efforts to the other side. The weird thing is, the intelligence on him indicates that, despite how powerful he is, he still likes to get his hands dirty. He's not some mafia don who orders hits and eats ravioli in the back of a dark pizzeria. He likes blood."

"A guy you know just told you all of this?" I ask. "You have one federal contact and he happens to know all of this stuff? That's a little incredible, George."

"I…" he pauses, "I have more than one source. And I'm owed a lot of favors."

I turn around to look at Bella. She's window shopping, or pretending to, respecting my privacy without accusing me of secrecy.

We've reached an understanding.

"What else do you know?" I ask. "From your incredibly well-placed sources."

"The only other thing I could get from my sources, who didn't feel real comfortable telling me what they did, was that there's some active investigation involving Blogis and money transfers to the Iranians. Some cash went through a bank that was under surveillance, and it got traced to Iran on one end, some of Blogis' people on the other. It was a lot of money."

"Makes sense."

"That makes sense?!" George sounds as though his head's about to explode. "What are you involved in, Jackson? Nanergetix, Bella Buell, nuclear detectors, and an Iranian-funded project involving a black market cartel? This makes your involvement with the governor seem like child's play."

"Yeah." I hadn't thought of it that way, but George is right.

"Is Blogis really dead?"

"Yes," I said. "Tell your source he's dead and floating in a river in southwest Germany."

"You're in southwest Germany?"

"Yep. On second thought, George, keep it under your hat for a news cycle or two. I promised you a story. You'll get it."

"Jackson, c'mon man. I've been patient. I've been providing you with a ton of good information. Give a dog a bone, brother."

"Didn't Sir Spencer give you enough of a bone, brother?"

"Wait, what?" George asks, startled. "How did you—"

"Just a guess. When did he call you?"

"About an hour ago," George sighs. "I did confirm some of it."

"How much of what you've been providing me this whole time has been from Sir Spencer?"

George is quiet.

"What did he pay you?" I should have seen this coming. George is always about George.

"He knows people at the networks," George whines. "He promised me interviews at MSNBC and Al Jazeera America. Maybe CBS."

"You sold your soul, your allegiance to me, for a shot at the network?"

"Jackson, please, I —"

I hang up and walk back toward Bella, tossing the phone into a trash can next to the picture window of the Absinthe shop.

"I've got our plan." I take her hand, steering her toward the Heidelberg Castle.

***

Bella's gripping my hand tightly as we navigate the steep cobblestone leading up to the castle. We're the only ones climbing our way up. Opposite us, a few hundred feet to the south, large clusters of tourists make their way down the long ramp back into the old city. The attraction is closing in a few minutes.

The castle itself is awash in an electric orange glow, the setting sun reflects off the river and the west facing stone facade of the centuries old fortress.

We began this journey a mile underground in a lab worthy of 22nd century science fiction. Now we're ending it atop the world in a crumbling edifice that predates the industrial revolution. Poetic.

"Come on up," calls a voice from above. "He's expecting you." It's Mack. He's bandaged and bruised, but armed and aiming his Ukrainian Fort-12 in our direction. His thumb is on the safety, his swollen, bruised eyes working hard not to make contact with Bella's.

Though Bella's eyebrows arch upward as though she's about to cry, her resolve is set solid in her clenched jaw. She doesn't want to make eye contact with him either.

"Mack," I say, "working for the dark side, eh?"

"Aren't we all, Jackson?" He waves us past him with the black matte steel of his double action pistol. "Last I checked you were on the payroll too."

I squeeze Bella's hand as we work our way to what's called the Karl Tower, the first of a series of crumbling stone structures that make up the remnants of the castle. We stop at a large open window looking south across the tops of coral colored roofs to the Neckar River. The water looks almost bronze as the sun sinks beneath the buildings to the west. It casts a looping shadow on the water from the ancient bridge connecting Old Town Heidelberg to the large homes on the other side of the river.

"Move along," Mack barks from behind us. I can hear the hitch of his prosthetics on the uneven stone path. "We're meeting the man up ahead."

He hasn't searched us!

Bella lets go of my hand and turns to face Mack. "I'm not going anywhere. I'm standing right here until you tell me why you betrayed me, why you betrayed my father by doing this."

Mack laughs and unconsciously lowers the gun before jerking it back into position, "Betrayed?" He steps toward Bella, and she steps back. "That's laughable. How did *I* betray *you*, Bella?"

"You gave me a blank drive." She holds up her index finger followed by her middle finger. "You helped Sir Spencer get the only part of the process I don't have," another raised finger, "and as of right now, you're pointing a gun at me."

Mack cracks his neck and closed his eyes for a moment, taking in a breath full of restraint. "If there is any betrayal here," he breathes, his eyes unafraid of Bella's now, "any lack of allegiance between us, it is on you and you alone."

"How is that, Mack?" she asks. "What did I do?"

"It's what you didn't do," he spits. "My wife is dying. You know this. The woman who treated you like a daughter is being devoured by her own body. Her cells are turning against her. The very core of who she is, evaporating right before my eyes. And what have you done to help her, Bella?"

"I —I"

"Nothing!" he roars, a fountain of spit spraying us. "You've done nothing. The care your father provided, the medical assistance he went out of his way to ensure my wife received ended the day he died."

"You never said —"

"Why would I have to say anything?" Venom drips from every word. "She reached her lifetime limit months before your father died. There was no help until he stepped in. I didn't *have* to ask him. I shouldn't have had to tell you."

"But why *wouldn't* you tell me?" her voice is up an octave and quavering. "Mack, that doesn't make any sense."

"I tried telling you." He wipes his mouth with the back of his left hand. "You were preoccupied. Then Sir Spencer asked me, out of the blue, about her health. *He* cared."

"This is about money?" Bella says. "This is about money for your wife's medical expenses?"

"It's about her LIFE!" he's at the edge of becoming unhinged, before closing his eyes again and taking a deep breath. "You were family, Bella," he says in a tone diametrically opposed to the one he took a moment earlier. "I thought I was family to you."

"Mack, you *are* fam—"

"I'm your assassin," he finishes. "In the midst of everything else in my life," he shakes his head, running his hand across the top of it, "you asked me to kill a man."

Bella has no response. She can't refute his argument.

"Now," he growls, "move along."

Bella hangs her head, tears running down her cheeks. She takes my hand to begin the march toward what might be our end.

***

Sir Spencer is a parasite. He senses weakness, and selfishness, and he preys upon it. For me, the weakness was freedom. I wanted some semblance of a life so badly, I'd joined forces with a man I knew deep down would betray me. I killed for that alliance. I maimed. I did it so that I could have what I wanted. However benevolent my need, I betrayed my own sense of justice to achieve it.

Bella joined forces with him out of a need to retain her power. She enlisted a man who, indirectly, killed her father, for the sake of proving her father wrong about her willingness to do what it took to succeed.

George wanted the story. He wanted the "get" so big it would land him a higher profile, higher paying television job that might come close to satisfying his unadulterated narcissism. He betrayed me to have a *chance* at that opportunity.

And Mack, poor Mack, seeking to save his terminally ill wife as much for himself as for her, turned against a girl he thought of as family. Too proud to ask for help, he turned to the first hand that offered it, no matter the stakes.

In each case, Sir Spencer was there to pick the ripening fruit from the tree. Each of us, he tucked into a basket and carried us, willingly, until we rotted.

Liho Blogis was wrong when he said that both sides could wear the white hat. Sir Spencer knew it not to be true because, in his world, everyone finds the black hat so much more attractive. In his world alliances are disposable. Allegiance is a matter of convenience.

Here, at his convenience, stand three pawns. We're not good foot soldiers, as my father's token would remind us, but rather played pieces moved and sacrificed as the game master sees fit.

Appropriate we are in a castle, bending knee to a knight.

"Jackson," he greets me with arms wide as he approaches from a dark corner of The Great Terrace. "Nice to see you, good man." He wraps his arms around me, his heft almost lifting me from my feet.

"And Bella," he smiles. "Always the beauty, regardless of the circumstance. Even the wayward strands of hair atop your head seem stylishly out of place, perfectly askew. Beautiful!" He genuflects for effect and then stands with his hands clasped behind his back.

The gray light of dusk makes it difficult to read his face, to gauge his expression. He steps from a faint light, back into a shadow, maybe sensing that I'm reading him.

"Mack," he says, "Come now. Stand over here with me. We need to keep keen watch on our compatriots here." We're standing at the edge of the terrace, our backs to the waist high stone wall.

"What's your play?" Bella asks. She must really be a *Homeland* fan.

"Good question," Sir Spencer says. "Worthy of a CEO. Or a former CEO. Either one. Take your pick."

Neither of us say anything, but Bella squeezes my hand. Her thumbnail digs into my skin.

"So," he says, "here's how it will go, my dear friends. I know you, Jackson, elicited the assistance of a young package clerk in Frankfurt." He must sense some involuntary reaction in my face because his widens into a broad grin. "Box 2929 was it?"

He found two of the pieces!!

Bella squeezes my hand again, and looks up at me. I don't look at her, but I can sense her glare. She thinks we're done for. She thinks it's over.

Sir Spencer pulls two silver hard drives from his coat pocket. "Yes, it was 2929. Which rhymes with gold mine, and wonderful find, and neutrino beam. No," he laughs, "it doesn't rhyme with beam. That was silly. But here they are. And that brings me to the lone remaining piece of the puzzle, which one of you holds on your person somewhere." He looks at Mack and motions for him to check us.

"Move away from the edge of the terrace, please," he says, "and raise your hands above your heads. I'm really very sorry for having to do this, but this is what's necessary. I have a very eager buyer and time is of the essence."

"Who's the buyer?" I raise my hand to shoulder level. I don't want my shirt lifting up above my waist.

"Germany."

"Germany?" Bella asks as Mack approaches her. "Why Germany?"

Sir Spencer shrugs. "It was them or Israel, and the Germans have more means at the moment."

"That doesn't make sense," I say.

"Of course it does," Sir Spencer laughs. "Why do you think the NSA was hacking Chancellor Angela Merkel's cell phone? They knew something was amiss. I've been fighting NSA taps on my electronics for years. Apparently German intelligence, the Bundesnachrichtendienst, isn't as good as my people. Whatever, they want the process. They're paying for it. I'll give it to them. Maybe I'll give it to the Israelis too. Nobody will be the wiser if two bidders have the process."

"Why not give it to everyone?" I ask. "You make money and everyone loses their nukes. It's peace everywhere."

"Ha!" he laughs again. "Jackson! Really? There's no money in peace."

"I've got it," Mack pulls Blogis' silver drive from Bella's pocket. He holds it up like a prize.

"Very good," says Sir Spencer. "Toss it here, good man."

Mack switches hands to toss the drive toward Spencer. During that split second, I reach into my waistband and pull the Smith & Wesson Governor, leveling it above Mack's hand as he lets go of the drive.

Pow! Pow! Pow!

Three rapid pulls of the revolver's trigger and the drive tumbles over the terrace wall, propelled ninety degrees in the wrong direction from the force of the shot shell that peppered the drive's internal magnetic platters. The final piece of the process disintegrates before the drive hits the tall grass twenty yards down the slope of the castle hill.

I turn to see Sir Spencer gasp, comically reaching for the drive long since destroyed.

"Are you kidding me?" Mack blasts at me. "All of this work, this pain, and you *destroy* it? I can't let that happen. I can't let you get away with that." Mack levels his weapon at me.

"Wait a moment now, Mack," Sir Spencer intervenes. "There's no need —"

Pop! Pop!

Two shots find their way into my chest. The searing pain burns, knocks the air from my lungs, and puts me flat against the ground. I feel like I've been punched with a hot poker.

"Mack!" Bella screams. "What have you done? Jackson? *Jackson?*"

I'm staring at a dark, starless sky, struggling to breathe, grabbing wildly at the holes in my body, when Bella grabs my head and cradles it her lap. "You'll be okay, Jackson."

"Now that was unnecessary," Sir Spencer says. "It's not as though we can find our way to a solution here, Mack."

Pop! Pop!

Bella screams and I'm sure I've been hit again, when there's a distant grunt and something cracks against the stone terrace flooring.

"Mack!" Bella screams. "Mack!"

"Mack's dead." Sir Spencer's large frame appears over my head, looking into my eyes and then at my wounds. "Shooting Jackson wasn't his decision to make."

"Call for help!" Bella yells. "Get Jackson some help!"

"You're in no position to demand anything from me," Sir Spencer says. He walks out of my line of sight, which is dimming with each passing second. "He just cost me hundreds of millions of dollars and at least two embarrassing phone calls."

The pulse against my neck is weakening. The searing heat is giving way to a chill running through my spine to my feet. The only warmth is a wet ooze below my collarbone. I must be losing a lot of blood.

Bella is stroking my head and crying, trying to keep me calm with a motherly "Shhh!" between sobs.

In the distance there's the rhythmic beep of someone punching numbers into a cell phone, then the distant two-tone wail of emergency sirens. My focus shifts from Bella's face to the empty sky above, my body feels as though it's sinking into stone, into Bella's hands, and everything goes dark.

✳✳✳

"Jackson?" whispers a soft voice close to my ear. "Jackson, are you awake?"

My eyes flutter against the light.

"You are awake!" Still a whisper. "Let me pull the shades so that you can see. It's bright outside. The light gives way to dark and my eyes readjust. This time I can see.

"Bella?"

"You're okay," she soothes. "The bullets both passed through. Neither of them hit any major vessels. You got so lucky. Just a broken collarbone." She sits bedside and grabs my hand in hers.

"How long…?"

"Two days. You've been here two days."

"What about the process?" I swallow against a thick, dry lump. "I killed it, right?"

"You killed it," she says. "It was like a quick draw from an old western. You made Swiss cheese out of the drive."

"No process then?"

"No." She rubs her thumbs against the back of my hand. "It's okay though. Nobody else will get it. I don't know, honestly. I'm just concerned about you at the moment."

"Your job?"

"Not important," she says. "I resigned."

"Spencer?"

"He disappeared," she says. "He's the one who called for help. He called the ambulance."

"Mack?"

"He's…"

"Dead?"

"Yes."

"I'm sorry."

"It's okay," she says. "It's not your fault. It's mine."

"Lots of blame for both of us," I say.

"We're quite a pair, right?"

A pair?

"Mr. Curtis is awake?" A voice from across the room. "Mr. Eugene Curtis?" A thick German accent, measured and precise.

"Yes," says Bella. "He is."

"Good," says a tall man dressed in a white coat, his eyes framed by circular frameless glasses. A thick reddish mustache covers his upper lip. "May I have a moment with him, Ms…"

"Analiese Muller." Bella lets go of my hand and stands to shake the doctor's. "I'm his girlfriend."

"Very well," says the physician. "I am Doctor Schulhof. I am here to check on Mr. Curtis here, and give you both an update on his health."

"Thank you, doctor," she says.

He thumbs an electronic tablet, stopping on a page, then thumbs through another two or three. "We have some good news for you, Mr. Curtis. The bullets passed through your body below your right clavicle, exiting at the interior edge of your scapula. You have slight fractures in both of these bones, which will take some time to heal. However, the vascular injuries were insignificant. I am told that your girlfriend, Ms. Muller, applied pressure to your wounds. That perhaps saved you from losing too much blood."

"All good news!" Bella looks exhausted despite the cheer in her voice. I can't imagine she's gotten much sleep.

"Yes," the doctor concurs. "However, we did find something unusual during an X-ray after you arrived."

Bella's expression changed, as though this is new information she'd not yet heard. "What is it?" she asks.

"You have had knee surgery, yes?"

I nod.

"Above the knee, which contains a lot of scar tissue, there seems to be an implanted device," he says, looking at the chart as he speaks.

"What kind of device?" Bella asks.

"It did not appear to be medically necessary upon a closer inspection." He looks up from the tablet and addresses me directly. "Are you in the military or do you work for the United States government?"

I shake my head. "Why?"

"You have a GPS tracking device in your leg," he says. "It's injected into the fatty tissue above the knee. Were you aware of this?"

Sir Spencer!

I shake my head.

"Do you know when someone might have injected or surgically implanted the device into your leg?"

I shake my head again. But I know. He did it when he drugged me and kidnapped me from that Sixth Street bar in Austin two years ago. It had to be then. He's known my every move since then.

A GPS TRACKER IN MY BODY!

I'm trying to hide what I'm thinking, but Bella senses it. Her hands are pulled to her face, covering her mouth, tears I would have thought had long since run out are again pooling in her eyes.

"Would you like us to take it out?" asks Doctor Schulhof. "We can do it with very little discomfort. Whoever is keeping track of your whereabouts will no longer be able to do so."

"Take it out." There's a post-operative rasp in my voice. "I want it out."

I want it out because I'm going to find him. I'm going to compel him to tell me what happened to my parents and why he chose to ruin my life. And this time, he won't see me coming.

EPILOGUE

Bella's salty lips are pressed gently against the small entry wound scar between my neck and shoulder. Her damp hair smells like a mix of ocean water and the conditioner she combed into her hair hours earlier.

"Does it hurt still?" She rests her chin on my chest and looks up at me with a smile. "If it does, I'll keep kissing it to make it better."

"I'm still in a lot of pain." I admire her beauty through the polarized lenses of my sunglasses. I can feel her throaty giggle against my body and she gives the scar another kiss before sliding up next to me on the sandy blanket.

"How long has it been since we escaped?" She turns her head to the side as if she's listening to my heartbeat.

"Two months."

Another North Shore wave crashes against the coral twenty-five feet from the shore of our cove.

"How long do you think we can hide here?" Bella asks this question every other day. And on the days she doesn't, she's thinking it.

"Is that a rhetorical question?" I ask.

A gust of ocean breeze brushes past us, curling the blanket around our legs.

"No," she says. "I just wonder what you're thinking."

"They'll find us," I tell her, the truth. "Whether it's Sir Spencer or the governor's goons, somebody will eventually show up."

"You forgot INTERPOL."

"Or INTERPOL."

Our violent bread crumbs in Ukraine and Germany are no doubt by now another obstacle to long term peace in the relative solitude of Haleiwa, Hawaii.

It wasn't difficult getting out of Germany. With Wolodymyr's handiwork and a private rental jet, we managed an easy getaway.

Bella resigned from Nanergetix on a conference call with her board and cashed out. She has a series of accounts in the Caymans and in Switzerland that hold the vast majority of her wealth. Wire transfers, in small, irregular amounts, to an account we share at the Bank of Hawaii have provided plenty of cash for our Spartan existence on Oahu.

I use the name Richard Denning. Bella's alias is Peggy Ryan. We borrowed the names from bit actors in the original *Hawaii 5-0*. Nobody's noticed.

We're renting a small one bedroom guest house for three hundred and fifty dollars a night. At my recommendation, Bella paid cash up front for six months. It's beachfront and secluded. Bella initially wanted to stay at a high-end resort because of the added security, but she relented when I suggested the paper trail would provide too much exposure.

Our days are split between scouring the internet, hiking in search of green sea turtles along the heavy deposits of rocks and coral that line the coast, and other, more private pursuits. Despite looking over my shoulder every other second, this is the happiest I've been since sipping that tainted beer on Sixth Street nearly two years ago. Bella has all but convinced me to forego vengeance in exchange for anonymity and a relationship with her. We both know our existence here is temporary, though secretly I like to pretend it's not.

Bella pushes herself from the blanket and sits with her legs tucked behind her. She's in a bikini top the color of the Pacific and a white sarong. Her olive skin is tanned a shade darker, her cheeks and nose pink from her refusal to use sunscreen. "You want some lunch? I was thinking Kono's."

Kono's is a breakfast and lunch joint on Kamehameha Highway not far from our bungalow. We eat there at least twice a week, and it's the closest we've come to assimilating into the culture here. I learned my lesson in San Antonio to avoid patterns of behaviors and public habits.

However, Kono's is too good to avoid. The Pig Bomber is an amazing burrito stuffed with kalua pig, rice, caramelized onions, and cheese. I almost forget I have no life when downing it. Bella lives for their coconut cream pie milkshakes. We sit on the bright blue picnic tables outside of the red frame restaurant alongside wild chickens that populate the islands.

"Sounds good." I slide my hand onto her thigh. "I haven't stuffed my face in at least three days."

"I'm really craving their waffles," she admits, "and a milkshake."

"Maybe you're pregnant," I joke.

She slaps my chest. "Hush. Not even funny."

"You're right, it's not."

We gather our blanket, shaking the sand downwind, and trek back to the guesthouse. Our feet sink to our ankles in the soft powder, squeaking with each step up the beach. Neither of us says anything until we've reached the thick overgrowth of palm and breadfruit trees.

"You read about Mack?" she asks, squeezing my hand with hers.

"I did," I nod. "So he survived after all?"

"That's what the article said." She steps in front of me on the narrowing path toward the house. "He was hospitalized for three weeks, but is being called a miracle man."

"Well, when you have a double amputee military veteran survive a violent 'mugging' at a popular German tourist attraction, it tends to make news."

"He supposedly left Landstuhl after he was stabilized," she says, stepping onto the wooden staircase that leads to the guesthouse's second floor entrance. "Now he's back in the states somewhere."

"Hiding from Sir Spencer?"

"Hiding from everyone." She pulls on the handle and tugs open the door. A cool rush of air greets us, carrying the scent of the pineapple lotion Bella generously applies to herself, and me, after showers. "The article claimed he was suffering from post-traumatic stress and the interview was conducted in an 'undisclosed' location."

"You forgive him?" I ask, stuffing the blanket into the stacked washing machine next to the kitchenette.

"I don't know," she says, leaning against the kitchen counter. "He tried to kill you. And he probably would have killed me too."

"But he didn't. And you have a history with him."

"What's with you?" she asks, folding her arms across her chest. "All of this forgiveness stuff? It's not like you."

"I don't know." I walk over to her and place my hands on her hips, tucking my thumbs into the sarong. "You got me thinking about it."

She looks me in the eyes and then brushes some sand from my forehead.

"You told me that my anger for Sir Spencer only hurts me," I explain. "You're right when you call the man a sociopath."

"He's a violent, egomaniacal, manipulative —"

"I know," I raise my hands in surrender, taking a step back.

Bella shrugs. "I'm just saying."

"Look, I know my quest to find *him* before he finds *me* is self-destructive."

"You actually listen to what I say?" she giggles. "I'm flattered."

"Every once in a while," I wink.

"So we're finished with trying to exact Hammurabi's Law?"

"It's Hammurabi's Co—" I stop. "Nevermind. Yes. We're finished with it."

"Until they find us," she reminds me.

"I guess," I sigh, "but we're prepared."

Bella inches toward me to wrap her arms around my back when my newest burner phone vibrates against the granite counter. The caller ID is blocked.

"Are you going to answer it?" Bella asks.

I pick up the phone, pulling it to my ear. "Richard Denning," I say.

There's silence, but I can tell that someone's on the line.

"Hello? You've reached Richard. Can I help you?"

"Richard is it?" the voice snarls. "Is that your name these days?"

"I'm sorry, I —"

"Don't belittle me with your games, Jackson," the caller spits. "I know who you are. And I'm coming for you." The voice is familiar, but I can't place it.

"Who is this?" I look at Bella, her reaction likely a reflection of mine. Her eyes are wide, mouth pursed.

"I'm going to find you and the rest of the process," he warns. "It's just a matter of time."

"I don't —"

"You *do* know," the caller says. "I'm the man who visited your home when you were young. I'm the man in the man in the photo with your father. I'm the one whose body you watched drift down the Neckar River." The line goes dead.

Liho Blogis.

He's alive. And he's coming for us.

THE END

EXCERPT FROM THE FORTHCOMING FINAL INSTALLMENT OF THE ALLEGIANCE TRILOGY: HIDDEN ALLEGIANCE

The sand squeaked underneath Liho Blogis' feet. The sun was barely a distorted reflection on the waves crashing against the coral outcrops dotting the inlet.

Blogis was aware of the noise and made efforts to more lightly tread as he moved up the beach on Oahu's North Shore. The crash of the waves, he thought, was enough to mask his approach.

They would never hear him coming.

Blogis thumbed the safety on the left side of his suppressed Makarov pistol. The so-called PM was Blogis' weapon of choice. He'd retrieved it from the cold, dead hand of a Soviet police officer in 1988 and it was as much a trophy as it was an effective bloodletter. It was heavy in his hand by modern standards, at twenty six ounces, and its blowback design was more accurate than pistols using a recoiling or articulated barrel.

A man's gun.

He'd surveilled the house on the inlet for three weeks; acting as a surfer, a tourist, a bum. The plastic surgery he'd undergone after having the bullet removed from his body provided ample cover from his targets.

They would not recognize his new nose, enhanced cheeks, or his longer, blond hair.

The small bungalow was fifty meters up a tangled hill, covered in palms and underbrush. There a was a single window lit from a lamp on the second floor. It was a hallway outside of the bedroom. He knew the targets typically arose in forty-five minutes.

Blogis, a student of many disciplines, was an amateur somnologist. Knowing the human sleep cycle was a valuable tool in his arsenal of intelligence and violence.

He knew that roughly ninety minutes after the couple fell asleep, they'd enter REM. Otherwise known as Stage Five, REM was dream sleep. If he timed it right, and he had so many times before on similar missions, he'd surprise the pair at their most vulnerable; during a long period of REM right before they awoke. With their voluntary muscles momentarily paralyzed, they'd be unable to quickly respond. By the time they knew what hit them, what hit them would kill them.

Blogis checked his watch before glancing over his shoulder. Nobody was on the beach, but there were the silhouetted bodies of a half dozen neoprene-suited surfers straddling their boards, bobbing rhythmically as they awaited a swell just beyond the mouth of the inlet.

There were so many parallels between surfing and his chosen line of work, Blogis thought. Both required unique skills, unmitigated patience, the love of control, and the urge to bridle powers much greater than oneself. Both required a tradecraft that was counterculture, a subset of rules and laws which were grossly misunderstood by anyone beyond the boundaries.

Blogis crouched in the palms, his feet digging into the dirt, and he momentarily lost himself in the surf, eyeing a lone warrior who braved a large wave gathering momentum behind him. The surfer popped from his chest onto his feet, crouched at first much as Blogis was, until he slipped into the brief curl of the water as it broke against the coral.

The surfer crashed against the loss of the wave's energy, and Blogis refocused on the bungalow. He checked his watch again and inhaled deeply, ready to initiate the task, when he heard a man's voice behind him.

"Howzit?" The man was smiling, his bright eyes contrasting his deeply tanned native skin. "I don't mean a bodda you, Brah." He was speaking Da Kine Pidgin, Hawaiian slang.

Blogis glanced back at the bungalow's lone lit window before spinning on the balls of his feet to face the interloper. He caught the surfer glimpse the Makarov and raised his finger to his pursed lips and stared down the dripping wet local.

"You cock-a-roach this hana?" the surfer whispered, a smile snaking across his face, revealing a toothy grin. His right shoulder bore a large, black patterned tattoo that stretched from his neck to his bicep, sloping across the top of his chest.

"Stealing?" Blogis tilted his head, keeping the Russian handgun at his side. For the moment. "You're wondering if I am here to break in and steal things?" His eyes narrowed.

"Fo'real," the surfer nodded, the smile disappearing. "I got a mo bettah way to do it."

"Do you?" Blogis looked past the local at the longboard stuck into the sand halfway to the tideline on the shore.

The surfer nodded again and Blogis nodded him up the hill, toward the back door.

The young man, who Blogis estimated no more than eighteen or nineteen years old, started toward the stranger. He'd climbed two or three steps when Blogis stopped him with a pair of suppressed slugs; one to the center of the boy's chest, the other in the small space between his thick eyebrows. That shot thumped the smile from the surfer's face and he crumpled to the sandy dirt, landing partly on a clump of silvery Hinahina.

Blogis scanned the beach and the surf. Nobody was close enough to see anything, so he returned to the mission at hand and inched quietly up a short set of wooden steps to the rear door. It was twelve-paneled door with a simple lock that Blogis handled with ease. He slipped inside, quietly pulling closed the door behind him.

He was in the small kitchen, the smell of pineapple and soap filling his nostrils while he got a better sense of his surroundings. Across from him was a granite counter and to his left a washing machine. He walked to the counter and saw a half-empty twenty ounce bottle of Dr. Pepper, a pair of cellphones plugged into an outlet, both of them blinking to indicate they were fully charged. Next to the sink, on the other side of the counter against the wall, was a wire basket full of mangos. An uncut pineapple sat next the basket. There was a juicer, taken apart with its plastic parts flipped upside down on a stack of paper towels.

They tried to make this a home. How naive.

Blogis moved to his right and around the floral-pattered love seat that separated the kitchenette from the small living area. An old steamer trunk served as a coffee table between the love seat and a wall mounted flat panel television. A laptop sat open on the trunk, its screen black and in sleep mode. Blogis walked past the television and into a narrow hallway. At the end of the hall was the door to the lone bedroom. He stepped quietly, Makarov primed, past the lit wall sconce to his left, a window at shoulder height to his right.

As he neared the bedroom door, he heard the soft rhythm of jazz, an alto saxophone chirping a riff against the backdrop of trombones, a double bass guitar, and drums. Blogis paused at the door, listening to the refrain before gripping the handle and turning it. His left shoulder pushed into the door and it opened into the room.

Underneath a thin yellow sheet was the shirtless man, on his back, left arm hanging off of the full-sized bed. Draped across him was the woman, sleeping in shorts and a loose tank top. Her long, tanned leg was wrapped around his thighs, her right hand on his chest, her face nuzzled into his neck. Her long, dark hair covered her face, but he knew who she was.

He slide alongside the bed, leaned over her, placed the barrel of the Makarov in the small of her back and whispered into her ear, "Bella."

He trailed the gun up her back and along her spine. "It's time to get reacquainted with your daddy."

Bella winced, her eyes still closed. But she didn't move. Neither did the man next to her, the one who'd saved her life too many times to count. Blogis had timed this perfectly.

He pushed the barrel into the back of her neck and pulled the trigger.

ACKNOWLEDGMENTS

First, foremost, and always I thank my wife, Courtney, for her support, guidance, and love. She is my muse. I also couldn't spend the hours and months it takes to craft these stories if it weren't for my children, Samantha and Luke. They give me hope that tomorrow will be better than today.

Thanks also to the wonderful team at Post Hill Press. It's a pleasure to work with such dedicated people. Michael Wilson and Anthony Ziccardi are saints for kindly responding to each of my emailed missives. I'm a reporter. I ask a lot of questions. Their belief in my work is both flattering and so appreciated.

To my editor, Felicia A. Sullivan...you rock. Please don't fix the ellipses. It's a convenient way to avoid using a semi-colon incorrectly.

A heartfelt thank you to my trusty beta-readers. Steven Konkoly, Curt Sullivant, Mike Harnage, Gina Graff, and Tim Heller read early drafts of my work, see through the mess, and guide me to a better book. Your comments, critiques, and hi-fives are invaluable.

Thanks to the great people at Murder By The Book in Houston for your unwavering support an promotion of my work. And to Tabatha Perry, you are too kind for your efforts to help the world discover Jackson Quick.

To my mom and dad, Sanders and Jeanne, my siblings Penny and Steven, and my in-laws Don and Linda, your love and viral marketing are better than any advertising campaign.

Lastly, to you the reader, I am indebted. Without you, Jackson Quick would have nobody with whom to share his adventures. I hope you'll be as excited to read the third installment of the ALLEGIANCE trilogy when HIDDEN ALLEGIANCE hits the shelves later this year.

ABOUT THE AUTHOR

Tom is a veteran television journalist and author who's spent the last 20-plus years covering the biggest stories of our time.

He's interviewed Presidents, cabinet members, and leaders in congress. He's reported live from the White House and Capitol Hill, Chernobyl, The Canadian Badlands, the barrios of Mexico City, Central America, and the Amazon Jungle.

Tom's covered five national political conventions. He has flown with presidential candidates, gone backstage at their rallies, and broken stories about them on television and online.

He was at the Pentagon while smoke still rose in the hours after 9/11 and was in the room when Secretary Colin Powell made his case to the U.N. Security Council for war against Iraq.

Tom lives in the Houston suburbs with his wife, Courtney, and their two children.

CPSIA information can be obtained at www.ICGtesting.com
Printed in the USA
BVOW02s2251140715

408045BV00004B/11/P